LEGEND *of*

The realm of Rokugan i
and mystics, dragons, magic, and divine ___ g
world where honor is stronger than steel.

The Seven Great Clans have defended and served
the Emperor of the Emerald Empire for a thousand
years, in battle and at the imperial court. While conflict
and political intrigue divide the clans, the true threat
awaits in the darkness of the Shadowlands, behind the
vast Kaiu Wall. There, in the twisted wastelands, an
evil corruption endlessly seeks the downfall of the
empire.

The rules of Rokugani society are strict. Uphold
your honor, lest you lose everything in pursuit of glory.

ALSO AVAILABLE

ARKHAM HORROR
Wrath of N'kai by Josh Reynolds
The Last Ritual by S A Sidor
Mask of Silver by Rosemary Jones
Litany of Dreams by Ari Marmell
The Devourer Below edited by Charlotte Llewelyn-Wells
Dark Origins: The Collected Novellas Volume 1

DESCENT: JOURNEYS IN THE DARK
The Doom of Fallowhearth by Robbie MacNiven
The Shield of Daqan by David Guymer
The Gates of Thelgrim by Robbie MacNiven

KEYFORGE
Tales from the Crucible edited by Charlotte Llewelyn-Wells
The Qubit Zirconium by M Darusha Wehm

LEGEND OF THE FIVE RINGS
Curse of Honor by David Annandale
Poison River by Josh Reynolds
The Night Parade of 100 Demons by Marie Brennan
Death's Kiss by Josh Reynolds

PANDEMIC
Patient Zero by Amanda Bridgeman

TWILIGHT IMPERIUM
The Fractured Void by Tim Pratt
The Necropolis Empire by Tim Pratt

ZOMBICIDE
Last Resort by Josh Reynolds

Legend of the Five Rings™

The Collected Novellas
Volume One

THE
GREAT CLANS
OF ROKUGAN

KATRINA OSTRANDER
ROBERT DENTON III
MARI MURDOCK
DANIEL LOVAT CLARK

ACONYTE®

First published by Aconyte Books in 2021

ISBN 978 1 83908 120 0

Ebook ISBN 978 1 83908 121 7

Cover art by Mauro Dal Bo

Rokugan map by Francesca Baerald

Distributed in North America by Simon & Schuster Inc, New York, USA

Printed in the United States of America

9 8 7 6 5 4 3 2 1

ACONYTE BOOKS

An imprint of Asmodee Entertainment Ltd

Mercury House, Shipstones Business Centre

North Gate, Nottingham NG7 7FN, UK

aconytebooks.com // twitter.com/aconytebooks

CONTENTS

CLIFFSIDE SHRINE

GROVE OF THE
FIVE MASTERS

Unicorn
Lands
Dragon Lands

Phoenix Lands

KHANBULAK

HISU MORI TORIDE

MORNING GLORY
CASTLE

Lion
Lands

CITY OF LIES

OTOSAN UCHI

←AL-ZAWIRA
12,500 LI WEST

S
h
i
n
o
m
e
n
F
o
r
e
s
t

Scorpion
Lands

KYŪDEN DOJI

KEEP OF
WHITE SAILS

COLD WIND CITY

Crab
Lands

S
o
u
t
h
e
r
n
C
r
a
n
e
Lands

GOTEI CITY

Islands of
Silk and Spice

The Shadowlands

Rokugan

ICE AND SNOW

KATRINA OSTRANDER

Special thanks to James Mendez Hodes for his invaluable expertise and guidance on this story.

CHAPTER ONE

"My lady Hotaru." Doji Inobu greeted her with a bow that was perfectly acceptable to make to a samurai of noble birth, but woefully inadequate to make to the lord of Kyūden Doji.

Which Hotaru was not, strictly speaking. She was only *acting* lord, and the palace's longtime fixtures such as Inobu were unlikely to let her forget it anytime soon.

Rather than answer with only a curt nod, she gave him a deep bow befitting an experienced orator and courtier. She no longer lived in the Kakita Dueling Academy, where she might draw her blade in a challenge, so she would resort to killing them with kindness instead.

"Your attendance comes as a surprise, my lady. I assure you, you needn't trouble yourself this morning. This palace's advisors have everything well in hand. Please, join your family's guests in the great hall."

Hotaru closed the sliding door behind her and composed a pleasant smile. "I appreciate your concern, but I shall stay, thank you." Hotaru took a seat at the low table and drew her folding fan from her sash. This deep into winter, she wouldn't need it to cool herself, but the cypress wood and silk stitching of the fan was a subtle reminder of her rank. "My family's guests and many relatives won't be offended if I join them in an hour."

"As you say," Inobu replied. He didn't have the status to defy her, who was heir to his liege, but his lack of agreement insinuated his disapproval.

Inobu bowed to the first of the gathered advisors who would provide their reports. Hotaru had made it just in time to be included in the daily briefing despite the "busyness" that had prevented Inobu from properly conveying the time and place to her. "Lord Koji, if you would."

The middle-aged shugenja, clad in formal priest robes and a high cap, cleared his throat. He was one of the few in the clan gifted with the ability to hear the spirits of the land, sky, and sea, called kami. "The currents of air and water are shifting. We foresee snowstorms coming these next few weeks..." he began.

Snow meant more days trapped within the palace's walls, crowded in with her family's guests, none of whom were important enough to attend the official Imperial Winter Court, either.

She'd begged to go this year, to no avail. There, she could have competed for prestige in the many tournaments that served as entertainment for the assembled samurai. She could have begun forging the friendships that she would need one day, when she would finally succeed her father as Crane Clan Champion.

But she was needed here, her father had assured her. The Winter Court was a den of vipers who would gladly poison a young samurai's reputation for a day of entertaining gossip, and she could still learn much from presiding over her family's court for the season, he had reasoned. It shouldn't have felt like a punishment, but when other clans' heirs were permitted to go...

She stopped herself from turning her fan over in her fingers and listened to the rest of Lord Koji's auguries in respectful silence.

"Lady Sun and Lord Moon will be at their height again soon. We can expect a king tide in a fortnight, Commodore Motoyashi."

The naval officer nodded. "I'll notify our crews."

Lastly, the shugenja reviewed his shrine keepers' preparedness for the Snow Festival. The acting lord would have a ceremonial part to play, but the palace seneschal, the seneschal's deputy, and their ministers clung tightly to the honors and responsibility of actually planning the event.

Inobu followed on with his own summation of the outings and demonstrations he had planned for the court, weather permitting. He would confer with their master steward and the seneschal to take account of the palace's stores and ensure they requested additional supplies from the storehouses if necessary. Again, Hotaru could do nothing but nod along at his reports. He had the matter well enough in hand without her questioning him or interfering. He'd given her no reason to doubt his competence – only his esteem of her.

Finally, Inobu asked Captain Asano of the palace guard and Commander Yukitori of the provincial infantry to report. Asano reviewed the reports from the palace's patrols, while Yukitori discussed the training efforts at her garrison. "We must begin to consider how many of our forces should be seconded to defend Toshi Ranbo. The Lion Clan's young lord, Akodo Arasou, will be sure to mount a counterattack to reclaim the castle."

Hotaru considered Akodo Toturi, Arasou's brother, a dear friend. Toturi was a thoughtful man, brilliant and slow to anger... but the two brothers were as opposite as fire and water. Arasou was always eager to fight. Even the Emperor's demand that he exchanged hostages with the Crane could do nothing to satisfy his appetite for war and glory. If only Toturi were the Lion

Champion, perhaps their clans would not have shed so much of each other's blood. But Toturi had forsaken Lion military affairs and traded the Akodo War College for a monastery.

"Hmm," Inobu pondered.

Hotaru was choosing her words to underline Arasou's aggression when Inobu declared, "Respectfully, this can wait until our lord returns."

But her father was wintering with the emperor far away in another clan's court, attending to the esteemed business of the Emerald Champion. Serving as the emperor's personal bodyguard, his chief law enforcer, and the commander of the Imperial Legions left little time for the needs of the Crane Clan and the Doji family, but her father had not yet relinquished the major decisions that concerned the clan and family. These advisors did not expect her to have opinions, much less to issue orders.

"Mobilization would not begin until late spring, in any case," Inobu reassured the commander.

"Very well," Yukitori said. Her frown was a small thing, but it spoke loudly to Hotaru.

If her father would not permit Hotaru to accompany him at the official Winter Court, then at least these advisors could cede some of the family's business to her. She couldn't prove herself if they wouldn't let her get involved with even the day-to-day affairs of the palace.

And, thanks to her friendship with Toturi, did she not have the best insight into Arasou's intentions?

She took a deep breath. "Commander Yukitori." Silence fell over the advisors. Motoyashi and Asano were unable to conceal their surprise that she had spoken up at all. "I was appointed acting lord of Kyūden Doji in my father's stead. Let me decide the matter of preparing troops from Kazenmuketsu Province."

Inobu's lips pressed together, barely concealing his irritation. "As I said, we do not need to make plans for several weeks yet. Commander Yukitori–"

Hotaru snapped her fan shut in warning. "If the commander is ready to begin preparations, wouldn't the clan benefit by having more time to ready our forces?" she pressed.

The advisors shifted uncomfortably.

Inobu drew himself up, readying to strike with a polite but firm rebuke, when footsteps rushed down the hallway and the sliding door opened with a sudden snap.

"My lady!" A soldier entered and bowed deeply. He was ostensibly addressing Hotaru, but his deference was directed toward the commander.

"What is the meaning of this interruption?" Yukitori demanded.

"I bear grave tidings." His head still low, the soldier approached and handed several folded papers to the commander before retreating to his original place. "One of the Mantis Clan fleets has overtaken the Keep of White Sails," he explained, while Yukitori paged through the letters one after another.

It was as though an earthquake had rocked the chamber. The advisors stared at the messenger in silence as they processed the news. Everyone assembled there was used to the frequent border skirmishes with their western neighbors the Lion Clan. They were ready to respond to an assault against one of the villages bordering the Osari Plains or even the castle-city of Toshi Ranbo itself. But for their coast to be under assault this way, and by a mere minor family of traders and smugglers...

"The Keep of White Sails... Lord Sasaki Okimoto commands the garrison there and oversees the signal fire pavilion, yes?" Hotaru asked. If she recalled her tutoring correctly, the Sasaki vassal family was sworn to her father. Their founder was a simple fisher who had rescued one of Hotaru's ancestors from a terrible storm at sea. As thanks, the fisherman had been elevated to the rank of samurai and granted the title to the Flying Fish Isles, an archipelago off the eastern coast of Oyomesan Province.

"That is correct, my lady," said Inobu. "But to think that a minor clan would be so brazen as to directly provoke us..."

"They are foolish, or delusional, or both," Motoyashi declared.

Yukitori finished the reports and handed them to Asano to read next. "It would be easy to push the Mantis from the keep in summer. Winter is another matter. We can assemble contingents of Doji troops, but... We might send word to the Daidoji to prepare reinforcements, both in terms of soldiers and ships. We'll need more than just your small fleet docked at Peaceful Village, commodore."

Motoyashi nodded gravely.

"Captain, run and get us maps of this region, will you?"

"Of course." Asano saluted Yukitori with a clenched fist and then departed the chamber.

Inobu rubbed his chin. "Hmm... Our greatest obstacle is not one of logistics, but of legality. Even if we are reclaiming a castle that is rightfully ours, we risk escalation. We cannot commit more than a scant number of troops against the Mantis Clan, lest we be seen as the aggressor. The emperor has extended his personal protection to all of the minor clans, the Mantis included."

Hotaru did not want to imagine the choices her father might be forced to make if the emperor's legions had to be turned against those of his own clan.

Koji finally spoke, his voice heavy with sorrow. "The laws of mortals are one consideration. The strictures of Heaven are another. War means death, and death is an affront to the kami. There is already enough suffering to be endured by samurai and commoner alike."

Koji was right, but that didn't mean he would be heard. The Asahina were pacifists in a clan in which half of the great families were devoted to the martial arts. How many times had he been overridden in this chamber? And how many more times would he be forced to watch the Crane march to battle?

"We all want peace, but if we don't deal with this swiftly, our enemies will think they have a chance," Yukitori warned. "Sometimes, we must fight to maintain the peace."

"And sometimes wars can be won with words alone," Inobu countered. "Let us send a delegation first."

"That may or may not work, depending on the Mantis's leader. Do we know who led the attack?"

The foot soldier answered, "According to the local fisherfolk, the flagship's banners were painted black with white lightning strikes."

"That could be the *Inazuma*. Captain Gendo commands that vessel," Motoyashi suggested.

"What do we know of him?"

"Not much. We can ask around our captains—"

"I have heard of him before," Hotaru ventured. Everyone turned. This time, their looks of surprise were tinged with curiosity.

She took a deep breath and drew herself up straighter. It might have been luck – or fate – that she knew the name. This was her chance to prove her usefulness. "When I was still a student, Uncle – I mean, Kakita Toshimoko – and I traveled to Gotei City on the Islands of Silk and Spice. We met some of the sailors from Captain Gendo's crew. They were bold, even for the Mantis, and they'd just returned from a successful raid against some Pavarron pirates. They shouldn't be discounted as warriors."

This was not the place for her to admit that she and her uncle had direct knowledge of their fighting from getting into a bout with some of the *Inazuma*'s sailors after an outrageously lucky roll in a game of Fortunes and Winds, so she left that particular detail out.

"Hmm. I see," Inobu said, still stroking his chin.

Asano returned with the maps, and they hurriedly spread them out before them.

"Still, how many ships – and sailors – would they have sent to take the keep and hold it?" Yukitori asked, pointing to the main island.

"That all depends on the conditions during the battle," Motoyashi admitted. "Was it a night raid, an attack under the cover of fog, or an assault in broad daylight?"

"'Twas an unnatural fog that rolled in with the dusk," the foot soldier reported. "We still don't know how many ships have docked in the Bay of White Sails."

Motoyashi swore. "Lady Doji," he said, fixing his gaze on Hotaru. "What can you tell us about their raid against the privateers?"

Now her usefulness would be determined. "Well… this was likely a boast on their part, but they claimed to have slaughtered everyone aboard without losing a single sailor."

"And now they have a walled keep with which to defend themselves," Asano pointed out. "Do we have any idea how many soldiers remain on the island as captives? And do we suspect they treated the Crane as brutally as they did the foreign sailors?"

"There have been no requests for ransom yet, but I can't see the Mantis leaving that money on the table, so to speak," Motoyashi said. "Even if they are bloodthirsty."

Yukitori butted in. "Then bring the Asahina shugenja to defend our troops."

Koji's face drained of color, but he seemed ready to send the request to his brother, the Asahina daimyō, regardless.

"Again, I say we must consider levying the Daidoji reserves from the surrounding provinces. Overwhelm the Mantis in a decisive assault."

"For an island raid? No, a few of the navy's best ships should suffice," Motoyashi countered.

"Perhaps we can make do with even fewer. Let them try to pit one of their warriors against a *kenshinzen*," Asano suggested. "Decide the matter in a duel to the death, and spare the forces of both sides." The kenshinzen were the most elite Kakita duelists in the land – and sometime assassins who wore a mantle of courtly etiquette to murder their victims in public. Uncle Toshimoko was probably the most legendary kenshinzen alive. Would they send him? More importantly, would he agree to do it? No one could order the Grey Crane around... or tell him to stay behind when he didn't want to.

"But if the Mantis live up to their infamous reputation, and they refuse to accept the outcome of the duel – or if the Daidoji ships or armies cannot retake the island–" Yukitori raised her voice "–we will look even weaker! We must get the champion's counsel."

Hotaru's heart thundered in her chest. How much longer would she be forced to defer to her father's counsel? Months? Years? "No!" She stood abruptly. She couldn't sit by and watch them bicker this way, or let this chance pass her by. She fought to steady her voice. "Lord Doji appointed *me* to serve as acting lord of this palace and this family. In the absence of the champion, and with no time to convene the council, only I can bring this matter to the lords of the Kakita, Daidoji, and Asahina."

Motoyashi looked as though he were about to challenge Hotaru, but he bit back his words. Yukitori didn't conceal the incredulous look on her face. Hotaru couldn't blame her. Yukitori had decades of experience as a commander, whereas Hotaru had only just graduated from the Kakita Dueling Academy – without earning the prestigious title of Topaz Champion, as her father had done, and his mother had done before him.

Yes, no doubt that was why her father had left her behind, and why the advisors of Kyūden Doji dismissed her authority.

But Hotaru was also sure that she couldn't let them make these decisions without her. They would only have more reason to ignore her in the future, and if anything went wrong, her father would have all the more reason to doubt her abilities – and her status as heir.

She needed to prove herself now, or she would forever be consigned to being left behind and having nothing of credit to her name. "It will take too long for us to hear back from my father, and we've no time to lose. Even if Lord Koji beseeches the air kami immediately, it will still take time for the swiftest of winds to carry the message all the way to Morning Glory Castle. We must decide now."

The advisors waited, and she quickly formulated a plan. "As my lords have pointed out, we should first seek a diplomatic solution. The Mantis have long been our friends. But in the case that a peace proves impossible..." she swallowed. "Then we must be ready."

Inobu was right. They could not employ direct military force against a minor clan without breaking Imperial law, even if that minor clan had been the aggressor. Worse, tensions could escalate, and a dispute involving a single castle could turn into several, or even draw their entire fleet into conflict. The Mantis Clan relied on the Crane Clan's rice to feed their people, and in exchange, they traded raw silk, spices, and exotic woods that could be fashioned into works of art sought after across the empire. It was pointless for the clans to waste their resources fighting, especially when the Crane had the Lion to worry about as well.

"Lord Inobu, request that Captain Gendo receive a delegation from us immediately. Commander, send word to General Daidoji Uji. Tell him to marshal his forces and begin preparations for a siege. Commodore, relay my orders to Admiral Hoshitoki to form a blockade around the island. Permit nothing in, nothing out. Tell them to capture or shoot down any messenger pigeons, if need be. We cannot allow the Mantis to anchor any more of their fleet in the bay."

For a moment, nobody moved or spoke. The acting lord of Kyūden Doji had just called a muster of troops in the dead of winter. There was frostbite to contend with, and considerable risk of troops getting snowbound in a blizzard or ships getting sunk in rough seas. But now that responsibility rested on her shoulders, not theirs.

"It will be done, my lady." Inobu bowed.

Already their scribes were transcribing her orders into official letters. One by one, she sealed them with her personal chop.

She handed them to the advisors, who would dispatch them to couriers who would deliver them as swiftly as their horses could carry them. For all their hurrying, the armies could only assemble so quickly, and if the weather did not cooperate, despite the prayers and entreaties of Koji and his fellow shugenja…

Any course she chose was a risk. But if she waited to hear from her father to ensure she was making the right decisions, the Mantis would have even more time to solidify their defenses. Any failure would come down on her head, now.

CHAPTER TWO

Six days passed. Togi, the messenger Inobu had dispatched to request an audience with the Mantis Clan captain, had not returned. No one was surprised when the seventh day brought the news they had all feared.

Hotaru awoke before dawn to her handservant informing her that Inobu had requested an audience. She changed out of her sleeping clothes into a white and blue coat and navy-blue *hakama* whose pleats were embroidered with plum blossoms. She pulled her white hair up into the simple ponytail she'd worn in her days at the Kakita Dueling Academy. It hadn't even been a year since she'd graduated, but it also felt like a lifetime ago.

In some respects, she'd been a different person then. She had still been known by her childhood name and was training to win her school's dueling tournament, which attracted contestants from across the Empire. Her father had privately told her how much he was looking forward to seeing her compete, how proud her mother would have been. That was before Hotaru had left for the front lines to win glory on a battlefield in addition to in the dueling ring. She'd returned home with neither.

But the messenger they had sent to arrange the delegation hadn't returned home at all.

Through the partly shuttered windows overlooking the sea, the horizon began to lighten with the first rays of Lady Sun. The faces of the advisors remained dark when they arrived. Inobu, Koji, Motoyashi, and Yukitori had exchanged their fanciful court robes for simpler garb. The palace servants quickly poured green tea alongside a simple breakfast of white rice, but no one ate.

"My lady, we have received the Mantis's response," Inobu said sadly, pushing a chest in front of her.

A metallic bite hung in the air. Hotaru didn't need to open the box to know that it contained Togi's head.

"You were right to call a muster, milady," Yukitori added.

Hotaru inclined her head. "I wish I had not been." Perhaps she shouldn't have tried to treat with Captain Gendo at all. It was right to try to resolve matters peaceably, but the failure meant one more death weighing on her shoulders.

Surely not everything had failed already. "Commodore Motoyashi – the blockade? Does it still hold?"

"Yes, my lady. Admiral Hoshitoki has the islands completely surrounded."

She didn't doubt that to be true, but it was a poorly kept secret that the Mantis Clan had some of the best smugglers among their crew. With the right ship, rowers, and weather, no blockade was truly impenetrable.

"Commander Yukitori, what of the infantry preparations?"

"The garrison of Kazenmuketsu Province stands ready. Reserve forces from Oyomesan and Gyōsha provinces are marshaling at Cold Wind City to set sail at your command. They will be ready within the week."

In a week, then, they could attempt a full-blown siege.

Inobu cleared his throat. "We have since received word back from our champion, as well." He motioned for Koji to speak.

The shugenja bowed deeply. "The champion said that he is prepared to beg the emperor's permission to leave the court and return to Kyūden Doji should Lady Hotaru's plan fail."

For the Emerald Champion to ask to forsake his Imperial duties was unthinkable, even if it was meant as reassurance.

The fan trembled in her fingers. She couldn't let her father down. She couldn't let their clan down. She met the eyes of Inobu. "Is it possible that the Mantis would receive the heir to the Crane Clan if they refused a delegation of lower status?"

"My lady, it is far too dangerous to risk sending you as well!"

Hotaru couldn't let herself sound desperate as she asked, "Other than that, what diplomatic options do we have left?" She'd be to blame for more deaths by the time a siege was over.

"Our most influential diplomats are away at the Imperial Winter Court, unfortunately, and it will take more time to reach out to our representatives on the Islands of Silk and Spice, but if they were to request an audience with Lord Yoritomo himself..." Inobu suggested.

The Crane were a Great Clan. They did not beg the lords of minor clans to call back their raiding parties from Crane Clan territories. For the Crane to demand a withdrawal would require them to back up their threat with action, rendering the time wasted.

Yet, did the Imperial law forbid the Great Clans from attacking a group of renegade pirates who illegally seized a keep and committed such vicious acts as beheading messengers? It was an argument that the best Crane magistrates could make in the courts across Rokugan – and probably win. The Mantis could save face by agreeing that Captain Gendo had acted independently.

The only casualty would be the Crane's relationship with the Mantis – and all the commerce that went with it.

"Then we have no choice but to strike decisively." She laid out the possible legal argument to Inobu, who quickly began running the theory through potential challenges and merits. Koji was silent, but his objection to the violence was clear.

Even if she did retake the castle, her father would be disappointed that she'd been forced to deploy their troops. Every Crane Clan casualty was a soldier they couldn't deploy to the Lion-Crane border. Every favor called in by the clan's diplomats was one fewer to call in against the Lion. Each a strike against her reputation and her legacy.

Hotaru almost didn't notice the sailor arrive and whisper something in Motoyashi's ear. Though the commodore didn't so much as flinch, the messenger assuredly had brought ill tidings.

"Beg pardon, my lady," Motoyashi apologized. "I have just received urgent news. One of the admiral's ships captured an Imperial vessel before it could reach the isles."

Her heart nearly stopped. Yes, she'd ordered a blockade, but to forbid an Imperial vessel…

Permit nothing in, nothing out. She should have been more specific. She couldn't afford any mistakes, much less a scandal.

"One of its passengers claims to be an emissary of the emperor."

Suddenly, the room was too warm, and the floor beneath her swayed. She'd known that her father would brief the emperor on the situation, but so far this was still a local matter to be settled between the Crane and Mantis alone. Involving the emperor made the Crane look weak, as though they were incapable of resolving their own disputes.

This was not her father's doing, then. But whose?

"Bring the emissary to the great hall immediately. I will receive them in court."

Her advisors practically leapt to their feet, emptying the room in rapid succession to make all the necessary preparations. Doji Inobu lingered behind for a moment before approaching Hotaru with a deep bow. He wanted something.

"My lady, should you see fit, it would be my honor and privilege to negotiate with the emissary on behalf of the Crane Clan." Of course it would be. It would also undercut any authority she'd won from her advisors.

"The Crane Clan appreciates your offer of service, Lord Inobu," Hotaru answered, keeping a level tone. It would be impolite not to acknowledge his dutifulness. His eyes brightened. "You have always been considered a loyal servant of my father."

He bowed, more deeply this time.

She rose and was about to cross the threshold into the hallway when she added, "Yet it must be me to receive the emissary. I shall see you in court in a few moments." She didn't slam the sliding door behind her, but Inobu winced as though she had.

Hopefully, she had quashed any notion he might have had to interject "on her behalf" during the reception. Now it was all up to her. She had to do this on her own.

The first task before her was to avoid being branded a traitor to the Empire.

"Presenting Her Excellency, the Lady Bayushi Kachiko, wife to the Scorpion Clan Champion and emissary on behalf of His Imperial Majesty Hantei the Thirty-Eighth," proclaimed the herald.

One of the vipers her father had warned her about had appeared at their very door.

All eyes were on Kachiko, but her stare was fixed on Hotaru. The sheer black lace that outlined the newcomer's cheekbones and brows was a mere suggestion of the traditional mask worn by all Scorpion Clan samurai. Four sharp, golden hair pins fanned out on each side of her oiled black hair. The morning light shimmered up and down the silhouette of her long, black and red silk kimono as she gracefully bowed to Hotaru. Her masked Scorpion Clan bodyguard bowed in tandem, like her shadow.

Hotaru's chest tightened, as though she were about to step down into the dueling ring. For a moment, she thought she saw a mischievous smirk play across the woman's lips.

Many a samurai in this court had whispered of Kachiko's treachery, including Hotaru's own uncle. Kachiko was called the most beautiful woman of the age. Samurai had dueled each other to the death to try to win her hand in marriage, it was said, and others had bankrupted themselves to earn her favor. Where she trod, she left ruined reputations and lives in her wake.

Her coming could be nothing but an ill omen.

"I thank you for your most gracious welcome, Lady Doji," she said, motioning with her opulent fan to the fully convened court, where samurai from all seven Great Clans, as well as a few minor ones, had gathered to see what Hotaru would do. "I sincerely appreciate the unexpected hospitality of the Crane."

The word *sincerely* cut like a knife. Hotaru relaxed her mouth and brows to maintain an impassive expression. She'd had only a few flights of stairs to compose an excuse that would save face for her clan and stand up in legal proceedings. Diverting an Imperial emissary on the emperor's business could, at its very worst, be considered treason. That the emissary was also a Scorpion made her even more dangerous, but Hotaru could not show even the slightest hint of fear.

She bowed low before resting her hands on her thighs, fan clutched in her right hand, as though she were the true lord of Kyūden Doji. Perhaps it was even convincing. "On behalf of the Crane Clan, allow me to extend my deepest apologies for any inconvenience, Lady Bayushi. However, your ship was entering dangerous waters, and we could not risk any harm befalling you during your voyage. We are sworn to protect the emperor's servants, after all."

The court shifted, murmuring, waiting to see if Kachiko would accept that interpretation of events. Should she testify against the Crane in the Imperial capital, who could oppose her? Her husband was famously the emperor's best friend, and he held considerable sway. Yet Hotaru's uncle Kakita Yoshi was the Imperial chancellor, and the Imperial advisor was Kakita Ryoku. Both of them owed allegiance to the Crane Clan Champion in addition to the emperor.

Hotaru spared a quick glance to Doji Inobu. He waited, watching to see if Hotaru would change her mind and defer to someone more experienced in dealing with Scorpion courtiers.

Finally, Kachiko replied, "Your clan's loyalty and service to the emperor is commendable, Lady Doji." Something twinkled in her eyes. "But may I ask, are the Flying Fish Isles indeed still under the protection of the Crane Clan?"

Her brazen insult was delicately wrapped in an innocuous question. If the emperor – or his emissary – publicly acknowledged that the Mantis now occupied the castle, his word was law, and the Crane's claims to the archipelago would dissolve, no matter how many centuries they'd stewarded them.

Hotaru could not allow that to happen. Without an unassailable response to solidify her clan's claim, she had to turn the questioning around. "What business is so pressing that you risk sailing through waters where there have been sightings of the *Inazuma*, a ship known for its brutal and bloody crew?" If Kachiko acknowledged the threat the Mantis posed, it would justify the Crane captain's actions and defend the Crane's claims to the islands.

"As fate would have it, my husband had delegated some matters to me that required me to stay in the capital for a few more weeks before joining His Imperial Majesty at the Winter Court," Kachiko answered, evading the question and the obvious trap. "Yet it seems my delay proved fortuitous."

Fortuitous was one word for it. Was it really her duties that had made her stay behind, or was this part of some scheme? The samurai of the Doji family knew how easy it was to conceal a half-truth in a single word, allowing the speaker to appear sincere in saying one thing while not precluding another meaning. "Some matters" could be interpreted in a thousand ways, all of which allowed Kachiko to ostensibly tell the truth.

Kachiko continued, "The emperor regrets to hear of the misunderstanding between his servants, and His Majesty has sent me to help resolve any lingering confusion."

There it was. She claimed to have come to arbitrate the dispute. If true, she had the authority to award the island to one clan or the other. There was no way to confirm whether she was really on the emperor's business, but it was also impossible to openly question an Imperial order.

Hotaru would have to win Kachiko to her side, then, and ensure her verdict favored the Crane. Bless the captain who had brought Kachiko here. She'd have to speak with Motoyashi to ensure the captain was recognized for their bravery as well as skill.

"It is a sign of His Imperial Majesty's beneficence and magnanimity that he sent you, Lady Bayushi," Hotaru played along. If Kachiko was lying – and those lies were ever brought to life – then publicly conflating the emperor's judgment with Kachiko's deception would only lead to a swifter and more scandalous downfall for her, as it would show how much she was willing to profit by the emperor's authority. "Surely, if anyone can find the solution to the Mantis Clan's confusion, it is you."

She could not allow Kachiko to continue on her way to the isles and work out some secret deal with the Mantis on her own. She could not hold the Scorpion woman here in the palace, but neither could Hotaru let her out of sight. The Crane's delegation may have been brutally rejected, but denying an audience with an Imperial emissary could bring the emperor's legions down upon the Mantis. Would they be so foolhardy?

Only one path lay before her, but it was far too reckless to meet with her father's approval. Yet she would be letting him down if she did nothing and let Kachiko go on her own to potentially award the island to the Mantis.

She'd have to tread this path perfectly, without a single misstep.

Hotaru rose and slowly descended the dais to stand before Kachiko. "As I said before, the Crane Clan will not allow any harm to come to you as long as you are in our lands or sailing upon our waters. I will see to this personally." She knelt down on one knee.

If Hotaru had caught Kachiko off guard, the Scorpion woman betrayed no sign, but her bodyguard shifted closer to her. "As you can see, I am already well protected, Lady Doji. I appreciate your offer, but—"

"I insist," Hotaru cut her off. It was a challenge.

Moments passed, and the eyes of those assembled were trained on Hotaru like arrows, waiting for her to falter. At the edge of her vision, her advisors silently conferred. They might think her reckless or impetuous, but Hotaru had no other recourse.

There was little Kachiko could say to deflect or deny Hotaru's insistence. They were too close in rank, and Hotaru held the power as lord of this palace, acting or otherwise.

"Very well," Kachiko answered. Her bodyguard would have to carry out her wishes with steel.

Hotaru rose to her feet as Kachiko's bodyguard stepped forward. His black mask covered his entire face, and even the whites of his eyes seemed veiled in shadow. Something in the way he lazily shrugged his shoulders made Hotaru think he might even be amused, although she could not see his smirk.

"However, my dear protector, Bayushi Nishiyo, has no doubt taken offense to your insinuation that he cannot properly defend me when we arrive at the Keep of White Sails," Kachiko said. "I'm afraid that you'll have to prove your superior technique with the sword in order to take his place at my side."

Hotaru had expected nothing less. She'd insulted his skills, after all. All she had to do was prove her technique's superiority over an unknown foe with an unknown fighting style and years of additional experience. In so doing, she would prove to Uncle Toshimoko and her father that she could have won the Topaz Championship if she had been there to compete in it. That their efforts to raise her well and pass on their skills had not been wasted. That she was a capable duelist worthy of the lineage of Kakita, the first Emerald Champion. And that in the not-too-distant future, she could defend her claim to the Clan Championship in the investiture tournament and win the right to wield Shukujo, the ancestral sword of the Crane Clan.

"I will," Hotaru said simply. But this audience hall wasn't the place for it. She looked to the castle's seneschal. "Prepare the gardens for our duel."

CHAPTER THREE

Hotaru could not be sure that the sound of the wind sighing through the pines wasn't the whispers of the assembled spectators. How many of them believed she would fail?

According to the gossip, Hotaru had missed the Topaz Championship because she'd been afraid to participate. Or perhaps the head instructor, Toshimoko, had held her back. Behind her back, they suggested that the daughter of the Emerald Champion was a failure. That she had completed her *gempuku*, her coming-of-age ceremony, in private rather than be bested publicly by duelists from other clans.

The truth was that she'd missed the tournament because she had been on the front lines, defending against the Lion Clan in Daidoji Uji's army, and her route to the tournament grounds had been cut off by Lion infantry. Even though that was public knowledge, many assumed it was a polite excuse. Her reputation was damaged, possibly irrevocably. Just as her father had warned it would be when she'd insisted on fighting alongside her clan before completing her gempuku.

If she failed now, she would only prove the rumors correct.

She might as well offer her retirement and withdraw to a monastery, forgoing her titles as well as her family.

At least there, she could no longer disappoint anybody except herself.

A cold breeze swept through the gardens. Hotaru had not bothered to wear a coat. She had kept her hands in her sleeves, though, as she couldn't afford to lose even a moment to stiff fingers.

A page approached bearing her sword, Elegance, sheathed and draped in fine silk. The page reverently held out the sword. Gently, Hotaru unfolded the silk and raised the scabbard with both hands.

The prized Ashidaka-forged blade had been passed down within her mother's family for generations. It had passed to her when she completed the trials required of her by the dueling academy and took her adult name. Toshimoko, her mother's brother, had promised she was worthy of it, as she had fought courageously on the front lines, but this was the first time she would dare to draw it. If the blade did not judge her worthy, it might refuse to be drawn.

Hotaru ignored the assembled crowds and turned to face the two Scorpion samurai. "The defender may name the terms of the duel."

"My bodyguard must be swift if they are to react in time to counter any threats. Let us see your quick-draw technique. To first strike," Kachiko suggested on behalf of her guardian.

"To first strike," Hotaru agreed. That didn't preclude the possibility that either of them would draw blood, or that a tragic accident could occur. Death was always a possibility when blades were drawn. Perhaps it would be better to die than to have to retire in shame.

The bodyguard nodded silently. Hotaru wouldn't put it past

the Scorpion Clan to cut out the tongues of some of their samurai if it would ensure they could not divulge the secrets of their clan. More likely, it was just an act, and the silence of the swordsman was meant to unsettle his opponents.

If it was working, she would not show it.

The Scorpion woman moved aside, a confident smile spreading on her face as she fanned herself idly.

The herald announced, "Bayushi Nishiyo has accepted the challenge by Doji Hotaru for the right to serve as bodyguard to the Imperial emissary Bayushi Kachiko during her time in Crane lands. The winner of this *iaijutsu* duel shall be the first to land a blow, as determined by all those gathered here as witnesses."

Hotaru stepped into the ring with her opponent and bowed, partially in apology for the insult she'd previously leveled at him, and partially in respect for the fighting spirit he would bring to this duel. It was not his fault that she needed to take his place.

Hotaru took a deep breath, crouched, and grasped her scabbard with her left hand. She kept her sword sheathed as she lowered her right hand on the grip.

The iaijutsu technique of the Kakita was designed for drawing and striking in a swift single motion. Timing was everything. Yet the Bayushi school of swordsmanship was known for speed as well. Like the strike of a scorpion, the duel would be over in the blink of an eye.

Nishiyo mirrored her, readying his scabbard for a fast draw.

Whose technique would prove the swifter?

Her opponent took a step forward, inviting Hotaru to answer him by stepping back.

She didn't move.

He came closer, one step at a time, inviting her to seize the chance to strike first. But she couldn't know how fast his reflexes were, and whether he could outmaneuver her if she drew first.

His mask was blank, yet it likely hid his smile. If he'd heard the rumors, too, no doubt he thought this would be easy. How many other bodyguards had he bested in Kachiko's service? One did not rise to become protector of an emissary without proving oneself, and Hotaru was still unproven in the eyes of the Empire.

What else was Nishiyo hiding? What was his secret to rising so high among the ranks?

Hotaru's eyes darted to his scabbard. It was slightly longer than was typical. Possibly the length of his sword was extended to match his height, and she would have to compensate for its length when they finally met in combat.

Unless that was what he wanted her to think. She couldn't know the sword's true length until it actually came free, and by then it would be too late. If it was shorter than she was accounting for, it would be a faster draw, and he'd beat her to first strike.

They were within range of each other, now. She could not let him see in her eyes that she suspected. If she blinked, she could miss the moment Nishiyo began to draw.

The wind rose, the pines swayed, and wisps of snow swirled around Nishiyo's feet. The breeze swept over her scabbard, her grip – threatening her balance.

That's when it came. Nishiyo darted forward and his scabbard opened to reveal the razor edge concealed inside.

She drew, slashing upward and reeling back as fast as she could to dodge his incoming blow, but too late.

There was a *whoosh* of cold air at the tip of her shoulder as the fabric of her robe parted like grass. She caught a cry in her throat before it could come free.

Heart pounding, she checked the tear to see if the Scorpion's sword had struck true. A properly whetted sword was so sharp that you might not feel the cut until you noticed it bleeding.

But whether he'd drawn blood wouldn't matter if she'd missed her target.

Behind her, something cracked, and clattered to the floor.

The crowd gasped.

Hotaru turned to see the Scorpion's mask on the ground, split in two. The handsome face of the Scorpion bodyguard was laid bare, a line of red crossing his nose.

They were nearly matched for speed, but Hotaru's blow had struck truer.

Nishiyo looked helplessly at the emissary, but he didn't bother to apologize. It would have been futile.

Kachiko's furious gaze met Hotaru's, and Hotaru's racing heart skipped a beat.

The herald beamed. "Doji Hotaru has landed a deeper cut and more lethal strike! She is the victor!"

The court buzzed with surprise and speculation. She'd won – they'd all witnessed it. The flames of gossip would lose their fuel.

She'd also disrupted Kachiko's plans. There was no telling what kind of revenge the Scorpion would try to exact. Hotaru would need to be on guard not just for the Mantis as they departed for the Keep of White Sails together. Their path would offer many more chances to stumble.

As various courtiers came to congratulate Hotaru, the Scorpion swordsman withdrew from the court chambers in disgrace, no longer having any purpose in staying. His fate wasn't enviable.

Now, it was up to her to avoid a similar fate, or worse.

Hotaru approached Kachiko once more, taking a knee again and offering up her blade to the woman. Kachiko's dark eyes were unreadable as they looked over her fan and down at Hotaru. This close to the woman, Hotaru caught notes of sandalwood and jasmine.

"On my honor as a samurai of the Crane Clan and by this sword, I swear to stay by your side, serve as your champion, protect you from harm, and give my life for yours if called upon to do so."

As Hotaru proclaimed her oath publicly, she placed her life in the hands of the very last woman she should trust.

What have I done?

CHAPTER FOUR

After enduring Nishiyo's humiliating public defeat, Kachiko had insisted that they be on their way to the island that same day. As Kachiko's new bodyguard, Hotaru had ceded her ability to host or command the emissary, and so her attendants packed her a bare-bones chest of clothes and effects that would have to serve her for an indeterminate length of time.

In her role as bodyguard, Hotaru couldn't be parted from her charge even to receive Commander Yukitori. She handed a servant hastily written instructions. *Wait for my signal. Do not move against the Mantis until I give the order.*

Now that diplomacy was once again an option, she could only allow the Crane to be drawn into a war with their island neighbors as a last resort.

Kachiko needn't stay a moment longer. She had done as custom required and presented herself to the palace's lord, and now that their meeting was over, she had no reason to remain. Her haste in leaving would sting the pride of the poets and performers eager to showcase their arts for an emissary of the emperor were Kachiko not so infamous and feared.

"Please send a message to my brother: tell him to do his best," Hotaru told her handservant Rie before departing from the inner keep gate for what could be the last time. It seemed like only yesterday she was traveling with Kuwanan to his new home in Lion lands. There, he was a student – and a hostage – of her clan's greatest rival as part of the peace negotiations meant to settle the tensions along the Lion-Crane border. If she met with the same fate as her messenger to the Keep of White Sails, her final words to her brother should be words of encouragement, as he would be the next to suffer the weight of responsibility as heir.

The wind picked up as they departed the palace. On the horizon gathered clouds dark and gray and laden with snow. Hotaru took her place across from Kachiko in the traveling cart, and when all their luggage had been packed on the nearby wagon, they set forth on the road to the castle town.

The Scorpion woman's stony silence was a wall between them. Hotaru would have to slowly dismantle that wall to have any hope of winning the emissary to her clan's side, starting with cordiality.

"It looks as though we will be met with snow before we depart for the isles, Your Excellency."

Kachiko remained silent.

"I'll miss the way the Fantastic Gardens of the Doji look when blanketed in snow, but I hear the Flying Fish Isles have their own beauty in winter. Has Your Excellency ever visited before?"

Kachiko still gave no response. Perhaps she needed a little more provocation. As impolitely as she dared, Hotaru said,

"The emperor must have a great deal of faith in you to have sent you on your own to mediate a peace at the Keep of White Sails."

It worked. The Scorpion woman spared her a glance. "Indeed, the emperor himself tasked me with this important mission; meanwhile, I am now protected by a duelist who did not compete in her academy's own tournament."

Of course Kachiko would have known her shame. But at least

now she could reply, "A duelist who did not compete in her academy's own tournament, but who proved superior to your previous guardian."

Hotaru and Kachiko braced themselves as the cart rumbled over several bumps in a row.

"I did not expect to find you at your family's palace," Kachiko said, changing course. "I thought that the Crane Clan heir would certainly be accompanying her father, the Emerald Champion, at Winter Court."

"It's true that I would rather be at the Winter Court," Hotaru admitted. "But it seems that fortune smiled upon us, and I was able to be here when I was needed."

Kachiko fanned herself indignantly. "I can assure you that I will not need you as an escort to the Keep of White Sails. The Mantis samurai will welcome me, and Imperial guards will see to my safety while negotiations are conducted."

Negotiations that had almost cut out the Crane Clan entirely, Hotaru noted. "You may be glad to have me by your side, after all," she said. "We presume that those of Lord Okimoto's retinue who did not die in the initial fighting were taken captive, and the Mantis beheaded the messenger we sent as well. We cannot expect them to play by the rules."

"And do you expect *me* to play by the rules?" She offered an upraised eyebrow.

"Absolutely not."

"Good," came Kachiko's reply. "Play the game, then. I look forward to seeing what kind of opponent you are." She offered a playful smile. "If you can even keep up."

Hotaru followed Kachiko onto the docked vessel, leaving the security of Crane lands behind. The contingent of Imperial guards awaiting Kachiko's return did not so much as remark on Hotaru's presence, but she was sure they were judging her nonetheless: *too young, too delicate, too naïve*. In theory, these guards were samurai belonging to the Imperial families – cadet branches of the Hantei line that had forsaken their claim to the Emerald Throne, as well as other lines that had sworn direct fealty to the first emperor. In reality, at least some of these guards were Scorpion spies, handpicked for this assignment by Kachiko.

No wonder Kachiko felt safe regardless of Hotaru's presence.

Yet they were polite enough. One of the sailors promised to bring her belongings to the bodyguard's quarters, which had already been cleared of Nishiyo's effects. Hotaru thanked the sailor and caught up with Kachiko in the passenger cabin at the stern of the main deck.

In the cabin, Kachiko politely asked a young woman to draw the blinds closed. Hotaru almost asked whether Kachiko wanted to miss the view of Kyūden Doji perched atop the white cliffs as they sailed out to sea, but surely the emissary knew what she was missing. Hotaru pushed aside the blinds to peer at the palace one last time. The feeling in her belly wasn't the thrill of adventure she'd known by Toshimoko's side, but it was too late to turn back now.

The light grew wan within the chamber, and Kachiko settled herself on a cushion beside a small writing desk. The young woman, who must have been Kachiko's handservant, brought her a collection of letters. Kachiko thanked the woman before she set about reading in silence, pointedly ignoring Hotaru's presence.

Hotaru settled into a cross-legged position to meditate. After she had failed horribly to learn inner stillness from her teachers at the academy, Toturi had taught her that meditation was not about shutting out the world, but about clearing the mind enough to truly let the world in. That, at least, Hotaru could do. As bodyguard, her principal duty was to remain alert for any threats, even while surrounded by other guards. Perhaps especially while surrounded by other guards. And when guarding a Scorpion.

The crew bustled on the main deck, shouting commands and adjusting the sails with the wind. It would be a full day's sail to the Flying Fish Isles if the wind was with them, and more if not. Commodore Motoyashi had sent word to the admiral – this time, the blockade would be sure to let the Imperial vessel through.

The next morning, the skies were clear and sunny. One side of the Keep of White Sails hung over sheer cliffs. The tip of the promontory was covered in frozen grass, and the pale cliff was marred by a single juniper tree that defied the relentless sea winds. It was a sight fit for a painting, but there was no time to truly appreciate it.

The wind was bitterly cold as they lowered themselves into the longboat. Across the bay, one- and two-masted ships crowded the meager number of berths, so the Imperial ship had been forced to drop its anchor offshore.

They were already within range of the Mantis's archers, but the gold and emerald Imperial standard flown on the ship's mast had granted them safe passage so far, as Kachiko had promised it would. Either the Mantis still respected the emperor's authority, or Kachiko had arranged things beforehand.

Hotaru stayed low to keep her balance, but she turned back to the ship to offer her hand to help Kachiko, whose kimono perilously restricted her movement. The Scorpion woman's hand was delicate and smooth, not roughened by years of sword practice like Hotaru's. Kachiko was the very picture of a courtly noblewoman – graceful and restrained and impossibly beautiful – while Hotaru was tall for a woman with a lean warrior's build. They were almost perfect opposites.

Hotaru reached her other hand around to steady Kachiko by the shoulder as she took her seat. This close, she caught Kachiko's scent of sandalwood and jasmine again, mixed with the salt of the sea air.

"Thank you," Kachiko offered unexpectedly as she released Hotaru's hand. Just yesterday, Kachiko had proudly declared that she would not need Hotaru's help.

"It is nothing," Hotaru replied. It was only her duty. She took the customary place of the bodyguard behind the lady. The cold wind had burned her cheeks to red.

A handful of other Imperial guards boarded the longboat after them, and their belongings followed suit. Waves lapped against the sides of the boat, and the spray of the sea felt like ice. Dark clouds still threatened on the horizon, promising to fulfill Koji's prediction. She shivered.

Though it seemed to take an eternity, eventually the sailors rowed them to the end of a wharf, where they were met by a dozen sailors dressed in heavy teal coats with red caps and belts – the bright colors of the Mantis Clan. They looked too jovial to be a real threat, but as the passengers disembarked, Hotaru braced herself for trouble.

The leader's unmistakable long red hair was pulled back in a messy bun. "We've been expecting you, m'lady Bayushi."

Hotaru's stomach plummeted. *Expecting* the emissary was different than *welcoming* her, but it explained their ease of passage in the bay.

Kachiko offered the slightest of smiles. "First Mate Seiyu, I presume?"

No wonder the first mate looked familiar. Seiyu of the *Inazuma*, reputed to be descended from a banyan tree spirit, was the sailor with whom Hotaru and Toshimoko had played Fortunes and Winds many years ago at Gotei City. The crew had called Seiyu their keel – the first mate kept the rest of them steady and shouldered the ship's heaviest burdens.

"Aye," Seiyu grinned, their smooth face dotted in freckles. "It's good to finally meet you," they said, exchanging bows with Kachiko. Their expression dropped as they spied Hotaru.

"But expecting that one, we weren't." Seiyu motioned to Hotaru with a jerk of their head. One of the other sailors in Seiyu's entourage, a large man with a full beard and a bald head, spit out a wad of chewing leaf.

She'd be happy to teach him a lesson in etiquette with the back of her blade, but as long as she served Kachiko, she'd have to endure this and many more incivilities.

"Come, Lady Doji," Kachiko commanded her. Hotaru bit back a curse and humbled herself by obeying.

"This is my bodyguard," Kachiko explained. The assembled Mantis glared at Hotaru as she passed them by. "And your name?" the emissary asked, approaching the one who'd spat.

The large sailor sprang to attention. "They call me Big Fish – but you can call me handsome."

"Very well, Big Fish," Kachiko said, ignoring his sophomoric flirtation. "Won't you be a dear and help me fetch my things? You'll be sure our belongings are transported carefully, won't you?"

She pointed her fan toward several large chests.

"I, well..." he stammered.

"Go on – help the mistress," Seiyu insisted, and waved him off.

"Feh," Big Fish grunted. He shot Hotaru another dirty look before turning to his task, which Hotaru returned with a smile.

Kachiko could have ignored the sailor who'd spat in Hotaru's direction, but instead she'd exacted a small revenge. Perhaps she had heeded Hotaru's warning, after all, and did not want to alienate her Crane protector. "Thank you," Hotaru murmured.

"It is nothing," Kachiko replied.

As the rest of the Imperial guards made to disembark, Seiyu

stopped them. "Sorry, sirs. We'll protect the emissary from here." The joviality of Seiyu's crew had turned to scornful glee. "This is the part when you turn around and go back to yer ship, aye?"

Kachiko betrayed no surprise, and for the second time in as many days, Hotaru wished she had not been right. The Mantis were overstepping to deprive Kachiko of her full complement of guards.

But the Mantis already outnumbered their party, and many more Mantis sailors were within shouting distance. No doubt Kachiko had made the same calculation. The emissary put up a hand to signal the Imperial guards to back down. "I will speak to the captain about this," she told them. "For now, please do as the first mate says. Wait for us on the ship."

The guards nodded obediently and prepared to return in the longboat.

As Kachiko and her bodyguard navigated the icy planks of the quay, Hotaru counted the Mantis ships docked in the bay. The Crane Clan navy would be hard pressed to assault the harbor directly. The keep and its towers were perfectly situated to rain down flaming arrows and equally deadly rocks from above if any ships attempted to dock without permission. The Mantis must have taken the Sasaki family samurai by surprise. It would have been impossible for the Sasaki to defend the harbor from invading ships if they couldn't see their enemy due to a fog, natural or otherwise.

Although Kachiko and Hotaru had set foot on solid ground again, to Hotaru, their standing felt more threatened than ever.

Ice gathered in corners and filled in gaps in the paths, promising a treacherous climb to the promontory where the keep stood. And yet, Kachiko did not so much as protest as they trudged up the trail. At one point, Hotaru instinctively reached out to steady Kachiko when she'd seemed to lose her footing, only for Kachiko to catch herself in time.

Gathered around braziers for warmth atop the castle walls, the other ships' crews eyed them warily as they approached each of the outer gates. The three-story castle had been built to defend the signal fire that guided ships to the harbor and to house the soldiers charged with protecting trade vessels and conducting rescues at sea.

Hotaru spared one last glance for the shrinking Imperial vessel. They were on their own now, fully at the mercy of the Mantis Clan. Only the Mantis's respect for the emperor – or Lady Bayushi herself – could guarantee their safety. That, and Hotaru's skills as a fighter.

They passed below the main gate of the keep and were conducted indoors at last, where they could warm their hands over a brazier's coals. Within the foyer, there were gashes and cuts in some of the wooden beams. On the floor were stains that looked too dark to have been just the natural coloring of the wood. The Sasaki samurai had struggled – and fallen.

"Please allow us to take your swords for polishing while you wait," offered one of the servants innocuously. In times of war, guests were forbidden from carrying any weapons – even their ceremonial *wakizashi* – into an official audience with a lord. But most courtiers had a small dagger for their personal protection hidden somewhere in their robes, and only the most brazen lord would have subjected an Imperial emissary to such an undignified search.

Hotaru looked for Kachiko's nod before relinquishing her swords and knives for the first time in her life. She'd spent her youth in Crane lands, as a welcome guest in other clans' lands, or traveling in places disrespectable enough that Hotaru and Toshimoko could get away with holding on to their weapons. Even while in Lion lands, the strictures of courtesy had allowed her to retain her wakizashi, the sword that marked her a samurai.

There was no telling when – or if – her blades would be returned to her.

"This way." One of the servants beckoned to Kachiko's handservant. The small woman disappeared with the rest of their belongings.

Seiyu led Hotaru and Kachiko down a hallway and to a side room. "The cap'n will call for you when he's ready," they added quickly, and they shut the sliding screen behind them. The sound of footsteps leaving was too soft. Some of the sailors who hadn't been assigned porter duty had been set as their guards.

The room was a place for castle furnishings to await their fate as well. Kimono stands, dressing tables, cabinets, and a Go table as well as other furniture and artwork had been stacked haphazardly on one side. Whatever the Mantis samurai had not been keen to keep in their new living quarters must have been brought here.

Kachiko took a seat in the center of the room and produced a small hand mirror, which she used to secure her hair back into place. Even buffeted by the wintry sea winds, she still looked impeccable, her high cheeks and dark eyes more befitting a painting than real life.

Hotaru was mindful not to let her gaze linger, and she looked away, but not before Kachiko noticed her. Hotaru's blood was finally returning to her face.

"Would you like to borrow my mirror?" Kachiko asked pleasantly.

"There's no need," Hotaru assured her. The last thing a bodyguard needed to care about was appearances.

"Indeed, you look the part of the wild warrior," Kachiko said playfully. "All the better to strike fear into the heart of Captain Gendo."

Hotaru couldn't help but smile. "I will take 'wild warrior' over 'haughty heir.'"

Kachiko chuckled at that. The emissary continued to touch up her makeup as the minutes passed them by. The longer they were made to wait, the more the captain was asserting his authority and importance over their own. Perhaps if it had been Kachiko alone, Gendo's reception would have been swift, but with a Crane in tow, there was no telling how many hours would pass before Gendo deigned to receive them. If Hotaru was to blame for Kachiko having to endure this, then the least she could do was offer some meager entertainment.

Hotaru gestured to the Go table stacked in the corner. "Do you play? I fear it may be some time before we are received."

"So do I. You might have caused something of a stir among our hosts." Kachiko looked as though she were considering. "I do play, but I am not sure if we are on the same level."

Kachiko's words left open to interpretation which of them was of higher level, but it was clear she wanted to see if Hotaru could keep up. "There is only one way to find out."

"Very well." She motioned to the Go set with her fan.

Hotaru set up the specially designed table in front of Kachiko and brought over the rest of the Go set, piece by piece. Go was a game treasured by courtier and warrior alike, as evidenced by the caliber of materials that went into the set. The two bowls were made of mulberry wood, with deep rings gracing the curves of the sides like ocean waves. Opening the lids revealed polished stones of black slate and white quartz.

"Would you like to play Black, Lady Doji?" Kachiko offered with a delicate gesture. Black went first, which was a significant boon to a weaker opponent.

Like most nobility, Hotaru had been taught how to play Go from a young age. She was a few years younger than Kachiko, but she didn't need to be patronized. "I'm not afraid to let the stones decide," Hotaru said pleasantly, dipping her fingers into the bowl to grab a handful of white stones before placing her hand back on the table.

"If you are sure…" Kachiko glanced up from Hotaru's hand to meet her eyes.

It is said that the eyes can speak as much as the mouth. Kachiko's eyes promised that she would not lose – this game, or the larger game they were both playing.

The emissary reached into the other bowl and placed a single black stone on the board, then another. *Even.*

Hotaru withdrew her hand, revealing an odd number of white stones. "You will play White, then," Kachiko smirked. "Impress me."

"As you command, Your Excellency," Hotaru replied, and set the two bowls on opposite corners.

The kaya-wood board stretched one and a half *shaku* between them, a grid of nineteen by nineteen intersecting lines. The star points sparkled with inlaid mother-of-pearl. No doubt the table itself was an heirloom of the Sasaki family, a means of entertainment through long winter nights or strong summer storms.

Her family's vassals had to be reinstalled in this castle. The heaviness of her duty weighed her down as she and Kachiko bowed to one another. The match had begun.

Kachiko took her time to consider her first move, and then picked up one of the black stones between her index and middle fingers. She set down her first stone with a loud *clack*. Her forcefulness couldn't be taken as anything other than a challenge. It was no different than the fighting spirit of Hotaru's classmates in the dueling academy – a confidence that some considered arrogance.

Hotaru responded with a conservative play. There was no reason to be hasty, and she knew little about her opponent. If the

Mantis delayed as long as she suspected they might, she might even be able to learn Kachiko's true purpose here. Or, at least, she could glean more about Kachiko's temperament firsthand, instead of relying solely on her infamous reputation. Who was the real woman behind the rumors and scandalous tales?

They played one stone after another, white and black, white and black, marking their territory until finally a group of Hotaru's white stones was surrounded by black on all sides but one. White had one liberty yet, which she would need to shore up or abandon.

"*Atari*," Kachiko announced as she cornered the white stone, as though Hotaru were a beginner.

Hotaru made her next move elsewhere and let Kachiko capture the white stones. It was a small sacrifice, but it had the intended effect of emboldening the Scorpion woman.

As the board filled with constellations of black and white stones, Kachiko seemed certain that each move she made was the right one. She didn't make mistakes, didn't cede territory she didn't intend to. She was in control, forcing Hotaru to react.

And why should she play any differently? She was the guest being received by the Mantis when Hotaru's delegation had been refused in blood. She was the emissary sent on the emperor's behalf to mediate peace. She was the wife of the emperor's best friend and closest confidante. She walked in the same circles as Hotaru's father, while Hotaru had been left behind.

Their game echoed the larger game Kachiko had invited her to play, only in that game, the lives of Crane and Mantis samurai were at stake in the place of mere stones.

Hotaru took a deep breath. Go could be played in contemplative silence, but that might allow the wall between them that had been lowered by an exchange of kindnesses to rise again. Hotaru needed to know what Kachiko wanted, and what measures she might take to ensure victory. And if she could convince Kachiko that they did not have to be opponents, perhaps the Scorpion could begin directing her competitive energy against the Mantis instead.

The next black stone announced itself loudly. Kachiko had cut off one of Hotaru's groups in an aggressive play. Hotaru accepted the loss of her stones with grace and a smile. "You really are an accomplished player."

There was only a moment's hesitation before Kachiko took Hotaru's stones off the board and placed them with the other captured white stones, but it was a hesitation, nonetheless. Perhaps it was possible that, ensconced as she was in the upper echelons of society where every word was political, Kachiko wasn't used to receiving sincere compliments.

Hotaru made her next move and said, "I imagine that your duties keep you quite busy, but even if you do not often get opportunities to play, it seems you are able to make the most of them to keep your skills honed."

"My duties keep me very busy indeed," came Kachiko's reply, as she set down another stone with an audible *click*. "It is not often that I am forced to pass the time with games of this sort."

"Of course," Hotaru said amiably, and she took another turn. "Perhaps the games of court are practice enough. Is Go not unlike a conversation, with each side taking its turn until one side makes an argument the other cannot refute?"

Kachiko let out a gentle laugh. "Did you read that line in a pillow book somewhere?"

Hotaru blushed. "No. It was something my sister taught me."

"Ah, yes. That does sound like something she would say, and she's not wrong. I dare say she's made quite a splash in the capital," Kachiko said, and made her own play.

Though Hotaru and her adopted older sister were very close, it was hard not to be jealous of Shizue's success in the highest tiers of society, or of her freedom to study as an artisan. But Hotaru had to keep talking, or Kachiko would know she'd touched a nerve, if she didn't already. "Is this the first time you've been granted the title of official Imperial emissary, or do you often act on behalf of His Imperial Majesty?"

Kachiko narrowed her eyes but didn't look up from the board. "From time to time, the emperor relies on my husband's assistance in official matters, and of course I am glad to help my liege in any way I can." The emperor likely relied on Bayushi Shoju for unofficial matters, too, but the important part was that Kachiko had refrained from answering either question. Hotaru still couldn't be sure whether Kachiko was representing the emperor's interests only, or the Scorpion's interests, too. Surely she would not dare to come here solely on her own behalf.

Yet nothing about the way Kachiko was playing this game suggested that she wasn't that bold.

"Of course." Hotaru couldn't accuse Kachiko of lying. She needed to come at the question from another angle. She studied the board, looking for other angles to attack there, and found one. Kachiko had left herself open to danger, but the play would expose Hotaru as well.

Hotaru placed her stone. *Seki.* Now they were at an impasse.

Kachiko began a contest on another part of the board, but her attention was focused on Hotaru now. Their eyes met once again, each looking for an opening in the other.

Sometimes, brutal honesty did more to disarm an opponent than the most cleverly concocted lie. "For my part, I am here to represent the Crane's interests, but I would be lying if I said I didn't hope to prevail, and thereby raise my standing in my father's eyes."

Kachiko's brown eyes darkened. "I am here to serve the emperor, not raise my standing," she said, but too defensively.

There it was – the lie. She had something to prove as well. Perhaps the two of them were not so opposite.

Kachiko placed another stone with an indignant *clack*, an aggressive but risky play. She sat rigid in her seat, waiting for Hotaru's counter.

Hotaru seized her chance and placed her stone to set Kachiko's group off-balance.

Now they were perfectly matched. Each of them could keep capturing the other's stone in the same fashion, locked in a cycle for eternity, but the rule of *kō* would not allow it. In this game, at least, Kachiko was forced to set her sights elsewhere.

Perhaps Hotaru could convince Kachiko to take her ambitions elsewhere, too.

The sliding door opened before Kachiko could respond, and Seiyu bowed before them both, more out of habit than actual courtesy. "The cap'n says you're to see him now."

A hint of Kachiko's irritation shone through at the Mantis's demand, and she got up a little too hurriedly.

"It would seem we are forced to end here," Hotaru said, rising to join Kachiko's side.

As they walked, Kachiko tapped her folded fan against her lips coyly. "Before we were interrupted, I saw more captured white stones than black."

Kachiko was willing to claim victory early, but Hotaru wouldn't consider the game a loss. "A lot can change in the end game," Hotaru reminded her gently. "We have many more moves to take yet."

CHAPTER FIVE

The Keep of White Sails stretched across the painted wall panels. Below the castle walls, a twisted and gnarled juniper tree clung to the rocky cliff face. High waves roiled beside the bluffs, and small dabs of paint evoked flocks of birds soaring above the bay. Golden rays emanated from the rising sun on the eastern horizon, but where they drew the eye sat a large, burly samurai, his legs splayed wide in the martial folding chair atop the single-step dais. A usurper.

The first mate stepped forward to serve as herald for the mockery of a court. "Kneel before Gendo, captain of the *Inazuma*, lord of the Keep of White Sails, blessed of Tobiuo-hime, legendary duelist of the Whirlwind Sickle style, raider of the south sea, conqueror of the Portugans, and son of the serpent Ikuji!"

Aside from captain, all of those titles had been self-granted, Hotaru was sure.

Gendo himself was a large man with a strong jaw and dark beard. Beside him, where the ceremonial armor of Sasaki Okimoto should have been, hung a bright-green cuirass and helmet. Two golden prongs rose up like antennae from the crest of the helmet, each nearly a shaku long. Red and teal thread coursed through the shoulder pads to match the silken under-armor Gendo was wearing, as if his clan were already at war and he might need to don the armor at any time.

A snide grin crawled up one side of his face as he watched Kachiko and Hotaru approach on their knees.

"Lady Bayushi Kachiko of the Scorpion Clan, emissary of His Imperial Majesty Hantei the Thirty-Eighth," the first mate announced, apparently educated enough to deliver a proper introduction when it counted.

Kachiko offered the captain a shallow bow. "May I also present my bodyguard and the heir to the Crane Clan, Lady Doji Hotaru."

Hotaru forced herself to follow suit with perfect politeness, but behind her back, someone snickered. Another Mantis sneered, "Didn't the Crane get the message?" Someone who sounded like Big Fish added, "They sent their *heir*? Are they idiots?"

Among the Mantis, the normal courtesies afforded to one's enemies didn't apply, it seemed. But revealing her annoyance was below a Crane.

"So, the Crane hides behind the Scorpion, fearing the might of the Mantis!" Gendo grinned as he leaned an elbow against his knee.

The Mantis samurai around them laughed heartily. Many looked as though they'd just stepped off their vessels, badly in need of a shave or a bath or both. The only respect this rabble afforded was to coin, it seemed.

"Regardless of our unexpected guest, let me welcome you, lovely Kachiko, to my seaside castle!"

Hotaru would have challenged his claim to these islands right then and there if she thought he would agree to duel civilly. He had no right to claim these isles, much less insult Kachiko by omitting her formal title.

"It would seem that the legends of your beauty pale in comparison to the truth."

Kachiko dipped her head. "You flatter me, surely," she said with a practiced grace worthy of a true noble.

"Do you call your host a liar?" Gendo joked. He let out a hearty chuckle. Kachiko did not dispute him further. "So, tell me. Have you brought the Crane with you so that she can formally cede these islands to the Mantis with you as a witness?" he then asked, still smiling.

The rest of the room erupted into laughter once again. Hotaru would not let them sense that they were getting to her – or that she feared Kachiko would do the very thing Gendo suggested.

"As you know, I am here to serve as a neutral arbitrator between your clans," Kachiko seemed to remind him. "Doji Hotaru is here to help ensure my protection, as it seems I was not permitted to bring my full complement of guards."

The mention of the guards was a jab – albeit a gentle one – against the Mantis, an insinuation of discourtesy. Was Kachiko ready to accept Hotaru's help, now that she had to choose between relying on the Crane or relying on the Mantis?

Gendo responded with a gruff *hrmph*. His amused look hardened into annoyance. "As the first mate no doubt explained, the Mantis can keep you plenty safe."

What Kachiko said now would determine all their fates.

"As you say, captain. I saw for myself the Mantis crews patrolling the harbor, but no sign of the Sasaki family samurai. Tell me, what has become of them? Who are you protecting me from, exactly?"

Gendo gripped the armrests of his chair. "Hah! To call the Sasaki *samurai* is generous… We came to collect the goods that were promised us, but the Sasaki turned their blades against us in a craven act of betrayal and greed!" He pointed in the direction of the bay, his voice full of false outrage. "When we defended ourselves against their onslaught, the Sasaki fled rather than face our might! Those who couldn't outrun us, we caught. We seized their ships to protect against a counterattack."

He was lying. The Sasaki family would *never* relinquish their post that way, and the signs of fighting they'd passed on their way to this chamber only confirmed that. Of course someone like Gendo would deny that he'd brazenly assaulted a Crane Clan holding. All of Rokugan knew the Mantis were liable to tell tall tales, and that one had to be careful when bargaining with members of the minor clan, but now she was sure that Gendo and his crew, at least, were simple pirates. A true samurai knew the importance of honesty, the strength of one's word, and the value of courtesy toward one's enemies.

"What a tragic misunderstanding," Kachiko said softly. "The emperor weeps for his servants," she lamented, without specifying which servants she was referring to. She was still playing Gendo and Hotaru both.

Gendo dipped his head in agreement. "But now that you've brought the Crane..." he gestured to Hotaru, "we can settle this quickly."

Kachiko's eyes focused on Gendo as he motioned for Seiyu to fetch ink, scroll, and brush. "One moment," she said, and lowered her fan. Her lips were drawn together in a tight, narrow line, her eyes too wide.

It was the first time Hotaru had seen Kachiko truly surprised. Was Captain Gendo going rogue? On instinct, Hotaru looked for the swords that should have been at her right, but she'd already surrendered them.

Kachiko continued, "I believe the testimony of the Sasaki family should also be heard before any *official* determination is made."

Kachiko had not fully sided with Gendo yet, which meant the

Crane had a chance. Hotaru could still prove her worth to her advisors, her clan, and her father.

Gendo almost growled in reply, "What is their word worth, after everything they've done? No – have the Crane representative sign the isles over to us as restitution, and let us be done with it!"

Hotaru braced herself, ready to fight off any who dared force her to put her seal on the scroll. Kachiko had to stop this, somehow. But why would she?

As his first mate unrolled the scroll before them, Kachiko snapped her fan shut in warning. "Do not forget, *captain*, that it is *I* who shall make the determination as to the stewardship of the Keep of White Sails and the Flying Fish Isles."

The captain met Kachiko's furious gaze. He didn't flinch.

This was her opening. "Your Excellency," Hotaru cut in. "As heir to their liege and sole representative of the Crane Clan, I would speak on the Sasaki family's behalf." The rest of the chamber shifted.

Hotaru took two steps forward, bowing first to Lady Kachiko and then to Captain Gendo in an offering of peace and respect. It was more than he deserved. "The Crane and Mantis have peaceably shared a sea for a thousand years," she began. She had to gloss over some disputes if she hoped to find common ground and win the sympathy of Gendo's crew. "The people of the Flying Fish Isles and those of the Islands of Silk and Spice are alike. Both are fisherfolk, sailors, traders, and loyal servants of the emperor."

It would feel good to call him a liar, but that would only undercut her efforts. Gendo needed to know what he was risking if he attempted to solidify his claim on the isles here and now.

"The Mantis Storm Fleet is mighty, but its sailors are reliant on the crops grown by the Crane to feed themselves on long voyages.

"In return, the Crane buy your goods and employ your many

captains-for-hire. There is no need to throw away an ally in the Crane like this and to cut off the chief source of the Mantis Clan's fortunes." Hotaru closed her eyes and mouthed a silent prayer to her ancestors that Gendo would see reason. She took a deep breath. "Release the Sasaki prisoners. Leave the isles in peace. If you do this, all can be forgotten and forgiven." She had said her piece. She could only hope she'd been persuasive.

A slow and mocking clap forced her to open her eyes. Gendo slouched in his chair, rubbing his hands together in amusement.

"Very nicely spoken, Crane! You almost had me moved. But that doesn't change the treachery committed by the Sasaki – a treachery you do not deny."

His outrageous claims weren't worth dignifying with a denial. Kachiko had to know that he was lying.

"Captain…" Kachiko warned. Her body was rigid, just as when she'd been put on the back foot while playing Go.

"I believe it is time for *Her Excellency* and I to continue this conversation – alone." He rose from his chair and extended a hand to invite Kachiko to his side. "What do you say to a private tour of the castle? The sunsets are striking from the top of the keep, I can assure you…" He gestured to Hotaru briefly. "Your bodyguard will be relieved to be reunited with her fellow Crane, I'm sure."

In the dungeons, he meant. As another captive, trapped and unable to serve her clan or her charge. The whispers would begin anew, ruining her reputation forever. She held her breath waiting for Kachiko to answer.

"I appreciate the offer, but I suspect that tonight's sunset will be marred by the encroaching clouds." Kachiko did not get up to accept his hand.

"Oh, but there are plenty of other artworks the Crane left behind that you could still admire, Kachiko." He kept his hand outstretched in a not-so-subtle invitation to spend the evening alone in his quarters.

"I am weary from the rough journey, and I think I shall retire early to my rooms if we have concluded our negotiations for the day." The tone wasn't playful, and she wasn't playing hard to get.

It was as firm a _no_ as she could offer without saying it outright. Even if Kachiko had previously worked out a deal with the Mantis, this had not been part of it.

Hotaru had to protect her after her move had left her exposed. "The Imperial emissary requires a bodyguard suitable to her rank at all times," she reminded Gendo, raising her voice to address them all. "To do anything else would be tantamount to an insult to His Imperial Majesty himself."

This was the moment of truth. If Kachiko shrugged off Hotaru's protection, she'd have the perfect opportunity to negotiate with the Mantis away from the Crane, and be back to where she'd started before Hotaru's interference. But Gendo's price for negotiations seemed clear now.

Kachiko met Hotaru's gaze. Let me protect you, Hotaru pleaded wordlessly. Kachiko's eyes softened.

At last, the emissary spoke. "Indeed," she agreed, lowering her fan into her lap. "As heir to the Crane Clan and daughter of the Emerald Champion, only Doji Hotaru has the standing to ensure the protection of an Imperial emissary. I insist that she remain by my side at all times during my stay."

Thank you, Hotaru said with her eyes, and Kachiko nodded almost imperceptibly. They were playing on the same side, for now. And Hotaru had not yet lost this game.

Upon the dais, Gendo stood, indignant. His crew braced for his outburst. "So be it, then! The Crane can flap about and squawk beside you for as long as you wish! You _both_ shall remain my guests until such time as the emperor compensates me for providing you hospitality. Ten thousand *koku* should suffice, I think."

Hotaru felt her mouth drop open. Surely, Kachiko had not come to this keep to be taken as a *hostage*, and ten thousand koku was an outrageous sum.

Hotaru's warrior instincts kicked in, and she shifted to keep Kachiko close. Kachiko leaned into her, recognizing a threat when she saw one.

"Captain–" Seiyu interrupted.

"Silence! We will speak after!"

Gendo's arrogance, insults, and threats were completely out of line. "How *dare* you and your ruffians make such demands upon your sovereign?" Hotaru snapped, standing to rebuke him. "How *dare* you disrupt the emperor's peace in this way, instigating a war with your closest neighbors and lying about the cause of this conflict? Why risk all that you have?"

Gendo's eyes went wide in shock and rage, and Seiyu stared.

"You would throw your good fortune and your allies to the winds? You would send a bald-faced message of contempt to His Imperial Majesty? Why? What good will this bring your clan? Think of the damage this would do to your clan's *reputation*!"

For a moment, the Mantis sailors surrounding them hesitated, and even Gendo was taken aback. Seiyu's gaze alternated between Gendo and Hotaru. Kachiko gently tugged at Hotaru's trousers to pull her back, as if to say, *Do not provoke him any further.*

"I was right to reject your fool delegation, you long-necked, preening hen," Gendo shouted, and took a step forward. "You and your kin are nothing but haughty and indignant! You come only to demand and threaten and lord over your minor clan cousins."

Kachiko rose to stand beside Hotaru. "Now listen here–"

Gendo cut her off. "First Mate Seiyu will see you to your quarters so that you can retire early."

Kachiko looked as though she'd been slapped in the face.

As she was an emissary, Gendo should have given her the chance to speak, but to deny her that, and worse, interrupt her…

He was no longer playing by the rules. Hotaru and Kachiko had lost their last liberty, and now their group of stones had been captured. But the game wasn't over yet.

Seiyu leapt from their seat, two other Mantis Clan samurai following them. Hotaru scanned the room for any other movement, or worse, aggression. Swords or no, she would teach them a lesson if they put hands on Kachiko, or if they tried to separate them.

"Stay close to me," Hotaru whispered.

Kachiko nodded and stepped beside her.

CHAPTER SIX

The inner keep was small compared to the palace she'd grown up in, and little art adorned the walls outside the main reception hall. The wooden pillars and beams were roughly carved and unevenly lacquered. The castle wasn't built for art, but for defense. Even the most skilled Daidoji soldiers would struggle to breach the walls without suffering serious casualties. A diplomatic solution could have saved hundreds of Crane lives, but it was plain now that Gendo would never have accepted a peaceful solution. He was eager for a fight.

Anger stung Hotaru's face as she followed Kachiko through the corridors, the dim roar of crashing waves the only sound besides their footsteps.

She'd tried her best, and it hadn't been enough. She may not have been sent to the dungeons, but she and Kachiko were still captives. Her father, the Emerald Champion, would be the one tasked with paying the ransom, if Hotaru couldn't find another solution soon. Once again, she would be deemed a failure and would prove her father right in having left her behind at Kyūden Doji.

They ascended a steep wooden stairway to the second floor

and turned a corner to a hallway, where Seiyu directed them to the middle room.

Maybe, just maybe, Seiyu had wanted to warn the captain against taking things too far. Hotaru could appeal to Seiyu, but that was a gamble. What if she'd misread Seiyu? What if they hadn't been warning the captain, after all? They'd have their excuse to lock her away for good.

A guard opened the sliding door for them to enter. A simple divider stood in the room's center, and there was no alcove. Their belongings had already been deposited here, and Kachiko's handservant was setting up for a lengthy stay.

"M'lady Bayushi will be staying here until…" Seiyu seemed to struggle for the right phrase, "until the cap'n has need of you again." They didn't have to say aloud that Hotaru and Kachiko risked the little freedom they had if any of them tried to sneak out.

Addressing Hotaru, Seiyu said, "Your room is just beyond this door." They gestured to a small panel on the left wall. For propriety, a dignitary such as Kachiko would be afforded privacy. Practically speaking, a bodyguard would be expected to sleep in the same room as their charge if they were in danger.

"Any questions?" Seiyu finally asked. Kachiko shook her head curtly. Seiyu shut the door behind them. Not all of the silhouettes left with them as they disappeared down the hallway. Kachiko and Hotaru were still under guard.

Hotaru didn't know what to say. Her coming along hadn't been part of Kachiko's plan, and now Captain Gendo had gone rogue, possibly because of her presence. She was responsible for Kachiko's safety, but she had only made the emissary less safe. She couldn't disappoint Kachiko, too.

She had to do what she could. Hotaru began her sweep for trapdoors, secret passages, and removable ceiling panels. The walls of Kyūden Doji hid a maze of passages for traveling invisibly from one part of the palace to another, both to keep servants out of view and to allow its inhabitants to discreetly conduct liaisons. A military castle like this one would have its own passageways for defending against a siege, but it was possible that these guest chambers were not connected – and were specifically intended for hostages or other guests who weren't afforded an escape route.

The far wall of the room was part of an overhang, making it more difficult for its occupants to try to escape by scaling the walls below. Opening the shutters, she looked out over sheer cliffs and the dark, cold sea beyond. A jump from this height would be certain death. The floor swayed beneath her.

Hotaru stole a glance at her charge. Kachiko busied herself by rearranging the belongings that her handservant had already set out. One piece at a time, she moved the pieces of her calligraphy set, shifting the brush, tray, inkstone, writing mat, and mulberry paper ever so slightly. It was the only power that remained to her.

Her sweep finished, Hotaru expected Kachiko to send her away. Surely Kachiko did not want her company. But a minute passed, and then another, and the dismissal didn't come. "What now?" Hotaru asked, waiting for the emissary's command.

Kachiko was silent for a long time as she untied a bundle of papers and began leafing through her correspondence. Finally, she asked, "Is this your first time being held for ransom?"

"It is," she said, but admitting so only made her feel even younger and less dependable. She took a cross-legged position between Kachiko and the sliding door. "I knew it was a possibility, but…"

"But you thought you could accompany me and convince the Mantis to retreat?"

What could she say? That she had believed Kachiko would negotiate away the isles if she hadn't come along? That she had believed herself the one to bring peace, to ask the Mantis to back down and spare lives on both sides? That she had wanted to prove herself worthy of being here and playing against Kachiko and Gendo?

Kachiko saved her from answering. "At least your words were sincere."

Hotaru felt herself blush. It shouldn't have felt so good to hear something resembling praise from someone as esteemed as Kachiko. "Sincerity won't sway someone like the captain," she said, reminding herself of their current predicament.

"Perhaps not," Kachiko agreed.

"But swaying the captain isn't the true reason I'm here," Hotaru admitted. "I will take every chance I can to help the Crane, but I'm here because I swore an oath to you. My chief duty is to keep you safe."

Kachiko's shoulders tensed at Hotaru's declaration, and she looked up from her correspondence. Quietly, she admitted, "So far, you have not failed in that."

Hotaru's heartbeat quickened. Kachiko had been so quick to dismiss her before, but now… Now she depended on Hotaru, as she had grudgingly admitted in the audience chamber.

Now, perhaps, Hotaru had strengthened her position enough to make her play. "Your plan failed, though."

"I beg your pardon?" Kachiko hadn't expected Hotaru to go on the offensive.

"The Mantis had been expecting you," Hotaru pointed out. "Captain Gendo seemed glad to see you until you refused to sign over the isles to him immediately. Based on his reaction, he didn't expect you to refuse."

"You assume many things," Kachiko replied, and she looked down at her letters again. But Kachiko did not say whether those assumptions were incorrect.

"Perhaps," Hotaru conceded. "Assumptions or no, Gendo has

made the conditions of negotiation clear. As expected, he was not playing by the rules. Let us play on the same side, at least."

"Very well. I'll let you in on the new plan." Kachiko started preparing her ink.

Relief washed over Hotaru. Perhaps her luck would win out, after all.

"You stay silent, and I'll handle this." Kachiko's words were a sudden blow, the kind they taught you to anticipate at the academy, but Hotaru had let down her guard. There was still something more at work for Kachiko to continue refusing her help, something that Hotaru couldn't unravel without additional insight.

"Yet there is one thing you can do to help, Lady Doji."

"Yes?" Hotaru asked, too eagerly.

"Make it through dinner without further offending our hosts, *hm*?" Kachiko's gentle smile was as close to a peace offering as Kachiko would allow herself right now, it seemed. Her tone suggested that Hotaru was perfectly capable of such a feat, if she wanted to see it through.

Hotaru smiled back. "I'll try." Maybe if she succeeded, she could win some of Kachiko's confidence.

As predicted, Captain Gendo "requested" their company at the evening meal, but both understood it to be a command.

Seiyu and their guards led Hotaru and Kachiko to a less formal chamber than the main audience hall. In summer, the large wooden panels could be opened to a balcony and a breathtaking view of the sea. In winter, the wind howled through the eaves of the keep, and waves crashed against the cliffs below.

The Mantis samurai sat with their backs to the walls of the room, leaving space beside the balcony doors for a few musicians who had not yet begun to play. Hotaru and Kachiko were seated a few paces away from Gendo, but not so far that they didn't have a clear view of the captain. They were too far away to speak with him, but if he so wished, he could still easily summon them to his side.

Dinner was served, with course upon course covered in so much spice that it drowned out the natural flavors of the ingredients, but Hotaru could not complain. Beside her, Kachiko wore a mask of propriety in addition to her signature black lace. If she was offended by the flavors, she gave no sign.

Hotaru forced herself to wolf down the food. A bodyguard shouldn't be savoring meals anyway.

As Kachiko ate, taking small bites in silence, servants wearing simple, drab-gray kimono circulated throughout the room attending to the whims of Gendo's crew – refilling sake cups, replacing empty dishes with yet more full bowls. If only Hotaru could speak with one without Kachiko's meddling, she might be able to learn something useful. Like an escape route that would let them get out – or let Crane Clan soldiers in.

The Mantis sailors boisterously accepted the drink, draining their cups before demanding a refill – except for one.

"Be careful how much you have," Seiyu warned some of their crew in between slow sips of sake. There could be several reasons to conserve the rice wine – whether to ration supplies for a prolonged siege, or simply to stay alert for a possible attack.

"Is that what the captain said?" a sailor snapped back.

Seiyu's eyes darkened, and they set down their cup purposefully. Seiyu opened their mouth to say something, but no words came out. They turned their attention elsewhere.

Was it possible that the crew wasn't equating the first mate's word with the captain's, and if so, why not? What had Seiyu wanted to say?

Steam rose from the sake cup the servant poured for Kachiko.

The sake was a rougher variety – cloudy white because it was unfiltered – and meant to be served chilled. Again, Hotaru could say nothing.

Sake jugs in hand, Big Fish and two other Mantis approached Kachiko. "So, milady," he crooned. Hotaru's stomach churned, and not from the meal. "You've visited the City of Lies, no doubt? Tell us about Teardrop Island."

"Yeah, I heard that it's a gambler's paradise!"

"And so many geisha. An entire island full!"

"Oh, I'm sure it's nothing compared to Gotei City…" Kachiko said shyly.

"That's not what we heard!"

They'd been ensnared, and now Kachiko had their full and complete attention. More Mantis gathered to hear her tales. Hotaru gratefully faded into the background, where she was less likely to give offense.

When the servant came to her, Hotaru refused the wine but accepted a cup of tea. Even engaged in conversation, Kachiko might overhear whatever words passed between her and the servant, unless…

There was one way, though it risked Kachiko's anger. Perhaps it would prove that Hotaru was a worthy opponent, after all.

"Have you heard of the annual spring revue held in the City of Lies?" Hotaru had caught the sailors' attention like a school of fish in a net. "There, the most famous up-and-coming performers each put on an act, but even more exclusive performances for samurai are held at the governor's mansion – where Lady Bayushi herself once danced." Where Kachiko had danced, and where one of the guests had ended up murdered, according to Uncle Toshimoko's tale. Once again, that part of the story was better left out. "As long as she is your guest here, it would be a shame for you to miss your chance to see her…"

Kachiko didn't stop smiling, laughing lightly between sips of sake. "Oh, Lady Doji, I assure you, my dancing is nothing special."

"But milady, you're legendary!" one of the sailors shouted.

Another sailor chimed in, "We've even heard of you as far as the Isles of Silk and Spice!"

"Indeed," the captain's deep voice cut through the shouts. "Won't you dance for us, as long as you're our *guest*?"

Perhaps this time, two guests would end up dead following Kachiko's performance: Hotaru for instigating this predicament, and Gendo for being Gendo.

"I would be glad to," Kachiko lied, and she made her way to the front of the crowd. She whispered something to the *biwa* player and flutist, who took up their instruments.

Kachiko took a seat in front of the balcony doors and bowed deeply, gently placing her closed fan on the floor in front of her. Even if the captain was a ruffian, Kachiko would not stoop to his level and forsake common courtesy.

The biwa player strummed the strings and began to sing.

"The spring moon rises above my lord's castle."

Kachiko slowly began to rise and reached out to grasp the fan. Her face impassive, she turned her gaze upward.

"But in the moonlight, all I can see is you."

Kachiko looked directly at Hotaru as she drew the closed fan to her mouth and drew herself up, one arm outstretched.

One of the more inebriated Mantis sailors had the gall to cheer, but Kachiko did not so much as flinch. Slowly, she turned her back to the crowd, raising her fan in an arc overhead and twisting it open in the same motion.

Hotaru motioned for one of the servants to refill her teacup.

"Your name," Hotaru commanded in a whisper, as the song soared.

"Gin, milady," the servant managed. The color drained out of her face as she poured.

"Gin. I'll keep you safe, but I need your help. Are there any ways in or out of this castle that the Mantis are not guarding?"

Gin kept her eyes down to not draw attention to herself. "Tunnels. Old ones. The cove. There was no warning, or else we would have–"

"Where?"

At that moment, the music cut off, and Kachiko snapped her fan open, her expression filled with longing. Gin slipped away before she could answer.

Kachiko's languorous dance and the music continued, her movements conveying the story of a married noblewoman who fell in love with another man at court. In Kachiko's eyes, the woman's longing burned, entranced by the flame of passion while fearing its destructive power.

Kachiko met Hotaru's eyes for the span of a heartbeat before Hotaru looked away. That dance wasn't meant for her – it was meant to win the crew to Kachiko's side, making them hesitate if the captain ordered them to raise a hand against Kachiko. She shouldn't have watched, but it had been too beautiful.

At last, the dance finished, and Kachiko gave a deep bow to the audience. The room erupted into bawdy cheers, and even Gendo dipped his head in recognition of Kachiko's talents. If Kachiko had not aspired to politics, she could have easily become a celebrity artisan, like Shizue.

Kachiko still wore a mask of pleasantness while she pointed her fan at Hotaru. "Did you know that Lady Hotaru spent a year at the Kakita Artisan Academy before studying as a duelist? All first-year students are taught to dance as well. Surely, it would be a rare treat to see a performance by the daughter of the legendary Doji Teinko. She was to the fan as the Grey Crane is to the sword."

Of course, Kachiko's revenge would be immediate, but it wasn't unjustified. Kachiko seemed to know a lot about Hotaru's past, but it was a courtier's business to know the histories of the scions of the clans. And the Scorpion had the benefit of the best spy network in the Empire, though they never admitted so in public.

Kachiko's sources were irrelevant, however – what mattered was not offending Gendo, even if that meant having to dance for him as well.

"Is that so?" Gendo asked, amused. "Well, well, well, it seems the Crane has some use, after all! Go on," he said, motioning for Hotaru to rise. "Entertain us."

There was no escaping Kachiko's and Gendo's insistence. Learning about the tunnels was worth suffering some embarrassment… and it would be embarrassing, she was certain. She was not half as skilled as Kachiko, and she had no business representing the artisan academy this way.

She made her way to the front of the room. There was only one dance whose steps she remembered well enough to avoid making a mockery of herself or the school whose reputation she now must uphold. It was the dance that had led Hotaru to want to study as an artisan in the first place, but she had never been able to perfect it.

Only Kachiko would recognize it, if even she had seen it before. Hotaru tried not to think about a master dancer such as Kachiko watching her meager attempt.

Trying to hide her nerves, she looked to the flutist and asked for the song.

As the melancholy melody slowly took flight, Hotaru's steps followed those of a young noblewoman walking wistfully along the garden paths once trod by her slain lover. With each step, she remembered the happiness they'd shared together, a fleeting moment in the seasons of their lives. A moment lost long ago.

In the moments when the noblewoman fondly recollected the past, Hotaru recalled the joy she felt on her first day in attendance at the dance school, after her mother had convinced her father to allow a future champion to study as an artisan. Even Satsume had smiled to see his daughter so glad.

That happiness had not been meant to last. Like the noblewoman, Hotaru walked a solitary path now.

The steps of the dance still belonged to her mother, but as she glided through the movements, she offered the performance as a prayer. Lady Teinko had been able to devote herself to the arts – to peace. After her tragic suicide, Hotaru had been forced to take up the sword, walking in the footsteps of her father. Perhaps, as bodyguard, it wasn't too late for Hotaru to use her sword for peace, and prove herself both to her parents and her clan.

Let me prevail here, she pleaded with her mother's ghost.

The flute's notes began to fade, as would the joyful memories of the noblewoman as time claimed them, until the room fell silent. Behind her, the balcony doors creaked in the wind.

Surely, the Mantis would have grown bored of the slow, solemn dance, but as she held the final pose, she thought she spied teary eyes among the audience. They might be little more than pirates, but perhaps even they had hearts that could be moved.

She felt Kachiko's eyes upon her as she bowed. When she looked up, she searched for the unspoken words in the Scorpion woman's gaze, but her eyes were unreadable once more.

That's when Hotaru spotted Gin hurrying away from Kachiko's side. Hotaru resumed her seat and pretended not to notice. She would have to trust in the loyalty of the Sasaki servants.

"You were beautiful," Kachiko said quietly, leaning in close to whisper it in her ear. They were the last words she'd expected to hear from her. Hotaru reminded herself that Kachiko was her opponent, but that didn't stop her heart from pounding. Hotaru looked straight ahead and did not reply.

It was not improper for a Crane duelist to offer to protect a Scorpion courtier. The Crane offered favors and gifts all the time to improve relations with other clans, all in the name of duty. But it was improper for bodyguard and charge to call one another beautiful. To let the words send one's heart racing. Such a thing would interfere with the samurai's duty to their clan.

Surely, Hotaru did not have feelings for Kachiko, and she was just lightheaded from the pressure of the performance. Surely, Kachiko had meant the performance was beautiful, not Hotaru herself. It was just some scheme meant to set Hotaru off-balance.

After finishing her cup of sake, Kachiko said to Hotaru, "I think I am ready to retire before Gendo requests an encore performance." Of course. Retiring now would also prevent Hotaru from speaking to Gin further. But until Kachiko was ready to work together, Hotaru would have to make do with what she'd found out so far.

Hotaru forced herself to nod and quickly concocted an excuse. She rose, made her way to Gendo, and bowed. "Captain, we hope you enjoyed our company tonight, but we are still weary from our travels, and I could not bear for someone as precious and talented as Lady Kachiko to become ill from overexertion – I am sure you would agree. Will you permit us to retire?"

Gendo weighed her words for a moment as he swirled the sake in his cup. How much did the captain enjoy toying with his hostages? Would he force them to stay in denial of the emissary's will, or would he still give her the deference she was due?

Finally, he waved them away. "Seiyu!" Gendo called. "Take these ladies away. They must rest if they are to keep up with the festivities of the Mantis for the foreseeable future."

The room laughed, but Hotaru only closed her eyes. Should she have told her soldiers not to wait for her signal, but to risk a rescue if they did not hear from her after so long a time?

It was too late now. She reopened her eyes to face the enemies surrounding them.

Before the laughter died down, Kachiko placed her fingers on Hotaru's shoulder, as though she were just using her bodyguard to steady her footing after too much wine. "I want you in my quarters tonight," she said in hushed tones. "You swore to protect me, and so you will."

"I–" she stopped herself, realizing all eyes were still on them. Of course they would be close, but this was… perfectly appropriate for a bodyguard, and still appropriate for an unmarried woman from a rival clan, Hotaru reminded herself. But after having watched Kachiko's dance… The thought of spending time alone together had taken on a different hue.

When Seiyu came to collect them, the first mate's face was grim.

The wind howled, and a cold draft swept through the room. Hotaru shivered, and she followed Seiyu through the lamplit corridors, keeping Kachiko close and her guard up.

CHAPTER SEVEN

Seiyu slid open the door to usher Hotaru and Kachiko inside their chambers. In the long corridor of the hallway, only one other soldier stood guard. If there was any chance that this soldier's sympathies mirrored Seiyu's – loyalty to the Mantis over Captain Gendo – Hotaru had to take it. The Crane did not give up on a potential ally so easily.

"Just a moment," Hotaru said to Seiyu, pausing before she crossed the threshold. "I wanted to ask you something."

Seiyu tensed, like their ship was steering into rough waters. Their eyes darted between Hotaru and the other guard.

"Do you remember me?" Hotaru asked, bowing, and gestured to the south. "We've met before, two years ago. Gotei City. You wouldn't forget Kakita Toshimoko, the Grey Crane – I was the student by his side."

Seiyu narrowed their eyes.

"What do you want?"

A true Doji courtier would be able to say the words that would mean one thing to Seiyu and another to the guard, but she didn't have time for perfect subtlety. Phrasing mutiny as a question was still dangerous, even if she could claim she wasn't inciting insurrection. "Is this the right course for your crew?" She gestured to the room that served as her and Kachiko's prison. "Isn't it a first mate's duty to warn a captain if storm clouds are on the horizon?"

"Don't tell me how to do my job, troublemaker," Seiyu warned. There it was: a flicker of hesitancy in their eyes. "Or you'll be able to retire to the dungeons next! Ha!" Seiyu earned a chuckle from the other guard.

"Aye, aye, sir." Hotaru put up her hands in surrender and smiled weakly as she stepped back into the room. "This room suits us just fine, thank you."

She closed the door between herself and Seiyu and let out a heavy sigh. She had to be careful, or she'd land herself and the first mate in chains.

As Hotaru turned around, the Scorpion woman was silent on the other side of the room's divider. Fabric whispered against fabric as the handservant helped Kachiko out of her most elaborate over-robes. The handservant moved the partition aside to open up the room again.

Even though Kachiko had only exchanged her many layers of finery for a simpler coat to guard against the chill in the room, it felt like when Hotaru had accidentally stumbled across Toshimoko alone with a geisha at the teahouse – she shouldn't be here. Hoping to dispel the awkwardness, she blurted, "First assignment accomplished: we made it through dinner."

Kachiko gave a soft laugh. She still wore several layers of elegant kimono, but she had let down her black-brown hair. She seemed to glide across the room before sitting beside the low table appointed with a small jug of sake and two cups.

"So we did. Thank you, Ayaka," she said to her handservant, before gesturing for Hotaru to join her at the table. "You are proving yourself to be an opponent of consideration, at least."

"You didn't expect to have to dance, you mean." Hotaru

offered a wry smile, but she held back from accepting Kachiko's invitation. She was still on her guard, especially after Kachiko's unexpected compliment.

"I'll grant you that it was clever."

Clever was a small victory alongside *sincere*, but she would take it. "Wouldn't it be easier if you could focus your efforts against a single opponent?"

"Perhaps… but who's to say I don't enjoy the occasional challenge?" Her tone was softer as she patted the spot diagonal from her.

Hotaru knew she should be careful to avoid seeming too close to her charge, but refusing Kachiko's overtures now would waste an opportunity to gain an ally. Relenting, she took a seat.

"And Gin? What did you want with her?" Hotaru asked.

"I wanted to check on her welfare, believe it or not. As a mere servant, she shouldn't have to be a part of a samurai's game."

As much as she wanted that to be true, she wasn't sure she could trust Kachiko on that point. "What about the guard?" she asked under her breath. Although eavesdropping was far below the dignity of a Crane, it was imperative to know how far one's words could carry at what volume.

"Ayaka mentioned that she noticed the guard was drowsy. I doubt the guard will remember anything we discuss tonight."

At least Hotaru hadn't felt any strange bouts of fatigue since becoming Kachiko's bodyguard, but all the more reason to be cautious.

This was their chance to speak without fear of being overheard. And a chance to convince Kachiko that she had more to gain by siding with the Crane than with the Mantis. "At dinner, we were at cross-purposes. I still don't know what you're planning to do next or what you intend to ask of the captain." What she was about to say felt like sacrificing territory on the board, but it was necessary in the long run. "I will say it again: if you let me in on your plan, I can help you. Isn't there anything that I or the Crane can do to help you get what you want in exchange for the island?" Hotaru had come here to prove her worth to her father, but even if the credit should go to Kachiko, it would be worth it if it helped the Crane recover the island and avoid a war.

"Are you asking if I am open to a bribe, or as you Crane call it, a 'gift'?" Kachiko responded casually as she filled each of their cups. "Surely you don't believe that I would be open to such enticements. I am here purely to represent the emperor's wishes for peace, and I must find the fairest solution for both parties."

Hotaru ignored the cup in front of her as well as Kachiko's hollow objection. "It is not a bribe to offer service to the emissary of the emperor – it is a samurai's duty." But she regretted the words instantly. She was simply reacting to Kachiko's play. She didn't need to defend her reputation to a woman whose reputation was mired in infamy. "If there's anything that I can do to help you…" Kachiko would recognize the difference between an offer to help her versus an offer to help the emissary.

Kachiko searched Hotaru's face. The Scorpion courtier seemed confused by something she found there, and her brows softened with sadness or pity. "Ah, Lady Hotaru."

Her heart skipped a beat at the use of her given name. It was an invitation to be more frank with one another, to strip away one of the levels of formality in their speech.

"I appreciate your willingness to help, but I can handle this on my own."

Her refusal made no sense. Kachiko could have set the price of helping the Crane as high as she wanted, and still Hotaru would have been forced to pay. "Of course you can, but you don't have to. I'm here."

"You're here, it's true," Kachiko answered carefully.

"Then why won't you accept my help?" Was there truly nothing Hotaru could offer that would outweigh what the captain could provide?

Kachiko turned the sake cup around in her fingers. "Because this is something only I can fix."

The word *fix* made Ayaka wince as though Kachiko had thrown her cup against the far wall. For Kachiko to admit that things needed fixing meant they were in deep trouble. But there was only so far Hotaru could push unless Kachiko trusted her more.

Kachiko looked at Hotaru's untouched cup and changed the subject. "It's not poison, if that's what you're wondering." Kachiko raised Hotaru's cup to her own lips and smiled. "If I'd wanted you dead, you wouldn't have made it to the isles." When she replaced the cup on the table, it was no longer full.

If Hotaru wanted Kachiko to trust her, she had to offer her trust in return. And Kachiko wasn't wrong. If half the rumors about Scorpion "handservants" were true, it would have been simple enough for Ayaka to murder Hotaru on the ship and dump her body overboard. So at least Hotaru had that going for her.

With a soft upturn of her hand, Kachiko gestured at Hotaru's cup. "I noticed that you abstained from wine at dinner, presumably on my account. I thought you might appreciate a chance to unwind."

Was that... kindness? It made no sense for Kachiko to stoop to manipulating Hotaru after she'd just unconditionally offered to help.

Hotaru took a sip. Smooth and slightly chilled, the sake must have come from Kachiko's personal stash. She hadn't enjoyed so fine a vintage since the summer, when a Yasuki representative brought a case of Friendly Traveler Sake to celebrate the Star Festival. "Thank you very much. This is wonderful." A gesture of kindness had to be appreciated, or it might not be offered again.

"You are very welcome," Kachiko replied. Her smile turned mischievous. "I know you were dying inside to see the Mantis drinking the castle's sake hot."

Hotaru almost choked as she took another sip, and blushed. "Was it so obvious?"

"Oh, not at all. You wore the strong, silent face of a bodyguard well." Kachiko squared her shoulders and furrowed her brows, pressing her lips into a thin line, her expression the same as when Toshimoko parodied Hotaru's father.

Hotaru couldn't help but laugh, and she had to set the cup down before she spilled any. She couldn't remember the last time she had laughed that honestly.

Kachiko relaxed her face back into a satisfied grin. "I've met enough Crane who are fancy about their sake, not to mention everything else."

"Hey! It seems I'm not the only one," Hotaru said, and held up the sake bottle to prove it.

Kachiko snatched the bottle from Hotaru and poured herself another cup. "It would be unseemly for the emperor's emissary to have anything less than highly cultured taste in wine," she said matter-of-factly.

"Oh, really?" Hotaru rested her elbow on the table. "You take me to believe that you prefer something on the rougher side? *Shōchū*, perhaps?"

"In truth, I find myself needing something stronger after dealing with fancy Crane all day."

Kachiko was giving her a hard time for fun, now. "You know as well as I that I haven't been nearly as fancy as the Crane you're used to in the capital. You can thank the Grey Crane for that." Hotaru gestured to all Kachiko's luggage. "And I assume all of that is needed after dealing with fancy Crane as well?" If Kachiko wanted to tease, Hotaru could oblige her in return.

"As I said, an Imperial emissary has certain appearances to maintain."

As Hotaru was about to voice her skepticism, the shutters banged against the window frame, startling her back to her senses.

It was just the wind, but it could have been an attacker. She and Kachiko were here as hostages, not as bodyguard and charge relaxing after a tiresome day. But for a moment, Kachiko had been able to let them forget the dire circumstances they found themselves in. For a moment, they had been able just to enjoy themselves.

"A little jumpy, are we?" Kachiko asked, her voice calm but her fingers trembling slightly.

"It was a reminder that I should focus on my duty."

"There you go, being all serious again."

"Someone has to be," she said, but there was a thin line between alertness and fearfulness. If she closed the shutters more securely, they wouldn't startle them in the night. She got up and tested the latch.

The icy wind threw the shutters open to the wintry night sky. The lights of the Crane blockade twinkled on the horizon, perhaps, or it was just moonlight on the waves, but it was far too cold for admiring the sight.

Frost burned her face as she reached for the shutters to draw them back closed. Then Kachiko was holding the shutters in place, so close that they could almost touch, and Hotaru could slide the fasteners into place on the top and bottom of the window. Most noblewomen wouldn't have bothered to get up, and instead of crying out at the sudden cold, Kachiko had sprung up to help.

Once again, Hotaru wondered at the woman Kachiko might be behind her mask, behind her efforts at appearances. "There, that should be better now, thanks to your help," Hotaru said.

Kachiko waved off the gratitude, as though she'd done nothing. "It's a shame that it's too cold to actually enjoy the view," she said instead, and retrieved a comb to smooth out her windblown hair. "I'll wager these islands are lovely in summer." Ayaka appeared to offer her lady help with the comb, but Kachiko waved her off.

"I'm certain they are," Hotaru finally agreed, trying to tuck her own hair back behind her ears. Summer felt like a lifetime away. If they could survive the next few days, Hotaru would worry about the summer. "Would you return here, after all this is over?"

"You make it sound as though I can go where I please," Kachiko said sharply, and then caught herself. As she pulled the comb through her long hair, she said more softly, "Even as emissary, I do not have that much power."

Hotaru nodded. Perhaps she had been too quick to be jealous of Kachiko's position.

Kachiko's gaze came to rest on her red comb, its wood carved with interlacing vines, like the Shosuro family crest. "Even if I were…" she trailed off, distracted.

"Even if you were…" Hotaru prompted her.

Kachiko started, and her cheeks turned a deep crimson below her mask. Master courtier or no, she had not meant to speak those words aloud. The stress of their situation had left her feeling raw and vulnerable, too. She did not need to reveal whatever it was that she had been about to say. But perhaps she secretly longed for someone to listen.

"You can tell me," Hotaru offered. "A burden is lighter if there are more to carry it."

Kachiko finished combing her hair and looked up at Hotaru. "And why should you care to carry my burdens?"

"Because I know what it's like to be forced to carry them yourself."

Kachiko sighed deeply. "What I was going to say was, even if

I were the Shosuro daimyō, I would only have so much power. I would answer to the Scorpion Clan Champion, but at least I would have more power in my own right. As it stands, my own young son will inherit the Bayushi lands and titles before me. Yes, for now I have some sway in the Imperial Court, thanks to my husband… But when he dies, what will be left for me? A life in my child's shadow? A life in the monastery?"

The words were cold water in her face. Hotaru would be daimyō of a great family and lord of a Great Clan. She would never live to see her titles passed on, nor would she retire unless it was under her own terms. Kachiko's power was dependent on others.

"Meanwhile, as heir to the Crane Clan, you wield tremendous influence, yet you willingly play bodyguard, a role far beneath you." Kachiko could barely conceal her jealousy.

It hadn't felt like wielding tremendous influence when Hotaru had to fight to be heard by her own advisors. Hotaru had had no choice but to stay behind in Crane lands, just as she had felt she must pledge herself to Kachiko in order to obtain even a chance at helping her clan. No, being heir had only meant constantly striving, and failing, to make her clan and her father proud.

"It is more complicated than that," Hotaru said softly.

"And so perhaps you understand my position," Kachiko replied, taking another sip of her sake. "But I still do not think you appreciate yours. One day, in the not-too-distant future, you'll be the champion of the Crane Clan and head of the Doji family. Your spouse will be subordinate to you. Your children will heed your word above all others. You'll have entire armies and navies under your command."

Kachiko was right. And yet… the demands of nobility had brought her to this room, where she was confined to wait unless she dared risk all three of their lives by escaping before they were ransomed back. She'd be risking many more lives if she called for the Crane to launch an attack. "That may be so, but it also means I'll be responsible for my clan, for my family, for my relatives, and for all who fight on my behalf." She felt her lip trembling. She couldn't let Kachiko see that it was overwhelming, that she was afraid of failing everyone, but maybe Kachiko would understand. Maybe Kachiko was willing to help shoulder the weight in return. "They all have their own idea of how I should lead. They'll have their own expectations of what kind of champion I should be." She felt her eyes watering, but couldn't stop herself.

"I think you underestimate yourself." Kachiko set down her cup. "You are sincere, clever, and determined. You still have not given up on swaying me to your side." She reached out to place a hand on Hotaru's shoulder.

Hotaru almost started at the warm touch, but when she placed her hand over Kachiko's in return, the weight of all her responsibility seemed to melt away. Kachiko knew what it was to tread a lonely and difficult path as well. Together, it would not be so lonely, or so difficult.

"And that you acknowledge your responsibility to your retainers shows you to be wiser than most lords, who feel entitled to power. Yet, I would still say that it is better to have too much responsibility – which you can delegate to people you can trust – than to have to fight to be afforded any." Kachiko gave her shoulder a gentle squeeze and withdrew her hand.

Kachiko was no warrior, but Hotaru could see in her eyes the battles she'd waged: the manipulations, the schemes. She felt she'd been forced to fight for power, but she couldn't see all that she already wielded.

"Kachiko – my lady," she quickly caught herself after the lapse of honorific. "I might not understand your unique position, or what you've had to do in order to get here, but you say it is important to delegate to people you can trust. Why not trust me?

Why not let me shoulder more than just your worries? Why not let me help with your plan?"

Kachiko did not hesitate in answering. "Because you are too pure and gentle, like freshly fallen snow. If you tread too often on snow, it will become icy over time. I am already like ice: cold and hardened and sharp."

Hotaru wanted to tell her she was wrong, but somehow, she knew that Kachiko was speaking the truth, at least about herself.

"Allow me to offer you another piece of advice: never trust a Scorpion." Kachiko withdrew from the table and summoned Ayaka to help her prepare for bed.

Hotaru almost asked for Kachiko to stay. The woman was wary of receiving help, of being beholden to another, but that didn't mean she didn't deserve someone to be there beside her.

Even ice can melt, Kachiko...

Kachiko disappeared behind the partition.

Hotaru was foolish for thinking that she should be the one to be beside Kachiko. She was overstepping her bounds as bodyguard, and even in the effort to gain an ally, she had said too much, admitted too much of her feelings. She would shame herself if she said any more.

Her face was too hot. There were smaller openings within the shutters that allowed one to look out a thin slit and get a much-needed breath of fresh air.

From this angle, she could see the cliffs of the rest of the promontory. Like the cliffs at Kyūden Doji, they were beautiful in the moonlight, but dangerous, too.

Mother. She felt a tear roll down. The sorrow of the dance came flooding back. *Rather than try to live up to everyone's expectations, you ended it all. You left Kuwanan and me alone.*

She'd had to be strong for her brother, for her father. She had to be strong now.

These cliffs… as painful as the memories were, there was something else familiar about them.

A twisted and gnarled juniper tree clung to the edge of the cliffs.

But there was no castle atop those bluffs, just walls.

The mural in the main hall showed the same juniper tree, only smaller. It wasn't depicting the castle as it was now. It memorialized an older keep, which had likely been abandoned and rebuilt. At least some of the tunnels Gin had mentioned must lead to that foundation.

She had to get the message to General Daidoji Uji, somehow. Then she wouldn't need to win Kachiko over to her side – she could save them both regardless. With the right wind and weather, like Koji's snowstorm, the Crane could launch a surprise attack and take the keep without having to risk the ascent from the bay.

There was some hope left. She just had to get the message out. She would figure out a way. If she couldn't… then she would once again be a disappointment.

Behind her, fabric rustled gently as Ayaka unrolled Kachiko's futon and repositioned the partition. The handservant bowed to Hotaru as she approached the table, stoppered the bottle of sake, and took away the cups. It was Hotaru's cue to prepare for the night as well.

One last time for good measure, she searched the room for secret doors in the walls and ceiling and found none. Between herself and Ayaka, they could keep Kachiko secure. The Mantis must have been more worried about them getting out than about others being able to sneak in.

But did the Mantis know about the old tunnels? If they didn't, the Crane could retake the castle by surprise, and avoid unnecessary bloodshed.

Hotaru lay down in front of the sliding doors without bothering to lay out a futon. It was the way of the bodyguard to sacrifice comfort so that they might get some rest but avoid a deeper slumber, thus remaining restless enough to hear any sounds of intruders. Ayaka lay on a thin mat between Kachiko and Hotaru, so that if any assassins made their way past Hotaru, they might yet be intercepted.

Hotaru was tired, though, in her soul. The Realm of Dreams gnawed at her as she kept tossing and turning. Many times, she awoke to the sound of waves – waves that could be carrying her father to these shores. The disappointment in his eyes burned her as his *naginata* cut swaths through their enemies, while Hotaru could not get to her feet, her arms and legs refusing to move.

In those dreams, she could only watch as Kachiko turned her back and disappeared into the shadows, forever.

She screamed, but no sound came out.

CHAPTER EIGHT

When she awoke, the window revealed a brightening sky. She must have fallen fully asleep, because she had to remember where she was. The faint scent of the sea air was familiar, but the dark room was spare, the plaster walls cracked. She reached for her swords before she remembered that they had been confiscated the day before.

At least she was not alone, but what good did it do if her only companion refused to work together?

Kachiko slept soundly. If she were like most courtiers Hotaru knew, she would sleep well past sunrise. A warrior's day, on the other hand, began at dawn, even if Hotaru didn't have the freedom to go outside to practice her forms.

For now, at least, it seemed the Mantis had no reason to want them dead. The two of them would be worth far more alive, anyway.

Hotaru drew herself up to a kneeling position. She could meditate to pass the time until her charge was ready to rise, and regain some of the clarity that she'd lost to a fitful sleep.

Or she could take a chance and try to find out what Kachiko needed to fix.

She squinted to focus in the darkness. Kachiko's makeup and jewelry, set aside from the night before, occupied the shelves of the lacquered travel cabinet that housed her belongings. On the writing desk lay Kachiko's calligraphy set and papers, a courtier's weapons and armor.

It was a gross violation of privacy and courtesy for anyone, even someone as close as a bodyguard, to go through another samurai's letters. A Crane should never even consider it, given the harm it could do to their reputation.

Yet… this might be Hotaru's only chance to uncover what Kachiko was plotting, as well as her true motives for serving as emissary. And she had to save them both from ransom before she irrevocably failed her father and her clan.

Silently, with one eye on Ayaka for any hint that she was stirring, Hotaru glided across the tatami mats in silence. She stopped just short of the desk.

Last night, Kachiko had shown a different side of herself to Hotaru: she knew what it was to feel trapped and alone. Perhaps they were mistaken to believe each other opponents. But could Kachiko be convinced to work with another, when she saw everything as a game with winners and losers?

And what of Hotaru's oath? She'd sworn to stay by Kachiko's side, serve as her champion, protect her from harm, and give her life for Kachiko's if called upon to do so. Yet Hotaru could not fulfill her duty to protect Kachiko from harm if she did not understand the dangers they faced, including those from Kachiko herself.

Forgive me. She began to read.

Most of the correspondence was mundane. Kachiko had countless contacts throughout the Empire, and when not in court together, courtiers kept in touch through letters. Hotaru only scanned their contents – she wouldn't dive any deeper than was necessary. Only the Keep of White Sails was pertinent to her duty as bodyguard, even if she and the Crane could gain tremendous advantage by seeing the social ledger of Kachiko's debts and favors.

At last, she found the letter she feared.

> *My dearest husband,*
>
> *I hope you have not worried overmuch about me. The matter concerning the Keep of White Sails is well in hand. When the Crane relinquish the Flying Fish Isles to the Mantis, the Scorpion should be among the first to recognize the minor clan's rising star, perhaps with an important appointment or two. I will send you more as I am able.*
> *Your wife,*
> *Kachiko*

Hotaru had been right to be suspicious. If it had already been the desire of the Scorpion Clan Champion and the emperor for the Mantis to have the keep, there would be no need for Kachiko to strategize with her husband now. Kachiko was acting on her own – this confirmed it – but Hotaru still did not know why.

Worse, Kachiko had written this in regular characters, as opposed to some cypher that only the inner circle of Scorpion nobles could understand. She wanted any fool who read this and thought themselves clever enough to have intercepted a message between the Scorpion Clan Champion and his wife to know on which side the coin would land, and to align themselves accordingly. If the other clans sided with Bayushi Shoju – and by extension the emperor, who was keen to trust his dear friend's advice – then they would avoid advising the emperor against his own wishes and refrain from making enemies of Yoritomo, the Mantis Clan Champion. The Crane would be isolated and forced to relent in this dispute.

But it wasn't too late. If Kachiko was trying to benefit by siding with the Mantis, Hotaru might still be able to sway her to benefit from the Crane instead. Even if Hotaru couldn't claim credit for the negotiation, at least she could protect the Crane's interests.

Hotaru couldn't steal or destroy the message. Kachiko would only rewrite it, and then give it to her handservant to deliver it at a later date, her suspicions raised. But if Kachiko intended for all Rokugan to see this on its way to Bayushi Shoju, then Hotaru could take advantage of that fact as well.

All her years practicing calligraphy and painting in spite of her father's wishes had led up to this moment. All she had to do was imitate Kachiko's brushwork to add a convincing postscript, one that was innocuous enough as to seem to have come from her if and when Shoju read it, but that would clearly convey the existence and location of the tunnels to Daidoji Uji's forces.

At least Kachiko understood what it was to be forced to play the game. Perhaps this would answer whether Hotaru was a worthy opponent.

Hurriedly, she sat and prepared the ink. Kachiko and Ayaka could awaken at any moment. More slowly, she inscribed the characters in Kachiko's cursive style:

> *Perhaps one day you will be able to see the cliffs overlooking the Bay of White Sails for yourself, as well as the ability of the Kakita artisans to depict their beauty on the castle's golden murals. Doji Hotaru said it reminded her of the castle in Kakita Kan'ami's play The Bloodless Beheading.*

Ayaka turned in her sleep, and then began to stretch. Hotaru was out of time, but what she'd already written would get the message across. She'd told her troops to wait for her signal. This would have to suffice.

"What are you writing?" came Kachiko's voice from behind her, too close.

The brush was still in her hand, the ink still wet on the page. Hotaru turned her head toward the voice.

Kachiko's bare face was mere inches from hers. She was even more beautiful without the black lace mask, and she was close enough to use her dagger if she wished. Her eyes swept over the characters with furious speed.

This was it. Kachiko would be furious with her. She'd squandered her chance at gaining Kachiko's trust, and had proven to be untrustworthy herself.

"Perhaps I was wrong about you, Hotaru," she said softly, her breath hot against Hotaru's ear.

"You see, I am not so pure, after all," Hotaru admitted, her voice cracking. A Doji was supposed to be so virtuous as to be untouchable in terms of reputation. Even if she had learned their ways, she was no Kakita to do as she liked so long as she could back up her words and deeds with steel. Sometimes, it was easy to forget, even if her father did not.

"No. I was wrong about whether you'd be able to keep up." Kachiko reached for the letter and reread the postscript. This close, the Scorpion woman's robes almost touched hers. Hotaru's heart pounded like a drum against her ribs.

She should have expected to be surprised by the Scorpion.

But if Kachiko wasn't angry, there was still a chance they could work together.

"What does this mean?" Kachiko asked. Hotaru almost smiled. If Kachiko did not already know about the mural or the tunnels, then it was possible that Gin had stayed loyal to the Crane.

"Tell me," Kachiko commanded.

For once, Hotaru had the upper hand. Kachiko would have to play nice for a time. "If I tell you, will we still be opponents?"

Kachiko looked deep into Hotaru's eyes, her face mere inches from hers. "As long as I am Scorpion and you are Crane, we will remain opponents," Kachiko replied.

Hotaru's heart sank. Both their clans served the emperor, and they could be more effective if they worked together – the Scorpion using their underhanded means when the Crane could not first succeed using more amicable methods. And a part of her didn't want to have to keep Kachiko at arm's length or treat her like an opponent. She wanted to continue talking freely with Kachiko, to have someone who would listen and understand and even give counsel.

"But in a game with multiple players, even opponents can work together to achieve a common goal," Kachiko conceded.

There was hope, then. Kachiko was right – she was being realistic – but there were places where their lonely paths could converge or run parallel for a time. Yet… "Should I trust you now?" Hotaru asked seriously. "Last night, you warned me never to trust a Scorpion."

"It is still good advice. But there's another side to it: 'A true friend in the Scorpion is more precious than anything.'"

The advice was contradictory. Or was it?

"Can I consider you a *true friend*?"

"Only you can answer that question."

Hotaru had to choose. She could refuse to tell Kachiko what she planned, and they could go on as they had been, with Kachiko refusing to work together. Or she could admit what she had done, what she knew, and what she hoped would happen.

She could only extend an offer of an alliance in good faith. Kachiko would have to decide whether she wanted to play a villain and sink to the expectations that surrounded her.

Hotaru wet the brush with ink again and reached for a fresh sheet. She began to commit her plans to paper – plans that could still be jeopardized if they were spoken aloud, especially if the guard were more awake now than last night.

"I see," Kachiko said simply, and then fed the papers to a lantern. "I can work with that."

"And you won't tell me how?"

"Not yet." In the lowest of whispers, Kachiko explained, "It is better for Gendo to think we are still enemies. The best way for you to continue acting suspicious of me is for you to keep up your guard." With that, she disappeared behind the partition again.

Hotaru cursed silently.

Kachiko returned unexpectedly with a small, butterfly-bound book. She'd donned her mask again.

"Here," she said, pressing the book into Hotaru's hands. "An act of trust deserves another. Bayushi's *Lies*. It contains the truest words you'll ever read. I know they teach it to Doji courtiers, but you probably only focused on Kakita's *The Sword* at the dueling academy."

"I have read *Lies* before, in fact," Hotaru countered. On top of her curriculum as a duelist, her father had bidden her complete a second set of studies to prepare her for her future duties as champion, which included many of the great texts of Rokugan, *Lies* included.

"But have you read a Scorpion's copy?" Kachiko smirked. "It's a more constructive use of your time than sitting with your eyes closed."

Hotaru wanted to protest, but at last she said, "Thank you." The book was far more than mere words on a page. Kachiko was allowing her a peek into the mind of a Scorpion, which would help them work together.

"It is nothing," Kachiko replied with a faint smile. Her gaze lingered too long on Hotaru before she looked away. "Now, I need to ready myself for a new day."

Kachiko turned her back to Hotaru while Ayaka made the final adjustment to the decorative sash clip on Kachiko's obi cord.

Hotaru couldn't hear what Kachiko whispered, but Ayaka bowed to her mistress and prepared to leave through the sliding door.

None of them expected it to open on its own. Seiyu's eyes filled with suspicion as they noticed Ayaka's hand outstretched to where the door handle would have been. "Were you planning to go somewhere?"

"Good morning," Kachiko said plainly, buying her handservant a moment to think.

"I was merely about to open the door for my mistress, First Mate Seiyu," Ayaka said, and Kachiko stood as though she were ready to leave. "And then I will be on my way to the servants' quarters to fetch a needle and thread to stitch my mistress's favorite robe, which tore while she was dancing for the captain last night."

Seiyu didn't budge from the doorway. "The cap'n gave strict orders that your maid must attend you at all times." They turned to address Kachiko directly. "Which means your maid can't be running errands for you. Someone can deliver thread if need be."

Kachiko tilted her head slightly, affecting innocence. "Surely my handservant can stay in my quarters, at least. She needn't accompany us while we attend the captain."

Most lords of the Great Clans would have their servants watch the other clans' servants if they sensed that some plan was afoot, rather than suffer their presence in the refined galleries of court. Even given the coarseness of the Mantis samurai and their gatherings, Ayaka would stick out like a fishing boat beside a luxury barge.

"Ah, but the captain insists," Seiyu replied. It shouldn't have surprised Kachiko that Gendo did not place the same value on etiquette as a Great Clan lord would.

Kachiko couldn't countermand Seiyu without being forced to bring it up with Seiyu's lord, which would only draw further suspicion upon their heads. But with Ayaka forced to stay close, how would she find a way to deliver the letter? Without the letter, the Crane wouldn't know how to avoid a costly siege.

Involving Seiyu hadn't been part of the plan, but Hotaru had no recourse. Moderating her voice so that it would be inaudible beyond the room, Hotaru rose and broke the silence. "There is one other errand that Ayaka was to run for us, but perhaps you can help us instead."

Fury radiated from Kachiko's perfectly serene face.

"We need your help getting a message to our ship," Hotaru explained.

"Absolutely not," Seiyu replied swiftly.

"Seiyu." This was her only chance. "I don't know if Gendo is acting on behalf of Lord Yoritomo, or if he is acting on his own initiative, but it doesn't matter. If someone were to testify that he was acting alone, the Crane would brand him a rogue captain and leave the rest of the Mantis Clan out of this. This doesn't need to get any bigger, or risk the lives and livelihoods of everyone who sails out of Gotei City."

"That's mutiny you're speaking of," Seiyu warned her, but they hadn't disagreed with anything Hotaru had said.

"You needn't let Gendo damage the reputation of the Mantis, or worse, bring the ire of the emperor upon them. Our clans can still be allies."

Kachiko watched Seiyu now, waiting to see what they would do.

"If you deliver a message for us, I can promise that the Crane will show forbearance toward you and the rest of the crew of the *Inazuma*. Your life – and the lives of your friends – needn't be gambled away like pennies."

Several warring emotions washed over Seiyu's face in

succession – they didn't have the courtier's practice to conceal what they were feeling.

"And as the heir to Kyūden Doji, I will owe you a great debt," Hotaru finished. "A fast ship, perhaps, fully equipped for battle, with a crew all your own." One didn't rise to become first mate without harboring at least some ambition.

Hotaru looked to Kachiko and Ayaka. *Please, Kachiko,* she pleaded with her eyes.

A long moment passed, and then finally Kachiko motioned for her handservant to produce the letter. Hotaru took it and then held out the message to Seiyu with both hands, a sign of respect and deference. Would the first mate accept this offer of peace?

"If you fear some sort of double cross, by all means read it," Kachiko suggested. "You'll see nothing that should make the Mantis unhappy." True, unless Seiyu were far more cunning than either Crane or Scorpion suspected. Having agreed to Hotaru's improvised plan, Kachiko turned her considerable talents toward its success. Her breezy affectation, her air of nonchalance, was carefully chosen for Seiyu's benefit, of that Hotaru was sure.

Seiyu stared at the letter for a long time. "I'll get your message to your ship, but that is all. Even if you get ransomed back in disgrace, you'll still hold up your end of the bargain – a fast ship, battle ready, with rights to dock and trade freely at *all* Crane ports."

The Daidoji Trading Council would be livid to lose the customs fees on a lifetime's worth of goods, but it was a small price to pay to help the clan save face. Hotaru would gladly trade one Crane ship to save a hundred. She nodded. "You shall have it."

Seiyu took the letter and stuffed it beneath the collar of their robes. "Come. We're late."

CHAPTER NINE

They were indeed late to the first meal of day. Hotaru expected a reprise of the evening gathering, but instead, they were led to one of the smaller reception rooms where only the captain awaited them. She wasn't sure whether to be grateful or even more guarded. His stern frown betrayed his impatience, but he said nothing, and Kachiko offered no excuse.

He reminded Hotaru of a villain out of a Kabuki play. A crimson silk belt was tied around the waist of his dark-teal robe, too colorful for the winter months. The right shoulder of his black coat hung loose, revealing a red leather vambrace – a casual hint at the prospect of violence. He finally offered a trace of a grin as Kachiko drew near. Hotaru and Ayaka followed silently behind.

If this was a second chance at diplomacy, trying to enlist Seiyu's help might have already ruined that chance. The first mate could very well turn over the message to Gendo right here and now, thereby sealing their fate. No wonder Kachiko had been furious.

Gendo offered Hotaru the bare minimum of courtesy by inclining his head as she took a seat beside her charge. Once again, she was only tolerated because Kachiko had insisted, and Gendo wasn't prepared to contradict Kachiko's sole demand – not yet, anyway.

All Hotaru had to do was get through the meal without giving Gendo the excuse he needed to separate them. Provided Seiyu delivered the message, it didn't matter what she did or didn't say here – the Daidoji mariners would decipher the message and then attack. If her luck hadn't completely soured, anyway.

Kachiko, however, was another matter. If she and Gendo reconciled their differences and agreed to a new plan, one that Kachiko thought would work better, what could Hotaru do to stop them?

"Are you feeling refreshed, my lady?" Gendo inquired. His tone suggested that he had seen right through their excuse to retire early the previous evening.

Kachiko couldn't complain about her accommodations without giving Gendo an opening to suggest alternative arrangements for them both. "Much more rested, yes," she replied. Gendo's crestfallen expression confirmed that wasn't the answer he'd been hoping to hear.

"Good, then," he said, recovering. "Then perhaps you are in a better state to resume negotiations." He gestured to the trays and bowls of rice, broth, grilled fish, and pickled fruits and vegetables that had been brought for them, as though he were still treating them as guests of honor and not petty hostages.

"Perhaps," Kachiko agreed, without allowing him any leverage.

"Let us eat first," he said, picking up his chopsticks and a bowl of rice. "As long as I hold the keep, the Mantis will ensure that you are taken care of."

Kachiko did not nod or agree, but she followed his lead and began to eat. He would have to work harder to win her back to his side. The Scorpion did not appear to be intimidated by the unspoken threat of privation if she did not accede to his wishes.

Several minutes passed in silence, with Hotaru and Ayaka finishing their meals first. Gendo finished soon thereafter, but

Kachiko seemed content to take her time, savoring each bite.

And buying herself more time to formulate a strategy.

"Ahhh..." Gendo sighed, patting his belly. "It seems the Sasaki family had good reason to jealously guard their fish. But was reneging on our deal worth the tragic bloodshed, I wonder?"

Gendo looked to Kachiko expectantly for a reply, but there was still rice in her bowl, and she did not look up.

The captain was too impatient to wait for her to finish before he opened up with his next line of attack. "Of course, the Mantis are committed to ensuring your safety while you are our guest. Who knows what sort of butchery the Crane Clan might be willing to resort to in order to cover up the disgraceful actions of their vassal?"

He spoke as if he were expecting a counterattack, but more likely he was trying to lure Hotaru or Kachiko into saying something that would confirm his suspicions. Hotaru wouldn't let him have the satisfaction.

Finally, Kachiko finished her last dish. "So far, it seems the Crane Clan's only foray onto the island was a lone messenger who was not well received," she said evenly, setting down her chopsticks. "Do you know what happened?" Her tone balanced inquisitiveness with accusation. Of course he knew what happened, but how would he explain it?

Gendo lowered his voice and said, "He came to this castle demanding outrageous concessions. His presumptuous words would have given any samurai great offense."

Stay quiet, Hotaru chided herself, as she slowly formed her hands into fists. That messenger, Togi, had been a dutiful servant of the Crane, and he had paid for it with his life.

"As you say," Kachiko allowed. "But I come here now on behalf of His Imperial Majesty, who wishes to see peace among all his subjects. I do not know that he would be pleased to hear that you are treating *his* holding as a roadhouse and demanding payment for the pleasure of hosting his servants. Surely it is a *privilege* to receive the emperor's emissary."

Although the clans each protected their own domains, every grain of rice in the fields and every grain of sand on the beaches belonged to the emperor, legally. The clans simply served as his esteemed custodians. One did not ask for recompense when hosting the emperor, his family, or his agents. Or rather, one could ask once, and then be swiftly relieved of all lands and titles.

"We would be glad to host you all winter long, at our own expense... All that we ask is that the Mantis be allowed to continue ensuring the protection of the Keep of White Sails. I swear on my ancestors – on stormy Osano-wo himself – that I would be honored to defend this keep in His Imperial Majesty's name, and glad to forget the injury dealt us by the treacherous Sasaki family. I would even release those surviving samurai back to their liege lords."

Kachiko raised her chin slightly and made a show of considering his bargain. Capitulating and ceding the isles to him in exchange for their freedom was the surer route. Holding out for Hotaru's plan to work was much riskier, and more likely to fail.

But Gendo did not understand the game Kachiko was playing. She would dictate the terms to him, or else there would be no terms at all. In the scenario offered by Gendo, Kachiko was the pawn, not the power broker. Gendo would have to try again with more favorable terms.

"I will think on it," was Kachiko's response.

"You *WHAT?*" Gendo exploded to his feet, red-faced and breathing hard. Hotaru was on her feet in the span of a breath.

"The Lady Bayushi has said *she will think on it*," Hotaru repeated. But would he insist that Kachiko think on it while imprisoned in the dungeons or in his private chambers?

Despite Hotaru's height, Gendo still had a few inches on her, and in hand-to-hand combat, his strength far outmatched hers. But if he wanted to be treated as a samurai, he had to act as one. Kachiko could end him if she provided an unflattering report to the capital. Lord Yoritomo would have no choice but to execute the brute who'd insulted the emperor's emissary.

Still seething, he managed, "Go, then. Think on it." He took a deep breath. "I will await your response."

"I thank you for your patience, my lord." Kachiko dipped her head and then rose.

Seiyu scrambled to their feet, seemingly eager to quit Gendo's presence before he lashed out at them as well. "This way," they said, and led the trio away from the furious and thwarted captain.

When Kachiko, Hotaru, and Ayaka were returned to their rooms and Seiyu had departed, the façade of Kachiko's pleasantness crumbled away. Her ire bubbled up to the surface, but unlike Gendo's blunt rage, her whispers were honed daggers. "I would have thought you smarter than this. You did not think that it would be wiser *not* to enlist the help of our captors?"

Hotaru was ready for her complaints, some of which were well taken. Under her breath, she explained, "Seiyu, and at least a few of the others, don't want to be a part of this plot. I could tell by the way the first mate almost spoke out against Gendo when we first arrived and by the way the crew dismissed Seiyu's warnings at dinner. I've gained us an ally. And our message may have gotten out that much sooner because Seiyu can move in parts of the castle we can't."

Kachiko was quiet for a moment, and then finally said, "You may have convinced them to help you, but just because you can gain someone's aid doesn't mean you should rely on them."

Because they may not do the job well enough, or succeed at all.

It was her father's voice speaking the words Kachiko had left unsaid. Perhaps it was why Kachiko was reticent to work with Hotaru.

"Sometimes you have to take a chance on someone." Barely above a whisper, she said, "The contents of the message itself are in the Mantis's favor, and it's highly doubtful Seiyu will decipher the allusions."

Surely, some sketches or studies of the mural existed at the Kakita Artisan Academy, which would tell Uji's forces where the old keep – and tunnels – had been. Kakita Kan'ami's play *The Bloodless Beheading* featured underground tunnels being used to break a siege. Now, she had to hope that the blockade would work once again, and the message would make its way to General Daidoji.

"Seiyu's death is on your hands if their treachery is discovered."

A lord's first duty is to protect their followers. "I will accept that responsibility, if it comes to that."

Something in Kachiko's eyes softened – a glimmer of guilt, or perhaps sorrow.

She'd spoken the question aloud before she could think to hold herself back: "How much tragedy do you bear responsibility for, Lady Kachiko?"

There was a long pause. Then, it sounded like Kachiko said, "Too much for one lifetime," but she said it so softly that Hotaru couldn't be sure.

Hotaru couldn't know what Kachiko had been forced to do on behalf of the Scorpion Clan. She couldn't know whether Emma-Ō would judge her sins less harshly if they were in service to her clan. Even the weight of a murder could be balanced out if more lives were saved as a result. But Hotaru suspected that Kachiko had done enough for her own ends to be worthy of one of the nine courts of Hell.

•••

Hotaru began *Lies* at the beginning and was only partway through when Ayaka started helping Kachiko dress for dinner. Every night, it seemed, Kachiko had a fresh outfit with which to dazzle. Hotaru had brought only what was necessary: one spare set of clothes that she could wear while the other was laundered, a painstaking process graciously completed by Ayaka. Both sets were of high-quality fabric and master craftsmanship, but they paled in comparison to the stunning brilliance of Kachiko's ensembles.

For a moment, Hotaru was reminded of the garish opulence of the courtesans she'd seen parading through the streets of the capital. No, the fashion sported by the courtesans was an over-the-top, cheaper version of the garments worn by the likes of Kachiko.

She was stunning, and Hotaru used Bayushi's *Lies* to keep herself from stealing too many looks at the beautiful woman.

Kachiko's copy of the book was annotated, so the going was slow. Was Kachiko in breach of some oath to the Scorpion Clan by allowing her to read it?

One line from *Lies* stood out so far: *Do not fear your enemies. Only a friend can betray you.*

But would a true friend betray you? Is that why they could be considered *true*?

It was possible that Kachiko was still keeping Hotaru at arm's length because their allegiances would be clearer if they remained as opponents – as enemies. But it didn't have to be that way. Although they served rival clans, they both served the emperor, in the end.

And they both knew what it was to be trapped and hurting. They would be stronger together than they would be apart.

Ayaka finished tying Kachiko's obi, and then they were ready to accept the summons for dinner.

A shout came from below them, and then more loud voices. Ayaka immediately put her ear to the floor and gave Kachiko a concerned look.

"What's happening?" Hotaru snapped the book closed.

Ayaka shut her eyes and put her hand over her other ear. Kachiko waited patiently for a few moments.

"It's an argument of some kind. Someone's angry. Others are riled up."

If Seiyu was involved, they might have to brace for the worst. "Do you think..." she trailed off.

Seeming to read Hotaru's mind, Kachiko said, "We should know soon. If Seiyu doesn't come to collect us for dinner, I think it would be wise to assume we no longer have an ally in them. Neither can we assume that the message made its way to its intended readers."

Hotaru nodded, but her heart was heavy. She hoped Seiyu was all right.

The wait was excruciating. After some time, a different guard than the previous night came with a small tray of food for the three of them. There was no sign of Seiyu or the other guard.

As dusk faded into night, Kachiko gave up on a possible summons and returned her outer robes to Ayaka. "We will need to be on guard tonight. If the first mate has been charged with insubordination, we may have earned the captain's wrath as well."

Hotaru swallowed. This was her fault for dragging Seiyu into their predicament. The first mate could face imprisonment, or much, much worse... And if Kachiko's letter hadn't made it off the island...

"Do not look so terrified, Lady Hotaru. Alive, we still have some value to Captain Gendo," she said, gesturing to the food that Ayaka was setting out for them.

She ate hungrily, without tasting the food. Kachiko was silent over the course of their shared meal. Ayaka reopened the shutters, but the moon and stars were gone, replaced only by dark clouds.

She prepared for a long night without sleep, and contemplated how she might fend off the Mantis long enough to get Kachiko to the tunnels if they had to make a break for it.

CHAPTER TEN

The dark clouds of the previous night brought with them a terrible storm. The winds buffeted the wings of the castle, and the very seas roared with the fury of a sea serpent. White snow clung to the cliff face, and the juniper tree strained to hold on.

Once again, Hotaru and Kachiko were not invited to join the captain for breakfast, but once again, a servant delivered a tray of simple food. Perhaps Gendo was waiting for Kachiko to send word that she was ready to make a deal.

"You should get some rest," Kachiko said when they had finished eating. "If we survived the night, Ayaka and I will be fine to survive the day."

"But..." But Kachiko was right. Hotaru would be of no use to any of them if she were too exhausted to protect them.

For the first time, she accepted Ayaka's offer of one of the futons, but with Kachiko's assent, she would stay in the main room so that she'd be close in case of escalation. Ayaka moved the partition to block out some of the natural light in that corner of the room.

Hotaru lay down to rest and forced herself to breathe through her belly in order to relax, paying attention only to her breath and the sound of waves. The anxious thoughts came anyway.

The rough seas meant that there was no chance of escape, and possibly no chance for the next day or the day after. Worse, the Crane Clan's blockade was still out there. How many would be lost to the depths because Hotaru hadn't been able to resolve this quickly enough? Would Daidoji Uji attempt to use the storm as cover for a surprise attack?

She'd known there were risks when she ordered Admiral Hoshitoki's fleet out to sea, but now the cost of her gamble was coming due. She'd have more than Seiyu's life on her conscience before the end of the night.

Lady Konishiko, Hotaru prayed. Her clan's foremost champion after its founders, Doji Konishiko had always been an underdog, but her ultimate sacrifice had helped save the Empire in its earliest days. She was one of the Crane's most blessed ancestors, a *shiryō* her descendants could pray to when times were bleak. *Please guide me to victory. Please help me find the strength.*

The Mantis might have Hotaru and Kachiko surrounded, but she could only hope that her clan's naval blockade was keeping them cornered in turn.

She turned to the other side and curled up against the cold. She shivered at the terrible shrieking of the wind. The very floor beneath them creaked and groaned.

She woke up several times throughout the day. Once, she half-awoke to find a red and black wool overcoat laid over her.

"*Aien kien.* We make for a strange pair, but it would seem fate has brought us together," said a familiar voice.

"As you say, mistress," another voice replied.

Kachiko…

The daylight faded early. As twilight descended on the castle, the sounds of cheers and drinking erupted from below. The time for dinner came, and Kachiko seemed almost ready to refuse the summons, but she bid Ayaka to help her dress anyway. Showing some resistance to the Mantis might help remind them that the emissary did not have to obey, but what leverage would that buy Kachiko and Hotaru?

With each setting of the sun, their chances seemed to darken with the night. Every day, it became increasingly likely that the ones to liberate them would be not Daidoji Uji's forces but the Imperial legions, come to deliver the ransom to Captain Gendo. Every day, it became increasingly likely that Hotaru would be humiliated in front of her father.

Yet it would not serve either of them for Hotaru to dwell in worry about the future. She needed to be here, in the now, where she could channel her worry into alertness for herself and her charge.

Certainly, she should not dwell on the words she'd overheard, or worry whether Kachiko returned the feelings that had been growing inside her since they'd departed for the isles. But if she did...

Hotaru shook her head. At least there would be hot sake to help ward against the chill that had settled into the castle. A little wouldn't hurt, and the wine might even settle her nerves.

"Shall we play a little game, my dear?" Kachiko offered, possibly to lift both their spirits in the face of their dire circumstances. "What do you think tonight's entertainments will be?"

The term of endearment made Hotaru's cheeks hot, but she overlooked it for both their sakes. "I rather hope they aren't relying on our dancing once again..."

"Agreed. Don't you think some Fortunes and Winds would be a little bit more fun?"

"Your Excellency..." Hotaru warned, in hopes of reminding Kachiko of their formal relationship. "Is gambling a seemly thing for an emissary of the emperor to engage in?" After she'd spoken the words, she realized they were her father's. Gambling certainly wasn't a seemly thing for the heir to the Crane Clan to engage in, but that hadn't stopped her and Uncle Toshimoko from fleecing some very drunk samurai a time or two.

"Who will see such shameful behavior? The other gamblers? The castle servants? Will you tell anyone?"

"No," Hotaru quickly replied. Kachiko had ignored her return to propriety.

"Perhaps we can even win enough to pay our way out of the captain's hospitality," Kachiko mused aloud.

"Or win ourselves a few new bruises." Despite her natural luck with the dice, Hotaru knew the attendant dangers of winning all too well. Now that she was older, she knew Toshimoko had probably cheated specifically in order to get Hotaru some real practice with hand-to-hand combat.

"But isn't that why you came? To protect me?" Kachiko teased.

Hotaru couldn't argue her on that point. She was sure every bodyguard had lamented their charge's willingness to rush headlong into danger at some point in the course of their service.

"It is," she said instead. "But that doesn't mean I approve of your asking for trouble."

"Now, now," Kachiko chided her. "Really, it will be they who are asking for trouble, once they start placing their wagers."

Finally, the invitation to dinner arrived. "The crew have been asking after you. Although Captain Gendo still awaits your decision, he doesn't think it fair to deprive the crew of their entertainments," the guard explained.

Hotaru rose. She would have her hands full tonight.

As it turned out, Kachiko wasn't wrong. Already, she'd cleaned out a third of the gathered crowd.

The mood had been somber when Hotaru and Kachiko

first arrived, and there had been no sign of Gendo or Seiyu. The atmosphere had quickly changed with a few overtures on Kachiko's part and a request for some livelier tunes from the musicians.

The sailors Kachiko had already ruined couldn't turn back now. They had to win back what they'd lost, so they were willingly stumbling further into her snare. Kachiko was more than happy to loan them the coin to keep them in the game, and she was doing a surprisingly good job of maintaining the accounts in her head.

In between rounds, Hotaru spared a glance to search for Gin or any of the Mantis samurai who had helped Seiyu bring them to their rooms originally, to no avail. Ayaka remained in the back of the room, dutifully staying within sight of her mistress. It was almost certain that Seiyu had been imprisoned, if they hadn't been keelhauled or forced to walk a plank off the cliffs. Hotaru shivered.

Kachiko was good at gambling without even needing to cheat. Toshimoko had done it time and time again, so Hotaru knew a few of the signs to look out for.

She still couldn't put it past the Scorpion, though, especially one who warned others of her untrustworthiness. Especially for a Scorpion who had gambled in the City of Lies and likely knew tricks Hotaru didn't. Especially when Kachiko was putting in extra effort to call over the servants to ensure the drinks were flowing freely. Seiyu's warning was long forgotten or happily ignored.

Was it possible that Kachiko was softening the Mantis sailors' defenses in case the Crane launched their assault tonight?

Could she possibly be helping Hotaru's cause?

It wasn't impossible, but it seemed too much to hope for...

"Where'd a dame learn to roll like that?" Big Fish demanded.

"I grew up a Shosuro, you know," Kachiko teased. "Ryokō Owari Toshi is only a short boat ride away. We're practically born with dice in our hands."

What the Mantis samurai probably didn't realize was how scandalous it was considered for a highly ranked courtier like Kachiko to engage in such uncouth behavior, much less excel at it. Because Fortunes and Winds was so popular on the Isles of Silk and Spice, he thought nothing of it.

"We could spend some quality time together on a boat ride, long or short," Big Fish offered, leering.

"Care to bet on it?" Kachiko offered, nonplussed. "I'll stake you."

"What about the preening Crane?" another Mantis asked. They meant Hotaru, although they were in their cups enough to have forgotten her name.

"I'll bet she has some coin. Come on, don't hold back from us. Get in the game!"

"Is that so? Are you sure 'bout that, Little Fish?" At Toshimoko's side, it'd been easier to affect the swagger of an overconfident young man than to fend off salacious advances while dressed as a woman. Luckily for Hotaru, she'd had the height and lean build to pull it off. Sometimes, she'd even gone by the name Hoturi to keep things simpler.

"'Little Fish'? This bodyguard of yours's got some nerve, milady. We'll show her…"

"Everyone in?" Kachiko checked as she began collecting bets from the samurai in the circle. Each participant had two bets: one for the round and one set aside for Lord Moon, which Kachiko left alone.

Hotaru caught Kachiko's gaze for a moment as she took Hotaru's coin. *Be careful,* she tried to say.

Kachiko only flashed a smile in response.

The dice passed to the next person, whose name Hotaru gleaned was Makoto. They scooped up the five dice – four white and one black – and began to shake them in their hands.

Everyone was able to win back some of their ante on a given roll, so the room was filled with cheers and encouragement.

Makoto blew on their cupped hands for good luck and rolled the dice while everyone held their breath.

"Seven Thunders!" they shouted, counting the results. The combination of four different element symbols on the white dice and a Seven Fortunes result on the black die was relatively easy to score, so it allowed people to keep their bet instead of losing it to the banker, while the person rolling won coin from the banker equal to their ante. In a gambling house, a hireling would serve as banker, but because Kachiko was the richest, she had the dubious privilege of serving as banker for the crowd.

The other samurai congratulated and thanked Makoto for rolling well, while others goaded them into trying harder next time.

Since the roller had won the bet, they were allowed to pass the dice. In this case, Makoto seemed glad to, and they thrust the cubes into Hotaru's outstretched palm.

"Don't let us down," Makoto warned, and patted her on the back. In the Esteemed Palaces of the Crane, such presumed congeniality would have earned someone a challenge to duel, but here, Hotaru had no recourse but to grin and bear it.

Someone shouted "Daikoku's belly!" and the rest of them laughed. It was a side bet against the current roller, and the Mantis were all too glad to be betting against the Crane.

She couldn't help but smile at the playful rivalry. *Time to teach them a lesson.*

Hotaru took the dice and gave them an earnest shake.

She dared to lock eyes with Kachiko as she shook the dice to the music, holding everyone in suspense.

Kachiko didn't look away this time, and she offered an actual smile.

Were they finally on the same side?

"Give it up and roll already!" someone jeered from the audience.

Hotaru outstretched her hands and let the dice fall.

North Wind, East Wind, West Wind, and South Wind on the white dice, with Lady Sun on the single black die. They called the combination *The Lady's Breath*. It was tied with the titular *Fortunes and Winds* combination for the best roll possible. And Hotaru had done it on her first turn, meaning that she won eight times her ante instead of the usual four.

"No way!" Big Fish shouted.

"Impossible!"

Everyone who had bet against her had to part with their coin, while only Kachiko was able to share in Hotaru's victory, collecting four times her own ante.

The audience groaned. "Cheater!" someone shouted, but the crowd didn't pursue the accusation. Kachiko made quick work of accepting the reluctantly offered coin and paying out to herself and Hotaru.

"Well played," Kachiko smiled. "It seems you have the luck of a lady on your side tonight."

Which lady did she mean? Kachiko? Surely not…

"Care to roll again?" Kachiko asked.

"I won't push my luck," she replied.

"Suit yourself," Kachiko shrugged, and she stretched out her hand to take the dice and pass them to the next roller on her left.

"Ante up," Kachiko reminded them, and the Mantis looked down to count themselves in. "Everyone in?" The room cheered in agreement.

"Big Fish is in it to win it!" someone shouted.

Once again, Hotaru could feel the heart in the Mantis crew. What they did, they did for each other.

"Here goes!" Big Fish shouted, and he rolled the dice around between his large hands. After much fanfare, he nearly smashed them against the wood of the floor. Hotaru winced, anticipating damage to the floor, the dice, or both.

Air, Earth, Fire, Water. Lord Moon.

Lord Moon had come to claim Big Fish's bet, as well as the ante he'd set aside "for Lord Moon."

"What is this?" Big Fish demanded.

"Bad luck, it seems. Such a shame," Kachiko said, and reached for the dice.

"She has to be cheating!" came a shout from the crowd.

"They're slippery! No wonder they had Seiyu fooled!" one of the other sailors jeered.

"You mainlanders are cheating!"

If Kachiko had cheated, Hotaru hadn't seen it, but that wasn't a guarantee that Kachiko hadn't – why would she, when all they had to do was hold out long enough for the Crane forces to attack?

"You scheming…!" Big Fish shouted, and he reached to grab Kachiko by the collar.

Hotaru was in front of her charge in an instant and intercepted the man's hand, but she quickly found herself being raised off her feet by the hulking Mantis samurai.

Before he could strengthen his stance, Hotaru punched him in the face, sending blood spraying.

Big Fish dropped her unceremoniously and clutched his probably broken nose.

Hotaru whirled around to grab Kachiko and make their escape, but Makoto and the other Mantis had already grabbed her by the arms and pulled her away from Hotaru.

"Bring her to the boss!" Big Fish yelled, still clutching his spurting face.

"KACHIKO!" Hotaru screamed, darting forward, but the Mantis were already lugging her toward the doors.

One of the Mantis had grabbed Hotaru by the ankle as she lunged for her charge, and she went down on the floor with a hard *thud*.

Despite the pain and dizziness, she lifted her head to watch as the Mantis escorted Kachiko out of the room, slamming the sliding doors shut behind them.

Her breath caught in her throat as she stifled a scream. She'd failed her only important task: keeping Kachiko safe.

The other Mantis began to surround her, towering over her, ready to give her a beating.

Big Fish raged as he kicked Hotaru in the ribs. "I'll kick 'The Lady's Breath' right out of you, you cheating wench!"

Another kick came, and then another, and Hotaru curled up into a ball to shield her vitals. She struggled to remain conscious through the pain.

If Kachiko had cheated, then why? What did she stand to gain from beggaring the Mantis Clan samurai? Hadn't she realized what kind of danger she would be in if she were caught? That Hotaru would be hard pressed to protect her against so many enemies?

Unless that had been the whole point. For the first time since their arrival, Kachiko had a private audience with Captain Gendo, away from Hotaru and able to bargain freely, having put Gendo on the defensive because of her refusals. Now she could dictate the terms as she pleased. Because she knew of the impending Crane attack, she could use that as leverage when dealing with Gendo.

Do not fear your enemies. Only a friend can betray you.

Kachiko... *is this what you were trying to warn me about?*

The pain threatened to overwhelm her, but she couldn't give up and let the Mantis imprison her without a fight. She forced herself to reach out and yank a leg, bringing a Mantis down into the fray with her and affording her the second she needed to get back to her feet, bruised and throbbing and breathless though she was.

She backed away from her attackers, moving slowly so that the balcony doors were behind her, gasping to refill her lungs. Her eyes darted around for Ayaka, perhaps her only ally, but she was nowhere to be seen.

That's when a shout of alarm went up from outside. She whirled around and threw open the balcony doors to let the blizzard in.

Through the ice and snow, through the obscured light of the braziers, she could barely make out the streaks of blue armor. The samurai of the Crane Clan had fought through the storm to answer her summons and take the Mantis by surprise.

CHAPTER ELEVEN

The wolfish expressions worn by the Mantis samurai evaporated, replaced by confusion as they looked for the source of the shouting.

Big Fish lowered his hand from his face, revealing a bloody mess. "Go check out that noise!" he shouted. "Shohei, Makoto, with me! We'll make sure this mainlander can't cause any more trouble." The Mantis were quick to obey, and the room emptied except for the trio, who looked ready to teach Hotaru a lesson.

Still finding her breath, Hotaru shifted into a flexible stance, prepared to flow around her attackers like a rushing stream. With the balcony behind her, she had an easy escape option open to her. She could reinforce the Crane Clan troops assaulting the keep and help them carry the day, winning glory for herself and praise from her father.

But Kachiko... If Hotaru allowed harm to come to the emperor's emissary, she would disappoint her clan and her father and – most importantly – herself.

The trio of Mantis samurai were approaching, fast, and her window to escape was closing.

Hotaru had sworn to be Kachiko's bodyguard. She was

responsible for the emissary's safety. She had to do her duty, even if Kachiko didn't think she was worth protecting – even if Kachiko lived up to her treacherous reputation.

She would act without fear, knowing full well the consequences of her actions. She would do what her oaths demanded, even if it cost her her life. She would prove herself a true friend – and perhaps something more.

Hotaru dove to the closest meal tray, grabbed a heavy bowl, and threw it at the head of Big Fish. He ducked out of the way just in time, and the ceramic shattered against the wall behind him.

She armed herself with the tray. Dishes clattered to the floor.

Shohei rushed toward her with a pair of *tonfa*, spinning the wooden stocks menacingly. Hotaru raised the tray at the last moment to block the blow and then used a sweeping kick to knock him off his feet.

She turned just in time to dodge Makoto's butterfly swords.

She dashed ahead to put some distance between herself and the bladed weapons, snatching a handful of coins and a jug of *awamori* as she went. She poured the jug's contents across the floor as she put her back to another wall.

She wasn't going to last very long at all, outnumbered and weaponless like this. "I don't know what happened to Seiyu, but you should know that the first mate had your best interests at heart!"

The sounds of battle drew nearer, distracting Makoto for a moment, though Big Fish was undeterred. After Shohei rose to his feet, the trio was still between her and the door to the rest of the keep.

"They were looking out for you – and the rest of the crew! Gendo is willing to risk all your lives for his gambit. And for what?"

Makoto and Shohei hesitated, but Big Fish wasn't going to listen to reason. He roared and charged at her. Timing her throw, she scattered the coins in his path and watched as he slipped and lost his balance on the wet hardwood floor, careening to the ground.

Without hesitation, Hotaru leapt atop him and smashed the awamori jug against his forehead, hard. The jug cracked as she brought it down once, twice, three times, until he no longer struggled.

She looked up at Makoto and Shohei, who stared in horror not at her, but at the castle servants armed with polearms and improvised weaponry in the doorway.

"We give up! We'll leave!" Makoto shouted. The two sailors fled onto the balcony and into the storm.

"Gin!" Hotaru shouted, recognizing the serving girl. She pulled herself off Big Fish and rushed to the castle's most loyal defenders. "Thank goodness you're all right!"

"Mistress!" Gin called out, a look of relief washing over her as she planted the butt of her naginata on the floor and bowed, the other servants following suit. Desperately, she looked up and said, "There's so much fighting. What do we do?"

"If you're up to it, go to the dungeons and free any of the Sasaki family members still held captive. Tell them we need to open the gates from the inside. Even if they're not armed, you'll need their strength. Before you go, make sure you free the redheaded Mantis named Seiyu as well. They're on our side, and they'll be able to offer the Mantis's surrender."

"Here," Gin offered, offering the naginata to Hotaru. "Lady Doji doesn't have a weapon of her own."

"Are you sure?"

"Yes! We would be proud for you to wield it!" Tears glimmered in Gin's eyes.

"I thank you. The Crane will not forget your service. All of you." She inclined her head.

The servants offered hurried bows and rushed to follow Hotaru's orders.

Abandoning the unconscious Big Fish to his fate, Hotaru followed the corridors to the middle stairwell and began the steep climb. She prayed she wasn't already too late.

The higher she ascended in the keep, the more fiercely the wind blew, and patches of ice had formed in the spaces between the shutters and the windowsills. Here and there, where a shutter had been left open, the fine snow swirled in the wind.

Most of the Mantis must have responded to the fighting in the courtyard surrounding the keep – she didn't encounter a soul as she clambered up one set of stairs and then another, careful not to catch her blade on the rafters. She passed by the body of the guard who'd been assigned to their room, a single red streak across his throat. Hotaru had been right to fear Ayaka, after all.

By the time she reached the lord's chambers on the third story, her ribs painfully reminded her of the beating she'd endured at the hands of the Mantis. She struggled to catch her breath, coughing to try to clear her throat. She pulled her hand away and saw red flecks. She didn't have much fight left in her.

Maybe that was part of the plan, too. Maybe she was playing right into Kachiko's hands, trying to do something foolish and getting herself killed in the process. It didn't matter.

Hotaru had made her decision, and she would live or die by it.

She threw open the sliding doors of the lord's chambers, searching for any sign of them.

"Kachiko!" she screamed, opening door after door. Her lungs ached, but she couldn't stop calling her name. "KACHIKO!"

At last, she threw open a final sliding door to find Captain Gendo standing over Kachiko's kneeling form.

"She's here," he laughed, half-crazed. "We're so glad you could finally join us."

The blades of his *kama* glinted in the lamplight, ready to strike the Scorpion down if Hotaru failed now.

"Release Kachiko to me!" Hotaru demanded. She lowered her naginata in a warning stance. Her weapon would afford her the advantage of range, but he was fully armored and uninjured, not to mention larger and stronger than she.

If they dueled, it would no doubt be to the death.

"I don't believe that will be possible. You see, Kachiko is an important ally of mine. And you are just a nuisance."

No, that couldn't be true. It was Kachiko and Hotaru who were allied now. Hotaru's heart fluttered as she searched Kachiko's eyes for the truth, but she found only fear.

"You are the one who separated your 'ally' from her guardian." Hotaru stepped forward with her right foot, leveling her blade between her eyes and her enemy's. She had outwitted Nishiyo.

She had gained Kachiko's trust. She had gotten word to her clan. She would not lose to Gendo now. "I, Doji Hotaru, daughter of Doji Satsume, heir to the Crane Clan, and acting lord of the Esteemed Palaces of the Crane, challenge you to a duel for the crime of kidnapping the emissary of the emperor!"

Gendo's eyes flashed with fury, and he readied his blades. "Very well, you foolish child!"

I am no child anymore. Hotaru charged ahead with a fearsome shout and thrust the blade forward with all her remaining strength. "You are the fool to underestimate me!"

Gendo jumped out of the way just in time, and Hotaru's blade pierced through the rice-paper door behind him. She drew the pole back to strike again, and this time, he was ready to defend against her with his bracer. The edge of her steel bounced off the armor plating harmlessly, and he brought his kama around to try to hook her weapon out of her grasp. She pulled away with only a moment to spare.

She had to be careful, or she could risk shattering her blade against his bracers. The confined space, too, meant that she couldn't make full use of the polearm's momentum without potentially catching her blade in a wooden beam or column. She needed to get him out into the open – onto the balcony.

He seized on her hesitation, swinging wildly with a kama, forcing her back into a wall. She sprang out of the way to avoid his other deadly blade but lost her footing.

He swung again, and with a desperate parry, she knocked one of the kama from his hand. But he was still too close.

With his free hand, he grabbed her by her hair and sent her flying through a screen panel, wood splintering against her face and stabbing at her sides.

To pause meant death. She sucked in a breath and forced herself back to her feet. She braced with her naginata just in time to use the long wooden haft to block the oncoming blade. His kama dug into the haft, but that also left him vulnerable. She kicked out with her right foot to plant it square in his chest, and he staggered back, pulling his blade with him.

She seized what might be her only chance. Flipping the haft in her grip, she arced the blade from the floor to his head, knocking the helmet off-kilter and dealing a concussive blow to his forehead, her blade grazing the thin layer of skin there.

She swapped her grip again, this time using the hooked butt of the pole to smash into his chest, sending him staggering backward and into a nearby desk.

She had to be wearing him down, but he pulled himself up just as quickly as she had. He labored to breathe, blood pouring from the cut on his forehead, dramatic in appearance but not a serious injury. She needed to get into a less confined space to be able to hit the gaps in his armor.

Keeping her naginata in Correct Eyes stance, she shouted

and lunged, her arms burning, forcing him to flee outdoors. She succeeded, but out on the balcony, the floor was already slick with ice.

Gendo skidded to a stop beside the railing and flashed a malicious grin, daring Hotaru to advance. She couldn't fail now.

Drawing up reserves of strength she didn't know she had and screaming in fury, she stabbed her naginata forward in a flurry of jabs, trying to set him off-balance for a finishing blow.

He had to leap away, tilting his head back and up, exposing his neck to the razor-sharp tip of her blade.

But he was a moment too fast for her tired arms, and he dodged out of the way just in time. He turned on his heel and dashed to Kachiko, who was watching them from one of the balcony's open doors. He grabbed the Scorpion woman with one hand and held her over the railing.

He gasped for breath as he screamed over the wind. "Either you grant me safe passage back to the Islands of Silk and Spice, or Kachiko sinks to the bottom of the sea!"

Hotaru didn't dare take another step forward. She thought of her mother. She couldn't stand to lose anyone else to the cliffs.

She wouldn't let him hurt Kachiko.

That left her no choice but to lay down her arms.

Was this what Kachiko had been waiting for all along? Hotaru's surrender?

No. There was something between them, something that had begun to melt Kachiko's cold heart.

Now it seemed her luck had run out, and it was time to pay the price. There would be no disappointment to suffer through soon.

As she lowered her naginata and kneeled, she looked up to Kachiko one last time.

Will you look to Gendo to gain the power you seek? Or will you be a true friend?

It might have been tears in Kachiko's eyes, or it might have been only the cold wind of the storm that made them water.

Kachiko's hand darted for her hidden dagger.

Gendo snapped his attention to Kachiko.

Hotaru surged forward.

Kachiko's blade plunged downward, and Gendo yowled in pain, but it wasn't a killing blow. Gendo grabbed Kachiko by the wrist, and she dropped the dagger with a gasp.

Hotaru thrust her naginata forward, and the blade pierced the soft flesh of his neck exposed between his helmet and breastplate.

Still rushing straight ahead, she let go of the haft and caught the Scorpion and the Mantis before they could tumble over the railing.

Hotaru pulled Kachiko away from the dying man. Gendo instinctively reached to his neck to cover the wound, but he couldn't stanch the gush of red. The light in his eyes faded.

The snowflakes melted in his hot blood.

He could no longer threaten either of them. They were safe at last.

"Are you all right?" Hotaru breathed, her voice hoarse. She clutched Kachiko tightly, afraid that so far up, a single gust could pull the small woman from her grasp.

"Never trust a Scorpion," Kachiko warned her again, her breathing ragged, but she held on to Hotaru tightly.

"I won't," Hotaru promised, and she cupped a hand to the woman's face. She could feel the tears coming, but it didn't matter that she was showing her emotions now, when it was only the two of them.

"Yet still you came for me," Kachiko said, bewildered. A single tear streamed down her cheek.

"Yes. As I swore I would." Hotaru offered a weak smile.

Amidst the ice and snow, she felt Kachiko's stiffness melt.

"You were true to your word."

Hotaru nodded and said, "Aien kien."

Kachiko blushed brightly.

On instinct, she brought Kachiko's face close. Would she pull away? Did she feel this, too? "Stay by my side," Hotaru whispered in a plea.

Kachiko stroked the side of Hotaru's face. Her answer was plain in her eyes, but she said the words aloud anyway, "I will. I promise."

Hotaru leaned in and kissed her fiercely. The weight of the past three days was swept away by the wind. They had each other. Nothing else in the world mattered.

When their lips finally parted, Kachiko met her eyes again, and Hotaru saw all the pain and hurt and sadness that Kachiko kept hidden behind the mask.

"I will protect you, always," Hotaru swore. "You don't have to be alone."

"Please," was all Kachiko could say before choking back a sob.

Hotaru pulled Kachiko into her arms and carried her back into the keep, out of the cold. It didn't matter how much she hurt. They were in this together, on the same side, at last. She held on tight to Kachiko as both their heartbeats steadied.

The samurai of the Crane Clan reached the top of the stairwell just in time, followed by a ragged-looking Seiyu, and Ayaka, a knife in her hand.

"Lady Doji!" one of the Crane shouted, saluting her with a rigid bow. "You're wounded."

"Yes," she admitted, "but Her Excellency is safe."

"We can take the emissary from here," one of the soldiers offered.

She didn't want to let go of Kachiko, but neither was she going to do either of them any good carrying on when she was already so drained. Perhaps they'd appeared too intimate, but it didn't matter. Hotaru had been doing her duty as bodyguard and had the bruises to prove it.

"Here," Hotaru relented, and she let Kachiko down gently. One of the female samurai helped steady Kachiko. She led the emissary aside, out of earshot of Hotaru. Kachiko stole a glance at Hotaru as they spoke.

"General Daidoji's forces have secured the castle," a soldier reported, "thanks in no small part to a message we intercepted from Bayushi Kachiko."

"And what of the Mantis? First Mate Seiyu?" Hotaru asked, beckoning the sailor forward.

Seiyu seemed shaken, but not broken. They'd probably suffered the most at Captain Gendo's hands for their betrayal. "The cap'n went rogue – this wasn't Lord Yoritomo's doing. Our crews have surrendered. May the emperor have mercy on us."

The soldier confirmed Seiyu's report with a nod of his head. "The Mantis gave up quickly, without putting up much of a fight. As soon as they saw this one," he said, nodding to Seiyu, "they threw down their arms."

Hotaru forced herself to smile thinly. "I'm glad," was all she said. "Thank you, Captain Seiyu."

Seiyu nodded, offering Hotaru a smile. "You're twice-lucky, you know that?"

Hotaru chuckled. "I am."

Hotaru looked to Kachiko, whose face brightened to see Ayaka. There were still tears in her eyes, and she shivered in the cold wind.

Neither of them were perfect, but they had found someone else who understood, who knew the same suffering. For now, the game was at an end. Hotaru had proven herself a formidable opponent. And she had upheld her duty to the end.

EPILOGUE

Dressed in a snow-white bridal kimono, Hotaru followed her father down the stony path to the shrine in silence. He had only returned to Kyūden Doji from the capital mere days before her wedding, and they hadn't had the chance to speak. Hotaru wasn't looking forward to explaining herself, nor had he summoned her to demand an explanation. Although the Crane still held the isles, she'd needlessly endangered herself and risked Daidoji Uji's best forces in her rescue. She'd appeared reckless.

To avoid such recklessness in the future, it was time for her to be married and produce an heir. She would wed Kitsune Kuzunobu in order to mend the feud that had begun with Uncle Toshimoko and to ensure the loyalty of the neighboring Fox Clan.

She did not complain. She'd done the right thing, even if she could not tell her father that it had been her makeshift alliance with a Scorpion and a forgery that had helped the Crane secure the Keep of White Sails. And if she could help heal the wounds that Toshimoko had regretted since she'd known him, then she would not hesitate to do that.

She did not have a better partner in mind. After all, Bayushi Kachiko was already wed.

Beneath the rooftop of the shrine to Doji-no-Kami, Hotaru sipped from the sake cup three times, then passed the cup to Kuzunobu, repeating the process twice with different-sized cups each time. Their parents did the same, symbolizing the seal between the Doji and Kitsune families.

Even though Kuzunobu was done up in all his finery, the waves of his soft brown hair made it seem like he had just returned from a walk in his family's beloved woods. He smelled of pine and fresh rain. His light-brown eyes seemed gold, reflecting the sacred altarpieces of the inner shrine.

Truly, Hotaru was lucky. Kuzunobu had wit, charm, and looks, but most importantly, he had been nothing but kind to her since he and his family had arrived at the palace with the spring thaw.

After the priest recited his blessing, they were wife and husband, and Kitsune Kuzunobu was officially Doji Kuzunobu, spouse to the future champion of the Crane Clan.

Toshimoko greeted them as they returned from the shrine. "Congratulations to my favorite niece." He looked at Kuzunobu and then said quietly, "I have never forgotten Lady Ryoden, and I am sorry."

Kuzunobu placed his hand on Hotaru's arm and nodded in return. "Now the Crane and the Fox will stand side by side."

If her marriage to Kuzunobu could bring peace to both their families, then it was a trifling sacrifice. Peace could be hard. A wedding seemed an easy path to reconciliation in comparison to what she'd endured at the Keep of White Sails. Love could still blossom between them, and if not, she at least respected Kuzunobu.

Despite her good fortune, Hotaru still hoped she was lucky enough that Kachiko would be in attendance as well. Invitations had been extended to all the other Great Clan Champions and their spouses, but whether the emissary who had helped thwart a pirate takeover of the Flying Fish Isles had time to attend a wedding reception was another matter entirely.

An eternity passed as she and Kuzunobu were presented to the visiting dignitaries and nobles. Satsume sat silently beside her in his Imperial emerald and gold robes with the crest of the Emerald Champion. As well-wishers approached the dais, they were entreating Satsume's good will far more than they were congratulating Doji Hotaru herself.

The herald announced Bayushi Kachiko and Hantei the Thirty-Eighth as they approached the bride and bridegroom.

Kuzunobu could barely contain his excitement, like a small dog being wagged by its tail. "Your Imperial Majesty!" he exclaimed, prostrating himself on the dais.

Hotaru followed suit, her heart racing. When she dared to raise her gaze, she saw Kachiko's slender form wrapped in a formal black kimono. Embroidered violets unfurled across her sleeves and hem – in the language of flowers, they symbolized honesty, which seemed like too much to hope for from the Scorpion. Kachiko's hair was pinned back neatly with delicate jewelry, simple and elegant. It was perhaps the first time the woman's elegance did not outshine Hotaru's.

Behind her black lace mask, Kachiko's dark eyes were once again fixed on Hotaru, betraying nothing, as though they had never shared that passionate kiss.

"Allow me to congratulate you both on behalf of the entire Scorpion Clan," Kachiko said pleasantly, bowing deeply to each of them in turn. "But truly, I must extend my thanks to your ladyship once again. From the beginning, Doji Hotaru had warned the Mantis crews of their leader's folly. It was thanks to her efforts that the Mantis were willing to surrender and there were so few casualties – and that I was protected as emissary."

Normally, the emperor did not need to speak in order to

convey his blessing – his mere presence was acclaim enough. But the Hantei bowed politely to the couple and then to Hotaru specifically. Hotaru flushed, bowing. She had been so fixated on Kachiko, she had almost forgotten the Son of Heaven was there.

"The Heavens thank you, Lady Doji Hotaru. Both for your mercy and for the protection you offered my servant."

She'd never dreamed that she would earn the emperor's praise, much less with all her clan present. This was perhaps the most precious gift Kachiko could have offered her on her wedding day.

She accepted the praise without demurring, for one did not contradict the emperor, even if humbleness was customary in every other case. Hotaru and Kuzunobu bowed even more deeply as Kachiko and the emperor departed.

"You have done well, Hotaru," her father said quietly, between well-wishers. "But you still have a long road ahead of you."

Hotaru looked out to the assembled Crane samurai, many of whom were congratulating Daidoji Uji on his exceptional assault on the Keep of White Sails.

"I know." The path she would take as future champion would not be easy.

Hours passed with seemingly endless spreads of food and wine, as ever more well-wishers came to pay their respects. As was custom, Hotaru changed her attire from the pure-white kimono to increasingly colorful robes three more times, highlighting the opulence of the Crane Clan and Hotaru's personal transition from sacred ceremony back to normal life.

As the party stretched into dusk, and the stone lanterns surrounding the courtyard were lit, she was returning from her third and final change of outfits when she spotted Kachiko walking on a path several paces away from the rest of the crowd.

She should restrain herself, having only just bound herself to Kuzunobu hours before. But this might be her only chance to see

Kachiko again alone. There were so many words between them that were still unsaid.

Against her better judgment, she followed Kachiko into the gardens. Petals of every hue lined the paths, drifting between the stones like snow. This maze of flowers and trees had worn many paths across her heart, and she knew which trails to take in order to cut off Kachiko before she made her way to the lake.

She found Kachiko standing in the shadow of a centuries-old cherry blossom tree, her dark form cutting a stark line against the dusky pastels of the gardens. A small stream babbled around the roots, and the flowers around them were strongly fragrant.

In a few days, all this beauty would be changed. This moment they had together was fleeting as well.

"You didn't claim credit for everything yourself," Hotaru began, not concealing the shock in her voice. Even if they had become something akin to friends, allies, or even lovers, that wouldn't have stopped Kachiko from seizing an opportunity when she saw one. "Why didn't you?" She expected a lie, or a half-truth at best.

Kachiko placed her fan in her obi and closed the distance between them. "Captain Gendo was acting at my behest, not Lord Yoritomo's."

Kachiko's words knocked the breath out of her as thoroughly as a kick to the belly during sparring practice. It was too bold a statement to be anything but the truth. And if it were true, then the deaths of those Crane Clan samurai lay at Kachiko's feet. She'd even been willing to draw the servants of the emperor into a war.

Hotaru had sworn to protect Kachiko, had been ready to make the ultimate sacrifice to her charge. And yet Kachiko was willing to throw away the lives of others in order to advance her own agendas. "I knew you were working for your own ends, but..." So that was what Kachiko had needed to fix. Did she think she could beg Hotaru's forgiveness now?

"Samurai serving my clan *died* because of you," Hotaru hissed. "Sasaki family samurai, my messenger… Why would you do such a thing?"

"That hadn't been part of the plan," Kachiko answered, her voice trembling. She was on the defensive, which was uncharacteristic for her. "The invocation of fog was supposed to allow Captain Gendo to take the castle without casualties. I didn't know he would be so brutal."

It was possible that Kachiko really hadn't known. But regardless of whether or not she was ignorant, innocent blood had been spilled because of her.

"Once the keep was safely in the hands of the *Inazuma*'s crew, I was to arrive to begin negotiations, which would stall until the Crane looked as though they could launch an attack at any moment. Then, I would announce Captain Gendo's withdrawal from the castle. The Mantis Clan would still have the bragging rights of having bested the Crane by taking the castle in the first place, and I would prove my usefulness to the emperor as arbiter of a peace."

It all made perfect sense. It should have been a simple matter to pull off. "But you didn't bank on my tagging along." Hotaru filled in the blanks, still shaking with anger.

"No. You ruined all my plans," Kachiko nodded.

Hotaru should just leave. She had a husband to attend to, and her clan, any of whom she could rely upon to be nobler than Kachiko. But none of them had understood her as Kachiko had.

"And yet, you wondered what sort of person I would be if I didn't have to claw my way to power on my own. By then, it was too late for you to help me. I couldn't drag you any deeper into the whirlpool of my own devising." Kachiko looked away to the lake in the distance.

"The last night in the castle, I didn't know what would happen to me – if Gendo would kill me and be done with it. I couldn't fathom that you would come for me, much less that you'd be willing to lay down your life for mine. I owe you an enormous debt."

Kachiko was a liar, a schemer who gambled with other people's lives. Hotaru had been right not to trust this woman from the outset.

"And the dice? Did you cheat the Mantis in order to speak with Gendo alone?"

"No," Kachiko breathed. "That was your luck, Hotaru. That was fate. Fate that the dice should land where they may, and fate that I had you there to protect me."

Despite everything, Kachiko had sided with Hotaru in the end. Hotaru would not have survived if Kachiko did not have some goodness in her, if she had not been willing to turn away from power when it was offered. It would have been easier to simply let Gendo escape at the end, but Kachiko had risked attacking Gendo in order to give Hotaru a chance to end him.

And she'd had to trust in Hotaru to save her when she'd failed to land a killing blow.

Kachiko had made terrible mistakes, but she was not unredeemable. Together, a Crane and a Scorpion, they could do more for the Empire than they could apart.

At Kachiko's side, Hotaru could remind the Scorpion what it meant to serve, what it meant to be a samurai who could be trusted. And that there were others who understood.

Perhaps, with Kachiko beside her, the Crane could remember what it was like to have someone help you when you were lost, to comfort you when you were hurting. To accept you for all your imperfections.

Hotaru's anger subsided as the spring breeze coursed through the branches, showering them in pink petals. "The debt is already repaid."

They had but moments left before someone else inevitably wandered into this part of the gardens. This was her chance to walk away, to turn her back on the Mother of Scorpions before it was too late and they were discovered together, too close for propriety. They both knew the scandal that would follow from even the suggestion that the heir to the Crane Clan was in love with the wife of the Scorpion Clan Champion. Both would be disgraced, possibly cast out by their clans.

Everything she had ever learned warned her to stay away from this woman, but now she only wanted to hold her close.

"Don't leave me alone. Stay by my side. Please," Kachiko whispered, giving voice to the part of her that shouldn't exist, the weakness that she wanted to deny. "I would fight by your side, not against you."

Never trust a Scorpion, Kachiko had warned her herself.

Hotaru drew up Kachiko's chin and traced a finger down her cheek.

Hotaru would trust the woman behind the mask.

She leaned in to kiss Kachiko amid a flurry of cherry blossoms.

THE SWORD AND THE SPIRITS

ROBERT DENTON III

*I wrote this for Christen, my wife,
my love, my best friend.*

CHAPTER ONE

With a sharp clack, Yūka's *bokken* clattered to the dōjō floor. She crumpled, pressing her hand against her right eye.

Hatsu dropped his own practice weapon and rushed to her side. "Let me see it," he ordered.

Blinking back tears, Yūka revealed the swollen welt across her cheek and forehead. Already the eye was beginning to bruise, a slow spread of midnight purple. "Will it scar?" came her tremulous voice.

The guilt was plain on Hatsu's face. "Why'd you drop your guard? I thought you had it!"

Yūka blinked up at him from the floor. She had nothing to say. Father had warned them not to get too carried away with sparring – that they had an important function this evening and would each have to make an appearance. She felt a hot sting as her eye swelled into a puffy thin slit. Father's anger was legendary; Hatsu would get a tongue lashing for sure. She sniffed, heat rising into her face.

Hatsu's disappointed expression crushed her rapid heart. "You've *got* to get tougher, Yūka-chan. Where you're going, there will be no room for softness."

Yūka started to cry. Her voice echoed through the empty dōjō.

Hatsu's face softened. He kneeled, working his *tenugui*, a hand towel presented to him by his sensei, out of his obi belt. He dabbed her tears like a pecking sparrow. The tenugui smelled like him: sandalwood and pine.

"I'm not strong like you, Nii-chan," she whispered. "If only I had your courage."

He smiled, and the dōjō seemed brighter. "You're stronger than you think, Yūka-chan."

He helped her to her feet as she tenderly palmed her eye. "Sorry for crying."

"That's fine." He placed his hand on her shoulder and made a serious face. "You can cry in the dōjō if you laugh on the battlefield."

Her chest swelled. She nodded. She would do better.

"That's enough for today," he said, going to retrieve his dropped bokken.

"One more." She had reassumed her stance, readying her wooden practice sword.

He grinned, falling into his own stance with proud eyes. "That's my little sister."

Shiba Tsukune opened her eyes. That had been long ago, in a similar place. Now, she had a different name. Now, she was here.

A downward strike disarmed her first attacker. The next strike, up and left, would have severed the arms of the second. She spun and knelt, slashing horizontally at the third, another dispatch. Two more strikes and she was back in her original position, the practice weapons of the final attackers clattering to the floor.

The five students bowed as Tsukune lowered her bokken. Her eyes lifted to an ancient banner hanging from the balcony, the banner of the dōjō, the Order of Chikai. A depiction of the

Phoenix *mon* blazed at its center, along with a string of words in the Shiba cipher: *when you are willing to sacrifice anything, only then can you be entrusted with the world.*

She started at the sound of clapping. A young man leaned against the nearby wall, his elaborate silks glowing as he smiled. "You are getting faster, Tsukune-sama."

Tsukune winced at the "sama" honorific. She was not used to it yet. She bowed. "Maybe our sparring is leaving a mark."

"Perhaps I've left several," he quipped with a wink. "But hopefully not."

As he approached, the students touched their foreheads to the floor and backed out of the room, leaving them alone.

"So I *am* improving," Tsukune failed to filter the hope from her voice.

His words slipped into the casual syntax, the dialect of friendship. "You're still pausing at the bottom. In dragon posture, the momentum should carry you back up. Be like a coiled spring."

Her shoulders slumping heavily, Tsukune nodded. She had to do better. "I will chisel this into my liver," she assured him.

He nodded, tucking his hands behind his back.

"Care to spar?" she offered, making her way to the weapon racks. She switched her bokken for a long *shinai*, a bamboo sword for contact practice. "Perhaps today I will finally beat you."

She paused, midbreath, at his plain expression.

"Another time perhaps," he said more seriously. "They're ready."

She stiffened. "Now?"

A nod.

Her grip tightened around the shinai. She drew a breath that did not feel deep enough. "I… shouldn't keep them waiting," she murmured, feeling the steady tap against her ribcage increase in frequency. The first impression was the only one that mattered.

"You're not going like that?" Tetsu inquired.

She glanced down at her sweaty practice kimono and *hakama*. There was no way she could appear as she was.

Tetsu chuckled. "Don't worry. I have something that will fit, and one of my servants is a seamstress. Any alterations won't take long."

She nodded. No breath seemed deep enough to still her jittering limbs.

"Are you nervous?"

The rattling of cicadas drifted in from outside.

She shook her head. "No. I'm fine. I'm ready." She managed a smile and abruptly turned to set the shinai back. "Lead the wa–"

As she turned, her shinai struck the bokken stand with a loud *thwack*. The stand teetered for a perilous moment before a cacophony thundered through the dōjō. Tsukune grimaced at her handiwork, practice weapons scattered across the floor.

"What happened?" came a shout from the doorway. Tsukune froze in the instructor's gaze as he slid open the door. His alarmed face softened into barely concealed exasperation.

Tetsu stepped between her and the instructor. "How careless of me! My apologies."

Guilt pricked Tsukune's heart, but she said nothing.

The instructor waved his hand. "It is fine. The stand was quite old. It would have happened sooner or later."

"I will commission a new one," said Tetsu.

Appeased, the instructor bowed deeply to Tsukune and left.

Tetsu affixed her with a knowing gaze. Sheepishly, she showed her teeth. "I might be a *little* nervous," she confessed.

"One can hardly tell," Tetsu replied.

Tetsu awaited her outside a dressing room, a thin paper *shōji* screen separating them. Tsukune watched his impatient outline through the screen as the handmaid, an older woman with gray-streaked hair, tied an elaborate bow into her obi. The woman rolled the shōji aside, and Tsukune jumped at the loud crack.

Tsukune's patterned kimono were contrasting layers of flame beneath a golden, broad-shouldered *kataginu* embroidered with the mon of the Phoenix. The handmaid's hasty addition, two draping sleeves swinging past her knees and attached with thick visible stitches, proclaimed her status as an eligible young lady. Looking up into Tetsu's appraising expression, Tsukune supposed she looked like some manner of awkward bird.

At last, he nodded. "Better. I'm not sure the color works."

The handmaid huffed. "Your red one was disassembled for cleaning, I'm afraid."

Tsukune tugged at one long sleeve and gasped as the cord partially unwound. An exasperated puff escaped the older woman's lips as she corrected it, resewing with deftness in defiance of her age.

"Her hair?" Tetsu asked, regarding her simple ponytail.

"No time," the handmaid replied, finishing the weave.

"What's wrong with my hair?" Tsukune asked.

The older woman chuckled and shook her head, as if the answer were obvious. Tsukune's questioning look at Tetsu's face found no answers.

"It's fine," he decided with a nod. "It's not like she's going to meet the *nakōdo.*"

"The jacket shoulders are too long," the handmaid observed.

Tsukune regarded the stiff cloth forming a pointed awning at her shoulders. They reminded her of pagoda roofs, of wings.

"She looks authoritative." She felt his gaze rake her one more time. "She'll need to," he added.

Perhaps, if she were lucky, she would fall into a hole on the way to the council chambers.

•••

Soon, they stood beneath a pagoda roof in the Garden of No Mind. The pink moss carpet swirled around islands of gray stone and bushy trees clustered with off-white loquat blooms. The sun was a gold-plated disk hovering low behind curtains of spotty rain.

"A fox's wedding," she murmured.

"Hm?" Tetsu's hands were tucked behind him.

"That's what they call it when it is raining while sunny. A fox's wedding."

"Who calls it that?"

Doubt swallowed her answer. "They do," she said and fidgeted with her sleeves.

She felt his shadow. Looking up, she met his eyes and froze. Gracefully, Tetsu pinched the cord attaching a swinging sleeve and pulled it free. The silk fell like an unfurled curtain, unburdening Tsukune's arm. He did the same with the other.

"Better?" Tetsu asked.

She flexed her arms in warm sunlight and nodded. In his returned smile, she swore she saw his sensei.

When the rain slowed, they left the pagoda's shade and crossed the pink moss, heading for the base of the sheer cliff overlooking the garden. The stone steps carved into the cliff face were still dry. They climbed in silence, Tsukune dragging behind Tetsu's shadow. The keening trill of the garden cicadas rattled in perfect tandem with Tsukune's heart.

At the top of the steps at the center of the Grove of the Five Masters stood an ancient oak tree, whose roots twisted around the entrance to an ancient stone teahouse with five sides. A depiction of the elements balanced in a circle nearly glowed on the shōji door. Tetsu slid it open. Beyond the doors of the far wall would be a spiraling staircase that led to a subterranean chamber.

Tsukune held her breath, as if to chain her heart and keep it from escaping. She looked away from the door and at the symbol on Tetsu's shoulder, the emblem of the Order of Chikai, the personal bodyguards of the Council of Five.

"What are they like?" she asked.

"Eccentric. You'll get used to them."

"What should I say? What—"

Tetsu offered an encouraging look. "Bow and show deference. Lead with the left, never the right. When they ask you something, answer honestly. Otherwise, just listen.

"You are here to witness so that, if you are called before the emperor, you may recall their decisions." His eyes trailed to her sword. "Be confident. Even if you do not feel it, you must try to appear that way."

"So, I should be more like you," she joked, her voice wavering.

He stared at her, unblinking, for a long time. "Yes," he finally said. "Like me."

She swallowed hard, pushing aside the sensation that she'd stepped on something he was trying to keep clean and hidden, or had opened a door that he'd meant to keep closed.

His eyes narrowed. "I accompanied sensei to meetings once or twice," he murmured, "but I've never been inside the council's chambers. I've never witnessed a champion's briefing."

He was staring at her sword. Bronze wings formed its *tsuba* handguard, the manta skin–wrapped handle was inlaid with pearls, and its sheath was exquisitely carved from a single piece of wood, as if feathers had simply petrified around the blade. The sword predated the katana, curving only gently, worn edge down in her belt. Every Phoenix Clan Champion, all the way back to Shiba himself, had once wielded it: Ofushikai, the ancestral sword of the Phoenix.

She knew, from his eyes, that he wanted it. That he felt it should have been his – the sword, the position, and the accolades. By all rights, it should have. Tetsu was the scion of the late Phoenix Clan Champion. Ujimitsu's teachings, his lessons, his techniques: they all lived on in Tetsu. That, for his age, Tetsu was the greatest warrior of the Shiba family and most promising among the Order of Chikai was no secret – certainly not among the students of the Chikai Academy, who whispered as much when they believed Tsukune was not listening. The same students spread rumors that Tsukune was not ready, that her appointment had been a mistake or, worse, political maneuvering. A young woman just past seventeen with no accolades would be far easier for the council to control than someone of Tetsu's reputation. Surely Ujimitsu's sword was intended for him.

But the sword had not chosen him. It had chosen her.

"You should go," he said abruptly. "They're waiting." His eyes never left the blade.

She bowed and left him at the entrance, glancing back just before the steps carried her out of sight. He never moved, his silhouette framed by the shōji doorway. Where she went, he could not follow. As she lowered herself into the chamber, she wondered if he would ever forgive her.

"This is unacceptable!" barked Isawa Tsuke. Beneath his fiery eyes, the mon of the Master of Fire nearly glowed on his immaculate robes. "Eju, this personal quest of yours has taken too much of the council's time. Just choose someone and be done with it!"

Tsukune snapped out of her daydream and looked down. Her scroll, for the notes of this meeting, was completely blank.

The ancient Master of Air took a tortured breath. He had the look of a man who hadn't done any eating or sleeping since he was young. "Your suggestion... explains... much."

Tsuke bristled. "You do not mean to imply I have elevated an unworthy student?"

The Master of Earth shrugged, ringing the wooden bells on his winged jacket. "I liked your last one better."

"I am not sure you are in a position to speak on the matter of apprentices, Rujo," quipped Tsuke.

The Earth Master darkened and did not reply.

When Tsukune was a child, she'd always looked up to the Elemental Masters, imagining them as sages whose hearts and minds were always in accord. Ruling the clan since the dawn of the Empire and the day Shiba bent his knee to Isawa, they represented the pinnacle of the priestly craft. Their word was beyond questioning, their judgment always unified. They couldn't be the same people who were shouting at each other around the meeting table in the chamber of Elemental Mastery.

"Can we return to the matter at hand?" asked Asako Azunami, the Water Master's piercing blue eyes twinkling against the twin waterfalls of black hair cascading from her cone-shaped hat.

"Naturally, Azunami." Tsuke laced his fingers. "Three days ago, Azunami and I attempted to purify a blight in the eastern Shiba farmlands. The water kami were silent; we had no choice but to burn the afflicted crops to contain the disease." The implications on the autumn taxes, and the coming winter, he left unsaid. "In contrast, just today a student attempted to invoke the fire kami and suffered several burns." He shook his head. "Every day, the elemental imbalance grows worse."

"The signs are everywhere," Azunami chimed in. "Floods, droughts, storms – without a doubt, it has spread to the provinces of other clans."

"We… must… act," Eju managed. "For the good… of the… Empire."

"Haste is not wise," Rujo spoke. "We still remember what

happened when Kaiyoko-sama attempted to correct the balance by herself. She was the strongest among us, her connection to the water kami unparalleled! Yet even with her insights, her ceremony had no effect."

"I would not say there was *no* effect," Tsuke remarked. "The Crane lands weathered a tsunami, after all."

The Masters paused, then collectively looked at Tsukune. Her face had gone white, and her brush slipped from limp fingers.

"Perhaps refrain from writing that part down," Azunami advised.

Ujina, the Master of Void, sighed. "We learned much about the imbalance from that ceremony, but that would be cold comfort to our allies."

The air grew somber. Tsukune had believed, like so many others, that Isawa Kaiyoko had retired willingly to study the *Tao of Shinsei*. Now, however, hearing this, she was not so sure the retirement had been voluntary.

Rujo broke the silence. "Are we sure there is no precedent? The rise and fall of the elements have always been part of the natural cycle. Perhaps this is no different."

"This has… never happened… before," Eju rasped. "Not even… since the dawn… of the Empire."

Tsuke scoffed. "You should know. You were there, after all."

Tsukune winced as Azunami hid a smirk poorly. Ujina placed his forehead in his hands. "Really, Tsuke. Try to remember your station." For his part, Eju gave no reaction.

"Then what is the cause?" Rujo challenged. "For all our time studying this imbalance, we seem no closer to discerning a pattern."

"Is it not obvious?" Tsuke said. "The kami are offended. For two hundred years, the Unicorn have compelled them with their *meishōdō* techniques, invoking them without suitable offerings in exchange. To those barbarians, the kami are merely spirits to be commanded, not divinities to be appeased. Their ignorance will have repercussions across the lands."

"Little good… has ever come… from beyond the Empire," Eju agreed. "Be it the meishōdō… of the Unicorn… or the sorcery… of the Yobanjin."

Tsukune darkened at the word. Yobanjin were the people dwelling beyond the northern border, descendants of those who would not bow to the emperor and thus were banished. Now, they were known for making raids against her people – the Phoenix.

"In the end there is little difference," Tsuke pressed. "They are both equally disrespectful of the spirits, too focused on the end result to care about the path chosen."

Rujo regarded Tsuke critically. "I did not realize you were an expert on gaijin sorcery, Tsuke, be it Yobanjin or that of the Unicorn."

Tsuke responded in an even tone. "A sword master cannot hide the root of their techniques from another sword master, only from beginners. Anyone who pays attention will know enough."

The Master of Void spoke, his voice rumbling low. "How fortunate, then, that the Unicorn will show their techniques to the Seppun Hidden Guard, at the emperor's command."

This silenced the table for a time.

Rujo leaned forward. "Your daughter warned the Seppun, Ujina. The Son of Heaven has decided not to forbid the Unicorn from practicing their arts. That no one is particularly pleased may well speak to the wisdom of his decision. In any case, there is nothing to be done about it now." He sat back, deflated. "Nothing except wait. Wait and watch."

Tsuke's expression spoke volumes of his displeasure.

"Forcing the kami to manifest without offerings could cause unpredictable behaviors," Azunami observed. "However, I do not think we can conclude meishōdō is responsible for the imbalance or Atsuko's prophecy. Not until we better understand the nature of meishōdō."

"You have a better theory?" Tsuke replied.

"Perhaps we are being punished." She looked around the table. "With so many omens, is it possible we have offended the Fortunes?"

Eju thumped a weathered hand. "All the more... reason... to act. Repentance... does not... come first..."

"Repentance for what?" Tsuke shook his head. "If this were divine punishment, then the signs would be obvious. The Fortunes would make it clear where the wrong occurred."

Tsukune spoke before realizing it. "Have we asked the other clans?"

As one the Masters turned, a wall of inquiring eyes.

Tsukune's heart raced, and she felt her palms grow slick, but she could not take it back now. Swallowing, she continued, "They may not have the same understanding of the elements, but their perspectives are unique. The Crane are our long-standing allies; their *shugenja* family, the Asahina, would gladly join forces and share their insights into the stars and oceans. The Lion may be assertive, but they are calculating, too, and can be made to see reason once they understand how the imbalance will affect them." She looked from one face to the next with growing confidence. "If we reach out to the other clans, this challenge could strengthen our bonds with the other shugenja families. With every shugenja family's expertise and perspective combined, the cause of the imbalance might be swiftly discovered."

The braziers popped, echoing through the chamber.

"Tsukune-sama," Tsuke said, leaning on the table to regard her openly, "the Lion have long looked upon our lands with jealous eyes. If they discerned we could not depend on the kami to defend ourselves, do you think they would sit idly by, or would they attempt to take them?"

Tsukune clenched her jaw. "Well..."

Azunami chimed in. "For an herbalist, all diseases are cured with herbs. For one who sets bones, all diseases are cured by realigning bones. In this way, when one chooses a doctor, one chooses one's illness." She regarded Tsukune with visible patience. "Are you so certain multiple specialized perspectives will reveal the truth? Or will more voices mean more noise?"

Tsukune sank in her seat. "I... I had not..."

Rujo shook his head. "If we reveal the existence of the imbalance before we have an answer, the Throne will respond as it did to Atsuko's prophecy. It is better that the Phoenix have an answer before we present the question. To do less would shame the clan."

"At least... she suggested... *something*!" Eju rasped. "This council... seems content... to do nothing... about it!"

As the discussion grew heated, Tsukune lowered her head and made a note not to interrupt a council meeting ever again.

As the Masters rose to leave, the tone of the room transformed. Azunami asked Rujo of his daughter's upcoming wedding. Isawa Tsuke helped the decrepit Air Master out of his seat, nodding at the old man's friendly whispers. Gone were the quips and resentment. They left their hostility at the table. This was the council Tsukune had imagined as a child.

She finally understood: at the table, their masks fell and they spoke freely, but once they left this room, the civility and unity resumed. They assumed the best of one another, regardless of what position the others had argued, or how vehemently anyone had disagreed.

Would this courtesy be extended to her?

Rujo and Tsuke lingered at the bottom of the steps. Washing her forearms in the stream nearby, Tsukune couldn't help but overhear their quiet exchange.

"I was out of line earlier," Tsuke said. "My apologies."

"Do not be concerned. I was foolish to take the boy as my apprentice," he sighed. "Perhaps Tadaka will see reason after the week is done."

She froze at Tadaka's name.

Rujo continued. Tsukune could not see his face, but from his voice, it sounded like he was frowning.

"He thinks I will not go through with it." A curt pause. "He is quite mistaken."

When finally alone, Tsukune sat and stared at Ofushikai in her hands. Her fingers wrapped experimentally around the hilt. Her thin fingers seemed mismatched for it: too frail, not large enough. She stared at the sword for a long time, waiting for something. Anything.

She lowered her lips to the bronze tsuba. "Are you there?" she whispered.

"I am," came a voice nearby.

Tsukune froze, then slowly turned. The Master of Void stood by the table, leaning on a cypress cane.

"Master Ujina!" She made a stiff bow. "A thousand pardons! I did not see you there."

"It is I who would apologize," he replied, then gestured to the side. "Do you mind? I would rather take the stairs, but there are a lot of them."

Tsukune nodded. Hooking his arm, she led him past the lift and up a vast flight of spiraling steps. They walked in silence until they emerged in the sunlit Garden of No Mind. Ujina thanked Tsukune, and they stood watching the pond for a while as the summer breeze stirred the butterburs.

"I spoke out of turn," Tsukune admitted.

"Out of turn, you say." He watched a dragonfly dance with a mosquito.

"It was not my intention to question the council. I only wish to be of some use. I should have said nothing."

"I am glad you said what you did. It needed to be said."

Her face slowly lit up. "Then you agree?" She thought for a moment. "If you mentioned this, it could convince the others. Your esteemed word–"

"I actually agree with the council," he said. "I am just glad you were willing to speak dissent."

"Oh. I see."

He looked up. The sun carved shadows into his wrinkled face. "You are young, Tsukune-sama. You see the world as you wish it to be. You believe involving the other clans will make this matter easier. Sadly, this is not so. It would achieve the opposite." She caught a glimpse of sadness behind his dark eyes. "The other clans may wish the best for the Empire, but they tend to themselves first. They would seek an advantage, and their games would only serve to make our task more difficult. While it is true that every clan holds a piece of wisdom, this task is only for the Phoenix."

"I understand."

"Your predecessor, Shiba Ujimitsu, was a very proactive champion. It is not well known, but he did not always agree with the council's decisions. Yet he always served. Now, we test our newest champion and wonder what kind of daimyō she will be."

"I've been wondering this myself," she murmured.

A nightingale keened and another answered.

"How is your son?" Tsukune asked suddenly.

"Headstrong and proud. Still."

"I overheard something," she admitted. "I wasn't sure what they were talking about, but they mentioned him."

Ujina sighed. "Yes. An unusual situation. As it turns out, my son challenged Master Rujo to a duel, and Rujo accepted. It shall be settled by season's end."

Tsukune's jaw went slack. "He... he what?"

"A disagreement stemming from his proposal to study with the Kuni. The council declined his proposal, and he blamed Rujo." He sighed again and rubbed his forehead. "You were the only one who could ever talk sense into him, you know. It is a shame you were not there to do so recently."

She clenched her jaw. "Where is he now?"

"He still has a duty to the council, so he was dispatched on an investigation. Some unusual occurrences at Sanpuku Seidō – Cliffside Shrine." He waved his hand. "Worry not. It is in the hands of the Fortunes."

She nodded absently.

"So," the Master said, "you and Ofushikai are becoming acquainted, yes?"

"In a manner of speaking." She glanced at the blade in her obi. "When it lets me."

"Has it spoken to you?"

"It has."

"What did it say?"

She felt as though she were kneeling in the dark before the shrine to Shiba, the weight of a new winged kataginu pressing down on her shoulders, the burden of the clan resting silently in her hands. She remembered that moment, looking into the blade, dozens of faces looking back...

"It said, 'You will never be alone.'"

The Void Master stroked his chin. "Interesting."

"Why me?"

The question surprised her, even though it had come from her own mouth. Ujina regarded her with a patient smile.

"Why me?" she repeated. "How does the sword choose?"

"I cannot say for certain," he finally replied. "Not even Elemental Masters have been able to discern a pattern. The sword chooses as it will."

"It should have been Tetsu." She regretted speaking the words as soon as they left her lips. Her face burned.

Ujina shrugged. "If the sword were meant for Tetsu, it would have chosen him. It did not. It chose you." He regarded her with starry eyes. "If you seek the answer why, look within."

Her hand absently curled over Ofushikai's too-large hilt.

A distant bell rang. It was the Hour of the Serpent. More appointments. Tsukune bowed and excused herself.

She paused and looked back. He was still watching the pond, the Void mon almost glowing white against the dark crimson of the back of his garment.

"Sanpuku Seidō," she called to him. "Where is that exactly?"

From his voice, Tsukune thought he might be smiling. "North. Garanto Province. One would find it on the tallest mountain in the range at the very edge of Phoenix territory." He paused. "Three days' travel. Perhaps four."

"Thank you," Tsukune said and bowed before leaving.

After some time, Ujina smiled at a butterbur leaf where a butterfly dried its dewy wings. His voice was just above a whisper. "We are even now, my friend."

CHAPTER TWO

In the Empire's darkest hour, Shinsei, the Little Teacher, came to the greatest priest, Isawa, for only the magic of his tribe could defeat and bind the fallen god, Fu Leng. Yet, Isawa refused. He could not abandon his people, and without his guidance, what would become of them? So Shiba, a living god, bent his knee before the mortal Isawa, making for him a sacred pledge. If Isawa would agree, if he would join the Seven Thunders, then Shiba's line would serve Isawa's forever...

"This way, Shiba-ue."

Tsukune flinched out of her daydreaming thoughts. The guide gestured ahead with her lantern. She followed, flushing when the guide turned away. She could almost hear Tetsu chiding, *"The Phoenix Champion should focus on the present, not daydream before her vassals!"*

She pulled her straw cloak tight against the sting of icy wind. Elsewhere, the autumn season had brought unexpected warmth, but here at the mountainous northern border, the cypresses were white with powdered snow and the pink orchids were heavy with frost. The road had long abandoned any pretense of having been maintained, comprising just mossy platforms of gray rock amid tall silver grass. If the sun had risen, and the wind had parted the trees just so, she would have had a clear view of the treetops of the

Isawa Woodlands, and perhaps even the glittering shore of the Sea of the Sun Goddess south of Castle Shiba.

Her guide paused on a raised rock platform and waited for her to catch up. Tan-skinned and round-faced, the guide was seemingly immune to the cold in a sleeveless white kimono tucked into vermilion hakama.

Tsukune sneezed and dabbed at her drippy nose with a knuckle. "Next time, I will wait until sunrise to climb a mountain."

The guide's chuckle caused her heart to skip, and she awkwardly joined in, reminding herself not to speak her private thoughts aloud.

They continued in silence until they rounded a tight corner. The guide's words dragged with the rural dialect. "Here's the mudslide."

The path beyond the lantern was marred by a wet, brown scar, as if a giant hand had scooped out a chunk of the mountain, leaving only enough crumbling stone and mud for one person to stand upon. "What did this?" Tsukune asked.

"A storm, I think." The guide looked apologetic. "Mountains hate roads, as it turns out."

The guide darted across, pausing to show Tsukune where she should place her feet. Tsukune removed her straw sandals before following, the cold ground stinging her soles.

Halfway across, she felt a breath on her neck. Turning, Tsukune stared into a yawning fissure, jagged with rock and churning with darkness. Beneath the wind's whistling, she heard silver chimes and something close to a whisper…

"Shiba-ue?"

Tsukune snapped back, meeting her guide's confused eyes. She blinked absently for a moment, then nodded that she was all right. They continued, Tsukune uncurling her hand from Ofushikai's hilt, which she had not realized she was grasping.

•••

Tsukune spotted her destination as the sun broke over the ridge: a complex of structures with red, flanged roofs clinging to the mountainside, balanced precariously over a vertical drop. If it had been one of her grandmother's wooden replicas of temple complexes, she'd have been scolded for placing it so close to the danger of the table's edge. Surely any moment it would slide off and into the foggy valley.

An arrow with a humming-bulb tip shrieked a keening whistle, echoing throughout the bowl of the ridge. "They'll be expecting you," the guide said. She gestured toward the dot of civilization on the rocky shelf. "Welcome to Sanpuku Seidō."

A small group of servants offered Tsukune obeisance before a shinden-style building near the monastery entrance. A quick thaw in a thermal spring bath, a warm layer of fresh clothes, and then she was standing before a sparse court painted with morning light from narrow windows, gazing at the three men awaiting her on the dais.

Only one returned her look, a middle-aged man in a winged jacket announcing him as the lord of the Kaito family estate and the high priest of the shrine. To his left, a boy closer to Tsukune's age watched the window and adjusted his pointed cap. The third was well past the age of retirement. He sat cross-legged in a seat of honor, deep wrinkles carved into his face, a long pipe tucked into his liver-spotted hand. Tsukune could smell sweet smoking leaf in his pipe's bowl.

The daimyō stood. "Welcome, Shiba Tsukune, daimyō of the honored Shiba. I am Kaito no Isawa Nobukai, daimyō of the humble Kaito vassals. On behalf of my family, I welcome you to Sanpuku Seidō." His head dipped. "I apologize for the state of the road. I trust it was not too much trouble?"

"An invigorating hike," Tsukune replied as she bowed. Her

hands felt naked without a gift, even though such a gesture was only required from visitors of lower station.

If he felt slighted, the lord didn't look it. "This is the first time in many decades that a Clan Champion has walked these halls. Congratulations on your recent appointment. I only just heard."

"Thank you. I will strive to be worthy of it."

Nobukai gestured to the young man. "This is my son, Uwazuru."

The boy gave a graceful bow, holding his cap with slender fingers. "Congratulations, Shiba-ue. It is an honor to meet a fellow servant of the Isawa." His sunny smile warmed his words. "I will see to your comfort while you are here. If you need anything, only ask."

"I am grateful," Tsukune replied. She then offered the old man a smile. "And this is your distinguished father?"

The old man grinned, eyes twinkling. Nobukai flushed. Tsukune's heart skipped, as if she'd tripped over a stone she hadn't seen.

"He is... an honored advisor," Nobukai explained.

"I am Asako Maezawa," came the withered sage's gravelly voice, "a man of little importance. Please take no offense at my slight bow, my lady. These old bones..."

"Worry not," Tsukune said. She imagined his story: here was one who had served his clan and should have retired to a monastery to reflect on the lessons of his life, but instead of accepting *inkyo*, he had chosen to remain in service. Her sensei had always spoken highly of such individuals. "Thank you, honored elder, for your service."

His laughter, choppy and unrefined, startled her. "There is some hope for this new generation, after all!"

"Please sit," Nobukai quickly offered. "I apologize for the inadequate finery, but in the mountains, you learn to make do."

Tsukune selected a cushion that afforded a full view of the

room. It was one of many *yōjimbō* habits that had made her former
job as a bodyguard easier. She set Ofushikai to her right, where it
would be harder to draw, as was polite. Servants entered with an
iron kettle and poured a fragrant liquid into plain ceramic cups.

"A blend unique to the Kaito," Nobukai explained.

The hot ceramic bit her fingertips, but she pressed her palms
against its circumference, soaking in the warmth. "You grow tea
this close to Heaven?"

"I'm afraid if something is wanted here, making it is the only
solution."

They talked for some time. Nobukai asked of her trip, about
the state of nearby provinces, and for news from the Imperial
capital. Tsukune answered what she could. She had not attended
many courts, but she knew enough to recognize social rituals.
One never spoke of business right away.

"So then," Nobukai said at last, "I must admit, I am both
honored and surprised today. No retinue, no messenger. Is
anything amiss, my lady?"

A cold breeze pricked her skin. "Not that I am aware of."

"Then to what do we owe the great honor of your presence?"

Tsukune set her cup aside. "While I am honored to visit your
esteemed family, I am here seeking one of your guests. His name
is Isawa Tadaka."

The old man's eyebrows rose at Tadaka's name. Nobukai
lifted his cup, his hand obscuring his lips. "It must be an urgent
message for the Phoenix Champion to deliver it in person. Sadly,
his assignment keeps him quite busy, and so far he has refused
guests." He sipped, set down his cup, and smiled. "If you relay the
council's message to me, I will ensure he receives it."

Tsukune looked from one set of expectant eyes to the next.
"There has been a misunderstanding," she said. "I am not here on
behalf of the council. My business with Tadaka is…"

She stopped. She'd dropped everything to travel halfway across Phoenix lands, unescorted, for personal business. Beneath their appraising eyes, Tsukune could almost hear their thoughts: *is this how the Phoenix Clan Champion spends her precious time?* She looked into her tea and saw a confused, foolish girl in a dark void.

"It is a personal matter," she finished. From outside came the nervous chatter of crickets.

"I see." Nobukai glanced at his son, then nodded. "Then please stay the night. Uwazuru will prepare your room. What little the Kaito can offer is at your disposal."

Outside Tadaka's quarters, Tsukune came upon a cluster of shrine maidens sweeping the veranda and casting glances at his balcony. It was time for his daily prostrations to the rising run, Amaterasu-ōmikami. They were hoping for a peek at him. Tsukune's heart sank into her belly. Was it like this every morning outside his window, maidens gathering like iris flowers hungry for the sun? He'd always been handsome, and the most gifted shugenja of his generation. In all the time they'd spent together, he'd never had a lack of admirers. And she'd only been assigned to him...

From their disappointed whispers, she discerned that his mysterious investigation had called him away to the mountain peak. *Damn*, she thought. Now she had time to pass, time the Kaito would doubtless think she was wasting.

She spent a short while practicing her morning *kata*, then sat in meditation. Usually, this was enough to still her restless heart. But not today, it seemed. *Maybe I could follow him*, she thought, looking up to where the mountain peak was obscured in thick clouds. He couldn't have gotten far. She might catch up if she left soon.

She shook this notion away. *Don't be foolish. What would they think, the Phoenix Champion chasing after him like that?* Even so, with energy brimming over, she could not just wait here.

Instead, she wandered about the open monastery. Tsukune stepped casually along the mazelike network of rickety bridges interconnecting the boxy structures, her touch light on the cylindrical prayer wheels lining the path cut from the mountain flats.

The Kaito were rustic people, soft-featured, a far cry from the angular faces and pronounced cheekbones common to the Isawa. They conversed in their rural dialect as they worked at the morning chores: sweeping the road, brushing snow from flanged eaves, or disassembling robes for cleaning. On one balcony, Tsukune spotted a few cutting their long hair into bangs, while another wove the gathered hair clippings into tiny ropes. Hair was sacred; these would be burned as offerings to the kami. The villagers' gossip and laughter mingled with their ceremonial movements, friendly teasing, and words of encouragement peppered with intellectual phrases and quotes from the *Tao of Shinsei*.

These are Isawa vassals? They seemed too unrefined, too openly emotional, less academic.

The truth was, she didn't know anything about the Kaito, other than the reputation of the acclaimed Kaito Shrine-Keeper School. Their lives were simple. Like hers had been, once.

A Kaito held her tiny daughter's hand as they passed, the little one grinning as her mother nodded politely, barely pausing in their daily lives. They hadn't recognized Tsukune. Wearing borrowed clothes, and with Ofushikai in her room, there was little about her that would distinguish her from a typical visitor. She felt normal.

She missed that feeling.

The monastery was no larger than a city block, ending abruptly at a stone precipice. A flock of wagtails flitted in an arrowhead pattern above, and Tsukune wondered what it was like to fly like that, far above all worldly concerns.

A volley of arrows arched through her field of vision, over the lip of the cliff and down. Tsukune identified the source, a line of students near the edge readying their bows under the supervision of a gray-haired instructor. In tandem they drew, pointing their arrows at the horizon, releasing together. Tsukune exhaled with them, her breath mimicking the collective snapping of their bows. It seemed like only yesterday that she had stood in a similar line.

The Kaito were vassals of the Isawa. Unlike the Kaito, the Isawa were shugenja, samurai who served physical and supernatural lords both, their souls knitted into the very fabric of the universe. While mere priests blindly repeated rituals to appease spirits, the shugenja knew the hearts of gods. They practiced *shugendō*, the prayers that could invoke the manifestation of spirits. To speak to and hear the kami, to ask for favors in exchange for offerings, was a gift only one in a thousand souls ever possessed.

However, while this gift offered shugenja considerable power over the elements, power that could be turned to martial ends, shugenja were sworn to peace. The Isawa did not carry weapons and fought only as a last resort. The use of the kami's blessings for violence was a distasteful notion. The more violent the emotions in a shugenja's heart, the more dangerous the spirits they invoked, until eventually the shugenja's prayers were answered not by kami, but by *kansen*, the corrupted spirits of Hell itself.

Another volley of arrows sailed overhead. Kaito were neither shugenja nor warriors, so what were they, exactly?

Beyond the monastery's edge, across a ravine, stood an ancient shrine. With fiery red columns and interlocking wooden beams holding up a stack of slanted roofs and a bell tower protruding from the eastern side, it looked hundreds of years older than the monastery, and perhaps just as large. A long, rickety wood-plank bridge crossed the harrowing drop of the ravine. The bridge deck rested not on ropes, as she'd initially thought, but on live wisteria vines woven together and rooted on either side. She crossed without pausing, her hand remaining on the handrail vine until her foot touched the other side.

At the outside pavilion, Tsukune ladled water over her hands and rinsed her mouth, then left her sandals on a little wooden shelf. The shrine's stone floor was cold against her bare feet. The rolling canvas walls opened onto a wide veranda overlooking the entire mountain range. Dozens of paper streamers hung low from the rafters, stirred by a lazy breeze, giving the impression of floating ghostly strands. A knee-high fence separated her from a wooden stage that extended to the back. Behind closed shōji doors would be the inner shrine and the sacred artifacts of the Kaito. During worship and festivals, these screens would be cast aside to reveal the objects of worship, like props on a kabuki stage.

That area was off-limits to non-priests. For her to step beyond the screens was forbidden.

Her barefoot path led her around to a cloistered garden. There she found a row of seven tiny shrines, like birdhouses, each elevated to shoulder height on a wooden pole.

She stopped at one with an indigo roof and a cloth bag swaying from its little porch. Kneeling before it, she withdrew a small offerings bag and produced a cone of incense and a pinch of salt mixed with ground barley. She laid these in an installed dish. It was not pure salt, and she could not light the incense, but this would not offend the Fortune of contentment. Taking her prayer beads, she clapped her palms twice and bowed.

"Hotei-no-Kami," she whispered, "I humbly beg your attention."

But when she closed her eyes, she saw the crimson, wind-torn robes of a man whose life she'd sworn to protect, his knees sunken deep into frigid snowbanks, his jagged breath frozen on blue lips. Alone and near death at the mountain peak. With no yōjimbō.

She sighed. The gesture was futile; there was no room in her heart for the Fortune to dwell.

A voice drifted into the garden. Tsukune thought she was imagining it at first, but as it grew in strength, she realized it was singing. It was unpracticed, but bright and silvery, like a rustic bell. She'd never heard a voice so beautiful, not even at the Setsuban festivals of her youth. Her concerns forgotten, she followed it back into the shrine.

A young woman in *miko* trappings was sweeping the veranda floor with a cane-handled broom. Tsukune noticed a splotchy discoloration on the girl's face, spreading from her brown eyes to the bridge of her nose. She sang as unabashedly as a *mejiro* bird, her black ponytail bobbing in rhythm. Unnoticed, each note plucking invisible strings in her chest, Tsukune stood at the door and listened.

> *"Night always falls first,*
> *Inside the valley.*
> *The sun is eager,*
> *It is always diving down.*
> *We two are like moths,*
> *Chasing the round moon.*
> *If the sun won't watch,*
> *Then we cannot trust ourselves.*
> *Night always falls first,*
> *Inside the valley.*
> *If not for that hill,*
> *We would have a bit more time."*

The broom clattered to the floor.

"Sorry!" Tsukune said. "I did not mean to startle you!"

Her face flushing, the girl laughed. "Serves me right. I should be more mindful."

"I did not want to interrupt." Tsukune smiled cautiously. "That's a beautiful song."

The girl awkwardly retrieved her broom. "Thank you. My grandmother used to sing it for me. It's an old song." She bowed. "I am Kaito Kosori."

"Shiba Tsukune." Her titles formed on her lips: *Phoenix Clan Champion, Daimyō of the Shiba Family, Protector of the Council, Keeper of the Tao*... Kosori made a toothy grin. The girl, like the others, did not know who she was. She felt normal. So she swallowed her titles, saying nothing more.

"Well met, Tsukune-san," said Kosori. "What brings you to Cliffside Shrine?"

"I came to see Isawa Tadaka."

"Ah, of course." She leaned on her broom. "He left this morning for the peak, alone. Wouldn't let anyone accompany him. He doesn't care much for advice, it seems." She sighed. "The handsome ones never do."

Tadaka clinging to a stone outcropping, a fragile red flame in an icy landscape. His foot slipping. The wind tearing away his voice.

Kosori's smile faded. "Oh. Sorry. I upset you."

Tsukune forced a smile. "It's fine. He *is* stubborn. Always has been."

Kosori looked at her sideways. "Are you and he...?" She crossed her fingers.

"No," Tsukune blurted. "Our fathers were friends. I was his yōjimbō for a time." She watched two moths dance around the broom. "But not anymore."

"I understood a Shiba yōjimbō served her charge until death."

"Not always," Tsukune whispered.

Kosori clicked her tongue. "Ah, my dumb mouth. Forgive me. It isn't my business." She looked away. "I should return to my work. Whatever is not finished today will mean more for tomorrow."

She pushed dust with her broom, avoiding Tsukune's gaze. Her feet dragged with her submissive gait. There was one like her at every dōjō. Someone whose purpose was to be at the bottom, the example, the one they whispered about and looked upon with pity. More servant than student. For a brief flash, the shrine became a dōjō in the lands of the Lion Clan, and it was Tsukune pushing dust beneath a hot face and her peers' snickering.

"May I help?" The words came unbidden, but the moment they left her mouth, she found that she desperately wanted to do anything but be alone with her thoughts.

Kosori cast her a skeptical glance. "You want to do chores?" Her eyes narrowed. "You're a guest. It would be unseemly."

"I've heard cleaning a shrine is good luck." She smiled sheepishly. "I could use some."

"I'm pretty sure it was a lazy priest who first said that," Kosori joked. She looked around, then offered Tsukune the broom. "Just don't tell anyone. I'd get another tongue-lashing."

Tsukune bowed as she accepted. "I'll consider it a favor."

Kosori again offered her a toothy grin. "Oh? Maybe I'll let you do all my chores, and you can owe me another!"

CHAPTER THREE

The time passed quickly, Tsukune's troubles falling away amid the comfort of familiar chores. Kosori sang as they worked, and Tsukune swept to the graceful lilt of her voice. Had Kosori been born in the city or among the court elite, she would surely have been classically trained to sing for daimyō. Kosori scrubbed at a stain with a willow-bark brush. Her path, like Tsukune's, had been decided by fate.

Tsukune swept these thoughts outside with the dust, whispering, "Bad spirits out."

"You've done this before," Kosori remarked.

"I used to sweep the dōjō all the time. We all did. It taught discipline."

"Ever clean rafters?"

Tsukune followed Kosori's eyes to a thick network of cobwebs resembling trapped smoke. She paled. "When was it last cleared?"

"Yesterday." Kosori chuckled at Tsukune's surprise. "I know. We have some diligent spiders. But so be it; shrine spiders are good luck."

Looking up, Tsukune's attention snagged on a massive rope

swinging above her in the doorway. It was fraying near the center, the hemp strands protruding in a short tangle.

Her mood darkened. "This *shimenawa* is frayed."

Kosori became serious. "Let me see." She gingerly tested the rope, holding up a vertical hand and whispering an apology to the spirit the rope appeased. Then she drew a small scrap of paper from her obi and affixed it to the tear. The tangled kanji on the surface vexed Tsukune's eyes.

"This rope dates back centuries," Kosori explained. "I've worried about it for some time."

"When will it be repaired?"

Kosori bit her lip. "It'll likely be replaced." She looked as though she might say more, but then shook her head. "In any case, this will have to last until the replacement can be procured."

Tsukune's eyes lingered on the tag for some time.

The midday meal was a bowl of rice and a heap of mountain cabbage. It was shredded, salted, and flattened between rocks until the water pressed out and the leaves were shriveled and tender. They took their lunch to the bridge and sat with their feet dangling off the edge. As they ate, Kosori pointed out villages and way stations beneath them. She held her chopsticks with her hand close to the tapered end, like a farmer or fisherman. Tsukune held hers closer to the back.

Kosori pointed at a thin column of smoke in the distance. "That's a Yobanjin settlement."

When the Empire first formed, there were some who would not swear fealty to the emperor. These banished people became the Yobanjin tribes populating the plateaus beyond the borders. A Yobanjin could be killed on sight for even stepping into the Empire.

"It must be close," Tsukune remarked.

Her expression faded. "When I was twelve a bunch of them raided the villages. It took weeks to restore the shrines they desecrated." Her hand gripped a vine. "Some villages have yet to recover."

"Do Yobanjin incursions happen often?"

Her eyes narrowed at the distant smoke. She didn't answer.

Tsukune lowered her bowl. "I saw some Yobanjin once."

Kosori regarded her with rapt attention. "Did you fight them?" A smirk cut into her cheek. "I heard they fight like demons."

On the western edge of Phoenix lands was a village whose name Tsukune had sworn to forget. She would never have known it existed had she not accompanied Tadaka there, breathing tensely as she watched five men for any hostile twitch. They stared through wooden masks, all except for their leader, whose hairy arms rippled out of his stiff tunic, teardrop-shaped earrings clacking around a tattooed face as he argued with Tadaka in a choppy tongue. They barked back and forth until Tadaka added two bolts of silk to the white bronze bars and a jar of powdered cinnabar. In turn, the man surrendered a fibrous scroll to the table. Only after they were gone with Tadaka's offerings did he scoop this up.

The knowledge within that scroll was priceless. This meant it was an unfair exchange to the Yobanjin, and therefore not a violation of Imperial decree, which defined "trade" as "fair exchange." So Tadaka had explained.

Focused on the past, she forgot the present. A chopstick slipped from her fingers, vanishing into the needle-thick canopy far below. She grimaced.

"You can have mine," Kosori immediately offered. "I can just–"

Tsukune snapped her remaining chopstick in two, then resumed eating. Morsels slipped through her weaker grip until she held the bowl to her mouth and shoveled.

Kosori watched with amusement. "You're a determined person, aren't you, Tsukune-san?"

"It's better to carry on," she said around a mouthful.

Finishing, they returned to the shrine for the last of Kosori's chores. Their progress dragged, but with Kosori singing and joking, Tsukune did not mind. The sun gilded the mountain range by the time they finished. "One final chore," Kosori said, dragging the screen walls shut. "The evening blessing."

"How can I help?" Tsukune asked.

She gestured toward an offset hall. "There's a room with some *yumi*. Bring me one and an onion-bulb arrow. I'll meet you here momentarily."

"You need a bow for an evening blessing?"

Kosori's bright affirmative nod banished any notion of jest.

The room was tucked to the side of a long hall near the garden. Asymmetrical bows of varying lengths leaned against a vertical rack, enough to line the entire wall. Some appeared quite ancient, the wood glossy and polished by countless fingertips. Tsukune selected the one she thought best for Kosori's height. Even when strung, it would tower over her.

The far side of the room afforded a view of the garden from a circular window. Tsukune froze in front of it, her eyes narrowing. The cypress beyond wore a blessed rope like a belt around its trunk. Affixed to this rope was a scrap of white, the black letters painful to behold.

Another one? Tsukune frowned. How many of the shrine's blessed ropes had these affixed tags? She remembered how swiftly Kosori had produced one for the rope hanging above the entrance. She'd been concerned, but not surprised. Were all the shimenawa falling apart?

Tsukune returned to the main room with heavy steps. Amber light filtered through the canvas, digging shadows out from every wrinkle in the wood. The paper streamers hanging from the ceiling looked yellow and splotchy in that light. Her nose wrinkled at the dust motes hanging in the stale air. Hadn't they swept and dusted all day?

A faint whistle stirred her ears. The streamers rustled like brittle leaves. The fine hairs on Tsukune's arms stood straight. The streamers undulated, then paused. She heard whispers – faint, distant, but unmistakable.

She brushed her hair away from her ears, slackened her jaw, and closed her eyes. The sound came into focus, wordless and nondirectional. A wheel in her belly turned, instinct spiking her in a specific direction. This was her *haragei*, her belly feeling. A yōjimbō trusted it above all other senses. She opened her eyes. She was facing the stage and the closed screen, behind which sat the inner chamber and the artifacts of the family, as in all other ancestral shrines.

Only priests could venture in there. By tradition, all others were forbidden.

But wasn't she the Phoenix Clan Champion? Tsukune bit her lip.

Stepping over the knee-high railing set her heart at a gallop. She crossed the stage like a child sneaking into her parents' room. The painted screen doors depicted a woman in the garments of a shrine maiden wielding a bow like a thin crescent moon. Tsukune felt the painting's eyes as she brought her ear to the seam between the closed screens. Multiple voices were talking over one another. She knew none of the words.

She pressed her palm into the textured paper. Just a gentle push and it would roll aside. No effort at all. Her cheek pressed against the screen. She held her breath.

"Tsukune-san?"

An icy jolt. The whispers were gone. The stale air, the dust, the sickly bronze light: all vanished. Everything was as it was before. She froze for several moments before turning into Kosori's uncomfortable gaze below the stage. She'd donned a padded chest protector and a three-fingered glove. She stared as though Tsukune had stolen a kami's offering.

Tsukune pushed guilty words through clenched teeth. "This... looks bad. Doesn't it?"

Kosori limply nodded.

Climbing down from the stage, Tsukune kept her eyes on the floor. An avalanche of excuses thundered through her mind. But what could she possibly say? Words seemed too brittle. What would Tetsu say? *He wouldn't have done it to begin with...*

"I won't tell," Kosori said, interrupting her thoughts. Then, as if nothing were awry, she looked pointedly at the screen. "Interesting tapestry, isn't it? It's quite old."

Tsukune stood in the coldness of her guilt. Kosori was inventing an excuse, allowing her to save face. She felt like a fish that had been thrown back from the net. "I've never seen one like it," she managed, looking grateful.

"That's Isawa Kaito," Kosori explained. "This shrine is in her honor."

Isawa Kaito. That would be the founder of the family. The woman on the painted screen drew her bow against a massive ogrelike creature. Time had faded both their faces.

Outside, Kosori strung the bow with an ease that defied her spindly arms. Tsukune watched with growing fascination as she nocked an arrow with a felted onion-bulb tip, bracing the massive bow against her knee for support. "I've only seen the arrow readied with the bow held vertically," Tsukune remarked.

"That is certainly more serene. But it forces one to turn the handle, which can weaken one's grip." Kosori brought the bow up above her head and paused. "A weak grip is distracting. If the mind is not on the target, then the arrow will go elsewhere. One must become an empty vessel in which the kami can dwell."

She shifted, pointing the arrow at the shrine's bell. A prayer tumbled from her lips.

Tsukune squinted. "That's perhaps five hundred *shaku*, and you're shooting in cold weather."

Kosori brought the bow to eye level, drawing the arrow to her cheek, the bow's maximum draw. Its mulberry and bamboo strained and bent until Tsukune felt Kosori's *ki* roaring like a wave desperate to break. She exhaled. The arrow launched, the force of the snap spinning the bow in Kosori's hand.

The bell rang. Birds took to the sky, their black silhouettes like inkblots on a firelit canvas. Kosori remained in her release posture. The chime echoed through the valley.

"All things considered," Tsukune said as they walked the grounds, "going up to it with a mallet would have worked as well."

Kosori chuckled. "Perhaps. But the kami prefer it this way."

"Is that so?"

Kosori's bashful gaze lowered. "You're the first outsider to see my shot, you know. Flawed as it is."

"Flawed?" Tsukune reeled. "I've known bushi twice your age who could not make that shot!"

"Any success belongs to my sensei." But her smile lingered.

The stood at the cliff's edge. The mountain range unfurled horizontally before them like a vast scroll. It was already night in the shadow-strewn valley, crickets singing among the pinpoints of light marking scattered villages.

"To aim is a delusion," Kosori said suddenly. "The arrow knows the way. So it is said."

"So," Tsukune said, "it is shugendō."

"It is for the kami, if that is what you mean." She faced the sun. "In ancient times, the bow was considered sacred. An arrow can divine the weather. A bowstring's twang can banish evil spirits.

Is it so strange that my family would hold the yumi in such high esteem?"

"I have known many Isawa, but none that venerate *kyūdō*."

"Kyūdō holds a place in all the Kaito family's traditions. Through practice, we grow closer to the kami and learn to sense them. And we use kyūdō in defense of Cliffside Shrine." She met Tsukune's eyes. "This shrine marks where a demon was felled by the arrow of Isawa Kaito herself."

"I haven't heard that story."

"Isawa Kaito was the first shrine keeper. All our techniques are derived from her insights. She did not have the shugenja's gift, but she knew how to consecrate a shrine and make herself a vessel for spirits. When she drew the bow, the kami would flock to her and guide her shots. One day, a demon came from the north, destroying villages and scattering helpless innocents. Kaito faced it alone, armed only with her bow and a handful of arrows. With the kami's help, she defeated it, giving her life to seal it away inside a well. When she died, the kami froze the well, trapping the demon inside. This shrine was erected in her memory. Ever since that day, our family trains shrine keepers, preserves Isawa Kaito's ways, and protects this shrine – just as she did."

Kosori stopped, eyes widening, then bowed. "Isawa Tadaka-sama! What brings you to the shrine at this hour?"

Tsukune's back went stiff. Isawa Tadaka stood just behind her, his amused expression nearly swallowed in the shadow of his cone-shaped hat. Broad-shouldered and well-muscled, he towered over them both.

"I'd heard Tsukune-sama was looking for me," he remarked. "I didn't want to keep the Phoenix Clan Champion waiting."

Tsukune shut her eyes. *Damn it.*

At first, Kosori did not seem to understand. But in the numb silence that followed, realization overtook her confused expression, which moved halfway to a grin by way of panic. "Ch-champion?" She stared at Tsukune. "You're the..."

What would be the point of explaining herself now? The damage was done. Tsukune stepped between them. "Thank you, Kosori-san, for keeping me company today."

Humiliation painted Kosori's features. "...Of course," she replied.

Tsukune watched her go, her lungs emptying into a sigh. She turned to Tadaka, who was blinking in confusion. If she could have set fire to his robes with her glare, she would have.

"She didn't know?" He arched an eyebrow. "You didn't tell her?"

"It didn't come up."

He folded his arms into his billowing sleeves, the gesture making his shoulder muscles ripple in a way that made her heart skip a beat. "My apologies," he said. "Although one might wonder why you would keep that secret." He smiled with his eyes. "It's good to see you, Tsukune. It has been a while."

In fact, it had been months. An entire season, come and gone. No letters. No visits. She'd been his bodyguard, his shadow, for almost a year and then... nothing. *Say something,* she thought. *Tell him you missed him.*

"We need to talk," she said. His eyes dimmed. She inwardly grimaced. *Nice job.*

"Then let's talk." He brushed past her, making for the shrine. "But I'm in the middle of my investigation, so if you have something to say, come along."

Her jaw clenched at the Phoenix crest embroidered on his back. Since the founding of the clan, the Isawa had led and the Shiba had followed. Now would be no different. She sprinted to catch up.

Tadaka paced the belfry, his hand rotating each polished orb of his prayer beads. He did that whenever he was thinking. He always had, for as long as she'd known him. He brushed the ancient bell, nostrils flaring as if following a scent. Then he moved to the banister, at the gap where the broken wood parted like a toothy maw. It made Tsukune's eye twitch. She wanted to pull him back. It wasn't safe so close to the edge.

"Here," he said. "She died in this spot."

"Did a spirit tell you that, or was it the broken railing?"

He smirked and pointed over the side. "If the fall were what killed her, then she would have died down there. Her vessel was empty before it touched the ground."

Which meant she – whoever *she* was – had died before she fell.

"Look at this place," Tadaka chided, tucking away his beads. "Ropes fraying, banisters breaking. And the filth!"

Jerking movement caught Tsukune's attention. A glistening centipede, its black body the length of her forearm, with dozens of red legs, clung to the wall inches from Tadaka's shoulder. Seeing it, he extended his hand. The creature crawled onto his palm. Tsukune's skin pricked as he craned the segmented beast over the balcony and onto the roof, where it crawled away.

"I suspect the Kaito daimyō will not like the report I am giving to the council," he said.

"Does the council usually take an interest in accidents at rural shrines?"

He cast her a knowing look. "The victim was Isawa Iwahaki. Lacking the aptitude for the Isawa Elemental School, she was sent here to train as a shrine keeper. Her death might have been overlooked but for a letter sent to Master Rujo."

Tsukune blinked. "A letter?"

"Anonymous. Signed with a moniker: Hototogisu." Lesser cuckoo. "So now we are here."

"Now *you* are here," Tsukune corrected. "Doing the job of a lesser council agent."

Tadaka shrugged. "It is an honor to serve the Masters in any capacity."

He was deflecting. She let her irritation show. "Will it be an honor to duel one?"

His eyes lit slowly, and he nodded. "Ah. So that's why you've come." He leaned against the wall and crossed his arms. "Go on."

"He's your sensei!" she blurted out. "It's disgraceful! What do you hope to gain?"

"I have reason to suspect the elemental imbalance is connected to recent attacks on the Kaiu Wall. If the Phoenix are to correct this, *someone* must study the Shadowlands."

Tsukune grimaced. To even speak the word was taboo. Nothing good ever came of mentioning the place where the twisted realm of evil touched all things.

Tadaka continued. "They would have recognized the wisdom of my proposal had my master not opened his jealous mouth."

"The Master of Earth is jealous of *you*?" Tsukune scoffed. "Do you hear yourself?"

"It is not hubris if it is true." His handsome face darkened. "For years, Rujo has taken credit for my research, presenting my findings as his own, and I said nothing. Only now that my deeds threaten to overshadow his own does he suddenly have a mind to protest!"

"He is your sensei!" Tsukune protested. "He taught you!"

Tadaka smirked. "I learned plenty on my own. When I defeat him, he will have no choice but to endorse my research. With the council's blessings, I will travel to Crab lands and learn the secrets of the Kuni shugenja. If the worst happens, the Phoenix will be ready."

"And if he defeats you," she said, "you'll be tossed to the winds. No one will even remember your name."

He didn't flinch. "That is not my destiny."

"What happened to you, Tadaka? You were always inquisitive, but you used to be humble. What changed?"

"The world," he replied. "We must change with it or be left behind."

Tsukune stepped forward. She grasped his sleeve. Her voice was almost a whisper. "I can't let you. Some doors are better left closed. Forget the proposal. Apologize to Master Rujo. I'm asking you to let it go. For me." She met his eyes. "Please."

His expression softened. For a moment they just stood there, he looking down at her, she looking up at him.

His eyes closed. "You cannot protect me, Tsukune. You are not my yōjimbō anymore."

Not his yōjimbō. Like a hammer, it split her heart in two.

"You think I wanted this?" she shouted at his back. "You think I did this on purpose? Your father said the sword chose me. Was I supposed to say no?"

He paused in the doorway. The last rays of the sun cast her shadow across the floor, as if it were reaching for him.

"We had plans," he said. "You could have said *something*."

Then he was gone. From the valley, the tangled screeches of roosting birds reached out and choked the serenity from the night.

CHAPTER FOUR

The rolling screen doors were cold against her palms. On its painted surface, a woman with a wooden face held the crescent moon in her hands. Tsukune's breath stirred the dusty shrine air and rattled the dry streamers hanging from the ceiling. The whispers on the other side slipped through the crack between the screens. She threw them open. A tsunami crashed through, flooding the world and breaking her.

She jolted. She was lying on a thin futon in a guest room. Outside the circular window, the night hummed. She exhaled slowly to lessen the hammering of her heart. A dream. Jumbled images falling from the dusty cupboards of her mind. Nothing more.

The night breeze chilled her. She made to tighten the collar of her sleeping jacket, but stopped when she felt an object in her fist. She sat up. Ofushikai rested in her clenched hands. Moonlight glinted along the carved feathers of its sheath. It had been on its stand when she went to bed. Had she taken it in her sleep?

They need you, Tsukune.

The words came unbidden to her mind, the voice not her own. She'd heard it once before in the shrine to Shiba in the presence of gossamer reflections...

She drew. A ringing note pierced the night.

The weightless steel was a band of light in her hand. Its curve was less noticeable than that of her mother's katana, the steel slightly thicker, but its flawless edge and mirrored surface defied its thousand years of age. She met her reflected eyes in the blade.

"Who needs me?" she asked. Then, "Should I stay another day?"

Outside, a cold wind ran invisible hands through evergreens and the banners of the monastery.

She sighed, feeding the blade to the sheath once more. "You said I would never be alone. So why do I feel more alone than ever?"

In the circular window, the pale moon watched her like a giant eye.

"Were you able to speak with Tadaka-sama yesterday?" Nobukai spoke without looking down from his seat on the tall stone.

"I was," Tsukune affirmed. With her back against the maple's trunk, she could watch three of the cloistered garden's five corners.

Servants brought the midday meal: a bowl of hot rice, a cup of clear broth, a dish of red pickled radish and cabbage called *fukujinzuke*, and a raw egg. Tsukune followed the daimyō's lead, cracking the egg directly into the rice and stirring this with chopsticks.

"I am extending my stay." She winced. "Assuming that is no inconvenience."

"None at all!" Nobukai replied. "You may stay as long as you'd like."

She watched the rice's heat softly cook her egg. "It will only be until Tadaka-sama's investigation is done."

"Ah yes. The girl," he sighed. "Tragic accident. She was a talented student, if headstrong. She was warned that the winds here could become unexpectedly strong."

Tadaka's words from the prior day echoed in her mind. *Her vessel was empty before it touched the ground.*

"It looked like she broke the belfry banister," Tsukune said.

Nobukai paused. "So you visited the shrine! I trust my niece did not chew off your ear?"

Tsukune hesitated. His niece? The only person there was...

A breeze rattled the purple leaves, revealing a hint of more sky. "So Kosori-san is your niece," she said.

"She didn't mention it?" He shrugged. "Yes. Her mother passed when she was very young. I took her in and raised her with my son."

"She impressed me," Tsukune said. "She taught me much of your ways. Her archery skill is commendable. And her voice..."

Nobukai's eyes shone proudly. "Kosori has her mother's voice. She was always singing as a child. We called her Little Hototogisu."

Tsukune's heart skipped. Lesser cuckoo. The moniker on the anonymous letter that Tadaka had mentioned. Curious.

"Perhaps you could see her again," Nobukai encouraged. "Your studious nature and respect for your elders may rub off on her."

His tone made Tsukune feel like a cat stroked in the wrong direction.

"I have some concerns about your shrine." The words came so suddenly, she wasn't entirely certain they were hers.

Nobukai stirred his food. "Oh?"

Once, Isawa Tadaka had led a tense negotiation with an easily offended Lion Clan samurai. Tsukune had listened from the other side of a paper screen, just close enough to intervene. She never had to. Tadaka's language had been careful. *How would he say this?* She gathered her thoughts.

"The shrines of southern provinces are exposed constantly to sea air. Due to the weathering effect, it has become custom to rebuild a shrine around its inner sanctum every century. Yet the wood and stone of Cliffside Shrine is as if it has never been replaced."

"Quite perceptive," Nobukai nodded. "I would expect no less of a Shiba yōjimbō."

"And of course, when shimenawa are frayed, they are swiftly replaced. So I have heard."

Nobukai set down his food. He was no longer smiling. "You heard correctly. Our own blessing ropes are ancient, dating from the shrine's dedication. I fear ours will soon break, and then the kami will have one fewer place in which to dwell."

Tsukune's eyes narrowed.

"You are not the first to suggest this, Tsukune-sama. If I had had my way, the shrine would have been rebuilt and the blessing ropes replaced the moment I became daimyō." He paused. "As it so happens, those ropes were created and blessed by an Elemental Master. The spirits have become accustomed to them, and so nothing less could replace them. As for the shrine itself, I needn't mention the expense, nor the challenge in transporting materials all the way up here." Another pause. "I mentioned this to the council, and although it has been some time, I am sure they are still considering."

The grass bent to the wind. Tsukune sat back. "I could mention it the next time I'm there."

Nobukai's face brightened. He dropped from the rock and pressed his forehead into the grass. "Thank you!" he said. "We would be eternally grateful!"

Tsukune blanched, wilting, looking anywhere but at the prostrated man before her.

As he rose, his eyes fixated on something behind her. Her instincts spun Tsukune in the same direction. A small, bulbous knob shook beneath a butterbur leaf, something inside stirring, the surface clear like glass. From within, a butterfly broke free, its sky-blue wings unfurling as it crawled to the arch of the leaf. Tsukune gasped.

"Exquisite," breathed Nobukai. "Such sights were rare in my grandparents' time, but our summers are longer now." He raised a reverent hand. "The wonders of the Empire are without number."

The little thing fanned its dewy wings.

"Of course," Nobukai continued, watching Tsukune, "its transformation must confuse it. Its whole life it was only a caterpillar, so close to the ground. Now it must be a butterfly."

Tsukune felt like an unfurled scroll. "As you say."

"Do you know how the Kaito family daimyō is chosen?"

She shook her head.

"Among the artifacts of Cliffside Shrine is a catalpa bow that once belonged to our family's founder. Named Mikazuki, it is said to be the home of an awakened kami, one that so adored High Priestess Kaito that it recognizes her children. Only the true family daimyō can string Mikazuki. For anyone else, the bow resists, and the string breaks." He regarded her sideways. "Of course, in order to discover you are the daimyō, you must be willing to try."

Her eyes widened. "Isawa Kaito's yumi chooses the Kaito daimyō?"

"There is no choosing. Mikazuki recognizes its wielder. I watched my relatives try, women and men I felt were far more worthy than I. Had I not attempted to string it, I would have never known Mikazuki was meant for me."

She remembered Ofushikai as it was placed in her hands, the sword unsheathing on its own, her breath caught among a sea of gasps.

"Partway up the mountain is a waterfall. I have often found it refreshing after a night of difficult sleep. Helps me to rebalance." He looked at her. "I will tell you where it is, just in case."

From beyond the garden came the sound of a bell, followed by cheers and shouts. "The midday offering," he explained. But from his furrowed brow, Tsukune could tell something was not right.

She followed him to the monastery square. There, a noisy crowd had gathered around a pear tree. At the center, Uwazuru was stringing his bow.

"It seems someone has challenged my son," said Nobukai.

"What is this?" Tsukune asked.

"An archery display to please the kami. Some use it as an opportunity to compete." He cast her a glance. "I realize some may disapprove." Many in the Isawa considered such displays to be ostentatious and disrespectful.

"Competition is healthy," she replied. "We did it all the time in the dōjō."

She caught his slight smile, though he tried to hide it.

The crowd quieted as the challenger stepped forward. Tsukune recognized her bobbing ponytail and the birthmark across her eye. Kosori tugged on her three-fingered glove and bowed to her cousin.

"They used to do this as children," Nobukai admitted, stroking his chin. "But I thought they had grown out of it. Why the renewed rivalry, I wonder?"

Tsukune blanched. Was this because she had complimented Kosori's archery?

Kosori pointed to a pear on a branch and nocked her arrow. She made an effortless release, and it fell to the ground. Polite clapping filled the square.

"Now Uwazuru must make the same shot," Nobukai explained. "Like in the Bowman's Wager."

Nobukai straightened. "Our family had a hand in the creation of that tradition."

Tsukune concealed a smirk. Her own sensei had once claimed the same thing.

After Uwazuru made the same shot and received the same applause, a woman waded into the crowd carrying a primitive helmet of soot-colored iron bands. Angry exclamations rose from the crowd, and someone threw a pear at it. "A Yobanjin lost this helmet!" the woman cried. "Here, Uwazuru! Show us how to properly treat it!"

Grinning, Uwazuru pointed his bow, drawing slowly. Tsukune could not comprehend his strategy. It was not a difficult target. But then he turned his wrists in opposite directions, twisting the string. He released, and the arrow smashed through the iron, the mangled tip emerging from the back. The crowd exploded with applause. Tsukune's jaw slackened. "How?"

"Twisting the draw," Nobukai said, demonstrating the movement with his hands. "In this way, one increases the tension in the string beyond what is normal. It increases power at the cost of accuracy. Or it would," he added, "if one did not have the kami to guide the arrow."

The crowd hushed. Kosori set her arrow. Even at this vantage, Tsukune saw her tremble.

"Yet it is not that easy," he continued. "The yumi is delicate. It will break if mishandled or pulled too hard. Instead, one must be gentle. Humble. One cannot command. One must ask."

Kosori released. The arrow broke through. Kosori blinked at her accomplishment, as if she could not quite believe it. As the crowd applauded, Kosori flashed Uwazuru a triumphant smile.

"There," said Nobukai. "She just made her mistake."

"Does someone have a coin?" Kosori called out.

"Here!" Someone pushed their way forward, offering a string of copper disks, each with a diamond-shaped hole punched from the center.

"Toss it up," Kosori said, loading her bow.

A pit formed in Tsukune's stomach. Even so, as the coin was flipped, somersaulting vertically above the crowd, she inhaled in tandem with Kosori's draw, hope filling her chest. *She'll land it,* Tsukune thought. *She wouldn't call the shot if she—*

The arrow slipped. The coin bounced on the ground, untouched.

Kosori's face turned the crimson shade of a mountain peach. Chilled, Tsukune felt as if she had been the one to pull the string herself.

"Let's try again," said Uwazuru. The crowd recovered the disk. He drew as it was tossed again, then released. A clear note rang, the coin spinning as the arrow struck it.

Beneath the cheers and Uwazuru's chanted name, Kosori's head sank. She turned suddenly, and her eyes locked with Tsukune's. Her face blanched. She spun away, but not before Tsukune caught her horrified expression. Nobukai said something, but his voice faded into the background as Tsukune gaped in dread at the unwitting role she had played in Kosori's humiliation.

"Shiba Tsukune-sama! I hope you are enjoying your afternoon!"

Tsukune paused, awkward and off guard, her bathing tunic folded under her arm. The old man from the previous day's court smiled at her from his seat on the rocks. The roar of the crashing waterfall behind him drowned out the bush warblers and mountain bugs.

She gave a stiff bow, tugging her kimono collar tighter. "Asako Maezawa-sama. Forgive my interruption, I didn't realize—"

"Bah!" The old man swatted the air. "I just finished. You will soon have it to yourself." He gestured to the top of the roaring waterfall. "These days, nothing else banishes the aches. Did you know these cascades were frozen until only a century ago?"

She shook her head and placed her bathing tunic on a flat stone, blinking in the spray. In his gentle and wrinkled smile, she dimly recalled her grandfather.

He gestured for her to join him at the water's edge. "How have you found the Kaito so far?"

"A little strange," she admitted, "but I am growing fond of them."

"Is that so?"

She cupped her hands. Icy water stung her palms. "At first I found their affinity for archery odd, but I'm starting to understand that they don't regard *kyūjutsu* as a purely martial practice. And they have an unabashed way about them that I find charming."

"When you've known them as long as I have, you come to adore their open innocence. The frog in the well knows nothing of the ocean, as the saying goes."

"You must have served them for some time."

"Oh, no. While I have history with the Kaito, my being here now is a recent development." He fished his pipe from his sleeve. "I serve on behalf of the Asako daimyō. My function is to advise Lord Nobukai on matters regarding Cliffside Shrine."

"The shrine?" Tsukune straightened. "Why would the Kaito require advice for their own shrine?"

Maezawa lit his pipe. "You've been there. Have you not noticed anything awry?"

She watched their wavering reflections for a time, then sat beside him. Their voices would not carry beyond the crashing waterfall. "I have," she admitted. "But I wasn't sure if I was imagining things."

"You are not," he replied. He seemed to be deciding something. "I understand you were trained among the Lion Clan?"

"Yes. The Akodo War College. I studied there for years, until…"

Even so far from home, even before the black-ribboned letter had come, she'd felt it. Like autumn leaves, she'd felt her soul grow lighter. That was how she'd known her brother was gone.

Her voice faltered, her throat closing. After all this time, she still couldn't speak of it.

"But after, you returned to the Shiba Guardian School."

She nodded.

Maezawa sat back and puffed as Tsukune waited. "So," he finally spoke again, "the yōjimbō training, it makes one observant, yes? Always watching for dangers? And as protectors of the Isawa, one also learns something of the kami?"

"These things are true," she said.

"So then, what have you noticed about Cliffside Shrine?"

She closed her eyes. She could see every crack in the ancient wood, hear the rattling of the brittle streamers, smell the rot and stale dust. "The shimenawa. They are fraying. I spoke with Nobukai about them today. He said the blessing ropes were simply aging."

"Blessing ropes, you say?"

"That is what he called them."

His knowing eyes twinkled. "But you know better, yes?"

She nodded darkly. "He thought I could not tell the difference. But we learn such things as yōjimbō to shugenja. They were ropes of *binding*. They make the walls not of houses, but of prisons."

"Very good," said Maezawa. "He underestimated you."

"There is something else," she continued. "I heard whispers."

His eyebrows climbed his wrinkled forehead. "Whispers? What did they say?"

"I'm not sure," she confessed. "I heard them once coming from the inner shrine, and before that, I heard them while climbing up the mountain."

His smile faltered for only a moment. "From all this, what might one conclude?"

"Kosori-san told me Isawa Kaito gave her life to seal away a demon. The Kaito's duty is to protect this shrine, which contains ropes of binding. There is nothing natural about the decay," she concluded. "Something is trying to escape the shrine."

"Astute." Maezawa tapped the bowl of his pipe. As he did, Tsukune thought she caught a glimpse of something etched on his palm, a black tattoo of some kind, perhaps an eye. But in the next moment it was obscured, and Tsukune could not confirm what she'd seen.

"Surely the Kaito realize this?" she asked.

"Some may suspect something is amiss, but they have chosen to say nothing of it."

Tsukune stood. "If they know, they should say something! To me! To the council!"

"And lose face in the clan?" Maezawa was smiling, but regarded her as one might a child. "Try to understand, Tsukune-sama. These people have lived in the mountains all their lives. It is not like the city, where resources are plentiful. The world has taught them self-reliance, to shoulder their burdens alone. To reveal their trouble would be to admit they cannot perform their duty. It is unthinkable for such a small family. So, they endure and carry on."

Tsukune frowned in spite of her understanding.

"In any case," Maezawa continued, "the council already knows. Do you not think it strange that the Masters would take interest in one student's death?" His voice lowered. "The truth is, people have been vanishing around that shrine for months now. At least eight have perished so far. Servants at first, then Kaito, then the student…"

The waterfall's spray grew suddenly colder. One was bad enough, a poor student with a lifetime before her, a door closed too soon. But eight? Eight souls lost for the Kaito's pride? Her kin. Her people. Gone. Tsukune's fist clenched. Unacceptable.

"Then Tadaka is merely confirming the council's suspicions," she said coldly.

"If only Nobukai would admit the problem, perhaps a disaster could be averted. I have advised him to do so for some time. But Tadaka's presence has caused Nobukai to hesitate, and the shrine's decay accelerated after his arrival. I fear he is inadvertently making things worse."

Tsukune shook her head. "That is not possible. Tadaka is a shugenja. His world and that of the kami are one."

"There is a darkness within him, Tsukune-sama. You have seen it yourself."

And she had seen it, just the other night. His stony look on the balcony, drinking the light, the way he'd just brushed her aside… Was this why the council had rejected his proposal?

She spoke carefully. "If I were to convince Tadaka to leave with me tonight and make his report, do you think you could make Nobukai see the wisdom of approaching the Masters?"

"Do you think you could do this?"

She looked at her uncertain reflection. When they were together, he'd made the decisions for them both. As a mere bodyguard, it was not a yōjimbō's place to say otherwise.

"I am not sure," she confessed. "The Shiba serve the Isawa, not the other way around."

Maezawa leaned back, looking her up and down. "My eyes play tricks. All this time, I thought you were the Phoenix Champion! If you were, you'd be sworn to protect the Isawa, and acting on behalf of the Kaito would be your duty."

She bit her lip. Things were not the same between them since she'd taken up Ofushikai. She had risen, while he had fallen from favor. He was colder now. The longer he stayed here, the darker his shadow would become. But if she did this, if she manipulated him or took charge, surely Tadaka would resent her forever.

Could she live with that? Knowing that the one person who had been there in her time of loss, the one who had given her purpose, who could set her blood aflame, wanted nothing more to do with her? Wetness bubbled up in her eyes. What could be worse than losing him for that?

Losing him to the darkness. To whatever the shrine imprisoned. That would be worse. Especially if she could have saved him.

Tsukune swallowed the knot in her throat and nodded. "I will do my best."

There was no time for *misogi* now. She turned to leave, casting Maezawa one final look. He was watching the waters, silent. Her heart churned with a final question. "Do you think the council will judge the Kaito harshly?" She recalled Kosori's guileless smile. *All of them?*

The back of his head rose. "We all have our roles to play, Tsukune-sama. The Asako heal, the Shiba protect, and the Isawa… *know*."

She did not understand. But perhaps she didn't need to.

CHAPTER FIVE

Tsukune nearly tumbled into Kosori as she rounded the corner. The girl was waiting outside her quarters, and she immediately doubled over in a steep bow. "I have come to beg mercy for my family."

Tsukune blinked, eyes wide. *What?* Before she could utter a bewildered word, Kosori dropped, palms up: a submissive gesture as old as the Empire. "How can I demonstrate my sincerity?"

Tsukune rolled open her door. "Not out here."

Kosori plopped herself down at the center of Tsukune's room and fidgeted with her prayer beads. Tsukune closed the door and rubbed her forehead. She didn't have time for this. She had to find Tadaka, convince him to leave with her, and...

And what? For that matter, how? The thought of pulling rank, of commanding him like a mere vassal, froze her blood. She could never do that. Why should he listen to his former yōjimbō when he would not even heed the word of his own sensei, an Elemental Master?

Kosori was staring. Tsukune looked to her window. How could she face the trusting girl now, with what she was about to do? But it surely had taken Kosori great courage to come like this, a mere samurai compared to Tsukune's rank as daimyō, risking a breach of etiquette. With all Kosori had done for her, was she not obligated to hear the girl out? Tsukune inwardly grimaced. What would Tetsu say, if he were here?

One opponent at a time, Tsukune-sama. No matter how large or sudden, that is how you defeat an ambush.

He was right, of course. She breathed slowly until the muscles in her neck relaxed. Finally, she spoke. "What did you mean just now?"

Kosori made a wry face. "I'm just the girl who cleans the shrine. I'm only good for pushing dust. But I am not daft. First came Maezawa, then a council representative. And now you, the Phoenix Clan Champion." Her fists tightened. "You came to decide my family's fate."

"You're mistaken," she whispered.

Confusion flickered across Kosori's features. "But… then why keep your identity secret? Why try to enter the inner shrine?"

Her face went hot. "I heard voices," she said. "As for my identity… well…"

"Voices?" The alarm in Kosori's voice, her pale face.

Tsukune's haragei spun. She sat before her. "Kosori, you must trust me. How long have you known the shrine's wards are failing?"

"Almost a year now." Shame pulled her gaze to the floor. "My *shufuku* was ten months ago." When Tsukune looked confused, she clarified, "My coming of age."

The regional dialect. "Your gempuku," Tsukune corrected.

"Due to my… underperformance… I was assigned to the shrine's upkeep. Cleaning and scrubbing every day, how could I not notice the ropes decaying? I knew something was wrong. But they didn't believe me! Whenever I brought it up, they said I was desperate for promotion, or trying to escape my duties."

She leaned forward. "It's true that I felt my lot was unfair, but I wouldn't lie about something so grave!"

"Did you ever approach your uncle about this?"

Kosori blanched. "So you know." She hesitated. "Yes. He forbade me to speak of it."

"Why?"

"I'm not sure. At first, I thought it was because he didn't believe me. But he's been visiting the shrine at night, reconsecrating, replacing blessed streamers, applying new wards. Still, this is not enough to keep it from escaping."

Tsukune's eyes narrowed. "The demon, you mean."

"That is one way to read the word. We pronounce it *ateru*. It's a kind of malicious spirit."

Tsukune produced paper and charcoal from her desk. "Show me."

She did not recognize the kanji Kosori drew, although it almost looked like the word for "blame". It was a rural word, a product of the regional dialect.

Kosori continued, "Isawa Kaito bound the ateru to a well in exchange for her life. The shrine was built to contain it. I don't know why the wards are failing now."

Tsukune's head reeled. "Are you telling me that your uncle knowingly kept the failing wards a secret from the Isawa, and instead sought to repair them himself?"

"He tried to preserve face while addressing the danger as best he could."

"Kosori," Tsukune said. "Eight people are dead."

The evening birdsong drew the sun below the horizon, lighting it aflame. Kosori shook in the amber light, struggling to maintain some dignity. Tsukune felt sorry for her. However, there was no denying that Nobukai had shown poor judgment in the execution of his duties. He had shamed his family and the Phoenix.

And the Kaito would be punished. All of them. Kosori's beads clacked as she fidgeted, her head stooped low. Just yesterday, in the shrine, their positions had been exchanged.

They need you, Tsukune.

Against the wall, on its stand, Ofushikai glowed in the twilight.

"All right," she said. "I think I can help things."

Kosori lifted her head.

"I believe the Kaito are not wholly responsible for these events. I am prepared to testify to this in defense of your family. However, Kosori-san, it will mean little if your uncle does not accept the blame and demonstrate his remorse. If you wish to do him any favors, you will convince him to approach the Council of Elemental Masters on his knees and ask for help. They may show lenience."

Kosori nodded eagerly. "I... I can never repay you." She bowed. "Thank you, Shiba-ue."

Tsukune winced. "Don't. Others may call me that, but for you, it is 'Tsukune-san.'" She offered a smile. "We're friends, aren't we?"

Kosori's eyes glimmered with a faint wet sheen. She sniffled and nodded.

Tsukune rose, donning her silk jacket. "Now I must find Tadaka."

"He's at the shrine," Kosori said, recomposing herself. "I passed him on my way here."

"Then I must go there and–"

She paused. And what, exactly? Somehow convince him to deliver a report that was sympathetic to the Kaito and laid the blame solely at their daimyō's feet? A man who had offered her sympathy, a man she'd promised to help?

Chase two hares, and you won't catch either.

She nodded. "Yes. One thing at a time. First, I find Tadaka. The rest will follow."

If Kosori wondered with whom Tsukune was speaking, she did not say so.

Tsukune hesitated by the door, then at the last moment, took Ofushikai from the stand. She tucked the sword between her obi's first and second layers, turning it so the edge faced downward, as suited blades predating the katana. Then she tucked in her *wakizashi* vertically.

Kosori stared at the ancient blade with wonder. "Is that–?"

"I do not plan to use it," Tsukune assured her. "I will need to look authoritative. Tadaka is… stoic."

"That is a polite way to say it," Kosori replied.

Two armed men passed Tsukune and Kosori on the dusky streets, sparing them not even a glance. When they were gone, Tsukune questioned Kosori with a look. "The guards of Cliffside Shrine," Kosori replied. "If I were to guess, I'd say they are reporting to my uncle."

Tsukune quickened her steps.

They found Tadaka partway across the swinging bridge, the last of the sun's rays tracing his outline. She called out, and he paused, waiting, face impassive beneath his cone-shaped hat.

"Good evening, Tsukune-sama," he said, his tone all business. "Out for an evening walk?" He glanced at Kosori. "And you brought your friend."

"What are you doing?" she blurted.

"I have a theory about the shrine pertaining to my investigation, but I must test it after dark." He resumed his steady walk. "Not that it concerns you."

"I know what's going on," she said, keeping stride with effort. "The other deaths, the decaying wards…"

"You know all of that, do you?"

"Listen. I know you think–" She stopped. There were whispers, layered and faint, but clear. She looked down into the ravine, where the jagged earth was parted, the gap seeming no wider than the space between two closed shōji doors...

"Tsukune?"

The whispers vanished. Even in his annoyed state, Tadaka's concern was clear.

She looked into his shadowy face. *There is a darkness inside him.*

"There are horses at the closest village," she said. "We can be at Kyūden Isawa within days. You have enough to give your report. We can deliver it together."

He shook his head. "Deliver yours, if you have one to give. Mine is not yet done." He gestured ahead, where dim light flickered behind the massive shrine's paper walls. "These events are not random circumstance. There is something even more sinister afoot, something that could affect all the Phoenix lands. And I intend to prove it."

"What are you talking about?" said Kosori.

Tsukune cringed. "Let me handle this," she told the girl as Kosori glared. She met Tadaka's eyes. "What do you believe you have found?"

Tadaka searched her face in the fading light. For a moment, his look was the same as when they had been together all those months ago. Then, he turned away. "Nothing for either of you. Go back. I must do this alone."

Tsukune looked at her hands. She'd been a fool to think she could reason with him. He wouldn't listen to her. He didn't take her seriously.

Did anyone? In that moment, she saw Tetsu's disappointed face. The way he stared at her sword. Like she didn't deserve it. Like she wasn't strong enough. Just a yōjimbō. Nothing more.

She gritted her teeth. Ofushikai had chosen her. She was Phoenix Clan Champion. Now, what was she going to do about it?

In three steps, she had tangled her fingers in his sleeve and balled her fist, pulling, forcing him to look at her. His annoyed expression melted into one of surprise. He tried to pull away, but she held him fast.

"This is the part of the Kabuki play I cannot stand, when the wise sage *could* tell the samurai what is about to happen, but chooses not to. It is the worst part of the play, don't you think?"

He frowned. "Perhaps he seeks to protect the samurai from things she doesn't understand."

"That is for me to decide, not you." Her heart raced, but she cast this aside, matching his eyes and not shrinking away. "I may not be your yōjimbō anymore, Tadaka-san, but I am your Clan Champion." *Even if we are no longer friends.* "If you have found something, then you will show me."

They stood there, opposed, like the sun and moon.

"Fine," he said and freed himself. Wordless, he continued across. Tsukune exhaled a tiny cloud.

"So," Kosori softly remarked, "you were just his yōjimbō?"

"Perhaps it was more complex than that," Tsukune admitted. Her heart was still racing, but it was exhilaration that pumped hot blood through her limbs now. She wasn't sure where her outburst had come from, but it felt good.

"Why are you following him? He doesn't want your help."

Tsukune looked out over the mountains set against the fading sky. She had no answer for that. "Once he finds what he needs, I will escort him back to the council. That is my duty, as is the protection of the Isawa." She glanced at Kosori. "That includes you, you know. You can go back if you wish. I do not want you to get in trouble with your uncle."

"He is in more trouble than I." She made a stern face. "I deserve to know what Tadaka thinks he has found. Besides," she added, "I'd like to see his face if he's wrong."

"So would I," Tsukune agreed. Although, she inwardly admitted, he rarely was.

The shrine at night retained little of its welcoming presence. Stone lanterns smoked with the cabbage-like scent of rapeseed oil, their glow not reaching far. The moon painted the shrine in pale tones and left corners dark. The paper streamers waved lazily from the rafters, giving the impression of spider silk. Tsukune's gaze was reflexively drawn to every twitching shadow, and she habitually positioned herself between the shadows and the others, her hand constantly flinching for her sword and then relaxing.

"Leave that sheathed," Tadaka advised. "A shrine is no place for a sword."

Tsukune swallowed her retort, that a shrine was where she had received the sword. She'd brought Ofushikai on impulse. Looking back on it now, she wondered why.

They stalked the shrine's rooms, Tadaka's beads swinging from his limp hand. Now and again, he would stop and tilt his head. Tsukune strained to listen, but no whispers came – only the wind and her own shaking breath.

Tadaka took a shimenawa and examined where it had frayed, then the paper tag affixed to it. "Did you make these?" he asked Kosori. She nodded. "You have some talent. Were the presence in this shrine weaker, these tags might have been adequate." He squinted at the tear, then held out the rope for the others to see. "Does this seem like the rope is unwinding itself from age, or does it appear as if it were being cut?"

"I'm sure I can't say," Kosori replied, but the jagged sawtooth pattern left no doubt in Tsukune's mind. She and Tadaka shared a knowing glance before he left the rope swinging.

Entering the southwestern room, Tsukune choked on dust. The moonlight through the open box-shaped skylight glinted off dust motes, and more white tags nearly glowed on their fraying ropes. The light flickered, and through the open skylight, a swarm of moths fluttered past, casting a single sprawling shadow. Tsukune nearly drew Ofushikai, then slowly relaxed.

The hairs on her neck were still standing when they entered the central chamber. Tadaka shook his head grimly. "Kosori-san, the presence in this shrine is very active. How could you have let things degenerate so far?"

Kosori's jaw clenched, and a crimson tint touched her cheeks.

"Leave her be," Tsukune said. "She did what she could."

Tadaka scoffed. "Did she, now? A few wards for the ropes? Scrubbing the floor?"

"She alerted the council." Tsukune smiled at her. "She is Hototogisu."

Kosori's mouth fell agape. "H-how did you know?"

"It was your childhood name. Your uncle told me."

Tadaka looked to Kosori with new eyes. "Ah, so you wrote that letter. I misjudged you, Kosori-san. My apologies."

Tsukune rolled her eyes. *And I have misjudged you as well, Tsukune-san. What a clever deduction!*

"You've learned what you need, then?" Kosori said. "We're done?"

Tadaka regarded the closed screen depicting Isawa Kaito. "Not quite," he replied and stepped onto the stage.

Kosori looked horrified. "You're going into the inner sanctum?"

"It is the one place I have not yet investigated." He whispered apologies as he placed a hand on the screen. Tsukune's heart thundered in her ears. She held her breath and braced for a crashing wave. He slid it open. Beyond, the world abruptly ended in void.

"Bring a candle," he said.

Kosori obeyed, procuring two from nearby and lighting

them with the lanterns. She hoisted herself onto the stage and surrendered a candle to the much taller man. Beyond the screen, the light revealed a deeper chamber and another set of doors. Tsukune felt like a taut bow, pulled in two directions. Tadaka knew she wouldn't follow. He strode beyond in a bubble of light. Kosori hesitantly went, leaving Tsukune behind.

Go, Tsukune! Now! Go!

The unbidden voice filled her limbs with urgent energy. She felt that she was standing before a closing door, and once it shut, she would never see the other side. She leapt onto the stage and passed the screen, not stopping until she was at the second set of doors.

In the wake of the shattered taboo, she looked up into Tadaka's surprised face and slowly smiled. *That's right,* she thought. *There's more to me than you believed, isn't there?* She was ready to counter any argument, but he offered none. Kosori exhaled with visible relief. "Behind me," Tsukune said, and slid the door aside.

The inner sanctum was vaster than she had anticipated, the polished floors and plain walls stretching well beyond the candle's reach. Dozens of paper wards lay flat against the ceiling. Silk lanterns, pale orbs on strings, hung in rows. An oil trough lined the walls, the spicy scent of cassia anointing oil ever-present. A row of dollhouses served as the shrines to the Kaito's honored ancestors.

"Is this the only interior room?" Tadaka asked, striding inside without hesitation.

Kosori timidly gestured into the dark. "The offering hall is that way. There are some rooms farther in the back. I'm normally not allowed in here," she added, casting Tsukune a meaningful look.

As Tadaka methodically stalked the chamber, Tsukune followed Kosori on a winding path. Small artifacts lay in designated spaces throughout the room. They paused by a shelf where an unstrung yumi was enshrined on a bow stand. It was ancient and tall, wrapped in rattan and adorned with silk tassels and a glittering bell. Kosori gasped when she saw it.

"Mikazuki," she breathed. "That's the bow of Kaito herself."

Other than the adornments, it looked like any other bow, if very old. "Have you ever seen it before now?" Tsukune asked.

"Only once," Kosori replied. She dipped her head reverently. "It only leaves the shrine when it is time to determine the new daimyō."

This is your family's Ofushikai, Tsukune thought.

Beneath was a small offerings bowl. Tsukune reached into her pouch and withdrew a spindle of incense, which she placed inside.

"You keep incense?" Kosori asked as Tsukune skillfully lit it with the candle.

"Of course. Every Shiba does. It's a long tradition." She inhaled the thin smoke. Aloeswood, cinnamon, and ginger lily. "Before a battle, it is customary to burn incense in one's helmet. That way, if your opponent takes your head, at least it will smell nice."

Tadaka grunted. At the center of the chamber was a short stone well. Shimenawa decorated its circumference, while a slanted roof sheltered the opening. "So, this is where Isawa Kaito bound the demon." Inside, Tadaka's candle glinted off untroubled waters.

Kosori gawked into the portal. "That's… not right," she muttered. "It should be frozen. The stories said…"

Tadaka's eyes fell to the back of the room, where his candle revealed an altar with a lidless lacquered box. His prayer beads were like a windswept porch swing. "Found it," he said.

Whispers. All at once, thundering. Tsukune could barely hear her own thoughts over the sudden layered voices.

Inside the box lay a dagger. Golden light thinly coated the splotchy ancient metal of the curved blade. Its handle was twice its length and appeared to be carved from bone. The voices stroked Tsukune's aching mind. Her fingers extended, reaching...

Don't!

She jerked back. The whispers stopped. Slowly she uncurled her fingers from the handle of Ofushikai, not recalling when she'd grabbed it.

Tadaka stuck the candle on a stand by the altar and wove his prayer beads around the fingers of his right hand. Although he looked grim, his eyes were victorious. "This may be the proof," he said. "I must bring this to the Masters."

"No!" Kosori's protest bounced through the chamber. "I can't let you take artifacts from the shrine!"

Tadaka spun. "Then you admit this is a Kaito family artifact?"

"Enough, Tadaka." Tsukune moved between them. "What is it?"

"I must study it to be certain," he said. "However, if I am correct, this dagger suggests the presence trapped here is not merely trying to escape. It is being aided." Tadaka glared at Kosori. "By your uncle."

Amber light filled Kosori's wide eyes. "That's not true." She met Tsukune's horrified stare. "It's not true!"

Tadaka continued, "I must investigate further, but daggers of such design dating from the fifth century were commonly used for blood offerings." He made a protective gesture. "If there truly is a demon sealed within this temple, then it is a denizen of Jigoku."

Only Tadaka would be so bold as to speak the name aloud. Jigoku was the Realm of Evil, the source of all corruption and the Shadowlands Taint. It was a labyrinthine maelstrom of pain and suffering, with rivers of blood, mountains of bone, and countless horrors.

Of course. That was why Tadaka would not let this go. If his

Shadowlands knowledge exposed the Kaito daimyō's misdeeds, then the Masters could never deny the validity of his research. They would have to accept his proposal.

And if he went, he would never come back. *There is a darkness inside him.* He'd be lost to her forever.

"You are mistaken!" Kosori trembled, her fists balled. "My uncle may have made mistakes, but he is not a *mahō-tsukai!*"

Tsukune winced at the word. Witch.

Anger flickered across Tadaka's features. "Oh, no? You believe the wards were ruined on their own?" He jutted a finger. "He hid a demon's awakening. To what end?"

"You could never understand! Without the shrine, the Kaito are nothing!"

Tadaka was stone-faced. "Perhaps the deaths were sacrifices."

Kosori hissed through clenched teeth, "Take. That. Back."

Now was no time for this. Tsukune opened her mouth. A sudden burst of pain popped behind her eyes, rattling her teeth. The floor seemed to warp beneath her feet. She staggered.

The weight of Tadaka's hand on her shoulder brought her back. "What is it?" His posturing was gone, only his concern remaining. "Breathe slowly, Tsukune."

She hadn't realized she was drawing rapid breaths. "I just need a moment."

"What is the meaning of this?"

Kaito no Isawa Nobukai stood at the door, wearing brocaded robes and an outraged expression. He was flanked by shrine keepers, paper lanterns, and bows. They unfurled to either side of him. The last to enter was tapping a pipe with a knotted hand, his old eyes looking disappointed to see the three youngsters within.

Tsukune spoke his name. "Asako Maezawa."

The old man sighed at Tadaka. "Disregarding the champion's

advice? I did not think even you were so stubborn." It was the first time Tsukune had seen him without a smile.

Nobukai's eyes flashed at his niece. "You let outsiders into the inner sanctum?" He stepped forward. "You must leave at once! All of you!"

"I am afraid that is impossible," Tadaka replied. "I have seen the dagger. You realize how this looks."

"It is not what you think! Come outside and I will explain."

"What is going on?" Tsukune demanded of Maezawa. Her hand twitched.

"Don't act rashly," he advised. "Violence in the shrine is unbecoming."

Her eyes narrowed. "Whose side are you on, exactly?"

"The Phoenix's," Maezawa replied.

"You are interrupting a ritual!" Nobukai said, his voice tinged with desperation. "If you do not leave–"

A flame floated at the center of the room, radiating a glowing violet light. It had not been there just before. Kosori looked as though she were staring into a dragon's maw.

"No!" cried Nobukai. "Not them! I beg you!" He fell to his knees. "This was not our deal!"

"Deal?" Tadaka thundered. "What deals have you made with this demon, Nobukai?"

Tsukune tensed. If the Kaito daimyō had made a pact with a demon, she would have to take his life, right here, right now.

The daimyō spoke with a defeated voice. "This was an appeasement ritual," he said. "You have just been mistaken for the offering."

A breeze stirred the hanging lanterns. They began to glow, a sickly pale glowworm purple. The flame expanded, assuming a vaguely humanoid form. Sweat dotted Tsukune's brow. It was becoming like a furnace.

"The wards will hold him," Nobukai shouted. "But you must leave now!"

Kosori's eyes glittered. "Uncle? Were the deaths really sacrifices to appease the ateru?"

Nobukai paled. "Who told you that? You cannot possibly believe such a thing!"

"I don't know what to believe. I thought you were trying to save our family's face and contain the ateru. But now I see you're trying to free it!"

"He is freeing himself!" Nobukai protested. "When the well thawed, he–" The daimyō gasped. His arms fell limply. "Now it is too late."

A resounding pop, and the flames peeled away. It was an emaciated human, translucent and floating. Its black hair and long mustache whipped violently around its head, as if trapped in invisible winds, but the triangular cloth tied to its forehead remained serene. Beneath a tattered white tunic of a style Tsukune did not recognize, its legs faded away at the ankles. A black flame was etched onto the creature's face. When it opened its eyes, the whites burned like fire, and a torrent of layered whispers thundered in Tsukune's ears.

"An *onryō*?" Tadaka thrust out his hand. "*That's* your demon? A vengeful ghost? The so-called 'ateru' is nothing more than a–"

He deflated, broad shoulders slumping, his mirthless voice dropping in volume. "Of course. What else could it have been?" As it was unrelated to Jigoku, defeating it would prove nothing to the council. There would never be a chance to convince them to support his proposal.

She would have felt sorry for him, if her yōjimbō instincts weren't roaring, turning her stomach into an oxcart wheel. The apparition's smile spread beyond its face's boundaries, splitting its head in two. "Tadaka!" she urged. "Stay behind me."

The shrine keepers were stringing bows. Nobukai drew a paper ward from his obi. "Begone, demon! Return from whence you came!"

"No," Tadaka spoke, his moment of self-pity falling away. "You had your chance." He drew a scroll, working off the bindings. "Now a representative of the council will handle this for good." He unfurled the paper and read, his voice like an echoing bell.

Tsukune looked from face to face. Nobukai held his breath. Kosori stared limply. They were almost hopeful. It was Maezawa's expression that made her heart quail. His knowing frown. His stoic resolution. Whatever Tadaka was attempting, the old man knew it would not work. And if that was so…

Its mouth parted. A thousand needles glinted in the light. It rushed forward, blurring, its elongated fingers rending the air as it issued a spectral scream.

No thought preceded action. Tsukune had drilled in this a thousand times. She stepped in the way of the creature's strike, shoving Tadaka behind her. Ofushikai sang a brilliant note as she freed it. She cleaved the ghost in half. It vanished like smoke.

Only after she'd remained in her attack stance for long moments did she return to a defensive posture, finally noticing the open horror on the faces of the others. She froze under their gaze, her mind catching up to her actions.

Tadaka seized her before she could reply, affixing her with stony eyes. "You drew the sword," he uttered. "In this blessed chamber, you drew steel." He stared up at the ceiling. "It is no longer sanctified."

As cold realization washed over her, the wards on the ceiling came away, falling gently like flakes of snow.

CHAPTER SIX

For a long time, no one moved. They searched the gloom beyond their impotent lanterns. Tsukune could not tell if she saw movement, or if these were merely tricks played by her straining eyes. There came a muted rumble from outside, followed by the drumming of wet fingers on the roof. A storm had broken, an oppressive blanket further dimming all senses.

Perhaps she'd banished it, after all. Tsukune swallowed and moved in front of Tadaka. No. If she had, then surely the unnatural viridian glow of the shrine's lanterns would have been extinguished, and Nobukai's face would not be so pale in the gloom.

Slowly, one of the shrine keepers began stringing their bow – *the pluck of a bowstring could banish spirits*. Having tied one end, he bent the yumi against the floor to string the other. It fought him, but he wrestled it into place, then gingerly grasped for the loop.

A screaming face bolted toward them from the dark.

The shrine keeper flinched. The bow slipped. There was a whipcrack sound, followed by a wet thud. In the dim lantern light, the bow limb protruded from his impaled, lifeless body.

The face vanished, its hot laughter echoing throughout the room.

She couldn't think. She couldn't move. She just stared at the dark pool slowly expanding.

The keepers dropped their bows and drew wands with paper streamers. They encircled Nobukai. Kosori, although unarmed, fell into their ranks.

A dark blur lashed out, swallowing up another keeper. His scream was abruptly silenced, followed by a hot splash. Tsukune vividly imagined a gutted fish.

She pressed her back into Tadaka's. He had drawn an agarwood rod and held it protectively. "It's toying with us," he told her. "It will pick us off, one by one."

"Can you do anything?" she asked.

"I'll need time," he replied.

Nobukai's voice rose above the din. "The anointing oil! Light it! Then it cannot hide!"

Kosori darted out, scooping up a dropped lantern. A sudden movement speared out from the dark, but another keeper threw themselves in the path and was wetly engulfed. Kosori spun and let go. The paper orb smashed into the stone trough. Flames spread quickly, tearing away the curtains of darkness. Tsukune readied her sword. She would throw herself at the ghost with all her power.

A wall of wooden faces stared back.

There were dozens, elongated and thin, their burial clothing splotchy and torn. They filled every corner, clinging to the walls like spiders. The eyes behind their burial masks were hateful coals. Among them, hands red and glistening, the ateru smiled.

The spectral wave crashed upon them. Tsukune lost herself in a sea of claws and screaming faces, the only light Ofushikai's flashing steel as it cleaved ethereal bodies, each cut shearing a ghost and leaving tendrils of fog. Hot blood splashed on her face. She didn't think. She just cut.

Then, Tadaka's rhythmic chanting rose above the mass. At the center of the violent storm, he held out his fragrant agarwood, and the ghosts broke around him like a diverging river. Tsukune cut her way toward him, deflecting, slicing. Every exertion slowed her a little more. In each brief pause between opponents, she saw no fewer of them.

So, this is why warriors prefer duels, she thought. *They are over instantly, while battles seem never ending.*

The Kaito fought valiantly, but with the grim resolution of inevitable death. There were too many ghosts. Nobukai darted from his dwindling circle to the bow stand where Mikazuki rested. It nearly scraped the ceiling as he pulled it free. With a wrist flick his bowstring was in his hands. The bow seemed to curve on its own at his touch.

A flash of light. Nobukai fell. The ancient bow clattered to the ground. A few moments later, so did his arm.

They leapt upon him. Tearing. Biting. Screaming. They drew red trails across his body. One reared back with animal eyes, reeling for the death strike.

"Don't touch him!" Kosori screamed. Clutched in her hands was a broom. She barreled into them, swiping with broad strokes. They recoiled, as if she were waving a torch. They formed a circle around her and her ruined uncle, stepping back when she threatened them with the broom, encroaching again when she swept at another.

Incredible. "How is that working?" Tsukune called out.

Tadaka's eyes looked urgently behind her. She turned, too late, toward the specter that was leaping, bony fingers reaching out toward her throat. There was no time to deflect or duck or do anything but numbly watch her own death. In that fossilized moment, she prayed that she would die on her face and not disgracefully on her back.

The strike never came. The ghost crashed into plated armor licked with white flames, impaled by a spear of radiant light. The crest of the Phoenix was a beacon on the newcomer's back. The armored warrior drew an ethereal blade and severed the ghost's head with a deft strike. The ghost burned up in heatless flames, ashes floating to brush Tsukune's cheek.

She recognized the newcomer's armor and knew the fighting style. She had seen them both in his student Tetsu. Her rescuer's name came to her lips. "Ujimitsu."

The fighting stopped. The ghosts paused in their assault, hateful eyes turned toward Tadaka. He was shouting, his agarwood rod clenched in both hands. "Oh kami, these ghosts defile your shrine!" he shouted. "They disgrace your presence! Will you do nothing? Expel them! Force them out of your sacred home! I beg you!"

As the ghosts leapt, Tadaka broke the rod in two.

The wooden floorboards beneath Tadaka's feet splintered and broke. A shimenawa rope snapped, cracking like a whip. It decapitated six ghosts, which dissolved into fog. Another snapped, banishing three more. A beam fell, the resulting shockwave scattering the fallen wards, each paper finding a ghostly victim and blinking it out of existence with just a touch.

In the pandemonium, the ateru lifted the bone-hilted dagger from the box. As he fed it into a sheath at his hip, less light seemed to pass through him. Then, a whiplike crack of a snapped shimenawa split him in two, breaking him into coils of fading smoke.

As the room finally stilled, Tadaka pulled a small book from the collar of his *haori* jacket. He flung it open, found a page, and tore it out. Flinging the book aside, he held the page aloft, shouted an incomprehensible word, and slammed the page onto the floor in front of him. More floorboards cracked. Something cold ran through Tsukune. Tears bubbled up from her eyes.

Silence. The ghosts were gone. Rainwater trickled from a crack in the ceiling. Wind stirred the singed and tattered wards. Lanterns hung split and jagged like limp jaws, and the scent of burnt oil lingered in the air. Only the well remained pristine and untouched, a grave marker in a quiet battlefield.

Tadaka fell to his knee. Tsukune rushed forward, fearing the worst – that one of the vengeful ghosts had managed to reach him. He staved her off with an outthrust hand. "I'm fine!" he barked, and then more softly, "I need only a moment." His hand came away from the paper he had slammed onto the floor. It was a simple illustrated page, but when Tsukune tried to read it, her vision blurred from unbidden tears.

"It is from the Radiant Sutra," Tadaka explained. "It contains a truth so painful that lost souls cannot bear to be near it. It will keep the ghosts away for now. But it will not last."

A thin red line traced down from Tadaka's lips. He touched the blood with a fingertip, then reached into his mouth and pulled out a broken tooth. It steamed, disintegrating in his palm.

"What have you done?" Tsukune whispered.

He could barely stand. "Our bodies are merely vessels composed of the five elements. To empower the earth kami of this shrine, I offered some earth of my own."

She went numb. "Where did you learn that?" came her hollow voice.

The kami and the Fortunes were not the only spirits that could answer prayers. There were darker forces in the world, forces that granted terrible power. They listened to any who reached for them, shugenja or no. But they accepted only blood. They stained the soul.

Had he learned this trick from his Shadowlands studies?

He seemed to read her thoughts. "I know how it looks. But it is not blood magic."

She looked at him meaningfully. "I can see how one might make that mistake."

He didn't reply.

Tsukune sheathed Ofushikai and gazed around. There were no survivors among the shrine keepers. Kosori hovered over Nobukai against the wall. "He's injured." She bound the daimyō's stump with his sleeve, but the red there was spreading at an alarming rate. "Hold still. Almost done."

"Don't waste your effort," Nobukai managed. "My life is finished."

"We need you," Kosori pleaded. "No one else can string Mikazuki."

"Look at me! I will never string a bow again."

She wrapped another cloth around the wound, almost frenzied. "The Agasha make wondrous prosthetics," she said. "I heard it from a guest once! Cypress wood. Ball-socket wrists with exchangeable hands. The Dragon would surely–"

"Kosori-san."

She stopped.

He gave no expression. "The art of archery is the art of letting go."

She fell away from him, trembling like a brittle leaf.

"I should never have meddled in this," Tsukune whispered.

Nobukai looked at her plainly. Razor cuts littered his face, and his right eye was dark crimson. "Spilled water will not return to the tray. What matters now is stopping him." He sighed. "And I fear you will have to do it alone."

Kosori's eyes popped open. "Maezawa-sama!" she cried. "He can heal you! He is of the Asako family. That's what they do. Maezawa will treat your wounds and–"

"Maezawa is not here," Tadaka observed.

Tsukune rose. He was not among the bodies. Had he even been here during the battle?

From outside, over the sound of the rain, came a loud snap, and then a cascade of crashes.

Tsukune sprinted through the shrine and into the falling sheets of rain. Each frenzied step brought another pang of growing dread. She skidded beneath the torii arch just as a second snap sounded, and the bridge crashed into the gaping ravine.

Maezawa stood on the other side. Even between the layered sheets of rain, a flash of lightning illuminated the serrated dagger he had hidden in his pipe and now held above his grim, weathered face.

"You've killed us!" Tsukune cried. But the thunder stole her words.

The old man shrugged with a remorseful look. Then, he turned away. The last she saw of him was the crest of the Asako on his back.

Tsukune stared at the space where the bridge had stood. Another flash illuminated the valley below. From that gash in the earth, she swore she heard a rush of tangled whispers.

CHAPTER SEVEN

"Maezawa cut the bridge," said Tsukune.

Kosori's damp eyes widened. Tadaka paled.

Nobukai laughed weakly. The red stain no longer spread, but his eyelids drooped, and every breath dragged between his pale lips. "It is too bad you could not convince Tadaka-sama to leave, Tsukune-sama. Otherwise, we might have lived beyond tonight."

Tsukune straightened. Nobukai had suggested the waterfall. Asako Maezawa had been waiting for her there. Talking to Tadaka had been his suggestion. "You were working together."

He closed his eyes. "I did not want to involve more outsiders. This is a Kaito family matter."

Her blood boiled. Was it simply the role of the Phoenix Clan Champion to be manipulated by everyone around her? Was this all they thought she was good for?

"Uncle," Kosori asked, "is there another way out?"

Nobukai shook his head. His words came in labored rasps. "This place was built to imprison the ateru. The bridge is the last defense. He has no feet, yet must walk regardless. That is part of his curse."

Wheels turned in Tadaka's head, his prayer beads clicking as he rotated them. "Yes. That's right. Onryō are a kind of ghost. So they cannot pass through salt circles, and they must avoid a lantern's light, and they are stronger at certain hours and weaker during others…"

"You forget," Nobukai interrupted, "other ghosts are punished by their sins. Onryō exist to punish the living. Such weaknesses do not apply to them." Seeing Tadaka's grim reaction, Nobukai laughed again. "It seems you have tested this water's depth with both feet, Tadaka-sama. I see now why Master Rujo thinks you are not ready."

Tadaka's eyes flashed. "What do you know about it?"

"We are a vassal family with a minor purpose far from civilization. The only reason the council would have sent you here would be as punishment. I wonder how you earned their ire."

So that was why the council sent Tadaka to this place. For challenging his own sensei, they wanted to teach him a lesson.

Amusement twinkled in Nobukai's weakening eyes. "You thought this place was taken by Jigoku, and I a mahō-tsukai. But you merely saw what you wanted to see. It is Tōshigoku that has claimed this place. Adjust your strategy accordingly."

Tōshigoku, the Realm of Slaughter, was a place of perpetual battle. Those who died with thoughts of revenge ended up there, compelled to fight senselessly for all eternity.

Tadaka bent until he was eye to eye with the fallen daimyō. "Crickets are breathing, Lord Nobukai." His gaze softened. "It is unwise to speak of those realms while so close to death, lest one of them take you."

"Speak of them I must! I must tell you what you are up against!" He gasped, eyes popping open. "But now there is no time."

Tears streamed down Kosori's face. "This is my fault."

"No," Nobukai said. "I am to blame. Me and my hubris." He coughed. His voice weakened. "I saw your efforts. The tags, the wards… But you are not strong enough to replace an Elemental Master, nor can you replicate the knowledge our family lost when we joined the Isawa."

Kosori's brow pinched. "But we came from the Isawa…"

"There is much you do not know," he continued, "but I have taught you none of it. I should have included you, told you what I was doing. I thought instead that I could spare you the danger, the pain…" He scoffed. "But I was foolish. Sun Tao once said, 'Try to save your soldiers, they will die. Plunge them into danger, they will live.'"

Tadaka prayed. "Emma-o, Fortune of Death, judge this soul fairly and lead him to his next reward…"

"Seek our past," Nobukai gasped. "Therein lies our future! Promise me, Kosori!"

Still grasping his hand, she nodded, her tears scattering like the ocean's spray.

He leaned back and whispered:

"Old men would tell me,
That death carried a blindfold,
And I believed them.
Yet with open eyes, I see,
His lantern, like the sun, sets."

Kaito no Isawa Nobukai breathed no longer. Kosori's head sank to her shoulders. She trembled, sniffling, as the rain fell outside.

"Cry, and he will hear you," Tadaka said.

She stopped.

"Cry, and he will remain, trying to comfort you. Bodiless, formless, never moving on to the next world. For him, you must endure."

Kosori stood and wiped her face with her forearm. "You killed him."

Tadaka held very still.

Her words came through clenched teeth. "If you hadn't stormed in here, none of this would have happened."

Tadaka stood to his full height, his shadow expanding against the wall. His eyes narrowed. "My orders come from the council. Choose your words wisely."

Kosori did not back down. She leaned in, fists clenched and shaking.

"Enough!" Tsukune shouted. "It's my fault. Look no further for the one to blame!"

They turned as one.

She was panting. She couldn't stop. Frenzied breaths tumbled from her dry mouth. She was shaking. Why was she shaking? Why did she think she could do this? What had possessed her to draw the sword? Now they were trapped. She'd trapped them. They would die here. Her eyes darted from one body to the next. Their blood was on her hands like a red iron weight coating her palms, dragging her, pushing her through the floor. Falling. Flying. An abyss.

"What's happening to her?" came Kosori's voice, but it was far away. Tsukune sat. She couldn't speak. She couldn't breathe. She was drowning, and the world was darkening, and she was empty, and everything was empty, and everything was broken, and nothing mattered, and–

"Tsukune!"

She jolted. Tadaka's face was inches away. His eyes were calm pools.

"We practiced for this," he said, soothing. "Do you remember? Breathe."

He inhaled. He exhaled. With his next breath, Tsukune followed. Inhaling. Exhaling. Slowly, again. With each breath the floor seemed a little more solid beneath her. She felt in control again. He smiled, relieved. In that moment, it almost felt like the months before. Like nothing had changed. But then his smile wavered, as if in realization, and the moment was gone.

She rose to her feet, accepting his help. Her heart still raced, her chest was tight, and she felt as if she'd been running for hours. But her thoughts were hers again. Kosori's heavy gaze was crushing. She looked as though she'd just watched Tsukune fall into a bottomless pit. In some ways, she had.

Tsukune spoke breathlessly, struggling around her continued panting. "I broke the wards. I passed through the forbidden screen. Whatever wall held the onryō back, I am the one who tore it down."

Do not rest in your own blame.

Tsukune's breath caught. Dim light glinted off Ofushikai's pearls.

"It was bound to happen," Tadaka said. "In any case, you did not thaw the well; I believe that is ultimately what freed them. The rest was inevitable."

We are but petals caught in the spring wind. We cannot say where we will land.

Tsukune regarded Kosori's confused face. "Even so, I acted without thinking. I have wronged you, Kosori. I am sorry."

Kosori looked away. "I … I need a moment."

Tsukune lowered her head as the girl left the room. Cold rain dripped from the ceiling, dabbing her cheek. She hadn't wanted Kosori to see her like that. It had been months since the last time. But nothing could be done about it now.

"What do we do?" she asked.

Tadaka folded his arms. "Spirits from the Realm of Slaughter are not my expertise, but the key to exorcising any ghost is understanding them. This is what we can safely assume: this shrine was meant to keep this so-called 'ateru' weak." He chewed around the rural word. "What I attributed to Jigoku's corrupting touch was actually the onryō's hatred slowly eroding the wards over time. The dagger, which I had mistaken for an artifact of Jigoku, must instead be one of Tōshigoku."

"What about the other ghosts?" Tsukune asked. "Who are they? Kaito's story told only of one demon. It makes no mention of any others."

"They are also onryō," Tadaka replied. "But lesser than him. It is as if–"

He stopped. The air was suddenly thick. Warm. A faint echo rippled through the shrine. Tsukune's skin broke out in goose pimples at the sound. It was laughter.

An orb blinked into being, a globe of sickly purple flame floating at the center of the room.

Tadaka paled. "Impossible. Could he have worn out the sutra already?"

A dozen more burst into being, casting the room in an unnaturally purple light. Tsukune squinted in the bonfire-like heat. "Behind me!" She grasped Ofushikai's handle, then hesitated. Would drawing it again only make things worse?

"No, behind me." Stepping forward, Tadaka wrapped his prayer beads around his wrist. "I don't care if they are from the Realm of Slaughter! They are still ghosts, susceptible to the sacred substances. Jade will hold them back." He clapped his hands three times. "Kami of earth, become like–"

His voiced trailed. He dropped his posture and thrust his hand into his drawstring pouch for a handful of coins, which he tossed on the floor. He gasped. "They're gone."

"Gone?" Tsukune started. "Who? The kami?"

The flames expanded, taking vaguely humanoid shapes.

Urgently, Tadaka clapped. It was as if he were applauding the floating balls in some bizarre performance. He was trying to attract the kami's attention. She caught his desperate look. "An offering! Something!"

She yanked the offerings bag from her obi. It wouldn't be enough.

Shadows danced across the wall. She scoured the destroyed room, throwing aside shelves and broken drawers. Empty. Nothing. This was a shrine – how could there be no more offerings?

"Forget it!" Tadaka shouted. He reached into his collar and jerked, snapping a thin strap from around his neck. The amulet in his palm, a green- and white-ribboned carving of a pheasant, shone with glossy light. Jade. Tadaka thrust the bauble into his coin pouch, drew it shut, then smashed a stone offering bowl onto the bag, over and over.

Movement behind her. Tsukune whirled. Kosori stood in the door, her face painted lavender. Tsukune looked back to the flames. "Go, Kosori! We'll hold them as long as we–"

The flames peeled away from the emaciated bodies, their burial clothes flowing in tandem with their wild hair. Their eyes burned behind their death masks.

Kosori darted for the corner as Tsukune grabbed Ofushikai. The ateru materialized, the bone dagger still in his sheath. His shark smile glinted under his long mustache.

Tadaka sprang to his feet. His amulet's remains, a mound of green powder, was cupped in his hand. Jade powder. He thrust it before him. The ateru's eyes narrowed. The ghosts hesitated.

"This is enough jade to tear all of you from the human realm!" he announced. "Take so much as a step, and I will–"

The ateru made a dismissive gesture. A gust scattered the jade powder into a dark corner. Tadaka blinked at his empty palm.

The ghosts laughed. The sound tore at Tsukune's ears and made her blood thick.

Tadaka clenched his fists. "Very well! Come all at once! I won't be humbled! Not by anyone!"

The leader floated forward. He spoke. His speech was thick

with an unfamiliar accent, his voice echoing as though through a narrow tunnel. "I am Ateru," he said. "Because you have amused me, I will make you a deal. Give us the girl, and you may leave."

The girl. Kosori.

"You can't have her," Tsukune said, gripping her sword. "I'll take your heads first."

Tadaka pulled a palm-length cylinder of wood from his obi. A *yawara*, his last resort. He made a fist around it. Nothing more needed to be said.

The ateru drew his knife. "Then die."

The spectral wave rushed forward. Tsukune braced for death.

Kosori stepped between them, a strung bow in her hand. She plucked the string. Then, the ghosts were gone.

Tsukune blinked at the moonlit room, not yet lowering her guard. But no attack came. Kosori lowered the bow. "A plucked bowstring can banish evil spirits," she said. "Even so, I wasn't sure it would work."

Tsukune relaxed. "You saved our lives."

Tadaka regarded the girl with wondering eyes. "You strung that bow? Just now?"

Kosori nodded. When Tadaka's expression did not change, she regarded the weapon more closely. Only then did Tsukune notice how old it appeared, the silk tassels adorning its curve, and its glittering bell. Mikazuki.

The realization hit Kosori like a thunderbolt. She tossed the bow like a hot iron. It landed in Tsukune's grip. The string snapped, nearly grazing Tsukune's cheek.

"I... I didn't mean to!" Kosori blurted. "I just strung the first one I could grab!"

A smile spread over Tsukune's face. "Doesn't this mean...?"

Tadaka nodded. "So that is why they wanted you. They hate the Kaito, and you are the Kaito family daimyō."

All color drained from Kosori's face.

Tsukune placed the bow in Kosori's limp hands. The girl just stared ahead, as if in a trance. It was a look, a feeling, Tsukune remembered well.

"We cannot fight them forever," Tadaka said as he gathered his fallen trinkets. "I must realign." They followed him to the main chamber. The rain was slowing, the wind stirring the hanging streamers. He sat in the lotus position, meditating.

Kosori seemed to be in a daze at the shrine's entrance, listening to the rain, hugging the ancestral bow. Her shoulders sagged listlessly, dark bags forming beneath her eyes. She was the future of the Kaito, fragile and flickering like a candle in the mountain's storm.

Tsukune gripped Ofushikai. She closed her eyes. She stood in a circle of peers within the shrine to Shiba as they passed the ancient blade from one to the other beneath the watchful eyes of the Void Master. The sword came to her, a woman with no glories to claim. She had never wanted them. She had anticipated a humble future: a peaceful life and a warrior's death were all she had ever desired. She extended the sword to Shiba Tetsu, Ujimitsu's own apprentice, and his eyes lit upon seeing its exquisite sheath. She knew the blade would choose him. Instead, it unsheathed itself in her hands.

She had wanted to protest, to say it was a mistake. But how could she question the Master of Void? And then she was alone beneath the statue of Shiba, her breath lost and her mind racing. Her rough hands were unfit to hold such a splendid blade. She could never be champion. She could never do this alone.

She remembered the hand on her shoulder. Drawing the blade. Seeing her reflection, and generations of Phoenix Clan Champions, their glowing bodies filtering the moonlight and casting no shadows.

You will never be alone, Tsukune.

Kosori's voice rose in the quiet chamber. It grew in strength, the noise of the rain seeming to match the tempo of her song:

> *"Do not cry, young maple tree,*
> *Although the storm strips your leaves.*
> *They paint Sazanami Lake,*
> *In such bright colors!*
> *Do not cry, Taiko River,*
> *Although the stones divide you.*
> *Someday the endless ocean*
> *Will join you again!"*

Tsukune opened her eyes. She wasn't going to let this be the end. Not while her heart was still beating, and she still drew breath.

When Kosori was quiet again, and the rain prevailed, Tadaka rose from his meditation. "The kami have returned." He looked to Kosori, then bowed his head. "My thanks."

Tsukune blinked at her. Kosori's song, had it called the kami back to the shrine?

For her part, Kosori seemed only mildly surprised at Tadaka's praise. Whatever resentment she had felt, she seemed to have set it aside. "What's the plan?" she asked.

"I will attempt to consecrate the shrine. It will no doubt be temporary, but we have few other options." He began taking scrolls from his satchel, unfurling them, and laying them at his feet. "Onryō are beings of extreme emotion. Their desire for slaughter offends the kami, who flee for more harmonious places. To succeed, I must convince the earth kami to remain. This will hold the onryō in place."

"What should we do?"

"String your bow," Tadaka replied. "Otherwise, nothing. I must do this alone."

Tsukune frowned. "Is there truly no way to help? Kosori's wards were powerful: you said this yourself. And surely I can at least search again for offerings?"

"Mere wards will not be of use. As for offerings..."

The steaming tooth. "No. Find another way."

"To consecrate this entire shrine at once, under these circumstances, would otherwise require a pile of offerings! If my technique, my research, can restore the balance here–"

"I forbid it."

He scoffed. "You forbid it? Really?" He crossed his arms. At his full height, the ceiling streamers nearly grazed his forehead. "Can you stop me?"

They both already knew the answer to that question. He would do whatever he wished. In this, and when they were together, he always had to be in control.

"Maybe I was never your yōjimbō," she whispered. "After all, you never let me save you."

His expression softened.

A resounding snap. The shimenawa at the entrance broke, swinging in two pieces. The paper streamers fluttered to the floor.

The room filled with floating orbs, painting the room in flickering iris. Tadaka cursed. Tsukune spun. Kosori lifted the bow. Her panic-lit face said everything. No string.

Tadaka grimly stepped into the center of the room. "Take the scrolls. Close the doors."

Unhesitating, Kosori scooped them up, scrambling to hold them all and her bow.

Tsukune grabbed his arm. "You can't–"

"You'll have to find a way to reconsecrate the shrine," he barked. "You and Kosori. I'll buy you as much time as I can."

The purpose of the yōjimbō was to die in place of their charge. A Shiba served their Isawa for life. She planted herself like a flag at his side.

He shoved her back. "You can't help me!" The pale light painted his desperate eyes.

"It should be me instead!" she shouted. "I'm your yōjimbō, whether you like it or not!"

"It's got nothing to do with that!" Tadaka barked back. "What will become of Ofushikai if you fall here? What will become of the Phoenix?"

Tsukune gritted her teeth. Ghostly forms encircled them.

"Is this a good time to argue?" Kosori asked, one foot halfway into the inner shrine.

Tadaka's shadow was tossed between flickering lights. As the flames increased, it grew darker. "What use am I otherwise?" Tsukune said. "At least let me do what I was trained to do! Someone else, someone more worthy, will become champion."

Tadaka's face broke into an anguished scowl. "Damn you, Tsukune! If you would only look past your own nose, you would see you are destined for this! That the sword chose wisely!"

Her gasp snuffed out her anger. He turned his back, his voice carrying a hesitant sting. "The way your peers look at you. How deeply you care about them. I will never have what you have." His voice wavered. "What you inspire in others is far greater than any feat you could accomplish alone. So, imagine what you could do if you were inspired by yourself!"

Now he was saying this. Here. In these circumstances, when she needed to be strong. "*Baka*," she whispered, a wet line trailing down her cheek.

As she followed Kosori away, beneath the crackling flames and steadily growing screams of otherworldly voices, she swore she heard his quiet murmuring. As she closed the shōji doors, she saw

Isawa Tadaka as a silhouette wreathed in jade flames. She shut the screen so forcefully, it cracked the frame. Then, silence.

You just killed him, she thought. *You killed him to save your own skin.* She clenched her teeth through a swelling film of tears. *Damn you, Tsukune. You're no better than Maezawa.*

Kosori dropped the scrolls and made for one of the keepers' bodies. There would be a bowstring there. Tsukune watched, swallowing around a lump in her throat. She blinked her tears away. *Kosori is what matters now. You must protect her.*

A flash of violet light. And there was the ateru, floating just before the well. Kosori froze, her eyes flicking to a bowstring just inches away. He followed her gaze and laid a hand on the bone-handled dagger.

"Go on," he said, jaw unhinging, voice echoing. "Try."

She steeled her gaze. "What do you want from me?"

His eyes burned hatefully. "The Kaito have forgotten, have they? That changes nothing. I have lost track of the hundreds of years I've waited for this moment. Nothing will sway me." A wreath of flames surrounded him. The room became a furnace. "If I have to cleave the mountain, I will see Momotsukihime's children utterly eradicated!" He drew his blade. "Starting with you!"

The first lesson of the Shiba yōjimbō was simple, yet overlooked by other schools. To be a good bodyguard, one needed not impressive defenses, nor speed to outpace the attacker, nor even the ability to detect danger. One needed only one thing: to be the greater of two threats. Tsukune screamed and threw herself upon him.

The ghost stepped out of her reach, but she did not relent. She ignored the burning in her joints and pressed forward. She needed only to buy Kosori time to string the bow. Nothing else mattered. She struck, again. Again.

He pinned her arm midstrike and drove the dagger into her shoulder.

The blade was a fire inside her. There was light behind her eyes, and for a moment, the world was an infinite battlefield stretching in all directions beneath a fire-brimmed sky.

Kosori strung the bow. She plucked.

The shockwave yanked the ghost away. The dagger carved a path through Tsukune, an arc of red splashing against the wall. Tsukune's strength left her. She stumbled, her head thudding hard against the roof of the well. She tumbled in. The water swallowed her up.

Dimly, she thought to swim. Her arms did not obey. Through her blurry vision, she saw a wavering portal above and a face that might have been Kosori's. It grew smaller and smaller.

Sinking, she thought. But she was too tired to care. The water was cool and dark. A red, cloudy trail followed her down. She felt that she was a part of it now.

Distantly, Kosori called her name. Then, she heard nothing at all.

CHAPTER EIGHT

Tsukune.

She scrunched her face. The voice was not her father, but it sounded like a father's voice. Concern and strictness and love.

You are sinking.

She didn't care. It was cool here. Quiet. The water soothed her aching limbs, cooled her tired eyes, and dulled all sensation, even the distant ache of her shoulder.

Wake up.

Why? It was still dark. Too early to awaken, too early–

AWAKEN.

Tsukune's eyes popped open. She was suspended in a wide octagonal shaft. Faint light filtered from above and below. Drowning. She was drowning!

She thrashed. Her lungs were bursting. Which way was up? The light dimmed. The paper balloon inside her tore open, and as the urge to breathe won control, she felt a final pang of shame. Hundreds of Phoenix Clan Champions, and she would be the first to lose the ancestral sword. It would fall from her limp fingers to the bottom. For that reason alone, this was a fitting end. Better that she should sink and never be seen again.

Her mouth opened. She inhaled. The water rushed in.

At first, she thought she was dreaming. She had breathed in oceans while dreaming before. But then her shoulder throbbed in hot pain. This was real.

From the first breath, she didn't stop inhaling. A steady stream of bubbles blew from her nostrils as she endlessly drank. Her water-filled lungs made her heavy and full, while the dreamlike quiet dark washed away all urgency.

Ofushikai. She would have gasped if she were not perpetually doing so. The iridescent pearls of its grip were glowing. The sword seemed more alive here, the wooden sheath young and newly carved, a gossamer aura refracting the filtered light. She drew the sword partway and watched thin shadows dancing on the gleaming steel, as if it were beneath the ocean shallows.

When the Empire was new, Shiba fell in love with a woman from beneath the sea, a mermaid named Tsumaru. Because she was a princess, their marriage briefly united the undersea kingdom of the Ningyo with the fledgling Shiba family. But as the years passed, she grew weak from her time away from the sea. After the Day of Thunder, when Shiba vanished in the Shadowlands, she dove into the sea below the cliffs of Castle Shiba, becoming a fish by the time she broke the waters.

The story from Tsukune's childhood replayed itself in her grandmother's voice, revealing one final detail. On their wedding day, Tsumaru presented a gift: a sword, forged by her own hands, using metals and techniques from the kingdom beneath the sea. This sword she named Ofushikai, a Ningyo word with an esoteric meaning. Tsumaru had made a sword that was stronger beneath the waves and allowed its wielder to breathe water as if it were air, because she knew she would someday return to the ocean. And when that day came, she wanted her husband to visit her.

A glowing bubble broke Tsukune's reverie. Far below was

a dim light. Returning the sword to its sheath, Tsukune swam down, mouth agape like a fish. The water grew warmer, and the light, a sickly purple, grew steadily brighter.

The bottom of the well was a box-shaped room, well lit, although Tsukune could not find the source. The water was like an *onsen*, hot and still. She had the sensation that she was standing in a doorway, both inside and outside. The walls were mortared stone, but now and again, whenever the light flickered, they seemed to vanish, revealing an infinite crow-picked battlefield. Her wound burned whenever it appeared.

She tensed. There was a body, waterlogged and swollen, staring sightlessly at the top of the shaft. It was mostly intact and well preserved. Its clothing was unfamiliar in origin, of fibrous cloth and leather belts. It had a strong jawline and a long mustache. There was fire tattooed on the man's mummified face. His hair was stacked into an elongated bun at the top of his head. A dagger sheath, bone white, was like a beacon against his black tunic. But there was no dagger. In his chest was an arrow, protruding like a planted flag.

So, this was the ateru banished by Isawa Kaito. Preserved by the ice for hundreds of years. Not a demon, but a human being.

A gentle current brushed her cheek. She followed it to a small opening, just large enough to squirm through. The source of the well.

She swam slowly and for some time. The tunnel grew dark, only the faint light of Ofushikai's pearls revealing the smooth stone walls polished by the current. At last, the floor ramped upward, and reaching, her arm broke the water's surface. She stood.

Ofushikai's light barely revealed an underground cavern. Tsukune had come up in the shallows of a subterranean river. A distant echo suggested waterfalls or cascades. She was in some hidden chamber beneath the shrine. Or so she hoped.

She sputtered. Bending over on mossy ground, she exhaled a

steady stream, her lungs emptying, until she was coughing, the noise echoing through the cavern. A cacophony of screeches signaled disturbed bats. She gasped a lungful of musty air. As she did, Ofushikai's light blinked out, leaving her in pitch dark.

She lay on her back, gasping, succumbing to her aches and pains. She was soaked and heavy and without the strength to move. A fire burned inside her arm socket. But her heart was still beating. Was she really alive? Had the Fortunes spared her in this forsaken place?

She laughed, sputtering, the cavern drinking the sound. No one would believe this, not Kosori, not…

Tsukune bolted up. Kosori. Tadaka. They were still in the shrine somewhere, fighting. Dying. She could not stay here.

As she achingly rose, the stalactites and rock formations dimly appeared before her. She thought her eyes had adjusted, but then she saw dancing shadows. There was a winding trail of candles leading deeper into the cave. Not knowing where else to go, she followed it with soggy steps. As she walked, candles spontaneously lit ahead of her, while those behind snuffed out.

They led her to a hollow chamber. A sudden flash assailed her as hundreds of candles lit at once. Shimenawa ropes with lightning-shaped tassels hugged stalagmites or swayed from a stone torii arch. A shrine was carved into the wall, decorated with ropes and dozens of tiny bells. Within the shrine sat a stone urn. Three hallways led deeper into this underground shrine.

She paused. Where did she go from here? Somewhere above, Tadaka was locked in a battle of wills with dozens of ghosts, and Kosori was alone with no one to defend her. Yet her urgency melted here, as if she had stepped into a place where time had no meaning.

The candlelight shifted from yellow to blue. Her hand darted to the sword, but her yōjimbō haragei was calm. There was no danger. As she relaxed, a pinprick of blue light coalesced before the shrine. It rapidly unfolded into a suit of glowing armor.

Tsukune paused at the familiar heraldry, recognizing the one who wore it, his kind eyes as iridescent as the sword's pearls.

"Ujimitsu."

She fell to her knees and placed her forehead on the ground. The spirit watched, saying nothing. She searched for words, but nothing seemed right to say. She had no secrets from him; he had been in the sword's reflection that day at Shiba's shrine, he had deflected the ghost's attack meant for her throat. He was never far from the sword, it seemed. Surely he had seen everything she had done.

"You have come to judge me," she uttered. "Very well. I know… that I am unworthy. I ruined the sanctity of the shrine. I freed an angry ghost. Priests are dead because of my actions. There is nothing I can do to atone." She offered the blade. "Please, find one more worthy. It should not be too challenging."

He approached, his hand hovering above the surrendered blade. *It is for the best,* she thought. She would make the four cuts when this was over.

Ignoring the sword, Ujimitsu's spirit laid his hand on her forehead.

Her world vanished.

"I see you both are acclimating. In time, you will unlock Ofushikai's full abilities."

Tsukune stood in the chamber of the Elemental Masters. There was the circular table with the five seats, the brilliant tapestries of the Elemental Academies hanging from the walls. How had she gotten here?

"Has it spoken to you?"

She turned toward the voice and recognized Isawa Ujina. Only gray had not yet stroked the temples of the Master of Void, nor had wrinkles yet set into his face. He tilted his head, expecting an answer.

She hesitated, then opened her mouth to reply.

"It has," came another voice.

Ujina had not been looking at her. He was looking *through* her.

Behind her, she saw a shorter man in elaborate wing-shouldered robes, topknot bobbing above an unremarkable, youthful face. Ujimitsu. Ofushikai rested in his inexpert hands. He didn't seem to notice her.

These events had already unfolded. She was just a spectral bystander to an immutable past.

"I've seen… visions," the young Ujimitsu confessed. "Dreams. I find them disturbing."

"They come from the sword?"

He looked confused. "Where else?"

Ujina nodded. "The Empire is strongest when the clans stand united, but only the Phoenix can show them the threat. You must prepare the clan for that day. That is your purpose."

Ujimitsu's eyes fell to the sword. Tsukune's eyes narrowed. Was he… trembling?

"Why me?" he asked.

Tsukune gasped.

Ujina regarded him curiously. "The sword chooses as it will, Ujimitsu. You know this."

"I am not a warrior. I am a painter! A woodcarver! I make portraits for newlyweds and toys for children!" Anguish washed over Ujimitsu's features. "It should have been Masumi! She is ten times the warrior I am. She understands the Tao where I can only scratch my head. Make her the champion, not me!" In the young champion's expression, Tsukune saw herself.

The Void Master shook his head. "That is not within my power. If the sword were meant for Masumi, it would have chosen her. The sword chose you."

Ujina smiled at him. "If you seek the answer why, look within."

• • •

Tsukune blinked. She was in the cavern once more, kneeling before the spirit of Ujimitsu. She blinked tears from her face. Her mind flooded with questions as her fingers curled around Ofushikai. She understood.

"It's your voice," she said. "All this time. You have been calling out to me. When I lose control, you call me back."

"They were your steps, not mine."

Her eyes widened. This voice came not from her mind. It bounced off the cavern walls and made the candles flicker and brighten. But it was the same.

"We are not born worthy. We *become* worthy. Our suffering is a flower, without meaning unless it blooms." He extended his arms like gossamer wings. "The Soul of Shiba knows its own. Trust it. Trust yourself. Be true to who you are and embrace whatever tests you. You will not always win. Repentance does not come first. But you should always try. Like unwrought metal, fearlessly embrace the flames and be changed."

Tsukune's heartbeat thundered through the cavern. Where once had been doubt, now a glowing light prevailed.

"Live. Die. Be reborn," Ujimistu smiled. "That is the way of the Phoenix."

Tsukune rose. She returned Ofushikai to her obi and met Ujimitsu's eyes. "I'll do my best."

The spirit vanished. The candles went out. Tsukune stood in the darkness of the hidden shrine. Soundless. Empty.

But she was not alone. Never alone.

CHAPTER NINE

The steps flew under Tsukune's feet as she ran, her heart pounding in her ears. Her first guess had been lucky; just a glimpse of spiral stairs leading up was enough to break her into a run. The twist was so narrow she had to take Ofushikai from her obi, lest it drag against the wall. Her body protested with each step, her tight muscles burning. Her shoulder wound had gone numb, the soreness just a hollow echo of before. These thoughts fell to the basement of her mind. They were unimportant, mere pond ripples compared to the sound of rain growing louder as she climbed. In her mind's eye, she saw Tadaka's silhouette as jade flames leapt at his attackers. She saw Kosori alone with the ateru. She pumped her legs harder and prayed to the Fortunes that this stairway would lead back to the shrine. That Tadaka and Kosori, like her, were somehow still alive.

Halfway up, a sound touched her ears. She stopped, straining to hear over the noise of her breathless panting. It was singing. Faint, distant, but clear. A rustic tune. Kosori's voice.

And she was running again, faster than her breath could carry.

The top opened to a square room lit by a masoned window. Sound ravaged the chamber, echoing rain and thunder, though

Kosori's voice was still clear. Tsukune sprinted to the far wall, a sliding door with the crest of the Kaito family. She yanked it, but it held shut. Icy daggers shot through her shoulder. She bit back the pain and the sudden rush of warmth against her side, trying again. Something was jammed in the sliding track, pinning it shut. She stepped back. Whispering an apology to whatever spirits watched, she ran and with all her remaining strength threw herself upon the wooden surface.

The door collapsed with a resounding crash. At once came the familiar musty smell of cobwebs and dust, and moonlight flooded in. Tsukune was back in the shrine. She praised the Fortunes.

As she stood, she felt a sudden swoosh by her cheek. An arrow stuck into the doorframe, splintering inches from her face. A second bit her arm and became embedded in the tight fibers of her kimono silk. "Stop!" she shouted hoarsely. "It's me!"

Kosori had just nocked a third arrow and drawn Mikazuki to full extension, the bow curving like the crescent spring moon. She was in the inner shrine. The door Tsukune had broken was the wall panel that backed Mikazuki's bow stand.

Recognition dawned across Kosori's features. "Tsukune?" She lowered the bow. Her face brightened. "Tsukune!"

She was across the room in seconds, arms around Tsukune in a warm embrace. Then Kosori remembered herself and drew back, red-faced. "I… I thought the worst." Her eyes twinkled. "You're alive. You're really alive!"

Tsukune smirked without energy. "So I am told."

"What happened? Where did you come from?"

She gestured limply at the hidden passage.

Kosori spared it only a brief glance before flicking her eyes at Tsukune's shoulder and a stain shades darker than her red silks. "You're bleeding!" she exclaimed.

"Oh?"

Kosori sat her by the well, setting the bow aside. Tsukune placed Ofushikai beside it. A glance at the well revealed her reflection. Waterlogged, with her ponytail undone, her disheveled kimono splotchy and stained, purple rings beneath her eyes, and the arrow protruding from her sleeve, she looked as though she'd crawled out of a watery grave. And, she supposed, she had.

She looked beyond at the complete disarray of the room. Arrows were stuck into rafters and walls. Broken furniture and wards were scattered everywhere. "What happened?"

"They tried to ambush me. They failed."

Tsukune nodded. "Where did you find arrows?"

"Under the floorboards," Kosori gestured. "Lots of stuff down there. Mostly arrows, but some incense and spices, too. Some gold plates," she added offhandedly.

"Gold plates? Too bad it wasn't something useful."

Kosori gestured to her shoulder. "Let me see."

"In the shrine? What if my blood touches the floor?"

Kosori made a wry face. "I think we're beyond that now."

Tsukune pulled her arm in through her sleeve and out of her collar. Red painted her shoulder and arm around a gaping wound and purple flesh. "Think it might scar?" she joked.

Kosori winced. "I think it may fall off. How have you not bled out?"

"I think he cauterized it," Tsukune replied. "The blade felt hot."

"Well, it's still bleeding. Although it looks clean." Kosori nodded. "I have just the thing."

As Kosori stepped away, Tsukune closed her eyes and felt the burn beneath her eyelids. Her arms were made of lead; her legs were sand-filled sacks. It had to be close to sunrise by now. Laying her head against the well, she looked at the closed screen separating this room from the main chamber. There was no noise from behind those doors. Nothing at all.

Returning, Kosori followed Tsukune's gaze. "I'm sure he's alright." She offered a stoic expression. Hopeful. "He is the scion of an Elemental Master."

Tsukune nodded. "I'm sure," she replied, ignoring the part of herself that felt this was a lie.

"All right, let's bandage this." Kosori held up a wad that looked like a charcoal-colored ball of cotton.

Tsukune grabbed her wrist. "What is *that?*"

"Cobwebs."

Tsukune gave her an incredulous look.

"It works. See?" Kosori extended her forearm. A vertical gash ran down her arm from palm to elbow. Something thick and clumpy lay against the wound, reddish brown and stuck to the skin. It moved organically with her flesh, like a scab.

Kosori smiled. "I told you spiders in a shrine were good luck!"

When Tsukune could stand, they each took a candle and she led Kosori through the passage in the wall. They descended the spiral stairs, Kosori breathless and wondering. "You did not know this was here?" Tsukune asked.

"If I had, I'd have led us down here. With all the wards and shimenawa, surely the onryō cannot follow."

When they came to the cavern shrine, Kosori's knees struck the ground. "That's Kaito's urn!" She lowered her head. "I never knew where we kept it ..."

After her prostrations, they explored the subterranean halls. One led to an armory containing dozens of arrows, some with jade tips and blessings tied to the shafts. Another led to a mushroom garden, a shimenawa encircling a dead log at the center.

The third was where they found the library. Bookshelves divided the room, with more set into the walls. Scroll cases stacked into pyramids filled many shelves. Others contained boxes with books inside. The herby smell of parchment permeated the room.

Kosori set Mikazuki against a wall and darted inside. "There must be thousands!" she proclaimed, her hands grazing the stacks. She peered into a wooden case left slightly ajar. "They're journals!" She lifted one, a coverless hemp-bound book with rustic lettering. "This is the personal journal of Isawa Tsuruko, Kaito's daughter! I didn't know this existed!"

"And these are star maps," Tsukune remarked, gesturing to a line of cylindrical cases that were labeled as such. "It seems the Kaito kept extensive records." On the same shelf sat cases marked with dates, some hundreds of years old. "These must be the histories of the Kaito." She paused. At the end of the shelf was a wooden mask. Tsukune took it. The old wood left dust on her fingertips. Looking into its featureless face, her mind leapt to another place, a village whose name she'd promised to forget. She'd last seen such a mask among the Yobanjin.

At the library's center sat a desk. Numerous documents were scattered across its surface: a floor plan of the shrine, numerous journals, some scrolls. They had been placed here recently. At the head sat an *emakimono*, a scroll combining pictures and text, intended to be unrolled and read horizontally. Kosori revealed the first section, an elaborate depiction of a woman in shrine maiden garments battling a demon. Isawa Kaito. Hands trembling, Kosori read the words aloud.

"If you are reading this, it is surely because you are the daimyō of our family. I leave this document for all future leaders of the Kaito so that they may know our true history." Kosori paused, brow pinching. "When the shrine is complete, I will hide this in the under-sanctum, the secret place my mother so often visited. Her deeds are recounted throughout these provinces, even spoken before the emperor himself. That story is an incomplete truth. With my heart and mind aligned, I write below the true story of our family's founding..."

Kosori's voice lowered until there was no sound at all. She advanced through the scroll, eyes darting from writing to pictures and back. Her lips trembled, mouthing words. Then, she stopped.

"That's... that's not possible."

Tsukune took the scroll from Kosori's limp hands. It unfurled, scrollbar clattering to the floor. "My mother was born Kaito no Momotsukihime," Tsukune read, "Princess of the Hyōketsu tribe of..."

The word seized her breath. "Yobanjin."

Kosori stared at Mikazuki. "That's... that's not..."

Tsukune continued. "Among the Hyōketsu, a princess and priestess are one and the same. Although my mother never possessed the gift of shugenja, she was a medium of spirits and the spiritual representative of her tribe. With this came an awesome responsibility to preserve sacred places. She always held this duty in great reverence.

"In her time, famine and misfortune led the Hyōketsu to stage raids against Isawa provinces, raids that grew bolder with every victory. Brief skirmishes to feed the tribe became extended campaigns to steal the wealth of Rokugani. And then came the visitor from their own Imperial Court, who paid the Hyōketsu to run daring attacks throughout Isawa lands..."

Tsukune clenched her jaw. Those words assured that this document could never leave this place. The accusation, levied against an Imperial official, would shame the emperor.

"My mother never approved of these raids. She was the lone dissenter among the tribe's leaders, including her betrothed. My mother watched with growing disgust as fields were burned, innocents killed, shrines defiled, and their sacred archery traditions, meant to honor the spirits, were instead converted to violence. She watched war change her people, quietly hating what they had become.

"But the Fortunes are always watching. One day they found the defenders ready; an army of Shiba, supported by Isawa blessings, backed them into a corner.

"This is why, to save her people, my mother betrayed them. In secret, she approached the Isawa with an offer: she would give the raiding tribe to them in exchange for a place among the Phoenix. For this, she and those who followed her became vassals of the Isawa. They were granted land in the mountains of Garanto Province." Tsukune looked up from the scroll. "Assimilation would have meant the death of her people's culture. She willingly chose that rather than let the violence continue."

Kosori's tremulous voice rose from the corner. "All my life, I was told we were Isawa. That our lower station did not matter, because our bloodline was prestigious, our duty sacred, our ways derived from the tribe of Isawa himself!" Tears ran freely down her face. "They were lies. We are conquered Yobanjin, founded by a betrayal! We were never Isawa. We are not even Phoenix."

Silence hung thick between them.

"Is that what you think?" Tsukune finally said. "What does this change? You are still children of the Phoenix, no matter your origins."

"Adopted children," she replied bitterly.

"Does that matter? Mikazuki does not seem to care. Why should I?" She leaned in, meeting the girl's wet stare. "I told you that I have seen Yobanjin, Kosori-san. When I did, I couldn't help but think they were not so different from us."

"The Elemental Masters might not see it that way."

The Asako heal, the Shiba protect, and the Isawa… know.

"I'd imagine they already know," Tsukune replied. Perhaps they already knew everything. The onryō. The eroding wards. They had sent Tadaka to punish him… but could she say they had not also anticipated this and sent him to stop it?

For that matter, had the Master of Void sent her, too? With the histories unfurled before her, it was impossible to tell what was due to guiding hands and what was merely fate.

Tsukune continued reading, "My mother's decision bypassed the council and was seen as treasonous. The Hyōketsu, like all Yobanjin, valued freedom over all else. Many would not bend their knee to their ancestral enemies. Among those who refused to join was my mother's betrothed: Ateru, the Demon of Wyvern Pass."

"Ateru," she repeated. The realization was like the final placement of a Go piece. "It's his name."

Tsukune knew the rest even before the scroll told her. Ateru could not forgive the betrayal. In his eyes, she'd laid their very identity at the altar of the Isawa, selling out her own people. She was a defector. The insult could never stand. And so, long after Kaito had taken an Isawa husband and established her line, he led the remaining Hyōketsu against her. Her death would wipe the disgrace from his people.

The body in the well. The arrow in its chest. The dagger…

"She didn't kill a demon," she murmured. "She killed her betrothed. Ateru. And with time, the true history forgotten, his name came to mean 'demon' in your dialect." Her chest tightened. "No wonder Ateru hates the Kaito. Betrayed, he died by her hand, never achieving his justice. He died lusting for revenge and was forgotten. His hatred must have…"

The flickering walls within the well. The infinite battlefield.

"…flung him into Tōshigoku. Kaito gave her life to trap him.

He's been frozen down there all these centuries, with all his followers, the entire Hyōketsu, as..."

Their screaming masked faces. Their reaching hands.

"Onryō." She paled. "He must have clawed his way back. And Tōshigoku is still waiting for him. That's what he wants. The destruction of the Kaito. Nothing less will do."

Kosori's eyes wavered. She was trembling. Tsukune watched the anguish crawl over her face, tanned and soft-featured, a far cry from those common to the Isawa. Grabbing the bow, she ran from the room, knocking the wooden case of journals off its perch. Books spilled across the floor.

Tsukune started to follow, but stopped. Tsuruko's journal had fallen open on a specific page, one visited so often the spine bent there naturally. Her eyes automatically read the practiced strokes in the Phoenix Clan cipher:

Again, I am awakened by Ateru's screams.

I have lost track of how many nights his cries and demands have kept me from sleep. When I do not reply, he lists the ways Mother wronged him. From the well, I hear him even now.

The Elemental Masters say there is little they can do. They could defeat him, but they are unwilling to deploy their power in this way; it would cause more harm than good, disrupting the harmony of the spirit realms. Even a pebble can cause waves. Invoking the earth and fire kami for battle in one place could result in a volcanic eruption elsewhere. No matter how people try to convince themselves that their actions have no repercussions, to turn their heads and deny the consequences, in this world, all things are connected.

Master Gensa is creating shimenawa that will constrain Ateru's reach, and Father's wards will quiet his voice. Gensa-sama warns that this is not a permanent solution. "A gardener

*who ignores their weeds dooms the garden," he said. Knowing
this, I wonder: if Ateru is silenced, will I sleep any better?*
  – *Kaito no Isawa Tsuruko, Month of the Ox, Isawa Calendar
    year 522*

Tsukune found Kosori in the inner sanctum. She was struggling
to remove Mikazuki's string, but the bow refused to bend, even
when Kosori pressed its arm against the floor.

Kosori noticed Tsukune and paused. "I can use another bow. I
don't need to use this one."

Tsukune just watched.

"It will be daylight soon," Kosori continued. "The onryō will
vanish in the sun, like a bad dream." She looked at the bow. "I'll
unstring it and put it back. Uwazuru will take it. He's a better
choice anyway."

"Kosori..." Tsukune spoke.

"You'll tell the Masters about the haunting! They'll fix the
wards! Everything will go back to how it was! As if nothing–"

"It doesn't work like that. A launched arrow cannot be
withdrawn."

Kosori grimaced. Her eye twitched, oh so slightly. Then
her expression broke, twin streams falling from her eyes. She
collapsed. On her knees, she hid her face in her hand, shaking from
emotion she could not contain. "I can't do this," she whispered. "I
can't. Not knowing it was a lie. Not knowing we wronged them. I
can't. I'm just not..."

Tsukune's heart twisted. "You have to, Kosori. There's no one
else."

Kosori scoffed. "I was the worst in my class. I couldn't fire a
bow without striking my cheek. I tried to learn, but nothing
stayed in. All I've ever wanted to do is sing. I never wanted to be a
shrine maiden! I had dreams!"

It was a shameful admission. Kosori looked away. "The only reason I even passed my shufuku was as a favor to my uncle. I've always burdened him. I shamed him even the moment I was born. Is there anything worse?"

Tsukune tried to smile. "But you've improved so much since then."

"How can I lead when they don't respect me? Uwazuru would be better. It should be him."

Tsukune shook her head. "The bow chose you. It–"

She stopped. The Void Master had said to look within. But he'd been wrong. It was here, in this place, that she finally understood.

"I'm not strong like you, Tsukune-sama." Tearful, Kosori looked into her eyes. "If only I had your courage."

Tsukune froze. The world fell away. *That is how she sees me?*

Like Tsukune had seen Ujimitsu. Strong. Certain. No room in his heart for doubt. The Master of Void had said he was a proactive champion. In every story she'd heard, he never hesitated.

And yet, he'd had his doubts. She knew that now. When the sword chose him, he'd been afraid. But had it made him any less strong? New air filled Tsukune's lungs. No. Moments of weakness did not lessen his legend. Just as Kosori was still strong now, in spite of her doubts. Just as–

She grabbed Kosori's shoulders. Their gazes locked. "Kosori! I am *terrified!*"

Kosori stared, wet eyes unblinking. The words tumbled freely, emptying her, growing lighter each syllable. "I don't know what I am doing. I wasn't ready for this. I wasn't even raised in the Shiba dōjō: I was traded to the Lion, trained as an Akodo until..." Her voice cracked, "...until I had to replace my brother."

"Tsukune..." Kosori murmured.

"I didn't excel. I would never have been anything more than a simple yōjimbō. And I was fine with that! I was happy in Tadaka's shadow! I wanted nothing more!" The emotion faded from Tsukune's face. "But none of that matters. Ofushikai chose *me*.

"And it is shameful to allow that moment to pass with inaction. What is a life but a mere handful of moments? We get so few of them. If I succumb, if I let my doubt drag me down, I will take the fate of my people with me. I cannot, I *will* not let that happen. I must..."

Kosori was smiling. Faintly, but just so. The words, her words, were echoed by voices only she could hear. Ofushikai was glowing.

Tsukune rose. Her voice filled the chamber, bolstered by the voices of countless others who had spoken the same. Hundreds of years shared this moment.

"We are but droplets in the river. We cannot say where the current will take us, for our paths are cast the moment we are born. But sometimes, when we are dashed upon the rocks, we might, for a moment, capture the sun."

A ring of glowing spirits surrounded them. They appeared as they had in life, young and old, expert and untested, ancient and modern. All unified by the same duty. All wearing the same knowing expression. All champions of the Phoenix Clan. Directly across, Ujimitsu nodded. Tsukune matched his smile.

"That is what it means to be a Phoenix."

The spirits were gone. Tsukune's hand grasped Ofushikai's hilt. It fit perfectly.

Kosori picked up her bow and the nearby bundle of arrows. Dark rings still glittered wet beneath her eyes. But there was fire behind them now. "I'll try to be worthy." She rubbed her face with her sleeve. "Sorry I cried."

"That's fine," Tsukune smirked. "You can cry in the dōjō if you laugh on the battlefield."

From the crack between the closed shōji doors came a thin unnatural light.

They saw it simultaneously: a glowing strip increasing in intensity. Tsukune could picture them: dozens of flaming orbs blinking into existence. Ateru was among them. The heat of his hatred seared even this far. She and Kosori exchanged one final look before they turned, resolutely, to the doors. Kosori readied a blessed arrow. Ofushikai sang a brilliant note as Tsukune freed it from the sheath.

The doors burst open.

CHAPTER TEN

The onryō were a glowing swarm of death. The stage was like a beach, and they were a sea rising to claim it. Tsukune cleaved through four just as they stepped over the threshold. Two more leapt at her exposed back. She made no attempt to duck from harm. Kosori's arrow blinked them away before they could touch her.

Then Tsukune planted herself in the doorframe, where no more than three could come at once. They rushed her in a relentless wave of burning eyes and masked faces. She struck, again and again, while Kosori picked off the ones that gave her trouble. She didn't flinch, not even when an arrow whizzed past her ear. Kosori's heart was beating in Tsukune's chest.

And then she spotted him. Rising above the ethereal throng, Ateru drew his dagger. The ghosts stopped. They appeared as they had in death, rays of light marking their mortal wounds.

Kosori called out. A shaft of purple light emanated from the well. Then came hands and ethereal bodies. The very ghosts they had just defeated.

"What now?" Kosori called out.

Tsukune grimaced. "Uh…"

Then she knew. And because Kosori knew her heart, so did she.

Kosori rushed forward and plucked her empty bowstring. The shockwave tore through the angry dead. The two women wedged through the path she cleared, Tsukune shearing away the last few onryō on the stage. Each slammed a shōji door, Kosori slapping a paper ward upon the screens. The ward stuck, but as the violet light on the other side grew brighter, the ward aged before their eyes.

They surveyed the room. Two dozen coal-fire eyes glared at them, Ateru in the back making twenty-six. Their hatred radiated from them, their ghostly farming implements and barbarian weapons gleaming in their hands. But they didn't charge the stage. It was silent as death, not even the storm outside making a sound.

Lying against the stage was Tadaka. Pale, his hat torn, his face bloody, he drew ragged breaths and didn't move. A fallen section of shimenawa rope, hastily encircled, separated him from the onryō. Tsukune ran instantly to his side, Kosori's arrow banishing the ghost that tried to intercept. Seeing him was like witnessing a sunrise after a prophecy of eternal night.

Tadaka's bruised eye looked up at her. "You look like you stepped out of your own grave."

"Find a mirror," she replied with a relieved smile.

"I couldn't stop them," he whispered. "They just reappear. Too many…"

"Save your energy." Her eyes darted for options.

Another arrow banished an opportunistic attacker. Tsukune leveled her gaze at Ateru. He grinned back with a shark's mouth.

"He's the demon," she remarked. "It is his body in the well. I've seen it."

"Is that so?"

Kosori let another arrow go, this one aimed at Ateru, but he batted it from the sky with a wind gust. His grin widened, splitting his face in two.

"What happens if I banish him?" Tsukune asked Tadaka.

The shugenja stirred. "All the others will vanish. But he'll just reappear."

"What if we last until sunrise?"

"The next evening it will happen all over again. We need a permanent solution."

Ateru's hateful eyes projected a challenge, his dagger flashing otherworldly light.

"It would buy more time." She rose. "I'll do what I can."

The doors to the inner shrine burst open as the ward finally failed. Kosori turned to the sudden rush of ghosts, slapping a paper streamer against the forehead of the first attacker. It popped like a bubble. "Go on!" she said. "I can deal with them."

The ghostly wave parted to let Tsukune through. She led with her sword. Amusement danced with hatred on Ateru's tattooed face as they circled one another. "You should have taken my offer."

Tsukune readied Ofushikai. "That remains to be seen."

They were enclosed in a ring of twisted faces. He took a bold step forward, testing her. She struck back. They both spun, avoiding each other.

"I know what you are, Ateru," she said. "I know why you're doing this."

"And yet you dare to defend them!" Ateru's dagger nicked Tsukune's face. "The children of traitors! What if it had been *your* people they betrayed?"

She jerked back, counterstriking. He danced around her attack and struck again. She barely deflected. He was faster than any human opponent. Her counters seemed to drag, her shoulder burning with every movement. He did not fear Ofushikai. What could she do to him?

His face brightened, looking into her eyes. "Now you're getting it. You can't win. All you know how to do is destroy. What good will that do against me, when I cannot be destroyed?"

"The weaker you are, the louder you bark."

His lips peeled back from shark's teeth. "I'll show you how weak I am."

A loud bang, like a prolonged crack of thunder, shook Tsukune's bones. The ceiling tore itself a jagged maw. Her eyes shut against the sudden curtain of rain.

Her belly wheel spun. She tumbled forward, his dagger edge raking against her ear. The rain droplets sizzled against Ateru's ethereal body.

She deflected a dagger strike intended for her throat, exposing her shoulder. Ateru grabbed it and dug his fingers into the wound. Tsukune's world bleached as ice and lightning shot through her. She collapsed, numb.

"You're done!" Ateru cried and drove the dagger down.

He yanked it back, away from Kosori's sudden arrow. A second grazed him, sizzling like enflamed paper. From the stage, devoid of enemies, Kosori pointed her final arrow at Ateru. Prayers tumbled from her lips. The arrow was glowing.

The body in the well. The arrow. Tsukune pointed to a spot on his chest. "Kosori! There!"

She let it fly. It struck into Ateru like a planted flag.

A spout of hot flame burst from where it landed. He did not vanish like before. Instead, he screamed. In that moment, Tsukune felt that she stood on the plain of endless battle.

Steam rose from the planted arrow. Ateru's face was like a split lantern. The bones in his back made peaks under his flesh. His body shook with tremors, as if struggling to maintain its form.

"Bitch!" he shrieked. "I will cut you to pieces and send them to Hell!" He pointed the dagger. "There! That is a daughter of the traitor Kaito! She is the one holding us prisoner! The key is in her guts!"

The onryō scrambled for the stage. Kosori pulled Mikazuki into a perfect crescent moon. But this would not save her: the first wave would be banished; the second would tear her apart. Tsukune pushed herself up. A crimson river flowed down her arm. She forced a foot beneath her. *Get up! Flank them! Force them to face you! Now! NOW!*

But she had no time.

The room shook with Ateru's laughter. "Prepare to meet your ancestors!"

"My ancestors," Kosori whispered, eyes lit from within, as if in epiphany.

She sang.

"Night always falls first,
Inside the valley.
The sun so eager,
It is always diving down."

A ghost froze still. It towered above her in its death shroud, mere inches away, its black hair unfurling, the gash across its chest bleeding spectral light. But no hatred shone behind its mask. Its eyes were confused, regarding Kosori with open wonder.

She spoke to it. "You remember that song, don't you? My grandmother used to sing it for me. She said her grandmother sang it for her."

Another leapt at her, screaming.

"We two are like moths,
Chasing the round moon.
If the sun won't watch,
Then we cannot trust ourselves."

It slowed to an uncertain trot, its guard lowering. Two more lowered their arms.

"This is a song from our people," Kosori said. "It is a Hyōketsu song. Remember it? Remember who you once were?"

Kosori's song touched all corners of the shrine. The orchid light softened, cooling to a faint blue. Spectral weapons clattered to the floor. Some of the onryō even sat at her feet, like children.

"Your ways were not lost," Kosori said. "Kaito no Momotsukihime kept them alive, folding them into the traditions of the shrine keepers and weaving them into folklore. She recorded your names in the family histories. You were not forgotten." She smiled at them. "We are kin. Our people are one. Remember."

The ghosts blinked with recognition. They made to remove their masks.

"Lies," Ateru growled.

Kosori flew into the wall and was pinned by an onryō's hand. It held her by her skull, its hand covering half of her face. Her limbs swung like a doll's. Mikazuki clattered to the floor.

No! Tsukune gritted against the pain, trying to rise. Her legs were wooden boards.

"They killed you," Ateru goaded the vengeful spirit. "They imprisoned you! If it is not true, why can't you leave?"

Kosori sang.

"Night always falls first,
Inside the valley.
The sun so eager,
It is always diving down."

The ghost let go. Kosori slumped to the floor, shaking. There were spectral burns where the ghost had touched her, luminescent flecks mingling with her birthmark. The ghosts lowered their guard. One clutched its shaking head.

"Kill her," Ateru said.

They climbed on top of her, shrieking, their thumbs pushed into her throat. Moonlight tears fell from their burning eyes.

Kosori croaked weakly. Tsukune could not hear the words.

"Enough!" Ateru leapt on the stage. "She speaks with two tongues! Crush her throat!"

Even as they choked her, she still mouthed the words. Every beat of Tsukune's heart surged urgency into her burning limbs. She pushed through a web of pain. Her eyes met Kosori's.

Instead of desperation, she saw knowing peace, a glimmer of hope.

They cannot be killed. Only appeased.

Of course.

Tsukune held her sword high. "Children of the Hyōketsu! Hear me!"

Spectral heads spun, dozens of coal-fire eyes lighting her at once.

"I am Shiba Tsukune, wielder of Ofushikai, champion of the Phoenix Clan! I am empowered to speak for the Elemental Masters; my word is law." She gestured to the spectral crowd. "You have been led astray, told that the Kaito have imprisoned you here. But it is your own anguish that ensnares you! The Kaito are your kin, and your ways live on with them."

The ghosts hesitated. Their eyes cleared.

Tsukune sheathed Ofushikai with a resounding snap. "And that makes you Phoenix!"

Tadaka's expression broke into open horror. She pushed this aside. They were onryō. They were Yobanjin. But they were also the Kaito's ancestors. The first ray of sunlight broke through the splintered ceiling, and as it graced the throng, the gossamer Phoenix crest appeared on their spectral clothing. Their masks fell away. They looked no different from Rokugani.

"I hereby acknowledge you as honored ancestors of the Kaito family, to be venerated and worshiped throughout these lands! Please take your rightful place and be remembered forever!"

The onryō vanished, no trace remaining behind.

Amaterasu's golden light touched the shrine in a gilded ray, painting the room in brilliant orange. Tadaka shook his head in disbelief. "How did you know that would work?"

"Kosori is the Kaito daimyō," Tsukune replied. "If she embraced her past, how could I not do the same?"

Coughing, Kosori stood. She smiled at Tsukune from her place on the stage.

Ateru rose behind her.

A cold rush. Tsukune started to yell, to sprint forward, but time fossilized around her. Kosori was smiling through her spectral burns, her eyes serene.

Then a red geyser burst from her neck. She struck the floor like a wet doll.

Heavy hands squeezed Tsukune's lungs. But she didn't hear her own scream. Ateru's knife glistened in the morning light.

"You think this is over?" he hissed. "There is no end to those the Phoenix have wronged!" He spun toward the inner sanctum. "I can always find more!" He bolted, a blur of mauve light, leaping in an arc and splashing into the well.

Tsukune stared at the pool forming around Kosori's unmoving body. It wasn't real. That hadn't just happened. Kosori was supposed to be the Kaito daimyō. She was chosen!

For you, it is "Tsukune-san." We're friends, aren't we?

There was no pain. Her wounds didn't matter. She opened her hand. Ofushikai leapt from the sheath of its own accord. Grasping the hilt, she marched into the inner sanctum. Beneath the waters of the well radiated a stormy violet light. She stepped onto the edge.

"Tsukune!" Tadaka shouted.

He was reaching for her, grasping, eyes flooded and overflowing. She'd never seen him like that before. He'd never really needed her. Had his posturing, his distant manner, been only a façade? Had he taken her for granted? Did he need her, after all?

It's too late, she thought. *I'm finishing this.*

She leapt in. Tadaka's voice, calling her name, fell away. The dark waters were cold. Tsukune embraced them.

CHAPTER ELEVEN

The well was a black ocean trench.

Ofushikai's pearls were an anglerfish's lure in the inky deep. Water filled Tsukune's lungs. She sank. Reaching out, her hand touched stone, the smooth texture of bricks followed by an unending sheet of cold metamorphic rock. But to her eyes, there was no wall. Only a churning mass of midnight clouds sculpted by sickly flashes, distant fluttering banners above the flashing tips of spears far below her.

Tōshigoku. The word came unbidden. The Realm of Slaughter churned just beyond her palm, as though she were separated by a pane of crystal ice.

"All she had to do was obey."

The voice came from everywhere. Ateru's. Tsukune spun and drew Ofushikai. The void consumed the blade's light.

"She was a mere priestess. What say did she have in matters of war?"

The water rippled. Her wheel was spinning.

"This happened because she stepped out of her place. She is to blame. When she killed me, she didn't even look at my face! She used a bow! A coward's weapon!"

The temperature rose. Hot water bubbled in her lungs. She tried to speak, but without air she had no voice, only bubbles trailing from her nostrils.

"I am an instrument of consequence. I will wipe out the Kaito and destroy all record of their existence. For what she did, for how I suffered, they will be forgotten as I was forgotten."

Her chest swelled. Her voice came like a bubble's pop. "She already paid her price."

The voice fell silent.

"She wanted to stop the senseless killing, your people and mine. She wanted to stop the desecration of sacred places. She knew that if she did nothing, the Hyōketsu would be wiped out. You are blaming her for your own mistakes." Her hands tightened around Ofushikai's hilt. "You are only angry because she wanted equal respect, and you thought that meant taking something from you. You are the one who would not listen. You led the Hyōketsu to their deaths. You don't want justice. You only want revenge."

"Little girl," the voice growled, "there is no difference."

A white flash. Her blood arced in the water. Her jaw cracked against the invisible wall.

Another. A sharp pain in her ribs. She lashed about, but found no opponent. Claws raked her thigh. The silk split and released a stream of red.

A knife hand from above. Her vision flickered. The abyss pulled her.

Ofushikai's reflection. In it, Ateru lunged.

She brought her blade up in time to catch his dagger. He pushed, driving her into the wall, pinning her flat. His shark maw opened, and she saw screaming faces in his throat. The water boiled around his spectral flesh.

"I have waited long enough! I will have my vengeance! They

thought they could bury me down here and forget. But I will not be silenced. My hate lives!" His eyes burned. "They may have forgotten the truth, but they remembered the demon!"

The water bubbled around her blade. Heat seared her cheek, boiling her flesh. Behind the violet cast of his spectral face was a screaming skull.

"And if I must burn every province, so be it! Even if it is raining spears and Jigoku itself has opened, I will wipe her line from Ningen-dō! *I will not be ignored!*"

He vanished. Tsukune sank, dragging, down to the bottom.

His voice was a whisper now. "Our sins are but shadows we drag along. Kaito's is inescapable. How long is the shadow of the Phoenix, I wonder?"

The floor pressed against her feet. She fell to a knee. Her vision blurred and her strength ebbed from her wounds. Shaking, fragile, she raised her head.

A battle unfolded around her like an animated mural. There were ancient warriors in broken armor, naked skeletons with spears, and dagger-wielding aristocrats still dressed in splendid silks. She saw tattered banners and clan crests: some she recognized, others she didn't. The beings killed each other, again and again, their white eyes wild, their faces without expression. Spectral blood, liquid of glowworm light, ran like a river. There were no sides. There was no reason. They were snakes eating their own tails. Above she saw turning oxcart wheels with screaming faces at their axles, each one set ablaze. Beyond the churning horde, something massive walked among them, snatching up bodies and biting off heads. It almost looked like a giant skeleton, but she could not be sure. All unfolded in complete silence.

Ateru stood between her and unfurled chaos. His back to her, he reached toward the phantom battlefield with his bone-hilted dagger.

"How many do you think will come when I call them? How many here have the Phoenix wronged? Daimyō? Families? Perhaps an entire clan." The dagger glowed. In the flicker of the light, the battlefield seemed less spectral, more real. Closer.

"Hero. Villain. What does it matter? All I care is that they are on my side. I will embrace anyone who hates the Phoenix." He glanced at her. "Look at you. You can't even stand." Back to the battlefield. "You are defeated for the same reason she was. You tried to defend people who were not your own." He held the dagger against the veil. "Ponder that in the next world."

He stopped. He turned.

Tsukune stood, ignoring her wounds, readying Ofushikai in her practiced stance.

"One more," she said.

His confident expression faded. His eyes widened. He held up his blade and called out to the Hyōketsu. Again and again. Nothing. For the first time, his coal-fire eyes deadened with dawning realization.

"They won't hear you from Yomi," Tsukune said. "They are Phoenix now."

He spun to the tapestry. The dagger shook impotently. Nothing.

"No one is coming," she said. "You are by yourself, Ateru. Whereas I..."

Looking up at the rafters where a gossamer woman pointed at the fraying rope.

Noticing the tree in the garden, where an armored man crossed his arms.

A spectral hand on her shoulder when she almost touched the bone-hilted dagger.

A wise sensei urging her to cross the forbidden screen.

Shiba Ujimitsu's smiling face.

A dozen spectral forms unfurled around her. Their armored

plates glowed with ethereal blue light, their shining blades reflecting on their serene faces. They each held a specter of Ofushikai. Like Phoenix Clan Champions.

She smiled. "…I am never alone."

His face twisted, his jaw distending with an animal roar. He lunged.

Her first strike knocked him aside. Her second shattered his dagger.

Her third cut him in two.

He screamed. Spectral blood, a splash of pearl against the ink, poured from his tear. As Tsukune followed through, a single droplet of his incandescent blood splashed into her right eye.

It was a white-hot shard, a spike driven into her socket. She gritted her teeth and blinked the lid, a trail of smoke snaking from beneath as she held her eye shut.

The battlefield rippled. Ateru jerked back, as if pulled in a riptide. His screams rattled Tsukune's teeth. With her good eye, she saw him pulled into that nightmarish tapestry beyond. Tōshigoku was finally claiming its own.

Then, he jerked forward and grabbed her kimono collar.

The current took her. She was being pulled in with him. She fought, leaning back, straining, clenching. She smelled fire and heard the crash of battle. Where Ateru's skeletal fingers gripped, the fabric curled and burned.

"I won't go alone!" he shouted, his voice filling her head. There was no hatred or desire for vengeance. Just fear, raw and cold. "I'll drag you there, too! I'll lash your soul to this realm! Unless you pull me back, unless–"

She leaned in. The current took them both.

He screamed. "You're insane! You'd willingly dive into that place?"

"If it will protect them from you, then absolutely." She looked into his confused eyes, her face serene and without regret. "My life, my soul, for the Phoenix."

As he screamed one final time, she closed her good eye, at peace with the world.

I cannot let you.

She opened her eye again. There was no current. She floated on the other side of the invisible veil. She was safe. But why?

And then she saw him. The glowing armor, the blue light, the serene face. Ujimitsu had tackled Ateru, throwing them both into the yawning void. Tōshigoku was hungry. It knew no difference between spectral dead.

His voice filled her mind one last time. *Thank you, Tsukune. Now my passing has purpose. Live on, and remind them what it means to be—*

The darkness swallowed them both. In her trembling hand, Ofushikai felt imperceptibly lighter.

As she floated numbly before the distant ethereal battleground, something stirred. She could not see it fully, for it was as if the planes were a painted lantern and the candle were slowly dimming. But she saw its silhouette, a massive suit of ebony armor, moving empty on its own. Two eyes, like lantern orbs, shone in the helm where its face should be, judging her. The hair on her forearms pricked up, and her heart waited to beat again. Guilt blanketed her soul.

Then its eyes softened. *No*, they seemed to say. *Not yet.*

Its gauntleted hand moved as if closing a shōji door. It, and the infinite battlefield, faded away.

One by one, the glowing champions collapsed into floating orbs. Like fireflies, they danced around the blade, casting their light against Tsukune's face. She watched them enter Ofushikai, melding with it like collecting mercury.

Ateru is gone, a voice said.

Another: *Tōshigoku is patient. It waited all this time.*

A third, more serene. *The Kaito's duty is complete now. The shrine is safe again.*

Tsukune let an air bubble give her a voice. "What of Ujimistu?"

There was a long silence.

Lost to us, a voice finally replied.

Despair pulled her eyes to the floor.

For now.

The last orb reabsorbed into the blade. As emptiness swelled in her chest again, Tsukune felt herself rising, limply, toward the surface of the well.

Tsukune pulled herself from the water with aching arms. Her tattered kimono clung wetly as she flopped to the shrine floor. Her hair formed a curtain around her face. The morning sun touched her skin, but she didn't feel it. She exhaled a stream and sat in a cold puddle, unmoving.

Six men formed a ring around her. They wore hooded cloaks emblazoned with a crest depicting an open eye. They held their naginata inches from her face, but made no motion to attack. They just watched.

Asako Maezawa stepped into the ring. "It's alright," he told them. "Stand down." He knelt beside her. "Tsukune-sama. What happened?"

She lifted her head. The curtain of hair parted from her face. They gasped. Tsukune's colorless right eye, flickering and translucent like a glowing orb, cast her face in a sickly light. Then, like a dying ember, the light faded.

"He's gone," she whispered limply. Her eyes swelled. "He's gone. He's gone."

Maezawa shook his head. "You poor child. What did they do to you?"

Realization broke her from her reverie. Beyond the ring, two others tended to Isawa Tadaka. He would not look at her. "Kosori!" he shouted. "He killed her. He–"

"Relax," Maezawa said reassuringly. "She lives."

Above her, the sky brightened.

He nodded. "It was close. Her spirit clung by only a thread. But I was able to save her."

She read his eyes. "You're not telling me everything."

His smile dampened. "The ghost. It… it touched her here, yes?" He gestured to his throat.

Tsukune's brow furrowed. "Why? What… what does that mean?"

Maezawa looked away.

Although it was morning, no matter how she strained, Tsukune could not hear the waking songs of the mountain birds.

CHAPTER TWELVE

Tsukune spent three weeks in a bed facing away from the unlucky directions. Servants came every day, washing her wounds, applying healing herbs, and rebandaging. They gave her a straw-colored tea that tasted of barley. When the pain of her broken ribs stole her sleep, the servants drew her curtains and gave her *chandu* to smoke. It didn't make the pain go away, but it made her stop caring and filled her with an energetic rush. At night they burned tea leaves and fennel in a burlap sack above her bed, until eventually, tired of the thick and smoke-filled air, she opened her window to let it out. When they discovered this, they said it was a good sign.

Most of all, they did not stare at her right eye, where her glossy iris had become a sickly purple. Each day her new reflection startled her less and less. She decided to wear her hair in a veil over the right side of her face. This seemed to make others more comfortable with it.

She tried walking again in the third week. Her joints were like planks, but soon she was performing her daily exercises, until finally the warden, distressed over the state of the floor mats, requested she try these outside.

By the shrine's precipice, construction of the new stone bridge was progressing swiftly. The scrapes and hammering of masons' tools resounded over the valley. It was a more expensive endeavor than the swinging bridge, but that was alright. Tsukune would ensure it didn't cost the Kaito anything.

There, she found Kosori. The girl was practicing her archery when Tsukune approached, a breeze seeming to lift the arrow to the target, dead center. Kosori whispered her thanks before realizing Tsukune was there. Her wide smile touched her shining eyes.

"Congratulations, Tsukune-san. You lived."

A shudder snaked down Tsukune's back. Pain rippled across Kosori's features when she spoke, her voice full of gravel and broken glass. It was barely more than a raspy whisper.

Pressure built in Tsukune's chest. Tears, bitter and hot, glossed her vision. Kosori's expression warmed, melting, and she shook her head urgently. She didn't want Tsukune to be upset.

But after this, how could Tsukune ever show her face to Kosori again? Kosori had loved to sing. It was her gift from the Fortunes. Hadn't Tsukune only been a curse to Kosori, when all Kosori had shown her was trust and kindness?

She looked away. "I'm sorry, Kosori. I… I ruined your life. I…"

Gentle hands on her shoulders. Kosori's eyes winced for a moment, no voice coming. But she mouthed the words, and Tsukune could hear them as clearly as if Kosori could speak.

"The art of archery is the art of letting go."

Shaking, Tsukune nodded. If Kosori did not hate her for this, then she supposed she shouldn't hate herself either. She stepped back, rubbed her face, and recomposed herself. "You're going to be a great daimyō, Lady Kosori." She paused. "Which is fortunate, because the Kaito family is receiving a new duty."

Kosori's brow furrowed. When Tsukune told her, she beamed and bowed low.

•••

Asako Maezawa bowed as Tsukune left Kosori to resume her practice. "It is good to see you up and about, Tsukune-sama. I'm glad you did not make a liar of me."

"You do that well enough yourself," she replied.

He laughed. "Well, I've had a long time to practice."

She showed no amusement.

"You'll be well enough to ride a horse in another week or so," he remarked. "Your recovery was very fast. How is your arm?" He looked at her shoulder. "I am still amazed you didn't realize your collarbone was broken."

She extended her arm and made a fist. "It feels too slow. Stiff. I can't pull it back all the way."

"You should recover most of the motion. I'm afraid it may never be *quite* the same. But you'll always know when it's about to rain!" His smile never dropped. "All things considered, you are quite lucky. It could have been worse."

"Like Kosori, you mean."

He nodded. "The ki of the meridian was disrupted beyond my ability to restore. I did what I could."

"What of Tadaka?" Her voice cracked at his name. "He recovered?"

"Completely." Maezawa scratched his ear. "He left a few weeks ago to deliver his report to the council. He expressed regret that he had to leave so suddenly. He... he did ask me to watch over you. He wanted to say goodbye in person but... well."

"He could not show his face."

Maezawa looked away. "As you say, Tsukune-sama."

Two dragonflies danced along the cliffside fringe. She sighed at the pinprick in her heart. "He wanted so badly to prove the council wrong. I tried to help, but he just pushed me away."

"To be completely fair to him, I would not be here if we had not suspected Jigoku's forces were at work. Thankfully, we were mistaken."

She regarded him sideways. "Who are 'we'? Some secret society within the Phoenix?"

"You could say that." His smile twitched. "Forgive my amusement that the council has not yet mentioned the Inquisitors in your presence. We watch for signs of corruption and act accordingly. Which naturally requires a certain degree of... discretion."

"How long have you been investigating Tadaka?" she asked.

The old man blinked. "Tadaka is not under investigation." He paused. "Should he be?"

She frowned. "You said there was a darkness within him."

"There is. Emotionally, he is quite burdened. It is obvious he cares a great deal about you, but now that things have changed for you both, he feels he must push you away. It is not healthy for him to be so dishonest about his feelings." He tilted his head. "What did you think I meant?"

"Never mind," she replied, cheeks reddening. Why didn't anyone ever speak plainly?

He shrugged. "In any case, we are grateful for your discovery. The histories of the Kaito will be quite useful to us. It is generous of Kosori to share them."

"I suspect the Kaito are done denying their past. A new wing will be erected in Cliffside Shrine for the worship of their oldest ancestors."

"There might be something in those documents for the council as well," he added. "It notes the exact date when the well began to thaw. It corresponds with when their waterfalls unfroze, and the mountain climate became more hospitable to certain insect wildlife."

"The elemental imbalance," Tsukune concluded. "It's been

happening for longer than we thought. The overactive fire kami is what melted the well and freed Ateru." She thought for a moment. "If the Kaito histories recorded this temperature change, why didn't they do anything?"

"They thought it was normal," Maezawa replied.

"Normal?"

Maezawa's splotchy eyes tilted to the cerulean sky. "Why wouldn't they? Anyone who remembers the well when it was frozen has long since retired. They are in monasteries or urns. Or else they're too stubborn for either." He chuckled. "In light of this, it makes sense that they would not recognize the warnings. It is the nature of man to proceed as if his actions have no consequences.

"That's the joke fate plays on mortals," he continued, meeting her gaze. "Even when old and withered, we are but children when fate takes us. Ten years to grow a tree, a hundred to produce a grove, and one thousand to educate a person. Only our experiences we treat as real. Anything else, we disregard." He looked back to the Heavens. "This world is merely the manifestation of the collective karma of all living beings, and karma is nothing more than consequences of thoughts and actions."

"Then you believe human beings are responsible for the elemental imbalance?" Tsukune asked. "That it is not a part of a natural cycle?"

"There is a natural cycle to the elements' rise and fall. But to say that our actions cannot impact the world is perhaps the haughtiest and most prideful thing I can think of." He sighed. "At least it worked out this time. Imagine if you were not here, Tsukune-sama. I dare not contemplate."

She stared at him for a long time.

"I should take your head," she whispered.

"You'd be justified," he agreed.

Her hand rested on her sword hilt. "You tried to kill us."

"You are within your rights. Go ahead."

He seemed frail. He was a candle wick that had burned too long.

"But know that I would do it again," he said. "I couldn't let him escape. If he did, he could have destroyed the Kaito. Would that satisfy his hatred? No. He would attack the villages. Would that sate him? No. He would attack the surrounding provinces. Then the Phoenix directly. Then the neighboring clans. And so on. People would die without knowing why, clutching to their confusion and hatred. How many more onryō would that create? How vast would Tōshigoku's numbers swell?" He shrugged. "Then again, perhaps not. Surely he would be defeated eventually. But I could not take that chance." He opened his palm and stared at the tattoo there, a wide-open eye. "The Asako's purpose is to heal. But sometimes, to save the body, one must cut off the arm. Thankfully, a severed arm can still grasp its sword.

"Anyway." Without looking at her, he pulled down his collar, exposing his neck. "Do what your honor demands. I commit myself to the next life."

Tsukune's grip tightened. She was justified, wasn't she? The Kaito would have defeated Ateru. The old man didn't have to cut the bridge and trap them inside. In fact, he was ultimately why Kosori lost her voice. It was treason, plain and simple. Attempting to cause the death of a Clan Champion was unforgivable. She had every right to take his life. What was a samurai if not an instrument of karma? To kill him here would be justice. Fair and–

From whence come these thoughts?

She stopped. The knuckles of her sword hand were white. Somewhere a bush warbler called, and another answered. Her right eye was tearing up. She touched the wetness. At her fingertips rested droplets of glowing moonlight.

She uncurled her fingers from Ofushikai. "It would be a waste," she said. Maezawa drew out his pipe. They both watched the northern mountains rake the passing clouds.

"I'm making you my personal advisor," Tsukune decided.

Surprised, he bowed. "I am humbled, my lady. I'll serve you as best I can."

"You haven't gotten off easy." She plucked the pipe from his hands and leaned in closely. Showed him her sickly purple eye. "Your life is mine now, such as it is. You'd best stick around for a little while longer."

Tsukune left, taking the pipe with her.

Maezawa blinked in her wake. In the distance, Kosori's arrow struck the bell of Cliffside Shrine. The chime resounded throughout the valley.

He smiled. "At last, the Phoenix Clan Champion. I wondered if she was going to show up."

EPILOGUE

"They are ready."

Tsukune turned. Her brocaded silks and pale hakama invoked a flame dancing above a blessed candle, her kataginu proudly displaying the crest of the Phoenix Champion. "Lead on," she said. Tetsu nodded.

Soon they stood beneath a pagoda roof in the Garden of No Mind. The dancing grasses had become golden tipped as autumn painted the lands in new colors. They climbed the steps to the stone teahouse. Rain was falling in spite of the sun.

"Hm," Tetsu remarked. "A fox's wedding."

She glanced at him with a smirk. "That's right. A fox's wedding."

When they reached the top, Tetsu reached into his satchel and withdrew a thin bound stack of pages. Tsukune brightened when she saw it. "That's all of them?"

"All but a collection of letters, which I am still assembling." Tetsu offered her the stack. "Ujimitsu-sama wrote in this journal every day since he drew Ofushikai. It contains many of his deepest insights."

She accepted it with grateful hands. "Thank you." She ran her fingers across the weathered pages. "I want to learn everything I can about him. I will return it soon."

Tetsu flashed a smile. "Keep it. It is yours. Sensei would have wanted that."

Their gazes lingered together. Leaves fell from the ancient oak at the center of the Grove of the Five Masters.

"I'm sorry, Tetsu-san." Tsukune kept her eye on the pond. "I know I can never replace him."

He would not look at her.

"And I know you would rather it was you that had been chosen. You are the better fighter, Tetsu. I need to work hard before I'll ever be at your level. I'm still not sure why the sword chose me." She looked to the sky. "But whatever the reason, I won't find it by hiding from my feelings, or trying to replace the others. I'm going to do things differently. I'm going to do my best." She smiled at him, the sunlight caught in her spectral eye. "How about you?"

Tetsu watched her enter the chamber of the Masters. "Me, too," he whispered. "Me, too."

The Masters took their seats as Tsukune entered. She approached confidently, stopping just beyond the lip of the table. Five Masters were here: Tsuke, Azunami, Eju...

No Rujo. The Earth Master was gone.

Seated in his place was Isawa Tadaka. His hands, fingers laced, rested on the stone table, his wide-brimmed conical hat nearly concealing his eyes. And there was something new: a crimson cloth wrapped around his face. On his chest was the jade-tinted crest of the Master of Earth.

Tsukune sighed. *I see.*

"Ah, Tadaka-san!" said Isawa Ujina as he sat beside his son. "I'm glad you could make it. I heard your caravan in Crab lands was delayed."

Tadaka's voice was only slightly muffled by the mask.

Legend of the Five Rings

"Temporary setbacks. I am used to them." He regarded her openly. "Hello, Tsukune. It has been some time."

"Congratulations on your recent appointment," she replied.

His eyes smiled.

"Now then," Ujina said, rapping the table with his cane. The Masters quieted. "You are the one who called this meeting, champion. What is this all about?"

As one, the Masters turned to her. Tadaka set his cheek on his hand, the amusement never leaving his eyes.

Taking a deep breath, she spoke.

"Honored Masters, recently unfolding events in Garanto Province have made clear the extent of the threat caused by the elemental imbalance. Our Empire is a garden where gods once walked, and as such, sacred places are without number. In light of what the fire imbalance unleashed in Cliffside Shrine, and knowing that many other shrines serve similar functions, I cannot imagine what else has been released."

"These are matters that the council has already considered," Tsuke replied.

Tsukune nodded. "I understand. I called this gathering to make clear my intentions." She met Tadaka's unflinching eyes. "I am launching my own investigation into the matter of the elemental imbalance. I have recruited the Kaito family for this purpose, as they have proven themselves in my eyes and won my confidence in this matter. Their orders are to investigate shrines, maintain the elemental order, and await the arrival of an Isawa shugenja to report their findings and set right whatever has been imbalanced. The Shiba family shall incur any unforeseen costs of this investigation, and it is my hope that by shouldering this duty, it will provide useful information for this council while freeing the Isawa from burdening distractions."

The Master of Water spoke. "This is not necessary, Tsukune-sama. This council and the Isawa have this matter well in hand. You needn't burden yourself."

"I am not asking permission. The Kaito have already begun."

Stunned silence prevailed for several moments.

"Outrageous!" Isawa Tsuke stood. "You have no such authority! The Kaito are an Isawa vassal."

"It does seem a little hasty," the Water Master agreed. "On what grounds did you believe you could do this?"

Tadaka watched her silently from the other side of the table. His eyes never left hers.

"My duty is to protect the Phoenix from all threats. The Phoenix's duty is to protect the Empire's spirit. A gardener who ignores their weeds dooms the garden. And so I have acted, and it is within my purview to do so." She lowered her head. "Even so, the Shiba bow to the Isawa, as always. I will stop if you so order." She let the light touch her spectral eye. "But only if."

Again, the chamber fell silent.

"Give her a chance," said Tadaka.

They all regarded him. His cheek still planted in his fist, he shrugged. "I see no reason to disallow a concurrent investigation. The Kaito are quite capable."

"It *could* provide useful information," Tsuke admitted.

The Water Master drummed her fingers. "Assuming knowledge of the existence of the elemental imbalance remains within the Phoenix until this council's approval to reveal it…" She leaned back. "Then I have no objections."

Tsuke crossed his arms. Then, after some time, he nodded.

"Then it is permitted," said Ujina. "The council wishes the Kaito great success in their new duty."

Tsukune bowed.

•••

She saw him again that evening. She was sitting by the butterburs, composing a letter to the Crane Clan Champion, when his tall shadow raked the pink moss and fluttering grasses, cicadas keening in his wake. She wasn't certain if he'd seen her or not. Even though he was silhouetted, the crest of the Earth Master glowed on his back beneath the golden cracks of dusk's breaking.

And for a brief moment, she saw herself beside him. They were laughing. Younger.

That is not your path anymore.

She closed her eyes. *I know.* When she opened them, he was gone.

There is a piece of Tōshigoku with you now. It will serve you or become your master. Your trials have only started. And one day, your soul will join us. You will be a guide for whoever is next.

The sun torched the horizon. Where its shadows touched, Tsukune saw firelights blinking into being, like a thousand tiny lanterns. Separate, they were frail. Together, they lit the gardens in defiance of the night.

So be it, she thought. Her fingers curled around Ofushikai. *I am not afraid anymore.*

My life, my soul, for the Phoenix.

WHISPERS OF SHADOW AND STEEL

MARI MURDOCK

CHAPTER ONE

Bayushi Yojiro chafed his hands together as his rickshaw crept along Mercantile Avenue in Ryokō Owari Toshi, the City of Lies. The Scorpion Clan rarely granted second chances, and his had come in the form of exile to the most indulgent – and dangerous – city in Rokugan. He shrank behind his high collar. What trap lurked behind the decadence?

The well-worn cobblestones of the famed Merchant Quarter were nearly invisible beneath the crowds of people bursting from shops and milling between tents. The pounding clamor of street musicians' cymbals shook the air, mingling with oppressive clouds of heavy perfume, cooking oil, and sweat. Around the merchants and buyers, teetering mountains of silks, dried tea leaves, exotic fruits, incense, lacquerware, and spices sprawled like the Spine of the World Mountains themselves. Voices clashed in the ruckus of trade, sellers bellowing prices and guaranteeing bargains, customers haggling and comparing quality. A red silk palanquin with a horned roof, belonging perhaps to some noble lady, sliced through the crowd. It disappeared as swiftly as it had come, born aloft by six heavily muscled servants, gliding above the market's commotion like a pleasure barge atop the writhing sea.

Travelers from all the Great Clans mingled in a chaos of hues. A Crane Clan noblewoman, dressed in a flowing blue kimono with a crown of silk flowers atop her white hair, inspected the artistry of some tapestries while her *yōjimbō* kept the crowds at bay. A pair of gruff Unicorn Clan warriors, trimmed in bear-fur boots and armed with sleek Moto scimitars, disputed the price for a cage of rare falcons. A towering Crab samurai with a missing ear elbowed everyone in his path as he followed the beckoning glances of *maiko* geisha in luxurious gowns, who giggled as they headed toward the ferry wharves to sail back to the Licensed Quarter.

Yojiro huddled in his rickshaw, overwhelmed by the swell and clangor of the masses, so different from the immaculate, spacious streets and neatly sorted bazaars of Otosan Uchi. He had left the capital city expecting difference, knowing Ryokō Owari's reputation for being "a gilded ruin", but this grinding disorder was proving oppressive. Perhaps Ryokō Owari Toshi – "Journey's End City" – was far enough away from the heavenly sovereign to avoid the emperor's celestial influence.

The darkness bothered Yojiro the most. Above his head rattled rows of the city's red and black Scorpion Clan banners and clusters of paper lanterns. These, strung between the unnaturally wide eaves of the sloped rooftops, crowded the air above, which seemed as full as the streets. They blocked much of the sunlight and cast long, deep shadows even at midday. The dimness played tricks on his eyes; when he passed a vendor, he thought she was selling human skulls. Only when a woman put one on her face did Yojiro realize they were actually theater masks. Another time, a horned *oni* emerged from a tofu shop, driving his hand to his katana. The demon was a child upon her father's shoulders, her horns two looped braids in her hair. Yojiro could only curse himself for being a fool so many times before he eventually stopped looking.

Yojiro's rickshaw puller, a sun-scorched peasant with a pocked face, eased to a halt, paused, and stared as though waiting for something. The buffeting wall of merchants and tourists among the goods and kiosks was as thick as ever, and he seemed hesitant to aggressively pitch himself into the swarm. He let go of the handrail to wipe sweat from his brow.

"We are almost at Shosuro Palace, magistrate," he croaked to Yojiro. "Just past this bazaar, through the Pious Gate, beyond the wall, and all the way–"

"Yes, thank you," Yojiro said, cutting off the man's exaggerated account of the route. Shosuro Palace's sloped granite foundation and crimson-tiled keep rose mere streets away, not more than half an hour's stroll. "I think I shall walk from here."

"No, no, no," the man objected, picking up the handrail again but making no effort to press on. "You said to the palace, so I will take you."

"I will still pay you for the rest of the journey," Yojiro assured the puller, ignoring the man's insistent greed. He drew a green silk purse from his pocket, a recess safely sewn deep in the breast of his black and crimson kimono. "I did say to the palace, so you will get that fare."

The rickshaw puller grinned stupidly, an air of self-congratulation at his slyness wrinkled into his pitted cheeks. The dim light crinkled the man's face into a more demonic visage than the little girl's. Yojiro ignored the impulse to squint, just to be sure. He tossed the man his coins and barely had time to step down into the street before the puller vanished, adeptly ducking into a dark alley, rickshaw and all.

This would never happen to an Emerald magistrate in Otosan Uchi. And this trick from a member of my own clan.

He folded his hands into his kimono sleeves and stepped into the masses.

I suppose that in a pit full of scorpions, some begin to eat one another.

As though instantiating his thoughts, the nimble fingers of a pickpocket suddenly tickled his side. Hand in Yojiro's side pocket, the small boy pretended to stare at a grotesque dancing dog. Yojiro let the tiny hand scuttle away disappointed. The child scampered toward the same alley as the rickshaw puller, and the peasant's pockmarked oni face jutted out from the shadows. He grabbed the boy by the collar, cursing and reaching inside his own kimono to indicate the location of Yojiro's purse. His eyes seethed with fury as he spotted Yojiro watching them from the crowd. The conspirators vanished into the dark alley again, like rats into their hole.

They aren't the only thieves.

Yojiro had already noticed dozens of tricksters in the bazaar, cheating customers and each other. Some used scales with false centers of balance or chains of differing metals to weight one side more than the other. Others used abacuses with fixed beads or movable bead columns to falsely calculate prices and cargo quantities. And nearly every merchant could deftly palm coins or cut purse strings. Some even tried to hide their affiliation with the Scorpion, masquerading as peddlers from minor clans, their exaggerated country dialects and cheap costumes with shoddily embroidered badgers or foxes actually fooling the tourists. Many, just like Yojiro's two rats, emerged from or disappeared into dark alleys flanked with looming walls and occluded by sweeping tile roofs. The dim shade of the narrow passageways concealed their movements, probably by design.

As one would expect from the Scorpion Clan's most visited city.

The Scorpion crest woven across the front of Yojiro's clothes suddenly felt heavy, a burden. Everyone could see it. Anyone might assume he was like those scorpions in the pit. A liar. Always concealing something. They might think this even though he was a samurai, sworn to uphold the sacred tenets of Bushidō, embracing virtues like righteousness, sincerity, honor. Virtues he would gladly give his life to uphold.

But what about your soul, Yojiro?

A disturbing memory wriggled in the back of his mind. Bleak trees wreathed with empty armor and broken blades. A frigid wind stirred the leaves, but all else lay still.

He immediately shoved it away.

A Scorpion banner flapped before him in the mild breeze. The crest's tail hung over him, as if about to strike, poised and waiting for the right moment.

Am I really one of them?

He wandered past a few more stands when the pickpocket, squat and skulking in the dimness like a goblin, appeared again. The boy casually snipped the strings of a tall Dragon Clan woman's coin pouch as he snuck by. In two strides, Yojiro was at his side, clutching his shoulder in a firm fist. Wordlessly, he snatched the money from the boy's fingers.

"Excuse me," Yojiro called to the woman. He held out her purse. "I am afraid you dropped this by accident."

The woman eyed Yojiro and the boy suspiciously, snatching her bag from him. "Yes, that is mine," she snapped, forcing it open to count her coins. Assured of its contents, she let her face soften. "Daikoku be praised for preserving my money. I shall say an extra prayer at his temple in thanks." She smiled until her eyes fell upon the Scorpion Clan crest on his clothes. She marched away with no second glance. Yojiro bit his lip. Perhaps it had been a poor choice to approach the Dragon, given the circumstances...

Yojiro had been sent to Ryokō Owari to arbitrate a scandal involving the Dragon Clan. Bayushi Aramoro, half-brother to the Scorpion Clan Champion, Bayushi Shoju, had been arrested for killing a minor Dragon official. The involvement of such a high-ranking samurai threatened the already strained diplomatic relations between the two clans.

"He stands accused of murder without cause," Akodo Toturi had explained in their private meeting back in Otosan Uchi. The Lion Clan samurai's generally inscrutable demeanor had cracked under the situation's strain; his eyes clouded as his mind reeled through possible resolutions. "Naturally, a minor death like this would result in few repercussions. However, the present moment finds this news most inopportune, coming on the heels of that *iaijutsu* duel between Kitsuki Shomon and Bayushi Gensato to resolve a public insult and amid suspicion that the Dragon petition about the Perfect Land Sect was sabotaged by Scorpion-spread gossip. Yes, the two clans are at each other's throats. I have heard rumors of annulments and even blatant violations of treaties between the two sides."

"It surely is not as bad as you say, Toturi-sama," Yojiro had said.

"Perhaps, but I received a personal visit from Kitsuki Yaruma, Dragon Clan liaison to the Imperial capital. He hinted at the possibility of trade embargoes against the Scorpion. Such a move would demand other political retaliation. This situation could very well spiral out of control for the Empire."

Yojiro had been confused. In his earlier meetings with Lady Kachiko and other Scorpion nobles about long-term diplomatic strategies, he had heard no whisper of intent to increase political difficulty with the Dragon. He also couldn't believe that Lord Shoju would let his own half-brother be implicated in such a petty ordeal as a minor official's death. Especially on the cusp of a major political battle. Let alone publicly! It simply was not their way. Too blatant. Too sloppy. If Aramoro had been caught and imprisoned, he had let himself be caught and imprisoned.

But what could our clan gain from such a scandal as the public killing of a minor Dragon official?

As if the Emerald Champion could read his mind, Toturi had answered, "Yojiro-san, I do not know what advantage the Scorpion hope for in implicating Aramoro in such trouble. However, you and I can guess that they have a plan in place. And you and I can also guess that Governor Shosuro Hyobu and her administrators will likely interfere with the investigations surrounding this incident. I have already addressed some of Yaruma's complaints by arranging for Aramoro to be held somewhere other than the Shosuro Palace dungeons, and I have ordered the city's Emerald magistrate, Otomo Seno, to take charge of the inquiry. However, I have need of further assurances on the matter."

"What would the Emerald Champion ask of me?"

"I know you have already done me a great favor, Yojiro-san, to the detriment of your reputation among your clan," he said, referring to the tournament of the Emerald Champion. Yojiro had tilted his head, as if ignorant of what Toturi referred to. As the tournament overseer, Yojiro had covertly warned Toturi of a Scorpion plot to sabotage the duel, helping Toturi win but losing the trust of his clan. To acknowledge such an act publicly would be admitting to acting against his clan. "I did no such favor, my lord," he said, warning Toturi with his eyes.

In turn, Toturi had hesitated, pausing to recant his improper assertion against Yojiro's honor.

"I must have been mistaken. Forgive me." A quick calculation troubled his face before he spoke again. "But I now ask you, for the sake of honor, will you go to Ryokō Owari Toshi as my representative, help in the investigation, and prevent any... interference?"

Toturi's request had pounded a sore spot in Yojiro's heart. His clan already mistrusted him. To challenge them with the Emerald Champion's authority would be political suicide.

His age-old conflict between loyalty to country and loyalty to clan had boiled within him once again, but he had answered the Emerald Champion without hesitation.

"I will do as you ask."

He was sincere in his desire to obey Toturi, to prevent dishonorable acts from impeding the investigation, but he could not afford another damning failure as far as the Scorpion were concerned.

"Uncle, you're hurting my shoulder!" the pickpocket hissed, wriggling in Yojiro's grip. He kicked Yojiro's shins to no effect. "Let me go!" A pit grew in Yojiro's stomach as he observed the child's grimy hair and pouting tears.

I have cheated this boy twice today.

Again, his responsibility as a samurai demanded action. Courtesy. Compassion. Yojiro scattered a few coins onto the ground for the urchin before releasing him. The boy scooped up the money and dashed away, disappearing into another rathole. A brazen ointment seller suddenly latched onto Yojiro's arm and shoved a box of pungent slime into his face. The acrid perfume of sulfur and fermenting ginger grated in his nose. "For your wrinkles!" the man cried. "Your troubles age you, sir. But today you are in luck! I discovered this special formula after being blessed by Jurōjin with a dream. A vision of longevity! This paste will dissolve all your sorrows—"

Flames suddenly erupted from a fried-noodle stand, causing nearby cages of monkeys to shriek. Yojiro took the interruption to flee, melting in the crowd.

Soon, he turned down Alabaster Street, hoping to skirt the rest of the bazaar's seething commotion, on his way to Shosuro

Palace. The avenue was narrow and infested with openings to tunneling alleys. As he walked briskly, he felt a prickle at the back of his neck. He hesitated. The dark corners were vacant, but out of the corner of his eye, it seemed a blood-red mist was lilting past the far end of the alley to his right. He turned. The alley was vacant: it was just an empty shadow.

Yojiro stopped walking, gripping his katana at the mouth of its scabbard.

"Who is there?" he called.

The skinny pickpocket slinked out of the shadows.

"Uncle, you forgot something," the boy called out, grinning in malicious amusement.

"What is that, child?"

Yojiro smelled the waft of gutter flesh too late. A pair of hands snaked under his arms and coiled up behind his head, pulling his grip from his katana's hilt and rendering his arms immobile in the air. The rank, wheezing breath and greasy skin of his captor identified him as the rickshaw puller. With ease, Yojiro slipped down, out of the man's grip, and slammed an elbow deep into his belly. The puller fell, gasping.

Yojiro turned to speak to the boy again, but the child was gone. Instead, the alley was now blocked by the red silk palanquin with the horned roof. Its six lumbering servants set it down and glared at Yojiro with brutish ferocity. From behind the crimson curtain, a sumptuously dressed man emerged. Strings of onyx beads wound about his neck and shoulders, and he had several golden teeth. The Scorpion Clan crest was embroidered across the collar and sleeves of his kimono, but the wicked gleam in his eye proved more revealing. This was evidently one of Ryokō Owari's crime lords.

"The child is right, magistrate," the man said, his voice calm, reassured: the tone of a man used to getting everything he wanted. He brandished a long, carnelian and brass pipe in the shape of a scorpion, its blue-gray smoke seeping between his sneering lips. "You forgot that this is not in your jurisdiction. As a citizen assigned to the neighborhood watch, I am the one obliged to mete out justice here. Isn't that right, Buyu?"

"Yes, Ikku-sama," the rickshaw puller confirmed, a hint of cringing fear in his voice. "This quarter is yours."

"Ha ha. He exaggerates," Ikku laughed. "But what you did to that poor boy – stealing his money – and just now to this rickshaw puller is inexcusable. In my duty to uphold this neighborhood's peace, I cannot tolerate robbers and brawlers. As a magistrate yourself, surely you must understand this."

Yojiro folded his hands into his sleeves, a feigned gesture of humility as he calculated the speed with which he could draw his sword should words not work. Despite his training, six guards in a narrow backstreet would prove difficult, and he had no idea what other minions Ikku might command forth from the shadows.

"Pardon my intrusion, sir," Yojiro said, ignoring the temptation to eye the other dark corners of the street. He needed confidence now. Composure. Delicacy. "I am unfamiliar with your local rules, having only just arrived in Ryokō Owari from the capital on official business for the Emerald Champion."

The crime lord smiled, his teeth glimmering in the dimness. He rudely pointed at Yojiro with his pipe. "Surely, coming from Otosan Uchi, you should know that not even Emerald magistrates are above the law."

"No, we are not," Yojiro agreed. "Then, I humbly ask forgiveness. I shall refrain from further troubling you and these humble people."

"Forgiveness is insufficient for justice's demands, magistrate," the crime lord chortled. He spilled the spent ashes in his pipe into the street and signaled his enforcers toward Yojiro with a casual gesture.

Yojiro lowered his stance slightly, centering his balance to react to an attack. "Perhaps I might ask Governor Hyobu to help me satisfy the demands of your justice. Doesn't her Thunder Guard enforce the governor's law here?"

"They could if they were here, but you are lucky I got to you first, magistrate. They are less… understanding than I am. The kami only know how many cells these Thunder Guard fill. How many bodies they leave behind. Since you have only slightly wronged these gentle citizens, I ask you pay a small fine to clear up this misunderstanding. Then you can avoid a more… enthusiastic punishment."

"His purse is in a breast pocket!" Buyu called out.

The crime lord nodded. His brutes were now within striking range. "Now, magistrate, you have a simple choice. Pay the fine and continue on your important 'official' business. Or…"

Yojiro grimaced. Duty demanded his mission take priority. Even if he could win this battle, angering a local crime lord might make his task more difficult, especially if he were to get caught up on the wrong side of the Thunder Guard. For now, he had to bend with the wind.

He drew his green purse and threw it. Ikku caught it, rubbing the coins inside, smirking.

"This is the right choice, magistrate," he said, climbing back into his palanquin. "Enjoy your stay in our city. I look forward to seeing you again."

The gang members dispersed, each disappearing into a different rathole, leaving Yojiro alone. Hopefully. He double-checked the shadows to see if the alleys were empty. Nothing moved, yet the exaggerated eaves of the surrounding buildings made the dark unfathomable from a few paces away.

Curse the architect.

Yojiro finally left Alabaster Street, the road ending in front of a twenty-foot stone wall, the perimeter separating the Merchant Quarter from the Noble Quarter. He approached the Pious Gate, an enormous entrance with lintels studded in gold flowers and carved with peacocks, tigers, and scorpions. Its imposing bronze-bound doors cast the illusion of an oasis in the midst of the bazaar's turmoil, promising refinement and order beyond its threshold. But Yojiro knew better.

If the Merchant Quarter is this city's den of thieves, then surely I will find Ryokō Owari's master deceivers in the Noble Quarter. If I am not careful, I may lose more than my purse.

CHAPTER TWO

Yojiro squinted in the faint light, the bare walls and exceptionally thick shōji paper of the window screens offering no sense of direction in the mazelike halls of Shosuro Palace. He only kept his bearings by noticing subtle blemishes in the cherry floorboards, but the dimness made those difficult to follow.

Even the palace is a dark alley.

He was escorted by a squad of four spear-wielding Thunder Guard soldiers and their captain, Shosuro Denmaru. Their red and black armor mingled with the shadows, and the crimson plumes atop their helmets trailed after them like bloody streams.

Did Ikku speak the truth about them?

Denmaru's wrinkles and a patch of fire-scarred flesh on the left side of his jaw gave his face the illusion of being carved from rough stone. A slight limp indicated an old injury on the same side, but the samurai's adjusted gait did nothing to hinder his balance or precision of footfall. His hands also bore scorch marks.

"How long have you been in the service of Governor Hyobu, captain?" Yojiro asked.

"Her whole career," he answered, his gaze fixed on their path through the labyrinth. "I was her yōjimbō before being assigned to the Thunder Guard when she became governor."

"She must put a great deal of faith in you to have kept you so close for over twenty years," Yojiro replied, hoping his compliment would soften the Shosuro samurai.

"Hyobu-sama does whatever is necessary," Denmaru grunted absently. "As do I."

"Naturally. I have heard great stories about the Thunder Guard," Yojiro continued. "Its long history boasts many impressive feats. Defending the city from Lion Clan invasions centuries ago. Battling the opium cartels. Breaking up smuggling rings. Saving the Noble Quarter from fires."

Denmaru did not flinch at the word "fire" as Yojiro had anticipated. Instead, the captain smiled with puckered lips, as if the word conjured a bittersweet memory. "The work of my comrades to control this city is indeed valiant."

"Surely, yours as well. It seems we in Otosan Uchi heard news of the last fire only… six or seven years ago."

The captain merely shrugged. "I helped."

Yojiro huddled back into his high collar. Toturi's request for him to prevent Scorpion interference specifically referred to working around Hyobu and her Thunder Guard, and this aloof conversation proved worrisome.

Would she be as difficult to work with?

Finally, the appearance of a lavish silk and cloth of gold curtain broke the uniformity of the hallways. Denmaru parted the brocade silently with a strong arm, revealing another dark room.

"Governor Hyobu is in here."

"Thank you, captain," Yojiro replied. "You have been an immense help."

The Thunder Guard and his infantry merely marched away, the darkness of the corridor swallowing them.

Yojiro entered the parlor, but the maze of gossamer canopies and tapestried hangings tangled in a pall of fragrant brazier smoke proved blinding. His eyes slowly attuned to the gloom, revealing the room's furnishings. Between the tangle of silk and drapery, decorative screens and curtains of ivory beads concealed all walls, masking the true size of the room. Every few paces revealed rearing dark brass statues of frolicking animals. Or dancers? Rare ebony porcelain vases balanced on every flat surface, filled with glinting paper poppies that seemed to shudder in the flickering candlelight in dizzying movements. Despite having only just entered, Yojiro felt that even the direction of the door might disappear if he were not careful.

"Excuse me, Governor Hyobu-sama," he called, blinking as he crept farther into the room. "I am Bayushi Yojiro, the Emerald magistrate newly arrived from Otosan Uchi."

Silence greeted his salutation. To be sure he was alone, Yojiro squinted again. None of the dim shapes moved.

He nearly stumbled upon a heap of silk cushions that blended seamlessly into a sumptuous rug, both half-hidden in the dimness. Beyond the strewn cushions stood scarlet-lacquered furniture arranged around a circular table. He drew close to examine its craftsmanship. An antique set, from the last century. Red cedarwood, probably sourced from the nearby Kinbō Province. Beautiful, though the lacquerwork was slightly flawed. He drew a curious finger along the minutely uneven paint layers on the back of a chair. But it was smooth, well cared for. The seats and divan had even been reupholstered with new silk, gold and pale jade threads marking them current with the present fashion season.

Yojiro moved to sit but froze as a tiny gleam of light caught his attention, like the twinkle in the eyes of a cat. He peered into the shadows. Nothing. The light had vanished. Or had he really seen it at all?

The points of his high, arching collar pricked the sides of his face, as if to spur his discomfort. He pulled at them, freeing his chin.

"My, you are as handsome as they say, aren't you?" The sudden, crooning voice split through the silence.

Yojiro blinked, his heart and breath tightening inside his ribs as he wildly scanned the parlor once more. Only the dark, lonely furnishings populated the room. A sheen of sweat prickled across his body.

She is toying with you. She is a Shosuro, after all, and they like their secret nets.

"Hyobu-sama," he began again, bowing formally to the dark. He reached into his sleeve to withdraw his papers of introduction. "My name is—"

"I heard you the first time, Yojiro-san," the unseen woman trilled, amusement curling her vowels as she uttered his name. "And no need for your papers. I have my own information."

A hand appeared, as if floating above the carpet, and slowly, the gentle curves of one of the brass statues sharpened into a stunning woman, graceful and sensuous in her middle age, swathed in layers of gold and crimson kimono despite the glowering heat of the braziers. She wore a black silk tulle veil over the lower half of her face instead of a mask. Her eyes, though slightly wilted by time, stared sharp and sparkling through the dimness. She had been administering to one of the vases, shaping its counterfeit bouquet with a tiny pair of shears. She beckoned Yojiro closer with a gold-lacquered fingernail. The heavy, spiced smells of poppy milk and plum wine wafted around her.

"It is a pleasure to meet you, Hyobu-sama," he said, bowing again, this time in her actual direction. "I hope I do not intrude on your busy schedule. Denmaru was kind enough to show me in."

Hyobu's lips curled behind her gossamer veil. "He is a dutiful servant. We were expecting you, of course."

"Then perhaps you know why I have come to Ryokō Owari."

"Yes," Hyobu replied, grasping his hands in an overly cordial manner, her skin hot against his. Yojiro had no idea where her snipping shears had gone. "I heard that you have come to my lovely city on urgent business, but you must make time to explore our Licensed Quarter. We have such pleasures to be enjoyed there. The finest wines. Gardens of the rarest flowers. Dramatic and glorious theater. The most meticulously trained *onna* geisha and *otoko geisha*. Everything to soothe or charm your senses."

"Another time, perhaps."

"Too bad. I heard the Cherry Petal Grove has just acquired a talented flautist."

Yojiro shook his head, politely. Hyobu shrugged and guided him to a seat. She then waved her hand, and immediately the mound of cushions stood. Yojiro's breath caught in his throat. The silken pillows had merely been a servant girl, kneeling prostrate upon the floor. She skipped across the room to retrieve a lacquered tea set. Returning, she poured him a generous cup of emerald-colored tea before retreating back to her post, again merging into the decor.

He cast his eyes around the room again for more surprises.

"I have heard interesting stories about you, Yojiro-san," the governor crooned, clicking her fingernails against the teacup. "I hear you are a masterful artisan. Carpentry, is it?"

"Carving, primarily, but it is only a hobby," he replied. "I have had no formal training."

"But I heard that you are talented beyond the need for a sensei. Last year, everyone spoke of a mahogany *inrō* box you made for your sister to hang from her obi that made every woman in the capital jealous."

"Surely, that was only due to Mikuru's kind praise of my work," he mumbled, the mention of his sister pricking his heart. Had Hyobu heard of their dissociation? "Do you mind if we speak about why I came? I do not wish to trespass upon your time."

"Well, since you are so adamant about business, instead of pleasure, I suppose we should get on with it," Hyobu said, delicately sipping her tea beneath her gossamer veil. "I am glad you have been sent to clear up this scandal surrounding Aramoro. It truly is unfortunate that he was caught up in the death of Kitsuki Obo."

"Then you already believe him to be innocent?" Yojiro asked, his tongue tickling from the strange tea blend.

"Don't you, Yojiro-san?"

Yojiro frowned. "I was sent by Champion Toturi to discover the truth."

Hyobu smiled coyly, her bright eyes narrowing. "Of course. The truth."

"Do you have any information concerning the circumstances of Kitsuki-sama's death that might aid me?"

"Not really," she laughed. "I generally leave matters of murder in Denmaru's hands."

Yojiro stiffened, the insinuation seeming too blatant.

"Oh?" Yojiro continued, shielding the newly broached skepticism from his voice and replacing it with interest. "He is investigating this case, then."

"He did at first. When the body was first discovered in the Fishers' Quarter. However, Champion Toturi has since commanded the case be left to the Emerald magistrates. To calm the cries of Dragon hatchlings, I suppose. You see, I have been receiving heated letters from Dragon Clan and Kitsuki family representatives all week. Pages and pages of complaints and bile. Though I am tired of their bawling, their letters have indicated several serious economic ramifications for my city."

"Such as?"

"Bans on Dragon trade ships entering our Bay of Drowned Honor. Normally, I would not balk at such threats. The Dragon have very few exports that I care about. Crystals. Monastery books. The occasional alchemical ingredients. You know, curios that only those with very specific tastes would enjoy. However, this threat may also bar us from their gold market, which, I'm afraid to admit, would be a severe blow. That market keeps us competitive with the other trade centers throughout Rokugan, and without it, my economy might just shrivel up."

She paused to sip more tea. She was pretending not to study Yojiro's eyes.

"Excuse my rambling concerns. They are nothing more than the fears of a pressed administrator. I am also aware of your concerns in this matter, Yojiro-san, since this case involves certain personal investments for you, too. Lady Kachiko has informed me extensively regarding what those might be," Governor Hyobu warbled nonchalantly.

A tiny spasm in Yojiro's chest threatened to unravel into despair at the mention of Bayushi Kachiko. That dark, bleeding memory rippled again.

The tournament of the Emerald Champion. The Lion Clan winning over the Scorpion. He winced, remembering how his clan had rejected him. "Failure," they had whispered. "Traitor." Even his own dear sister Mikuru. At his request, she had been ready to risk her own life for the part she played to secure a Scorpion victory. When his plan failed, rendering her sacrifice for naught, she refused to speak to him ever again. But beyond becoming a social outcast, the pain – that searing shame – came from the look Kachiko had given him. Her dark eyes. Deep and alive, like fiery pools of pitch. She had even taken off her mask to stare, intense and hateful, into his own face. She had looked so beautiful, even in her fury, the grace of her cheeks only enriched by her ire.

"Your failure was unfortunate, Yojiro," she had said, her usually refined, alluring diplomacy poisoned in her disgust. "You play at maintaining your integrity, but where is the honor when a master has an unreliable servant? Your failure betrayed my trust, Yojiro. You betrayed me."

Had he truly betrayed her? His resolve to serve Rokugan, to serve the Empire over the Scorpion, might have held. He had, after all, devotedly accomplished his duty to the emperor as his Emerald magistrate. He had righted a wrong under Heaven. He had restored balance, harmony, justice. He had upheld his oaths to follow Bushidō...

Yet Kachiko's dark eyes still haunted him. Her look pierced his heart with a hundred hot needles. Beyond the fire of her wrath glimmered a shard of hurt. A wound, bruised and bleeding. He had inflicted it. His failure had inflicted it.

He had betrayed Kachiko. For that, he could not forgive himself.

And she had reminded him that the Scorpion Clan could not forgive it, either. She had dismissed him, then held him back for a final message.

"Do not fail me again, Yojiro. To fail twice might mark you a traitor. Traitor's Grove is such a cold place. I would hate to have to visit you there."

In her indifferent mention of Kachiko, Governor Hyobu had been reminding him what was really at stake here in Ryokō Owari. Should he fail, Scorpion *shugenja* would bind his soul to a tree in Traitor's Grove. His final resting place would be in the forest hung with the belongings of other Scorpion traitors, a living tomb wherein he could be tormented for all eternity, unable to advance to the afterlife. A bleak reminder to future generations of Scorpion of the cost for betraying their clan.

Yojiro wrenched the memory away from his eyes.

This is like the Unicorn Clan parable about the hare caught between the serpent and the hawk, isn't it? Either choice means death… To fail the Scorpion would mean having my soul stolen from me. But to free Aramoro might mean abandoning my oaths to uphold Bushidō, blaspheming under Heaven and losing my soul. Why must my clan duty ever be at odds with my duty to Rokugan?

"The Mother of Scorpions wishes you luck in your endeavors here," Governor Hyobu continued, clipping the final tangles of his reverie, taunting him.

Yojiro blushed but did not look away, meeting her challenge with a clenched jaw. "Then I carry her blessing with me. And as an Emerald magistrate, representative of our Emerald Champion and our joint master the emperor, Son of Heaven, I carry celestial blessings as well."

Hyobu laughed, her clever eyes narrowing into crescents of delight. "I can see why Lady Kachiko adores you. You are so amusing. Well, if you will protect my city by clearing up this Kitsuki business, I do not see why I should not also add my blessing to theirs. You have my aid. Denmaru is at your service."

"I thank you humbly, Hyobu-sama. However, I could not intrude upon your generosity," he replied, remembering his promise to Toturi. He switched into the furtive language of the court. Delicacy and tact. "I am sure that you and your retainers have much more pressing tasks in this blossoming city than to assist me in such a lowly inquest. I would hate for you and your agents to trouble yourselves."

Hyobu's brows furrowed, though her smile never left her face. "I see. I thank you for your humble thoughtfulness, but as this is my city, I should make a poor governor if I neglected the small tasks. And I would make a poor hostess if I were to simply abandon you in your work."

"Not at all, Hyobu-sama. Instead, you have been a most generous hostess, and from what I have seen of your city, an exceptionally adept leader. No, you would do me great honor if you would trust me with this humble assignment. It would allow me to redeem myself in the eyes of my peers," Yojiro insisted.

Hyobu sniffed, unable to further deny his requests without insulting him. "Your skills garner my confidence, Yojiro-san. At least allow me to assign Denmaru to you as a guide to the city and its workings."

"I am sure that the city's Emerald magistrate and his *yoriki* are more than capable of helping me."

"Ah yes, Otomo Seno-sama and his investigators," Hyobu chuckled, her dry, delighted sarcasm calming her frustration at his outmaneuvering. "He is quite the warrior for truth and justice here in Ryokō Owari. Always thinking. Always planning. You can take your letters of introduction to the manor of the Emerald magistrate to find him. I hear he has made such… interesting improvements to the place."

"Thank you, Hyobu-sama." Yojiro stood, bowing to her politely, though not cordially. He turned to find the door.

"Oh, and Yojiro-san, you may want to visit our Temple Quarter and make an offering at the Temple of Daikoku," Hyobu added, standing and plopping an empty green silk purse onto the table. It was his. "I heard from Denmaru that you… accidentally dropped this. Do be more careful."

CHAPTER THREE

As Yojiro passed out of the shadow of Shosuro Palace on his way to the Emerald magistrate's estate, he walked by the magnificent mansions and lush gardens of the Noble Quarter, wary of the odd mirage that seemed to hang in the air. Unlike the Merchant Quarter, this district lay quiet, its few pedestrians silent, not even conferring with one another. A few local dignitaries nodded to him as they passed, only the careful click of their steps echoing after him. Every door and window was shut, all trees and shrubs trimmed to perfection, every cobblestone level and swept. It was all too clean, artificial, like the immaculate skin of a mask.

Yojiro turned a corner, nearly colliding with a man dressed all in black. He leaped back to avoid a crash, his heart pounding. He blinked. The street was empty.

The congested skyline of stunning towers and decorative roofs with pitched eaves crumpled the light of a sinking sun, casting jagged, toothlike shadows on the cobblestones. Many of them, out of the corner of his eye, looked like the faded outline of a person's silhouette. One would never know if one was being followed.

This district trades dark alleys for illusions. I can't even trust my own shadow here.

He paused, mid-shudder.

Could Denmaru or his squad be following me now?

Yojiro rubbed his eyes. Each shadow still loomed, a possible threat, though he still couldn't see a person casting one. He squeezed a fist around his katana.

Just be ready for anything. If I keep worrying, these tricks of the light will be the end of me.

Even if the Thunder Guard was following him, he had nothing to hide from them. He and Hyobu had the same goal. She had obviously received a letter from Kachiko informing her of Yojiro's potential fate in Traitor's Grove, which meant she knew his interests hinged on a favorable Scorpion Clan outcome. Her aims were similar, the potential political threat to her city necessitating a diplomatic triumph over the Dragon by clearing up the scandal. And she had insisted that Yojiro accept her help.

Yet, her words seemed too obvious. "I generally leave matters of murder in Denmaru's hands." Why take such a risk? Was she merely testing his loyalty? Was the Thunder Guard somehow involved, or had she simply referred to their role as her law enforcers? If Ikku's words were to be trusted in any way, the Thunder Guard had a reputation for merciless, perhaps even corrupt, practices. Could that be under Hyobu's command? Was Ikku one of her minions? Yojiro's purse had certainly made its swift way to her. Or had Denmaru really retrieved Yojiro's purse from the crime lord? According to Ikku's side of the story, they certainly seemed at odds. Regardless, he must be wary of the whole lot of them for now.

What is Kachiko hoping I do in the face of all these Scorpion secrets?

Yojiro finally reached the manor of the Emerald magistrate.

The massive three-story building wrapped around a hollow courtyard open to the street. Unlike other civic centers, which featured traditional Rokugani architecture, this building had no angular roof, no windows, and no shōji screen doors or sliding exterior walls. Instead, the structure was a solid square encasement of pine, like an enormous wooden chest. In contrast to the ugly, ascetic building design, the center of the courtyard featured a large garden waterfall cascading over obelisks made from stacks of square stone blocks. The water flowed into a pool ringed in black marble that bore the inscription "Ritsuryō", the word for Rokugani traditional law.

Near this waterfall, on a stone dais, knelt a rail-thin man swaddled in a pale-green kimono. The Otomo family crest of four coiled snakes was emblazoned across the chest, marking him as a member of one of the Imperial families, those related to the emperor or counted among his closest followers. However, this Otomo crest was inside an emerald orb, the official marking of an Emerald magistrate. A black, polished *kanmuri* hat sat pinned upon his gray head, and dark facial hair framed his stern mouth, granting him a regal yet sinister look. He perched behind a tiny bamboo desk scattered with stacks of official papers and scrolls, which he busily perused, occasionally making notes with the flick of a brush. A single man inside an enormous wooden fortress.

Yojiro approached, handing his letter of introduction to a nearby attendant.

"Otomo Seno-sama, I presume." Yojiro bowed low before his fellow magistrate. "I am Bayushi Yojiro, the Emerald magistrate from Otosan Uchi. I was sent here by the Emerald Champion to aid you in your ongoing investigation of Kitsuki Obo's death."

Seno briefly looked up from his papers, setting down his brush on a plain, square inkstone. His bleak eyes scanned Yojiro before he took the letter of introduction and read it. His mouth puckered. Somewhat loud over the sound of the waterfall, his voice was cold, with a restrained, polite malice.

"You must speak up if I am to hear you, Bayushi-sama." He waved his hand in the direction of the splashing water. "The spies of your clan necessitate this trick."

Yojiro blinked, the Otomo's blunt insinuation rendering him momentarily speechless. "Pardon me?"

"Scorpion spies," Seno said simply, taking up his brush again, finishing some notes in the margin of a scroll. "This city is swarming with them: there is an eavesdropper in every corner. Their presence has required that many measures be taken to maintain peace of mind and peace of city, and this waterfall ensures my privacy in the execution of my duties." With this, he once more eyed Yojiro warily, subtly leaning away as if afraid of being stung.

Yojiro paused, a protest forming on his lips, but he maintained his courtly respect and composure. He smiled before answering, "I understand that the exaggerated reputation of my clan might alarm you into a state of perpetual concern, Seno-sama. However, you must forgive my skepticism. I have never known such precautions to seem necessary, let alone be taken, even in Otosan Uchi."

"Are you suggesting that I am paranoid, Bayushi-sama?" Seno frowned, his bony chest puffing up in egotistic agitation as he flung down Yojiro's introduction letter. "Having been Emerald magistrate in this city for nearly three decades, I have witnessed plenty of proof of your clan's 'reputation'. Especially here, where the agents of the Scorpion seem to cling to our very shadows! Dozens of spies, lurking. Behind every corner. Inside every crack. Watching. Listening. Biding their time..."

A stone formed between Yojiro's ribs, sinking slowly into his belly. He silently groaned.

Did I sound just as absurd when I told myself these same things about the Thunder Guard moments ago? Fear makes fools of us, does it not? I must learn to bridle my worry.

"...The construction of this waterfall was my idea, Bayushi-sama, and since its implementation, we have had no disclosures of internal information circulated. Not a single drop of water escapes this bottle! And this is but one of many ingenious initiatives, numerous in every sector. For example, just look what I have done to the manor. Not a hiding place in it. You see, my policies maintain the peace. I am truly the greatest force in the progressive fight against ninja scum that Rokugan has ever seen."

At this, Yojiro almost couldn't contain a burst of laughter. "Please excuse my ignorance, but did you say 'ninja'?" He hid his mouth in his high collar. His mirth at the ridiculous notion and the accompanying pomposity of the magistrate nearly rendered him rude. "Otomo-sama, forgive me, but everyone knows that ninja are not real – merely an oft-told tale circulated by gossipmongers and by storytellers looking for listeners' gold."

Yojiro immediately regretted this statement of fact as Seno's face lightened to a shade of enraged gray.

"This is exactly what I expect from a Scorpion," the magistrate growled, barely restraining himself from pointing at Yojiro. "I know your kind, Bayushi-sama. Nothing but deceptions and excuses, ruses and feints. And you come here believing I am fool enough to accept your tricks just because you have a mandate from the Emerald Champion, but I will not. I am prepared for what you might do here to hide the truth, to save face, to protect your clan's ninja conspiracy–"

Seno's insult was cut short by the swift approach of a contingent of *dōshin* wearing leather caps, who dragged several ragged criminals in chains behind them. The guards were led by a samurai wearing slate-colored *hakama* trousers and a sage kimono bearing the crest of the Seppun, another Imperial family. She briefly laid her light-brown eyes on Yojiro before addressing Seno with a deep, formal bow.

"Otomo-sama. We have arrested the leaders of the Storm Tigers in our raid on the wharf near Moment's Edge Bridge, just as you commanded. We managed to capture all of them at a sake house."

Seno's face lit up in bitter pleasure at the news. "Bayushi-sama, this is my yoriki Seppun Motome-san, a servant who enacts my orders."

The woman flinched ever so slightly at Seno's subordination of her, reducing her status as an Imperial law enforcer for his administration to a mere act of servitude. The old Otomo noticed nothing, grinning and pointing at the prisoners.

"And it seems she has brought proof of the effectiveness of my methods." Seno nearly jeered as he took Motome's report, eyeing Yojiro with glee. "I am proud to show this to you, Bayushi-sama. These villains belong to an elite gang of ninja operating on the outskirts of the Fishers' Quarter. With this capture, I am one step closer to destroying the ninja activity in Ryokō Owari."

Yojiro swallowed the rest of his humor, though it threatened to burst from within him. The "ninja gang" stank of rotting rice and fish guts and were obviously drunk, nearly reeling over themselves. Dressed in threadbare kimono with the Scorpion Clan insignia clumsily stitched all over them, these ragtag criminals were clearly mere ruffians. They probably hustled the occasional laborer in the poorest parts of town, but crime lords they were not, let alone fabled ninja.

Among the group, Yojiro spotted Buyu, the rickshaw puller. *Ninja indeed.*

Though Seno continued to grin stupidly, bragging about his

conquest, the look on Motome's face suggested reticence to join Seno in his expression of triumph at the arrest. The Seppun yoriki had her mouth clamped into a tight line of silent seething, an expression that looked long practiced, probably from years of compounded, unvoiced disagreements with Seno's exaggerations. A slight flush in her cheeks hinted at her embarrassment at Seno's assertion that these reprobates were ninja. A flicker in her eye marked distrust, though of Seno or himself, Yojiro was not yet sure.

"Guards, take the criminals to Ryokō Owari Prison. You can press them for their confessions after they have sobered up," Seno ordered, self-adulation plastered on his withered face. He turned to Motome and handed her Yojiro's introduction letter. "Motome-san, you are ordered by Akodo Toturi-sama, our illustrious Emerald Champion, to include this Scorpion representative in your investigation of the death of Kitsuki Obo. However, despite Toturi-sama's confidence in Bayushi-sama, I do not trust as easily. I personally charge you with watching him carefully, and I will hold you responsible for all his actions. Make sure he does not intervene. And that he does not trick you."

With a nod, he dismissed them both and continued to work on his stack of papers.

Yojiro swallowed, hesitant to walk away from the Otomo Emerald magistrate just yet. He had casually, effortlessly insulted a fellow magistrate and a Great Clan in public. What kind of tactless, ill-bred official was this Otomo?

Perhaps all his yelling over this ridiculous waterfall has made him a brave fox among the chickens. But brave foxes eventually catch arrows.

"If you would accompany me, Yojiro-sama," Motome said, tucking Toturi's letter into her sleeve for later perusal. "We can confer in my office at Ji-u Reformatory."

Yojiro shot a final annoyed glance at Seno before following Motome onto the street, heading north, back toward the Merchant Quarter through a different gate. He studied her as they walked. The yoriki stood nearly two heads shorter than himself, yet the severity of her light eyes and scowl lent her an intimidating presence. She never opened her mouth unnecessarily. Probably due to her crooked teeth. She kept her short hair tightly secured in a bun at the base of her skull. Though her katana hilt was woven with pristine silk cords, unworn from lack of use, the strong muscles in her hands indicated that she was still trained in some form of martial skill. Perhaps in the *jitte* – one was tucked into her obi – though the two-pronged sword breaker was often carried more as a symbol of a yoriki's authority than for actual fighting.

"I have heard of you, you know," Motome said, interrupting his scrutiny. Her voice was taut with civility and caution. "I heard you are called 'the only honest Scorpion.'"

"An interesting epithet, is it not?" Yojiro replied. "Given to me by the courtiers in Otosan Uchi. It has definitely proved helpful in my career at court."

Motome frowned. "Then it is not true?" She was indeed careful, picking apart his responses for possible motives and meanings.

"You do not believe my reputation?"

"I do not believe many things," she replied, tucking her arms behind her back. "I have lived long enough among the Imperial families and their political façades, and my duties as yoriki bring me in close contact with the full gamut of swindlers, perjurers, and gossipmongers. For me, actions indicate more truth than a tactful excuse or a well-spun story. Or the gossip of reputation."

Her candidness surprised him. He laughed. "Then I suppose, Motome-san, that as a rule, you do not trust people like me."

"No, I do not." She hesitated, turning to look him in the eye. Despite the chill of her expression, the color of her eyes was warm, almost golden. "But I want to. Especially if we are to work together to discover the mysteries behind this murder. It is just that my experiences in this city with…" She paused as though to avoid saying "Scorpion", "…people will not allow for it."

"I understand. Thank you for your candor, Motome-san. If you truly want to trust me, remember that reputations often stem from actions, not merely gossip. I hope that mine will earn your confidence before we part ways."

Motome smiled. "I hope that, too."

"Speaking of liars and storytellers, I noticed your doubt at Otomo-sama's insistence that those Storm Tigers are ninja. That is a foolish tale, to be sure," he said, remembering Buyu for his incompetence and unsubtlety in the Merchant Quarter. "And it seems as though you do not trust Otomo-sama with regard to much more than that."

"What? Oh… no… He is my superior," she stammered, picking her way through the honorable reply. "There are no contradictions between his beliefs and mine. We really do have a problem here in Ryokō Owari…"

"With ninja?" Yojiro said skeptically.

"With *shinobi*."

The word landed like a blow to Yojiro's gut, paralyzing his whole body. Shinobi? Ninja had been an interesting bit of fictional flair. However, the word "shinobi" evoked the most illegal, even unthinkable, of criminal activities. These legendary master saboteurs and assassins were only spoken of in whispers, and Yojiro had never even heard them mentioned out loud by anyone outside his own clan.

"That is impossible, Motome-san," Yojiro said, his voice deepening to a harsh whisper at her confession. The anxious chill of an irrational fear shuddered down his spine. "The existence of shinobi would imply that the Great Clans are making pernicious affronts to Bushidō, abandoning their honor. Such activities would be in direct conflict with ancient Imperial edicts. No clan would dare stoop to such immorality."

Motome clenched her firsts, as if readying for a physical attack. "Regardless of what might be true in normal society, in the safety of Otosan Uchi, as a yoriki in Ryokō Owari, I have seen enough to warrant my assertion. I intend to help Otomo-sama uncover their secrets," she declared, her brow furrowed. "And I intend to prove they exist."

Yojiro stared at the investigator, bewildered by her revelation. Her forthrightness unnerved him, but he did not know why.

Could she possibly have ulterior motives in blatantly making such a ridiculous claim? If she were a Scorpion, I could anticipate such a bold move being used to draw some secret from me, to put me on the defensive – to frighten me, even. Like Hyobu. But she is a Seppun. She seems so harmless. Still, there is nothing harmless about mentioning shinobi.

The pair walked in silence through the Gate of Condescension, reentering the Merchant Quarter with its dark alleys. The budding Hour of the Rooster had called forth promoters of the Licensed Quarter, who mixed among the throngs of people, ringing bells and clacking wooden dowels together, shouting promises of wine, gambling, and plays for the night's entertainment. The setting sun made the already-dark roads even gloomier, so traders and vendors lit the hanging street lanterns, casting an abundance of new shadows across the crowded streets. Gangs of firefighters appeared to monitor their blocks, eyeing the lanterns and the people with disdain, sacks of sand or barrels of water at their feet. The emergence of these bullying neighborhood watchers seemed to warrant extra caution, as the Thunder Guard started to make their rounds, and many samurai and nobles now traveled with their yōjimbō.

However, though everyone towered above her, Motome strolled without hesitation through the throngs. Her reputation, whatever that might be, seemed to keep her quite safe. As she walked by, several merchants vanished into alleys at the sight of her, casting rueful looks in her direction. She merely ambled along, paying them no heed, her arms folded behind her back, her jitte poking out of her obi farther than before, somewhat ominously.

"You are obviously very adept at your work, Motome-san," Yojiro said finally, after they turned down Jade Street, finding themselves alone on the quieter lane. "You command the respect of everyone in this quarter."

"It is not me but my station they respect," Motome explained quickly, modestly blushing at the compliment as if unused to any form of recognition.

"Possibly," Yojiro replied. He kept his voice down. "If I may be as honest as you have been with me, I will admit that your previous... declaration came as quite the shock."

She cocked her head, listening intently, though keeping a watchful eye on the alleys.

"Shinobi have not been reality for centuries," Yojiro continued. "So long, in fact, that they are a matter that many now consider only myth."

Motome continued to stroll ahead, her attention mostly on their surroundings, ignoring his explanations. Propriety never left her voice. "You know, Yojiro-sama, I am no liar. What I say always contains all the truth I know. I hope you will give me the benefit of your respect in this matter before we begin our task."

Preventing a grimace from creeping onto his face, Yojiro nodded, opting to defer to her as leader of their investigation and keep further doubts to himself. He would play along for now.

"In fact, we shall start at that point," Motome stated, pulling out a scroll from her obi. It contained an inquiry painting of the face of a man with a small mouth and wispy facial hair. The brushstrokes were fairly well composed – done by someone with training, probably from a Crane art academy – so Yojiro trusted the spite he could see in the portrait's eyes.

"This is Kitsuki Obo, the man whose murder you have come here to help me resolve. He was found in the Fishers' Quarter over two weeks ago, stabbed to death in a sewer gutter."

"Who was he?"

"Kitsuki-sama had been acting as a gold-trade minister for the last twelve years, representing Dragon interests with customers in the Merchant and Fishers' Quarters. However, this was merely a façade."

"Oh?" Yojiro frowned at the detachment with which Motome said this. She was rather calm for someone investigating the secret life of a dead man.

"Yes. He had been acting as my personal informant for about ten of those twelve years, specifically notifying me of shinobi activity in the city."

Yojiro dared another ill-timed laugh. "And you trusted him? Why?"

"Kitsuki-sama was a trained investigator."

Yojiro could not believe his ears. This was the third preposterous thing he had heard in the last hour. The Kitsuki family of the Dragon Clan oversaw an elite magisterial investigation school whose famed ability to scrutinize a scene and deduce the truth from even the tiniest detail rivaled even that of shugenja. For Motome to command such an ally would have been invaluable. His loss would have been equally devastating. Their ten years of correspondence could have made her privy to some of this city's deepest of secrets. Now, Hyobu's insistence on Denmaru's involvement made sense. Motome could be at the heart of something that not just Hyobu but the entire Scorpion Clan would want to keep hidden.

Yojiro now understood why he had been commanded to come here. The murder of a Kitsuki investigator in Ryokō Owari meant that this investigation was dangerous to the Scorpion, given the charge against Aramoro. It made Motome their worst enemy. Against his better judgment, his instinct toward duty, honor, and truth, Yojiro's mind had already begun a defensive analysis of her, constructing ways to conceal his intentions and actions from his new partner, examining her weaknesses and potential points of exploitation.

Torn between the halves of his eternal paradox, Yojiro stared into the painted eyes of Kitsuki Obo's portrait. Their inky blackness nearly professed the sinister plot beginning to emerge.

To contain this scandal, to save my clan, I may need to stay several steps ahead of Motome. I will need to discover the truth behind this murder before she does. Shinobi or not.

CHAPTER FOUR

Moments before sunset, the pair arrived at the Ji-u Reformatory on the western bank of the Merchant Quarter near the Bridge of Drunken Lovers. The small compound had thick, towering white-pine walls and an iron gate stained dark with age, a solemn fortress amid the lively markets. The tiny stronghold, built by farmers several centuries before Ryokō Owari was established, had once contained a rice vault for storing reserves for use by the Scorpion samurai during long campaigns. The vault was now used as a prison for higher-caste criminals with minimum security requirements. This had earned it the name "ji-u," referring to the gracious rain that blessed crops in Ryokō Province; it was a popular pun on "jiyū," the word for freedom.

In addition to the underground vault, the compound had a gravel courtyard that housed a few ancient administrative buildings and another one of Seno's spy-deterring waterfalls. This one was inscribed with the word "Meiyo": honor, the first precept of Rokugani law, deriving, of course, from the Bushidō tenet. Yojiro could guess that the Ryokō Owari Prison, where Buyu and the Storm Tigers had been taken, had a matching waterfall with the second precept, "Jihaku", the principle of confession, inscribed.

"How long have you been working for Magistrate Otomo?"

"Nearly fifteen years. I was appointed as his yoriki just after my graduation from the Seppun School of Magistrates."

"I have heard that the Seppun train some of the best magistrates when it comes to investigation."

Motome blushed again at the praise. "The school is very good, but you are mistaken in including me among the ranks of great investigators."

"We shall see. Fifteen years' experience is quite the accomplishment."

She smiled. "Perhaps. What about you? How long have you been Emerald magistrate in Otosan Uchi?"

"Six years."

"So, you were appointed by Champion Doji Satsume, then."

Yojiro remembered the late Emerald Champion, the one Toturi had replaced. The old Crane samurai had been strict, devoted. "Yes."

"Both Satsume-sama and Toturi-sama trust you," Motome observed, more to herself than to Yojiro. "Do you have friends?"

Now it was Yojiro's turn to blush. "Friends? Well, I–"

"Oh, curse my curiosity," Motome stuttered, shaking her head as if coming to her senses. She bowed apologetically. "I did not mean to interrogate you. I was… writing your character profile in my head. A matter of habit, I'm afraid. Please forgive me."

"It is quite all right," Yojiro replied, the answers to her questions starting to gnaw inside him. Did he have friends? He spent more time with Lady Kachiko than anyone else, but he would hardly consider her a friend. Their relationship was more… professional? More complicated, anyway. He listed the people at court who were friendly to him.

"I suppose I can consider Toturi-sama my friend," he replied slowly. "We respect one another."

"Yes, I suppose friends should respect one another," Motome said, her smile drooping.

Yojiro frowned. He had not considered it. Besides Mikuru, who would no longer speak to him, he truly had no one. Scorpion were repelled by his honesty, and few others accepted him, because an honest Scorpion was too much of an anomaly. Maybe that was why he spent so much time carving, making trinkets, whittling toys. He was just... alone.

They entered the largest building in the courtyard: a worn, gray outbuilding with the Scorpion crest in ancient, sun-bleached paint above the sliding door. The prickling stench of mildew greeted them, the air musty from the lack of windows. Numerous oil lamps filled the halls and rooms, enough to blind the eye as they rounded corners and to suck the already-stale air out of the rooms. No doubt more of Seno's ingenious schemes to catch ninja.

As they descended a heavy, split-post draw ramp down into the vault, Yojiro crouched slightly to avoid the low ceiling. The cells were made of fist-thick, red-pine lattices, like cages for wild animals, the holes only large enough for an eye to peer through. However, as this prison housed high-ranking, genteel criminals, they were sanitary, even mildly furnished. Beds. Chairs. The occasional desk. Despite the accommodations, Yojiro could see bleak expressions behind the bars. Ministers. Priests. Courtiers. People used to luxuries, who could not appreciate merely a dry bed and a clean floor.

Why did Aramoro let himself get put into a place like this? Did he and Kachiko plan this?

His worries gnawed inside him as he and Motome arrived at her office, which she unlocked with a heavy iron key from her brass ring. Despite her rank and ability, Seno had tucked her away in this dungeon, deep within the prison vault. However, she hinted at no irritation at the location. She clearly took care of the tiny room. The walls were crowded with perfectly organized shelves of scrolls and iron-bound chests, not a speck of dust visible.

No tatami mats had been installed, likely due to mold growing in the damp, so Motome set out a pair of lavender *zabuton* pillows for them to kneel upon. Then, carefully, she hung her pair of swords, katana and *wakizashi*, upon a plain wooden rack. Her jitte also went on its own little stand.

"I would offer you some refreshment, but I command no amenities here at this prison," Motome apologized, regret at the social impropriety pinching her eyebrows. "Please forgive me."

"There is nothing to forgive," Yojiro assured her. He first knelt politely in *seiza* position upon the cushion, but she gestured that he could relax.

"I have all the materials from the murder investigation in here," she explained, unlocking a pine chest with a key from her brass ring. She withdrew scrolls, letters, wooden boxes, and even a basket of bloodied clothes from it, setting each article carefully upon her low desk. She watched him with hawkish vigilance, as though afraid he would take something. He ignored her suspicion as he examined the articles.

"Did you collect them yourself? Or did you get them from Captain Denmaru?" Yojiro asked, referring to what Hyobu had said about turning over the case.

Motome's face hardened into a defensive scowl. "Yes, Captain Denmaru gave me some of these articles."

"I did not mean to offend by implying incompetence on your part," Yojiro apologized. "Rather, I heard from Governor Hyobu that he was originally investigating the Kitsuki's death."

"And I was implying… never mind," Motome bit her lip,

rethinking her statements. "Captain Denmaru and I have often quarreled. As a representative of the Emerald magistrate, my attempts to uphold Imperial law sometimes clash with his enforcement of local law. We sometimes have not seen eye to eye in the execution of our duties."

"Confusion in the lines of jurisdiction?"

"More than that," Motome explained. "Sometimes I wonder if he may have purposely hindered some of my investigations."

"This is a grave suspicion, Motome-san. What has given you such an impression?"

"Forgive my directness, Yojiro-sama. In the past, I merely experienced obstacles that have caused me to wonder; untimely arrests of my witnesses, damage to evidence, and killings of my suspects. Many of these instances involved the Thunder Guard in some way. Some of them may have been merely unfortunate accidents, but part of me remains skeptical. Otomo-sama has also often protested against Captain Denmaru, having had some of his own efforts obstructed."

"Seemingly obstructed, you mean?"

Motome turned her face away, the shame of her allegations burning across her face. "I am sorry, Yojiro-sama. The only reason I mention this at all is due to our partnership. I have long come to expect interference from Hyobu and her Thunder Guard, and you might need to as well, even if we have no proof."

Motome bit her lip again.

Yojiro sank down into his high collar to think. The Scorpion carefully trained the Shosuro to work in secret, so the fact that Motome had no proof of whatever she feared did not surprise him. Surely, this was the interference Toturi also feared, probably having heard reports from Seno himself. Yet, despite everyone's suspicions about Hyobu and Denmaru, including his own, Yojiro knew that Motome shared some of Seno's bias against the

Scorpion. She was almost aware of it herself, the old Otomo's paranoia undoubtedly making it clearer by the day, but that prejudice was sure to still color her judgment.

I need to bide my time. Wait. And watch.

"Thank you, Motome-san," he finally said to repair her embarrassment. "If I have reason to suspect Captain Denmaru, I shall share it with you, as you have found reason to share your inner thoughts with me. Since I am a newcomer, I cannot yet pass any judgments, and I look forward to becoming more acquainted with the facts, as you are."

The yoriki stared at him, astonished at his willingness to ignore her improperly critical outburst. "That is generous of you."

"Not at all," he replied. "We shall proceed as we can, regardless of the obstacles."

Gently, he pulled close some of the articles from her investigation. A large porcelain urn containing Kitsuki Obo's cremated remains, sealed with wax. A yellow silk coin purse with a ragged lining. An ivory case containing Obo's signature chop. A jade ring with a dragon's head etched into its surface. A tiny brass key. Some identification papers speckled with blood. At the bottom of the pile, a few letters of introduction from the appropriate Dragon Clan officials and Kitsuki gold mine owners. He scanned their contents, reading about Obo's duties as one of many trade ministers representing Dragon trade interests in the area.

These articles give no indication of why the Scorpion would have any interest in him. He seems as powerless and inconsequential as any other low-ranking samurai retainer.

Yojiro next picked his way through the basket. Obo's kimono was a very simple green and yellow layered garment with no embroidery and only a cotton lining. The sides had been reseamed about a palm's length in from the garment's original width, as if the kimono had previously belonged to a much larger man, becoming a secondhand castoff. Bloodstains followed several tears in the silk, congregating in a pattern. There had been three quick strikes: precise slashes near the neck, belly, and groin. The Swiftness of Shadows technique. Aramoro's fighting style.

Yojiro's body nearly recoiled from the clothing as though it carried a plague.

Had Aramoro truly killed Obo? If so, then Yojiro would not be determining and sharing the truth, as he had hoped. That would surely lead to the Traitor's Grove. Could that have been Aramoro and Kachiko's plan all along? To use Aramoro's crime to force Yojiro to dishonor himself, anticipating that the truth would force him to lie? It could not be as twisted as that.

He dropped the clothes back into the basket. The garments fell in a way that concealed Aramoro's slash pattern. He gritted his teeth.

Lies are unnecessary if one can simply speak around the truth.

"Motome-san, how do you know that Kitsuki-sama received training from the Kitsuki School of Investigation?" Yojiro asked, trying to ignore his subconscious deception.

Motome sat back on her cushion, her slight wince indicating that Obo's loss had not been painless.

"I first met Kitsuki-sama about ten years ago at a tavern in the North Rim neighborhood in Fishers' Quarter. I was there investigating burglaries. He heard that I was Otomo-sama's personal yoriki and approached me, asking me to help him. He seemed somewhat unnerved. Frantic, really. He told me someone was following him. Trying to kill him. He kept looking over his shoulder and seemed scared of his own shadow."

"Those sentiments seem natural here in Ryokō Owari," Yojiro observed. "I felt that same disorientation when I arrived earlier today. Otomo-sama's own fear seems to have blossomed from a similar effect."

"No, this was different. Kitsuki-sama kept muttering strange nonsense about shinobi. Roof climbers. Ambushes. Poison. Assassins. At first, I thought he was merely a raving drunkard, but he showed me a piece of paper with a strange symbol on it, a kind of serpentine pattern of knotted strokes and crescents." Motome hesitated a moment to stare at Yojiro with her honey-colored eyes. After a deep breath to clear the suspicion wrinkled in her forehead, she continued, "He told me that the picture was a dark Scorpion secret, something he would be killed for if the Scorpion knew he had it. I was still unsure, but he kept repeating himself in such incredible earnest. That I needed to help him. That he was not safe. I told him we could talk when he was sober, hoping he would make more sense later, so I left him overnight.

"The next morning, I visited the inn where he was staying, a place called the Fortuitous Wind. He did not quite remember me, probably due to the drunkenness. I repeated what he had told me the night before, the story about the Scorpion killing him, and he denied that, too. He only acknowledged that I spoke the truth after I mentioned his drawing of that strange symbol. He invited me in and confessed that he had been sent to Ryokō Owari by his masters at the Kitsuki School of Investigation to observe covert Scorpion activity. Anything illegal or incriminating."

"How do you know that he was telling the truth?"

"He showed me his secret identification papers and his instructions from the investigator school. They were signed by the Kitsuki family daimyō."

"Do you have those documents here?"

"No, they were not on his person when he died," Motome explained, somewhat defiantly in the face of Yojiro's question. "But I am sure we can find them if we search his room at the inn. Otomo-sama has yet to sign a search warrant for me. He has been busy with other investigations."

Oh yes, the dangerous Storm Tiger ninja gang.

"Anyway, when Kitsuki-sama showed me those documents, he said that he had started to gather information regarding Scorpion shinobi. My reaction to him was similar to yours. I laughed at him and went back to thinking that perhaps this was just some joke or hallucinatory ravings. Even with all the crime here in Ryokō Owari, I could not believe that the samurai of a Great Clan would flagrantly violate the Imperial edict that forbids the use of shinobi. But he said that he was not a liar, just as earnestly I insisted that to you, Yojiro-sama. He asked if I would help him."

"And you said you would?"

"This was about the time when Otomo-sama developed an interest in ninja activity. He had mentioned seeing spies inside the manor, which spurred his fierce campaigns against them. I thought that by helping Kitsuki-sama, I could help Otomo-sama's efforts as well. So, I told Kitsuki-sama I would."

"Did he ever explain what the strange symbol was?" Yojiro asked, almost more confused by the story than enlightened. What strange Scorpion secrets had the two of them stumbled upon?

"He said something about a coded picture. An image that the shinobi could use to leave messages in plain sight for each other. I think it looked more like a tattoo. However, I could be mistaken. I only saw it once. In fact, I did not see Kitsuki-sama again after that day, owing to the secrecy of our missions. He did keep in contact, however, sending me messages every few months hidden in my packages from my laundress." Motome opened a small wooden box that contained dozens of slips of paper no wider than her little finger. Yojiro selected a handful and scanned their contents.

"Scouted Blossom Dock. Followed but lost him at the Bay of Drowned Honor."

"Counted four, maybe five, potential suspects while watching Alabaster Street. Talking about poisoned opium."

"Gathering planned. Rooftop of Temple of Amaterasu. Date undetermined. Will observe the area."

"Shadows sighted. Iron Wharf. Hour of the Ox. Escaped again."

The rest of them were similar. Places. Times. Shadows and rumors from all over the city, each one eluding Obo's firm grasp. There were no real patterns, no linked facts, no actual substantive accomplishments. In fact, Yojiro saw no real evidence of shinobi in the messages, only reports so vague that they stank of a productive incompetence, much like Seno's own ninja-hunting activities. The bumbling reports of a man pretending to work.

However, another possibility surfaced as Yojiro read through more of them, remembering Motome's story about a drunk, paranoid Kitsuki investigator afraid of his own shadow, afraid of death. Perhaps chasing ghosts had twisted Obo, goading him to obsessively attempt to prove the impossible: that shinobi exist. His shame and fear of the truth, perhaps, had driven him to paranoia and delusion. Maybe Motome's naïve, conveniently timed faith in his story had reset his deluding self-assurances.

Yojiro looked over the slips again, noting the careful handwriting, Motome's added dates on the backs, the chop marks that matched Obo's signature. The only glimmer of proof that shinobi existed was Motome's mention of the painting Obo had showed her at their first meeting. If only Yojiro could find it, or someone who might know about it.

"Thank you for sharing this with me, Motome-san," Yojiro said, helping her return the evidence back to the chest. "Please excuse my continued skepticism of the shinobi component. These slips are an interesting collection, but I think that perhaps they need to be sorted to make more sense to my slow sensibilities. Maybe we will find something more obvious after we search Kitsuki-sama's apartment. In the meantime, I think it is time to move on to Aramoro-sama's involvement."

"Of course. I will arrange for an interrogation immediately." She handed him a scroll before rising and rushing to the door. "This report details what I have found thus far that implicates Aramoro-sama in the death of Kitsuki Obo."

Half an hour later, Yojiro pinched his lips to smother a weak, watery unease that was creeping into his chest as the guards led Aramoro into the interrogation room. The accused killer's cruel mouth dangled in a mocking smile, a perversion of the oni mask that usually covered the bottom half of his face. Yojiro dared not look away.

"It is good to see you again, Aramoro-sama," he began.

"Yes, it is," Aramoro snickered, dark humor painting his sharp eyes. "The honest Scorpion descends to the City of Lies. Good indeed."

"I come at the command of the Emerald Champion to aid in investigating your involvement in the issue at hand."

"If that's what you believe..." Aramoro trailed off, his leer deepening. "Where's the Seppun woman?"

"Since her report said you were rather quiet during her interviews with you, I suggested that you might say more without her here."

"Fine." Without taking his eyes off Yojiro, he addressed the guards. "You may leave us. I have much to discuss with my fellow Scorpion."

Yojiro nodded at the order, a bit unnerved that Aramoro so smoothly assumed command over everyone around him, even when he was in chains. The guards sidled out, brusquely barring the heavy door behind them to lock the two Scorpion in. Aramoro slumped himself down onto his zabuton, refusing to bend his knees in polite seiza. Yojiro ignored it.

"I have a few questions to ask you," he began. "I would like to hear your version of the events behind Kitsuki Obo's dea–"

"You know, I talked to your sister just before I left Otosan Uchi," Aramoro interrupted, chuckling. "Do you know what she called you, Yojiro? After the tournament?"

"That does not concern our present topic–"

"She called you a lapdog to a lion. One with an emerald collar. Is that not a delightful picture? So fierce."

Yojiro ignored the provocation. "Why are you here in Ryokō Owari? I was not aware that Lord Shoju gave you freedom to travel."

"I wouldn't call this freedom," Aramoro snapped, swishing a finger around to point at the thick walls. "No air. Too much light from these damned lanterns. Half-wit sentries to watch me sleep and piss."

"As far as I am aware, you have not been mistreated while in Otomo Seno-sama's custody."

"I wasn't mistreated until they locked me up with you, you servile worm."

Yojiro frowned.

"Yes, you would be the one Toturi would pick," Aramoro grumbled, still enjoying the power of his jabs. "You're so honorable. So… trustworthy."

Aramoro's bitterness recalled the tournament of the Emerald Champion, and Yojiro stiffened inside his high collar.

Does Aramoro know I warned Toturi?

He attempted to fathom a spark of knowledge inside Aramoro's reddened eyes but only saw the samurai making his own calculations.

No. He's searching me, too. He only suspects. How could someone so alert allow himself to get caught?

"Why are you in this city, Aramoro-sama?"

"To suffer my humiliating defeat in exile, of course. I fled Otosan Uchi for my reputation's sake. If I must hide, why not crawl into the cave with the best pleasure courts in Rokugan in it?"

"And how do you account for your involvement in Kitsuki Obo's murder?"

"Bad fortune," Aramoro said, obviously amused. "We were guests at the same inn. He ended up dead, and it seems his bad luck is trying to drag me down with him. Perhaps I have not been saying enough prayers to Fukurokujin for daily deliverance."

"Did you know him?"

"No."

"Motome-san's report indicates several witnesses saw you speaking with the Kitsuki the day before he was found dead in the street."

Aramoro smiled, his angular teeth glistening in the lamplight. "Bad fortune, indeed."

"Her report also suggests that your clothes had blood on them."

"A shaving accident."

"As you are the Whisper of Steel, a shaving accident seems unlikely," Yojiro said, growing tired and angry at the samurai's deflections. Aramoro was obviously lying, but Yojiro could not tell if he was lying for the sake of the clan or out of spite. Either way, his lies were an unnecessary obstacle. "Aramoro-sama, an honest answer from you would make my duties much easier."

Suddenly, Aramoro's face hardened into a frightening scowl. "Is that why you fail at your duty? Because you think it should be easy? No, Yojiro. Betrayal is easy. And you are lower than selfish swine spit if you believe you are superior to those of us who sacrifice everything for the clan."

This stung more than all Aramoro's past insults. No matter how he defended the actions he had taken during the tournament of the Emerald Champion, the Scorpion would only ever see it as disloyalty. He had undone their treachery, but he had also slighted their Mother of Scorpions with his failure.

Yojiro stood, rising above Aramoro's cheap blows, and knocked on the door to signal the guards to unlock it. "I will return when you are ready to talk, Aramoro-sama."

He left the room without a second glance. Motome stood outside, waiting for him, holding an armful of writing utensils for composing a report about his conversation with Aramoro.

"Did he tell you anything useful?" she asked. "Or did he just laugh in your face like he did to me?"

Yojiro stared at Motome a moment, relief unknotting his stomach. During the last several hours, working with this Seppun yoriki had been so simple compared to the layers of tricks, feints, and plots inherent in dealing with his own clan. Aramoro. Hyobu and Denmaru. Even the pathetic Ikku demanded precautions, discernments, wary responses. He smiled. For the first time, it seemed, he knew what trust felt like.

CHAPTER FIVE

Yojiro returned to the estate of the Emerald magistrate the next day to ask Seno for the search warrant. Motome was already in the waterfall courtyard. She crouched, almost in a combat stance, fierce anger contorting her face. The old Emerald magistrate took no notice as he studied several thick scrolls stacked upon his tiny bamboo desk.

"Ah, Bayushi-sama," Seno sneered over the loudness of the falling water. "You are just in time. I was telling Motome-san that the Storm Tigers have confessed their despicable crimes."

"Those fools admitted to being ninja?" Yojiro asked, incredulous. Under the law, if they gave verbal testimony, they could be condemned and punished, even if no physical evidence could be found to prove their guilt.

"Yes, finally. They were loath to relinquish their wicked secrets, but my perseverance was rewarded after I sent an interrogator."

"They confessed under torture?"

"And now he is planning their executions!" Motome shouted. Had there been no waterfall, she might have been reprimanded for defiance. Her eyes pleaded with Yojiro, the shame of her participation smoldering inside her.

"There is no precedent in our archives for how ninja ought to be executed," Seno said, ignoring Motome and scouring his law scrolls. "However, I think boiling them alive might be just."

"No," Yojiro argued. "You cannot do this."

"Bayushi-sama," Seno snapped, his bony face growing gaunter with indignation. He folded his arms, glaring at the Scorpion magistrate. "These criminals are under my jurisdiction, so I shall be their judge. You have no control over anything in this city except for that pathetic investigation Toturi-sama allows you to play with. You would do well to remember this."

Lightning fast, Yojiro raced through the situation in his mind. Buyu and the others were not ninja. Merely ruffians. Seno's obsession had stretched too far. Executing them for worse crimes than their own would be a grave injustice, a mockery of the law.

But I will gain no ground fighting him. In fact, I may lose it if, in his rage, he refuses to issue our search warrant. My first duty is to uncover Obo's secrets, for my clan. However, Bushidō demands I fight to prevent this injustice, and as his equal in rank, only I can.

"Otomo-sama," Yojiro began, selecting his words with the utmost care. He could not afford the convenient slip of a lie with Motome watching. "I am afraid that in my haste, I did not communicate myself well. Please forgive me."

"Oh?" Seno said, his chin wrinkled with bitterness.

"Yes, I did not intend to defy your prerogative or your power over this city. As Emerald magistrate of Ryokō Owari, you have Heaven's blessing to enforce and judge the sacred laws of our land here. I simply thought that perhaps, since this is an exceptional situation, you should inform Toturi-sama of your achievement first. After all, no Emerald magistrate has successfully captured ninja in eight or nine centuries. He may want to inspect your prisoners before you execute them."

Seno stroked the black hair on his chin, pondering, though suspicious of the Scorpion's supposition. "What trick are you playing, Bayushi-sama?"

"No trick, Otomo-sama. I merely present the possible consequences of your success. Toturi-sama may want to make an example of you and your efforts for other magistrates."

"Yojiro-sama is right, Otomo-sama," Motome added, catching on to his ploy and adding to the bait. She knelt before Seno in humble supplication. "Please allow me to write a letter to Toturi-sama, telling him of our accomplishment here."

"No. I shall write the letter of my accomplishment," Seno asserted, greedy excitement causing his hands to tremble. "Yes, Toturi-sama will want to hear of my victory for justice. Such important news surely will interest him."

Moments later, Seno scraped an inkstick into an enormous black puddle on his inkstone for a long letter while Motome and Yojiro left, bearing away their search warrant.

"Thank you," Motome muttered. Despite their success in saving the Storm Tigers, her voice was low, soft with dejection, her warm eyes wet with a repentant sorrow. "How foolish I was. My part in this wretched business was dishonorable."

"You obeyed your lord, loyally fulfilling your duty, Motome-san," Yojiro reassured her.

"Yes, but I defied his judgment, his authority. I was so afraid of my mistake that I became a disobedient servant. I fought against my master."

"But your compassion and integrity were noble..." Yojiro stopped. His tongue grew leaden. She had done exactly what he had done to Kachiko, and she longed for reprimand. They both defied their masters' authority, seeking to undo their personal mistakes. Motome to save the Storm Tigers a cruel fate. Yojiro for his own honor. They had righted the treacherous wrongs of their masters, but was there dishonor in such disobedience? Were there karmic consequences for defying even a wicked lord?

Was Aramoro right? Am I merely justifying my disloyalty? Motome is prepared to sacrifice her honor for Seno. Am I not willing to sacrifice myself for my clan? To suffer for duty?

Yojiro winced at the implications. He had considered himself selfless, righteous, pure. But now, he could see the stain upon his skin that Aramoro had spat upon, the one that disgusted Kachiko. He shook his head. *Can I be just and a Scorpion at the same time?*

In spite of his initial hesitation, Yojiro and Motome rode a rickshaw to the Fishers' Quarter to find the inn where Obo had spent the last twelve years. The Fortuitous Wind, a derelict two-story guesthouse, squatted inside a back alley near the docks. Generations of dead fish and unbathed fisherfolk had pressed their oily scent into every board and brick, and the gutters along the alley ran brown with constant trickles of fish guts draining into the Bay of Drowned Honor. The entire district was nearly black as dusk that morning, the sky engulfed in the reeking smoke from innumerable cooking fires and smokehouses. Sailors, butchers, vendors, smokers, and cooks scuttled past to process their catches before rot sank in.

Surely a Dragon Clan gold trader could afford better accommodations. Especially if he really was funded by the Kitsuki School of Investigation. Why did Obo choose to live here? Was the location inconspicuous? Closer to shinobi activity?

The last thought made him laugh at himself.

You are starting to sound like Seno.

Outside the inn, a few filthy urchins played in the street puddles. They eyed Motome but thought better of throwing sludge balls when they saw Yojiro.

They must know not to disturb a well-dressed Scorpion.

"I need to go speak with another witness to finish my report," Motome mumbled, pointing to a man across the alleyway smoking gray squid over a filthy brick oven. "Go show the innkeeper our warrant, and I will meet you in there."

Yojiro lingered a moment as Motome crossed the street, watching her engage the fish smoker. He seemed shy, almost unwilling to speak to her, so she loosened her purse and dropped a few coins into his hand. She saw Yojiro still standing there, so she waved him away, turning back to the laborer.

It seemed a little strange that she suddenly trusted him enough to be autonomous. Was it a show of faith? What were they talking about?

Yojiro slid open the door of the Fortuitous Wind and stepped inside. He only had a moment to dodge a filthy dishrag that splatted against the wall near his head. His hand whipped to his katana, silencing a chorus of accompanying guffaws. A roomful of wide-eyed sailors stared back at him, guilt freezing their faces at their mistake. Seeing Yojiro's fine silk, they crumpled back into private conversations, cautiously eyeing the spot where he stood.

"Oh no!" an old man shouted, running and smearing the greasy smudge on the wall with another rag. He could barely hide an overly playful grin at his joke, even if it had gone amiss. He jumped up and down, trying to mop up the final slimy spot. "Forgive me, sir! We thought that Ebi-kun was back for more!"

The room buzzed with nervous laughter. The sailors were crowded around tables in the small common room, drinking weak sake and sour tea from chipped cups. The walls had other oily splatters, and the floor slipped beneath his sandals, which he dared not remove at the door. Juniper-scented oil lamps sat smoking everywhere, trying vainly to stave off the smell of fish, turning the air thick and gracelessly pungent.

The old man, still giggling to himself, skipped past Yojiro to finish his table rounds with a teapot. He wore a cloth cap over his balding head, liver spots freckled his face, and he boasted but a few teeth, browned with age. Despite his many years, the man's back was unbent, his gait spry.

"Excuse me, Uncle," Yojiro addressed him, assuming he was the proprietor of the inn. "Forgive my intrusion. I have come as a representative of the Emerald magistrate."

"The Emerald magistrate?" the old man gasped, a gnarled hand rising to his mouth. His melodramatic tone sounded flippant. "What does old man Otomo want here?"

Yojiro's brow furrowed. As a samurai, he had never been addressed with such boldness from a peasant, let alone one who would casually refer to a superior with such nonchalance and disrespect. In fact, Yojiro did not know old men of any class who talked like that.

"I have a search warrant to inspect the room formerly tenanted by Kitsuki Obo."

"Obo-sama? But what would you want with – ah! Ebi-kun!" the old man squealed. A young man entered wearing a fisherman's short *kosode* and a black scarf looped around his neck. The owner flung the dishrag anew, joined by several sailors throwing rubbish or hats or cups. However, the target merely darted aside and between them with unusual dexterity, the articles splattering and smashing to the floor. The room again filled with roars of amusement.

"You need a new game, Jin-sama," the young man scolded, shaking his head, though a silent delight colored his dark eyes. "I win again."

"No, no, no," the old man Jin nagged. "We will hit you one of these days, Ebi-kun. You are such a cheat!"

More mannerisms that ill-befitted his age emerged in the old man with Ebi's entrance. A delicate wrist flick with the teapot. A sway to the hips. A flirtatious eye.

Yojiro interrupted their conversation, grasping the innkeeper's soft arm gently. "Excuse me, Jin-san."

"What do you want?" Ebi demanded, coming close, nearly springing between the two of them in defense.

"He comes from the Emerald magistrate," Jin explained hurriedly, waving his hand to calm Ebi. "Here to talk about Obo-sama. No need to worry. I will take care of it."

Both Jin and Ebi referred to the Kitsuki by his first name. So, they knew him well.

The fisherman stood down but kept mistrustful eyes fixed on Yojiro. He sat down at a nearby table and began whispering with the sailors.

"Perhaps we can talk in another room, somewhere more private," Yojiro suggested, pointing to the sliding doors of the back rooms.

Jin nodded, sharing a final, wary glance with Ebi before leading the way. "Of course. Please follow me."

They went into a tiny storeroom stuffed with rank futon mattresses and cheap linens, a tiny window netted with cobwebs admitting the only light. Yojiro shut the door behind them. Jin shrank into the corner, growing somewhat shy, rubbing his hands together and biting his lip.

"Forgive my eagerness," Yojiro began, quite sure of his deduction now. Jin was not a man but a woman. A young woman. "I have serious business I would like to conduct in your fine establishment. It is yours, is it not?"

"Oh yes, it is." Jin's demure unease made her previous caprice all the more telling.

"Well, you seem to care for it with such youthful vigor," Yojiro said pointedly. "However, I am sure that since you do not see many of my rank or status here often, you might be concerned to know that your… performance of duty toward me was somewhat lacking. An earnest member of your station would do well to remember differences of class conduct and act accordingly."

Jin had started to sweat tiny drops, but a childish pride was also beginning to harden her jaw. "You… observe well."

"And, if I might add one more piece of advice," Yojiro continued. "A man, especially a man of venerable years, ought to act with more dignity when in the presence of young, handsome men. I have never seen old men tease quite as you do, and I cannot say I find it appropriate for your role."

"I understand your meaning," Jin said, sulkily, as a child caught stealing pressed-sugar candy. "You honor me with the lesson. I shall… act, as you say, more in line with my age, station, and gender."

"I might suggest spending more time with aged men, to learn their ways."

Jin smiled, that flirtatious sparkle lighting up the eyes again. "Are you volunteering to show me those ways?"

Yojiro grinned. "I am not that old."

"Of course not. Old men never think they are when in the right company."

Yojiro smiled and bowed to the young woman, a small respect for her growing. She was an excellent Soshi shugenja. Her illusion had been quite good with its extreme attention to detail, tricking even him at first. However, her poor acting had shattered that mask far too easily. Still in training, perhaps, making the innkeeper Jin a practice role. She must have a clever sensei. An inn constantly full of strangers made for a perfect training ground, where mistakes and inconsistencies might pass unnoticed.

"Now, to business," he continued, showing her his magisterial identification papers and search warrant. "I am Bayushi Yojiro,

Emerald magistrate from Otosan Uchi. I come not only on behalf of the Emerald Champion himself but also on behalf of Governor Hyobu to work with local authorities in investigating Kitsuki Obo-sama's death."

"I see," the young woman said, still in her old man's voice, though it had deepened somewhat with an anxious guilt.

"Did you get to know him well while working here?"

"Yes…" the shugenja trailed off, growing graver at the question. "In a way."

"What way?"

Before she could answer, the door suddenly slid open, and Ebi, a suspicious glower marring his face, marched into their small meeting space. He strode directly between them, hiding the young woman behind him.

"Someone is here to see you, sir," he said, pointing back out in the common room at Motome.

"There you are, Yojiro-sama," the Seppun samurai said. Her eyebrows arched at finding them in a closet, but she held her tongue. "Shall we inspect Kitsuki-sama's room?"

Yojiro nodded, stepping out. The false Jin gave them a key and directions to Obo's apartment before returning to her customers, this time more carefully hunching her back and hobbling her step.

As they walked toward the stairs to the second floor, Motome touched Yojiro's arm lightly. "Did you notice anything strange about that young fisherman?" she whispered.

"Beyond his marvelous reflexes and irritability, no," Yojiro confessed, creasing his brow. "What did you see?"

"Nothing really," she confessed. "Except that he is the cleanest fisherman I ever saw. He doesn't even stink."

Yojiro looked over his shoulder back at Ebi, who still fixed a sharp glare upon him. As far as Yojiro could tell, the man wore no illusion. However, he was missing the calluses on his hands that came from the constant wear of rope and net. He was also not nearly as sun scorched as the other fisherfolk and sailors in the common room.

How odd. Jin. Ebi. Obo. Three people under one roof with secret selves…

"What did your witness across the street say?" Yojiro asked as they found Obo's room and entered using the key. The cramped chamber, though significantly cleaner than the rest of the Fortuitous Wind, had mold-soiled tatami mats and a narrow sliding window. A fine layer of dust and stray soot from outside coated the chest of drawers, desk, and folded futon. No one had been in here in weeks.

"He said he had seen the Kitsuki many times over the last ten years," answered Motome, taking note of the furnishings, careful not to disturb too much yet. "They never spoke, but he said there were neighborhood rumors about why he had decided to live in North Rim instead in the Merchant Quarter like the other trade ministers. Something about associating with street orphans who eventually were never seen again. As far as I can tell, it was merely vulgar gossip."

"Are you sure?" Yojiro asked. Every new detail about this man was stranger than the last. "What if he were a child stealer?"

Motome's face grew steely, her thin lips quivering in a sudden rage. "Street children disappear all the time, and do you know who is to blame? Scorpion crime lords. Scorpion toughs. They have sucked this city's marrow to dust. Opium eaters. Thieves. Whoremongers. Living in this wretched city has showed me to what depraved depths your clan's lies and manipulations sink. And when someone tries to stop you, to loosen some of your chokeholds around our throats, they end up dead!"

Her unexpected outburst ended as quickly as it had sprung. She looked away, her cheeks crimson in embarrassment. Yojiro stood, uneasily watching as the tense moment stretched into silence. He sank behind his collar.

Was this a distraction? An emotional attempt at changing the subject? She had wanted to talk to the fish smoker in private, so perhaps she was hiding what their conversation had truly been about. He tried to read her body to confirm, but the stiff shoulders angled away from him, and her sinking jaw spoke of pain. Her posture huddled around her heart.

"Motome-san," he started, unsure of what to say. He swallowed.

"Forgive me," Motome muttered, squeezing the handle of her jitte with a shaking fist. "That witness went missing the day Otomo-sama assigned me to take over the case from Captain Denmaru. Another inconvenient obstruction. I was angry. Now, being in Kitsuki-sama's room reminds me too much… of how I must now do all this alone. The loss of a comrade-in-arms against this dark, lying city is difficult."

Yojiro's first instincts were to lie, to attempt to save face for his clan, but there was no point in defending his clan in light of her experience. Ryōkō Owari Toshi was plagued by all that she said it was. In fact, he was there to be part of it. Kachiko had made sure of that. In the end, no matter how much he wanted to be honest with Motome – as honest as she ever had been with him, even to her humiliation – no matter how conflicted he was in his soul, he would need to race her to the truth, to absolve Aramoro by any means necessary, to hide any hint of Scorpion guilt. He knew he would be forced to betray her.

I can only commit to tell her the truth where I can. No more.

"You know, Motome-san," he started again, his heart still heavy. He looked her straight in the eyes and tempered his voice to an even pitch, just as any good liar is trained to. "I am on your side."

Her chin tightened as her teeth ground together. She let out a strained breath, and her cheeks softened as she relented.

"Perhaps," she muttered, turning her back to him. "We shall see."

Together, they made a careful dissection of the room. The drawers were stuffed with many sets of used kimono, all altered to fit, like Obo's death clothes had been. They also found a shaving mirror and razor, several pairs of geta with worn soles, small jars of medicinal ointment, and a volume of the *Tao of Shinsei*, bound in green and yellow silk – Dragon colors. The pages felt crisp and the spine was unstretched.

The only other bit of furniture was a magnolia-wood desk with a deep red lacquer finish. Not quite master grade, but clever work. The legs were fashioned like the squat claws of a tortoise, the edges etched with wildflowers native to Yuma Province, indicative of Soshi artisans. Though it was not odd for Obo to have had a Scorpion-made desk, as he had been living in a Scorpion city, the uncommon expense of this particular extravagance clashed with his threadbare, secondhand lifestyle. The light yet strong wood of magnolia trees was cultivated exclusively for decorative crafts, making it a costly piece.

Perhaps this was the only luxury he was allowed. It certainly is only conspicuous to those allowed within this room.

The drawers were locked, but Motome had brought Obo's tiny brass key, which fit. Despite getting past the locks, the drawers were lodged shut. With a quick jerk, Yojiro wrenched a drawer out, sending papers and brushes bursting onto the floor. Files on gold pricing, scrolls, and loose slips of paper like Motome's messages had been crammed into every space inside the desk, with ink bottles and ragged brushes wedged in between the gaps. Yojiro scanned the mess for the Scorpion symbol Obo had showed Motome at their first meeting. Seeing nothing similar, he fished out a particularly well-worn notebook tucked carefully in the back of one drawer and flipped through the pages. Place names appeared. House of the Plum Blossom, House of the Morning Star, House of Foreign Stories – geisha houses from Ryokō Owari's Licensed Quarter. Next to the locations were names, printed in tiny characters, along with dates scattered over the last ten years.

"It seems our trade minister was a frequenter of pleasure houses," Yojiro said, handing Motome the ledger. "The names of his favored geisha performers, perhaps?"

Motome scanned the lists. "I don't know. We should take all his documents back to the magistrate's manor so we can reference them against the police archives. There is too much here to properly address in one sitting, anyway."

Yojiro nodded, gathering the papers that had fallen beneath the desk. Crouching beneath, he paused to look for a tradesperson's marking for the piece. The bottom was unmarked by any guild, trade school, or craftsperson. Yojiro froze. Unmarked work often meant secret work. He ran his hand over the smooth grain. As his fingers climbed up the sides, he felt a tiny, raised bump. A nearly invisible switch had been fashioned into the side, probably a latch for a false bottom.

Yojiro's heart sank as he stood from beneath the desk.

A need to lie so soon. Mere moments after my commitment to be honest.

Motome was bundling the documents into easily transportable packets, oblivious of his discovery. She had been so honest with him, even about her inability to trust him. And she wanted to trust him, even made efforts toward overcoming her reticence, such as granting him a private audience with Aramoro as a show of faith. How could he return her efforts with treachery?

His mouth almost opened of its own accord, but he clamped his lips shut, struggling to smother the news.

Kachiko's mournful threat played across his mind again.

"The Traitor's Grove is such a cold place. I would hate to have to visit you there."

Failure meant more than death. Failure meant losing his soul. If Obo's desk had been Dragon made, he would not have to hide it. But... this development was too risky a coincidence.

Perhaps honesty is worth the price. Aramoro spoke of sacrifice for clan loyalty, but perhaps I can make that same sacrifice for... Who am I making this sacrifice for?

Rokugan. Rokugan was his treasure. The emperor, his master. If Yojiro were affixed to a tree, he could not defend the Empire. As the only honest Scorpion, there were things only he could do to save it. He could not fail again if he wanted to continue to serve.

He turned his back on the desk and silently unfastened the window before kneeling to help Motome.

I will come back tonight to open the desk. Alone.

CHAPTER SIX

The Hour of the Rat lay silent as Yojiro slipped into the backstreet in the Fishers' Quarter. District lanterns had long been extinguished, and only the occasional feral cat prowled the viscous darkness. The suffocating daytime smoke had died down, letting the stench of fish bloom in the hot night air. The moon glistened in the street slime, and amorphous clouds conjured waxing and waning shapes in the alleys. Yojiro's eyes had grown somewhat accustomed to the shadows, as he had walked in darkness all the way from his room in Shosuro Palace, through the deserted Merchant Quarter, to the North Rim. Worried about a Thunder Guard spy, he had bound his feet with sandal coverings woven from hemp cords to smother the sounds of his footfalls and had covered the glint of his lacquered scabbards with black woolen stockings before sneaking out.

The stinking alleyway beneath Obo's window was narrow enough for Yojiro to climb between the walls, so he pressed one hand and knee against each side, gently easing himself up to the second story. Pushing tightly against either wall, his arms burned, his muscles less limber after years in a magistrate's chair. Inching up between the two buildings, he finally reached the window. He let go of the walls, using only his knees and feet to wedge himself securely in place. His legs trembled with his weight, so he quickly wormed his fingernails into the casement to open it.

The wood squealed. He froze, waiting in silence. Long, heavy minutes passed before he could assure himself that no one heard. Drawing a candle from his sleeve, he ground the wax into the wood channel, working by feel in the darkness. His legs continued to tremble with tension. His breath shortened.

Bishamon-no-Kami, help me.

Slowly, he tested the window again. The wood creaked much more quietly. It would have to do. His knees shivered, seizing up. As his legs gave out, Yojiro snapped the window open and leaped into the room. He tumbled lightly across the tatami, landing on his hands and knees. Again, he waited, straining against the silence to hear if anyone stirred. Nothing.

He dared to catch his breath and muttered a silent prayer of thanks to the Fortune of Strength, for bolstering him. Adding more wax to the casement, he shut it again, silently.

He used his fire striker to light the candle and crept to the desk. The flame glowed hot in the deep red stain, reflecting his own face as if he were submerged in a pool of blood. He knelt to inspect the secret switch. The craftsman had hidden the tiny button, scarcely larger than a grain of rice, in a swirl of the magnolia, the natural wood lines drawing attention away from it. However, concealment often was not enough to protect secrets. Gingerly, he pressed the switch with the bottom of the candle instead of his finger. As he expected, a short, silver needle emerged, triggered by the pressure, stabbing the wax harmlessly and leaving a milky drop behind.

Scorpion venom.

A secret panel dropped from the bottom of the desk, revealing a shallow drawer with an iron ring handle. He grasped it and pulled slowly, listening for any more mechanisms inside that might signal more traps. Nothing more clicked. Inside the drawer lay stacked packets of letters, a black silk-bound book, and Obo's identification stamped by the chop of the Kitsuki family daimyō, which Motome had mentioned before. The letters were addressed to Obo from the Kitsuki School of Investigation and carefully arranged by date. He opened the most recent one, dated only a month before Obo's death.

"Greetings, my pupil. Your last communiqué regarding the illegal activities of these Storm Tigers has been relayed to our superiors. We were worried after hearing rumors that they were mere street toughs, but at your assurance, we have updated our records."

Yojiro shook his head. *The Kitsuki investigators have a reputation for being so precise. How could they be fooled? Was Obo truly a fraud, only chasing phantoms in his delusion, like Seno?*

"We have a new task for you," the letter continued, "one that takes precedence for its danger. Another interesting rumor has come to our attention, one circulating through the Scorpion spy network. Our informant tells us that Soshi Ezo, the shadow master, is still alive, and that he is in Ryokō Owari. If this is true, find him. If he only faked his death ten years ago, then his dangerous art of…"

Yojiro paused, unsure of how to read the next word, having never seen it before. The characters were "shadow" and "form," but that introduced a paradox. Shadows had no form.

Shadow form? Is it read kagegata? *Kagenari?*

"…then his dangerous art of kagenari has been thriving all this time. Do not engage him. He is possibly the most dangerous shinobi the Scorpion have yet produced. Until next month,

"Kitsuki Jusai."

Yojiro's heart stopped, his mind rapidly drawing lines between the letter's implications. He did not know Soshi Ezo, or what a shadow master could possibly be, but if this letter was authentic, then the Kitsuki investigators believed Ezo to be a shinobi. Did this confirm Motome's story? Somehow, they had discovered this from Scorpion spies, which not only meant that the Dragon had infiltrated his clan but that they now assuredly knew that the Scorpion used shinobi.

He scanned the paper, the calligraphy, struggling to find any stroke, any defect that could discredit the letter as a fraud. It did not follow Obo's handwriting, even if disguised. The outside was worn and scuffed, as if the letter had actually been transported a long distance. The paper matched none of the paper found within the desk. The signature? He snatched up Obo's secret identification papers again. The chop marks matched, reading "Kitsuki Jusai, the Kitsuki family daimyō." Yojiro paled. As an Emerald magistrate, he had seen this chop mark several times in passing. The letters were genuine.

Yojiro shoved the letter into his pocket, as if burying it could erase the message. But the words echoed inside his skull. Scorpion shinobi. His breath rattled. His clan retained samurai who had abandoned the laws of Bushidō.

What else did Kachiko not tell me? Does she even know?

Yojiro grasped the notebook bound in black silk, thumbing through the pages. These seemed to be Obo's investigation notes, charting his efforts from the day he arrived until his death, a span of twelve years. Settling into this new, dark city. Exploring the different districts, particularly the Merchant Quarter with its blatant crime. Observing the hierarchies of street and firefighter gangs contending with each other and bribing the Thunder Guard. Meeting and judging Otomo Seno as a capable though unwise magistrate. Locating the opium dens sanctioned by

Hyobu. Yojiro hovered over the pages near the time when Obo first met and started working with Motome ten years ago.

"The shadows move without the flicker of flames," Obo had written, his characters large and unbalanced – wild, even. "There are eyes in all the alleys. I turn corners, footfalls promising me someone is there, but no one ever is. Ever since I left that wicked temple, they have followed me. These moving, stalking, suffocating shadows! It's this city! This lying city with its festering sores! It's to blame. This lying city will be my death."

The words sounded like Yojiro's own terror of Ryokō Owari from yesterday. Shapes and shades fooling the eyes, the mind conjuring faces for the silhouettes, never knowing if someone was following. From the sound of it, Obo must have been hallucinating, seeing shinobi in every shadow. Yojiro turned the page to the next entry.

"I will now be working with Seppun Motome, yoriki to Seno," the log read, the handwriting suddenly calmer, returning to its tight, careful characters. "She is driven by ethics, not as perceptive as she thinks, too eagerly dazzled by hope's bright star. Her connection to Seno may prove useful."

Yojiro blinked, reading the notes again. Something had changed. He searched for the root of a torn page, but there was none. Obo had simply moved on, his paranoia cured. He scanned pages again. He was missing something.

What changed after Obo met Motome?

The faint hiss of a dagger was Yojiro's only warning.

He flung himself back, away from the downward thrust aimed for his head. His fumbling feet caused him to drop the candle and book, and the darkness splashed thick around him, rippling with his fear as he drew his wakizashi with hot fingers. He couldn't remember the last time he had wielded a blade in defense of his life. It slipped in his hands.

Calm yourself! Listen. Act!

His anxious commands crowded his reaction time. A smooth stroke to his left shredded his kimono, and Yojiro only had a moment to flinch before his legs danced away in a half-remembered fighting reflex. The wind of another blow sliced toward his right side, and he caught his enemy's blade with his own, scratching up a vain illumination of sparks.

My luck won't last. I must leave now!

Leaping away from his assailant, he tumbled toward the window, but his opponent had anticipated his move and stood there, already waiting.

He's too fast!

Yojiro sprang to the door, fumbling with the lock only a moment before flinging open the shōji screen to reveal the burst of moonlight in the hall. A second assailant leaped from behind the puddle of light, crashing into Yojiro, who barely lifted his weapon in time to block a heart-aimed slash. The force shoved him back. Yojiro flinched, waiting for a blow from his rearward attacker. But it never came. The space behind him was empty.

He dared not wait at the mercy of two attackers, so Yojiro ducked beneath the dagger of his forward foe into the hall and bounded toward the stairs. He had only just leaped down a few steps before a jolt on the stairs below divulged the presence of a third attacker, rushing up to meet him. He skittered back up the steps, avoiding four sharp thrusts, the last of which slammed into the wood near his foot. He instinctively kicked the blade away, which clanged down into the dark, and he launched himself straight into his attacker's body.

His body slam met with empty air. He toppled down the rest of the stairs with a crash, knocking the wind from himself. The blood pounded in his ears, and he shook his head to clear it, hoping to catch a hint of the three attackers. Through the flood of adrenaline, he could only make out the light footfalls of a single one.

Where did the others go?

Yojiro bounded to his feet, circling away from the sound. However, the sound leaped, as if by echo, from before him to behind him, and Yojiro had to dive forward to avoid a blow to his back.

Impossible. How can he move through me like a ghost?

A chill curled behind Yojiro's eyes before plunging deep into his stomach as he remembered Obo's letter from his sensei.

Kagenari. Shadow taking form.

His opponent could move in the darkness, melting into the very shadows as through a doorway, only to reemerge in another place, another patch of black, in an instant to catch him at the right place.

I need light!

He sped into the common room, straining to hear to give himself an instant's notice. Nearly knocking over the table, he seized an oil lamp, and with fumbling fingers attempted to light it. A tickle of body heat flared behind him, and Yojiro rolled forward over the tabletop, dropping the lamp with a crash. He flung himself to another table, hitting his fire striker in an instant and lighting a new lamp. The flame danced for one moment before Yojiro dashed it to the floor, igniting the spilled juniper oil.

The shadows scattered, wavering across the room as the fire sputtered, giving the shadow-walker no clear paths. A black-swathed man stood opposite Yojiro, retrieved dagger in hand. Though his face was covered, surprise flickered in his eyes.

My chance!

Yojiro sprang, switching his wakizashi for his katana in a lightening-swift stroke, the larger chamber giving him more space to move. He slashed at his attacker, aiming for his head.

The shinobi ducked, tumbling forward to fight at closer range with his dagger. However, Yojiro was ready, dropping his sword to the floor to catch the man's arm as it swept upward toward his belly. He twisted to the side, avoiding the blade and tearing the man's sleeve. Yojiro whipped the cloth down the arm, tangling the dagger and the man's wrist with the torn rags. The naked arm had a strange scar running down the sun-bronzed skin of the upper bicep. There was a pattern, almost like words, serpentine with pointed arcs all along it, as if it were a kind of message branded onto the flesh. Yojiro, snapping the shinobi's wrist down toward the floor, drew his wakizashi to lop off his attacker's head.

Suddenly, Jin the innkeeper appeared, brandishing a *tantō* knife. Her liver-spotted old-man face knotted in determined anger, she thrust at Yojiro's side. Forced to dodge, he redirected his death blow and swung again, preparing this time to slice them both in half. At the same time, she kicked out at Yojiro's hand, releasing his grip on the shadow-walker, who untangled his wrist and freed his dagger. They ducked beneath Yojiro's blow. The innkeeper then leaped between them, crouching into a defensive stance and shielding the shadow-walker with her body, her tantō gleaming in the firelight.

Breathing hard, she nodded to Yojiro, a pleading gesture of good faith.

"Yojiro-sama," she panted.

He hesitated. She swallowed hard and muttered something beneath her breath. Suddenly, her old man's visage melted in the firelight, the illusion falling away as she released her invocation. Her smooth, round cheeks emerged from the gaunt, yellow face, and dewy eyes sparkled past the innkeeper's cloudy, wrinkled ones. A long ponytail swung from the back of her head.

She slowly spun, turning her back to Yojiro to face his attacker, and pointed her blade at him.

"Takao," she whispered, her real voice high and melodic. "Do not kill him."

"Move out of the way, Aoi," Takao hissed, raising his dagger against her. "He has seen too much."

The fire still blazed around them, keeping Yojiro safe from the shadows for the moment, but to be sure, he backed up carefully into the wall, leaving no space for a surprise attack.

"Perhaps he can help us. We are all alone. Sensei's other students have all fled, abandoning us. We need support from our clan. Better yet, Yojiro-sama is the Emerald magistrate from Otosan Uchi."

Rage flooded the young man's eyes. "Aramoro came from Otosan Uchi, too, Aoi. They must have worked together to kill sensei! Don't you see? The clan cares nothing about us."

Yojiro balked at Takao's claim. Obo was their sensei? What was a Dragon Clan samurai doing training Scorpion Clan students? The tangle of revelations left no time to unravel all the threads.

"I did not work with Aramoro," Yojiro explained. "I was sent here to investigate Kitsuki-sama's death. To find out what happened to him. If you know, please tell me. I can only help you if I understand."

"See, Takao? He is here to aid us. We must turn to the clan. We cannot do this alone."

But Takao shook his head. "If you want to spare him, you tell him nothing," he warned, tucking his dagger into a cloth sheath at his side. "As the only remaining senior student of our school, I command it."

Aoi opened her mouth again but, out of respect for Takao, her elder, said nothing. The young couple stared at one another, silence stretching between them. Finally, she nodded, looking apologetically at Yojiro.

"I am sorry, Yojiro-sama. This is our secret."

She went into the back room and returned with a bucket of sand to spread all over the fire. As the grit smothered the flames, darkness returned. In the dimness, Yojiro thought he saw Takao wrap his arm around Aoi's waist.

"Do not return here, Yojiro," Takao said, his words tight with anger. "Or my duty will be to kill you."

The couple left the room, going upstairs to Obo's quarters. Yojiro heard them shuffle through the desk for a moment, and then all was silent. Yojiro exhaled as though he had been holding his breath through the entire ordeal. His body still quivered with adrenaline, his arms and legs hot from battle, but his face numb. He had survived. Thank the gods.

Yojiro recovered his katana from the floor and lumbered out the front door. The moon sparkled on its blade, illuminating the dark alley with a tiny spark. To have let it touch the ground, especially that filthy floor in there, had been disrespectful to the ancestors who had wielded it before him. However, the necessary move had saved his life. Another enigma.

Should I be punished for this as well?

The conflict was eternal.

He looked up, his eyes again unused to the dark. The world was black. The darkness, a wall for Yojiro. A path for Takao. Kagenari. Shadow taking form. Honor. Dishonor. Lies. Truth. Yojiro felt as if his body were bound up, restricted in all ways, a hundred million filaments constricting his arms, his heart, his soul, dictating his destiny. He stared at the sword, wishing he could slice through them all. Cut his way through to freedom.

As Yojiro left the Fortuitous Wind, he knew Takao was watching. Like Obo, he could feel eyes from the shadows.

CHAPTER SEVEN

As Yojiro returned to Shosuro Palace, the night heat cooled. The Hour of the Rat waned into the Hour of the Ox, and the moon sank over the jagged skyline. He slunk along the night-stained gardens and terraces of the Noble Quarter, bruised and somewhat ashamed about his visit to the Fortuitous Wind. He had lost the contents of Obo's desk except for a single letter. The discoveries he did make, such as Aoi and Takao's relationship with Obo, had only revealed more questions than answers. Why would a Kitsuki investigator come to Ryokō Owari with the intention of finding shinobi, become beset with hallucinatory nightmares while looking, make allies with a yoriki of the Emerald magistrate, and then lie to her and his superiors? What was Obo's purpose? And why did he have pupils? What could he possibly have been teaching them?

Takao's kagenari disturbed him the most. Yojiro had never seen sorcery such as this before, which seemed to avoid the use of kami altogether. It was similar to what he had heard the most powerful users of Void were capable of, but Takao was clearly no Ishiken of the Phoenix Clan. Where did he learn to use it? Was he shinobi? He was clearly trained for assassination techniques. If he was, for whom? Scorpion? Dragon? Someone else? The excursion had merely multiplied Obo's secrets, and his death hid them all.

The questions rattled inside his mind as Yojiro approached the main gate, which was, oddly, still open. The sound of footfalls echoed just inside the outer walls, so he hid himself in the warped shadow of a nearby white-lilac tree.

Shadows work both ways.

About a dozen Thunder Guard with spears emerged, Captain Denmaru leading the way, his marred face scowling in the sinking moonlight. The Thunder Guard captain and his soldiers uniformly marched out into the street and waited. Denmaru sniffed the night air, as if testing the wind. Yojiro held his breath, realizing the stink of the Fishers' Quarter gutter probably still marred his sandals. He pressed himself deeper into the lilac's trunk, praying the tree's perfume could mask his location. Denmaru continued to survey the night a moment longer before more footsteps sounded, coming toward the palace. The governor appeared, sitting in a hanging, open-air sedan chair borne by two servants, accompanied by her own contingent from the Thunder Guard. She nodded to Denmaru as they approached.

"He was at the Theater of Summer Flowers tonight, at a performance of *The Floating World*," she said, her honeyed voice bright with amusement. "That Yasuki play was indeed a most rare treat. It is the only refined thing the Crab Clan have ever produced."

"Why was he there?"

"It seems the magistrate and I share the same passion for the theater as an alibi. He brought a whole troop of his dōshin, too. Either he was worried about being attacked by the actors, or he was desperate for company."

"Or he is making an arrest," Denmaru offered, his voice low with caution. "Was the Seppun woman with him?"

"You know your mark well," Hyobu crooned. "No, she was not, which is why I think he intends something more… exhilarating. One of his personal projects."

A few Thunder Guard soldiers fidgeted on their feet at those words, as if they held grave meaning. They turned to observe Denmaru's reaction. Their captain merely nodded.

"Where is he now?"

"He went to the Scarlet Tent after the performance, but I do not know how long he will stay there," Hyobu replied, tilting her head as if she heard something in the distance. She looked out into the skyline. "Opium eaters are not good witnesses."

"As you say."

"And how is our guest?"

"He went for a midnight stroll."

Hyobu let out a small, surprised laugh. "I wonder if he went to the Licensed Quarter, after all, and I just missed him. If he did, then his night promises to be eventful. Hopefully, in the right way. Do be careful, captain. The fool makes for an easy pawn, but you know he has his dangerous moments."

The Thunder Guard captain bowed, and he and his contingent sped down the street in the direction Hyobu had just come from. She followed them with her eyes until they turned the corner, headed west. Then she disappeared with her guards into the castle courtyard, the enormous doors of the gate shutting behind them.

Yojiro crept out from his shadow, the urge to follow Denmaru drawing his footsteps back away from the palace.

Had they been talking about Seno? Why did he need an alibi? What did Hyobu mean about the personal project? And witnesses? Motome's words about Thunder Guard interference came to mind. She hadn't had evidence for her accusations, but could this be an opportunity to confirm her suspicions? Hyobu certainly had sent Denmaru to thwart someone… but whom? And why?

Yojiro stripped off his fishy sandal coverings and concealed them beneath some nearby hydrangeas.

It was time to stare into the soul of Governor Hyobu and her Thunder Guard captain.

Despite the late hour, the small ferry boats to Teardrop Island still teemed with crowds of wealthy sailors, samurai, and nobility, as the staff and services of the Licensed Quarter never slept. As Yojiro disembarked at the wharf on the northern tip of the isle, the air around him trembled with music and laughter. The sounds of shamisen, drums, flutes, koto, and singers swelled like a restless wind, the pulse of passionate excitement and abandon. Perfumes of a thousand flowers, oil lamps, and bodies mixed with the invisible, earthy miasma of opium. In front of every tavern, teahouse, gambling parlor, theater, and geisha house, each one painted with the brightest hues, stood sumptuously dressed attendants, beckoning and enticing visitors with promised pleasures beyond their doors. Unlike the rest of the city, Teardrop Island was illumined with legions of lanterns, a new canopy of stars that cast no dread shadows but gladdened every corner with light.

Between him and the district, the crowds of visitors bottlenecked on both sides of the enormous Swords Polished Gate, the entrance into the entertainment paradise. Festooned with hundreds of flowers and gold paper banners, the gate was more of an enormous antechamber where several dozen muscled guards checked each guest for weapons. Maiko geisha milled around the arriving guests, cordially inviting the newcomers in after they surrendered their weapons for "polishing" during the stay.

Yojiro traded his swords for a sea-ivory token with a teardrop and a number carved into its surface, and immediately, a geisha apprentice in pink robes and sparkling silver hair ornaments scattered across her ebony wig singled him out. She gently took his elbow and led him through the gate with dainty steps.

"Good evening, sir," she whispered, sliding back one fold of his raised collar with a poised finger so her gentle, coaxing voice could reach his ear. Her breath tickled his face. "My name is Heaven's Lily, and it is my joy and honor to be your guide during your visit tonight."

"Do I look that lost?" he asked, feigning the charisma of a wealthy pleasure seeker. Inside, he almost recoiled from her attention.

How convenient. A personal spy for every patron.

"No one is lost here," she chuckled, her crimson lips curled like loops of silk ribbon around her pearly teeth. "On Teardrop Island, you belong everywhere. Where do you see yourself tonight, samurai-sama? The theater? A teahouse? A private moonlit garden?"

Yojiro shook his head, raising his hand in protest. "No, I am actually looking for someone. An acquaintance."

She smiled sweetly, but her jaw stiffened at his words. "Well, we can certainly look for them. Tell me what they like, and I will surely know where they might be."

"Yes, thank you, Heaven's Lily," Yojiro said, slipping some money into her hands. "But I do not think I will need your guidance tonight."

Her shoulders drooped slightly. "Are you sure? There are plenty of lovely places that I could show you tonight."

"That will not be necessary," he insisted. "I will find my own way."

The apprentice geisha bowed respectfully and deposited the coins into her purse before wandering back through the throngs of the Swords Polished Gate for a new visitor.

Yojiro waded through the rivers of people into the heart of the island. He cut through the mazelike lushness of the Island

Garden, strolling past a pair of lovers sharing the cool air beneath blooming wisteria arbors. He skirted a carousing group of young Lion Clan samurai who tumbled out of a sake house and avoided a cloud of singers thronging around a Tortoise Clan samurai who sang refrains of epic poems with them as he passed out coins. Though Yojiro wandered in and around and between the licensed establishments, he did not see even a glimpse of Seno or Denmaru.

As he withdrew from peeking inside a fortune teller's shop, a squat, one-story building, covered in red silk banners to mimic a Unicorn nomadic cloth hut, caught his eye.

The Scarlet Tent?

Yojiro approached, and just as he grasped the shōji screen, the door silently slid open a crack. Tendrils of opium-laced steam wafted out into the cool night air. Red light gleamed ominously from the gap, and the melancholy strum of the *biwa* echoed from within.

He cautiously opened the door to the opium den wider, revealing a small, low-ceilinged, blossom-garlanded room aglow in red lantern light. Several steaming water pipes glimmered like black towers on the floor, surrounded by lavish couches and cushions strewn with opulently dressed bodies. A few moved their heads to look at Yojiro, but they immediately shut their eyes, their thoughts lilting away on the rivers of rapture pulsing in their blood. Only the musician, a slender boy with delicate wrists and meticulous fingers, acknowledged his entrance.

"Welcome," he said, strumming his hypnotic rhythm. "Come and indulge."

Yojiro edged back out the door. None of the bodies were Seno or Denmaru, nor did the building have any other exit to suggest separate rooms or back doors.

An icy apprehension nipped the inside of his stomach.

Was this a trap? Did Hyobu merely fool me into coming here?

Yojiro leaned his back against the wall of the opium den, scanning each nearby shadow, door, and shrubbery for surprises. Ragged moments passed, and eventually, his heart eased back down to its normal gait.

"Strange night," came a weak voice from inside the Scarlet Tent. A man with long, silvery hair and a blue fan absently swished fireflies away from the door as he emerged. He opened a tiny porcelain case and smeared a glob of poppy tar onto his finger, which he subsequently rolled into a ball between his finger and thumb. He then stuck the pill to the roof of his mouth and sighed. "The Thunder Guard did the same thing you did. Took one look and vanished."

Was this part of the trap?

He felt the visceral panic of helplessness without his swords at his side. He balled his fists.

"You saw the Thunder Guard?" Yojiro asked, careful to keep his eyes on his surroundings. "Where did they go?"

"They went that way, toward that glow of sunrise," the opium eater mumbled, pointing to the sky where an orange spark shone above the rooftop of another nearby geisha house.

"That is not east," Yojiro mumbled, staring as the orange stain in the black sky.

Fire?

He wandered toward the direction of the flames. They were still small yet, barely larger than Hyobu's sedan chair. Manageable, but no one had seen them yet.

Suddenly, an elderly gentleman slammed into him, knocking them both onto the street. The bruises from his fight with Takao screamed in pain at the new agitation, but he leaped to his feet, offering his hand to the poor man.

"Please forgive me, sir!" Yojiro babbled, pulling the man from the ground and proceeding to dust off the man's silk clothes. There were singe marks all over him. Then, the Otomo crest with the magisterial green orb stopped him dead. It was Otomo Seno.

"Scorpion!" Seno barked, his face livid as he straightened his hat. "How dare you? First, I see that skulking, stalking Thunder Guard captain, and now I run into you! The two of you are in league! Both of you! Conspirators!"

Yojiro took a step back. "Forgive me, Otomo-sama, I meant no offense. I was merely in a hurry to help–"

"Arrest him!" Seno yelled, throwing his hands in the air. Seno's half-dozen dōshin eyed each other warily, but they shuffled forward. "Ninja conspirator!"

"But look at the fire," Yojiro contended, his voice rising. He pointed in the direction of the flames.

The roof lay dark.

At first, Yojiro stared, his eyes wide in incredulous panic, but he realized that someone must have already extinguished the flames. The telling, lingering smell of the fire still hung thick in the air, right in front of him.

"You helped start the fire, you say?" Seno asked, his furious red face turning even more scarlet. His frustrated anger suddenly melted into the sneering belligerence of victory. "I knew there was something evil about you, Bayushi. Arrest him!"

The dōshin grasped his arms tightly and marched him toward the Swords Polished Gate. A sizeable crowd of curious onlookers stared at them. In the sea of faces, Yojiro spotted Denmaru and his Thunder Guard. They locked eyes for one moment, the gruff Shosuro captain's face twisted in slight amusement. He turned his back and walked away.

CHAPTER EIGHT

Day dawned mere hours later in Ryokō Owari Prison, but the sun made no difference in the light of Seno's blinding lamps to ward against ninja. Yojiro had sat on his heels those few hours in his cell, a squat filthy cage strewn with hay. It was not tall enough to stand in, but he didn't dare sit in the grime or let his guard down.

He shared company with the Storm Tigers, though the ruffians scarcely moved, even as dawn rose. Their bodies were broken and bleeding from their interrogation the day before, the one that had convicted them as ninja. Several Storm Tigers had mangled hands or feet, while others had sustained a variety of flesh wounds and burn marks. Buyu, the pitiful rickshaw puller, had fewer marks, probably having given up his confession easily.

Yojiro could not banish the memory of Denmaru's smile. The gloat of a trap well sprung? Yet, the events had only developed as a random set of accidents. Yojiro's detour to Teardrop Island. Running into Seno. Seno arresting him out of anger. Denmaru's appearance right at the end.

Conspirators, Seno had called them. Ninja conspirators.

Could Hyobu and Denmaru have orchestrated it all?

As if conjured from the air, the cell block doors opened, and the Thunder Guard captain entered, a few infantry in tow, carrying spears.

"Good morning, Yojiro-sama," he said disinterestedly, motioning for one of Seno's dōshin to unlock the cell. The guard was hesitant until Denmaru flashed an edict signed by Hyobu in his face. Yojiro's swords hung from his obi beside his own. "Governor Hyobu has heard of your arrest and has judged, upon review of the events last night, that according to her laws, your apprehension was a mere magisterial misunderstanding. You are free to go."

"Wait, Captain Denmaru." Yojiro stepped over Buyu's still-snoring form and out of the cell. He bowed once in forced thanks and took his swords back, but propriety could not overcome his scowl as they met eye to eye. The night had drained his patient etiquette. "What happened last night?"

Denmaru's eyes narrowed in annoyance at Yojiro's question. "A magisterial misunderstanding."

"But what were you doing there last night?" Yojiro nearly demanded, his endurance wearing thin. "The fire? The arrest? What did you do to Otomo-sama that made him lash out at me? What were you and Governor Hyobu plotting?"

The captain's eyes grew stonier than his skin. His jaw tightened, and he nearly raised a scarred hand as if to strike Yojiro, but one of his soldiers grunted and he lowered it. "You should know better than to accuse a fellow Scorpion. You sound more and more like that fool Otomo."

"Then tell me, captain."

"If you are looking for shadows, you will find them," he hissed. "And you may just burn your whole world down trying to get rid of them."

• • •

Frustration gnawed at Yojiro as he approached Motome's office in the vault. He wished he could erase the night before. One Scorpion Clan secret had sprouted after another, choking him with their dishonor like foul weeds. Shinobi. Sabotage. Hedonism. Murder.

Luckily, his high collar concealed the deep-purple welt on his jawline from his tumble down the stairs at the Fortuitous Wind, so Motome wouldn't know how much it battered him, inside and out.

"You did not sleep," Motome observed, looking up only briefly from her work on a map of Ryokō Owari Toshi spread out over her desk. She busily marked it with red ink, occasionally referencing Obo's geisha-house log. Sticking silver needles into the wood of the walls, she had pinned up all Obo's desk documents they had gathered the day before, grouping and fanning them out by content. She had also pinned all her tiny slip messages from Obo near them, creating a woven timeline of papers.

She must have spent all night doing it. And she was concerned that *he* hadn't slept.

"Did you go out last night?" she asked, pausing in her work a moment to stare at him. The warmth in her eyes revealed more interest than suspicion.

Yojiro was in no mood for lies this morning. "Yes."

"And?"

"I learned Ryokō Owari is dangerous at night."

Motome only just stifled a laugh. "Yes. It is. You were robbed, weren't you?"

Yojiro smirked, her bluntness putting him at ease. Honesty was indeed a simpler way to live. "After a fashion. That was the second time in two days."

"What?" Her eyes grew wide and round.

He grimaced, embarrassed at her incredulous tone. Maybe he was being too honest.

"Perhaps the Fortune of Wealth is displeased with you, Yojiro-sama. You should visit his temple and make an offering to appease him. I can show you the way if you would like."

Yojiro flushed. No one had ever offered to accompany him on a private outing. Not even Mikuru, who had been too busy living her own life, following her own duties. He wasn't sure how to respond. Decorum dictated that he decline, at least once, for humility's sake. But he did want to go with her. How did one respond beyond the polite, detached refusal?

"I would be grateful, Motome-san, if your offer was in earnest."

"Of course. We have reason to go to the Temple Quarter anyway."

"Oh?" Yojiro cocked his head in surprise.

She pointed to Obo's slips pinned to the wall. "I organized them, as you suggested, and I found a pattern. The log mentions locations scattered all over Ryokō Owari, but Kitsuki-sama mentions the Temple of Amaterasu the most, in the greatest detail."

Yojiro shook his head. Obo had been lying to Motome, just like he had been lying to his superiors at the Kitsuki School of Investigation. "I am not sure that you can trust those slips, Motome-san."

"No, listen to me," Motome growled, knitting her eyebrows in frustration. "I know you still do not believe that there are shinobi. You believe that Kitsuki-sama was fanatical, driven by fear, perhaps like Otomo-sama. But this is important."

Yojiro, cowed by her anger, lowered his eyes. "Forgive me. Please go on."

Motome puckered her mouth in sour satisfaction. She pointed to the slips she had marked in red ink. "Kitsuki-sama's messages about the Temple of Amaterasu all occur on the first day of the month."

Yojiro's jaw dropped open. "What?"

She pointed to the wall, indicating one slip that mentioned the temple.

"Gathering planned. Rooftop of Temple of Amaterasu. Date undetermined. Will observe the area."

She lifted the slip, exposing the other side.

"The Month of the Ox, first day."

"He did not send them to me consistently, but whenever he mentioned that temple, the message arrived on the first day of a new month, and those arrived almost every month." She pointed and flipped through the ten years' worth of red-marked slips.

"Northern garden. Temple of Amaterasu. Two figures congregating near the okame cherry trees. The Month of the Hare, first day."

"Temple of Amaterasu courtyard. Footprints on the wall. Someone tried to climb the roof. First day of the Month of the Rooster."

"But why that day?" Yojiro asked, his mind picking apart the weeks and days of their lunar calendar to find some inkling of Obo's obsession with the Temple of Amaterasu. Perhaps Obo merely developed a cyclical system to trick her, to vary his lies over the months.

"I am not sure," she said, picking up Obo's pleasure-house ledger. "But look at this." Opening the book to a page she had marked in red ink and pointing, she revealed the same pattern. On the same days of the month, there were entries of:

"Month of the Ox, first day. House of the Plum Blossom. Funa."

"Month of the Hare, first day. House of the Crashing Wave. Nobu."

"Month of the Rooster, first day. House of the Morning Star. Aoi."

Aoi? It can't be.

Yojiro tore the ledger from Motome's grasp and scoured the names she had circled in red. Names of all genders. Each associated with a pleasure house. Each date coinciding with a date on one of Obo's messages to Motome, as if he had attended the pleasure house the same day he reported going to the Temple of Amaterasu.

The date next to Aoi's name was only just over a year ago. Had she worked in a geisha house until just recently? Perhaps it was not the same person. However, none of the names in the log repeated. Could Obo know two people named Aoi, both a geisha and his student?

Being so fixated on Denmaru, he had not thought to ask the geisha proprietors on Teardrop Island about these names.

"I am sure that we will find something to tie all of these together if we go to the Temple Quarter," Motome said, folding her arms and leaning back on her zabuton. Her excitement made her body tremble, though her cheeks were drooping slightly from exhaustion.

Yojiro shook his head in disbelief, smiling. "Motome-san. You are an exceptional investigator."

She flapped her hand. "No, no, you flatter me, Yojiro-sama," she laughed, modestly. She stood to tuck her swords and jitte into her obi. "I am merely stubborn. I wanted you to believe in Kitsuki-sama's shinobi story so much that I stayed awake all night, obsessing. Perhaps I am learning well under Otomo-sama's example."

Yojiro opened the door for her, not sure if he should smile at the irony of her words or grimace after last night. "I think he would do well to learn from yours."

•••

The golden Temple Quarter lay east of the Merchant Quarter, a true opposite side of the coin. While the markets were a maze of dark alleys, this district dedicated to the gods was bathed in sunlight. Wide streets flowed between tranquil meditation parks filled with glassy lotus ponds and raked stone gardens.

Studding the roads were peaked shrines and temples devoted to the Ten Thousand Fortunes. Some sanctuaries, tiny as paper fans, housed collections of stone statues of the kami dressed in silk shawls and woven grass talismans for good luck. Larger temples and shrines dedicated to the Seven Fortunes contained enormous bronze or gold statues and boasted their own worship halls filled with whole congregations of reverent followers.

Towering above them all, however, was the immense, thirteen-tiered shining pagoda of Daikoku-no-Kami, whose shadow was said to bless all it touched. The Temple of Daikoku retained nearly one hundred monks, whose daily chanting and prayers rang in the air, blending with the sandalwood and aloe incense smoke that fluttered throughout the quarter.

Yojiro and Motome had only just entered the district, passing a courtyard fountain where novice priests sat in contemplation, when Yojiro spotted Ikku's red palanquin. Instead of lurking in the shadows, the crimson silk carriage boldly passed by on the arms of its bearers. Hovering in the distance, it continued behind an enormous bronze bell hung from a gray cypress belfry, headed in the direction of the Temple of Daikoku.

What could he be doing here?

"Did you hear me, Yojiro-sama?" Motome asked, pointing the opposite way. "The Temple of Amaterasu is down this street."

"Excuse me. I thought I saw someone I recognized," Yojiro apologized. The palanquin was gone. "Please, lead the way."

As they rounded the corner of an incense shop, a sharp light burned Yojiro's eyes. His hand shot up to shield himself. High above his head, at the height of an enormous camphor tree, hung a dazzling spherical mirror crowned with a golden ring of fiery rays. The mirror rested on a thick brass minaret in the center of the temple's shimmering limestone courtyard, with seven sacred buildings gathered about it. Motome led the way to the smallest of the buildings, drawing another search warrant from her sleeve. She had done much more work than he had realized.

"Excuse me, venerable sir," she said, approaching and bowing to a shugenja garbed in robes of intense saffron. He wore a straw, mushroom-like hat upon his head, which shielded his eyes from his surroundings, and he plied garnet prayer beads with calm, methodical fingers. "We come from the Emerald magistrate to investigate particular circumstances surrounding a deceased Dragon Clan minister. His name was Kitsuki Obo, and we have reason to believe he might have come here often."

"Everyone comes here," the priest answered, an aloof smokiness to his voice. He did not look at them, merely staring into the shade of his hat, avoiding the distractions of the physical world. "This is the temple where we honor Lady Sun's light. The mother of the kami blesses all, and they in turn come to thank her."

Motome nodded, more out of delicacy than sincerity. "Of course. We have come to inquire after one of her worshippers, someone who came monthly, perhaps."

"Her light blinds. Her light heals," the priest continued, his voice taking on the reverent intonations of a chant. "And so, all come to worship her, to see what she reveals in them."

Motome looked at Yojiro, unsure of what to do. He shrugged. If the priest was lost in the loop of his liturgy, this could take time. Finally, she waved him on, indicating that she would speak to the priest while Yojiro searched the rest of the complex. He nodded, slowly backing away from the conversation to avoid offending the priest.

He wandered toward the nearest of the seven shrines: a two-story, white-walled sacred hall with a black roof forked with spires along the top. White-pine plaques marked the building as having been dedicated in honor of both Amaterasu and Onnotangu, Sun and Moon, mother and father to the kami.

As he entered the sanctuary, taking off his shoes, he saw in lieu of a statue an enormous mural carved into golden *kiri* wood. The masterful relief mimicked the sky, with swirls and stars. Inlaid across its surface, round glass mirrors representing Amaterasu chased intricately carved ivory disks representing Onnotangu. Lord Moon waxed and waned in its phases, its black side covered in a roughly hewn ebony.

The relief told the story of the Moon, the fickle lover whose passions cooled in jealousy over Lady Sun's love for their children. Eventually, the envious Moon grew completely black, extinguishing his love for her, which marked the day he betrayed Amaterasu and swallowed their kami children. The complete ebony disk, the night with no light, marked when Amaterasu wept for her children.

Yojiro stared at this last disk. The blackest night. Despite the despair of the black moon, from this night emerged hope, as Amaterasu had saved her final child – the kami Hantei, blessed ancestor of the emperor's family – from being swallowed in order to save his siblings. The Rokugani marked the black moon as the start of their lunar calendar in deference to Hantei, the Blessed Son of Heaven, who saved the kami and grew to rule Rokugan. The first day of every new month.

As he studied the artistically rough edges of the final ebony disk, a flaw emerged. There, in the center of the disk, concealed in the black eddies of the carving, was a secret switch no larger than the tip of his little finger.

Yojiro swallowed. *Scorpion craftsmanship, again.*

But he was sharing the shrine with an old shugenja who lay prostrate, praying to the kami, her forehead touching the smooth elm floor. She muttered her swift, complex prayers, barely pausing for breath. Yojiro cleared his throat, but she did not move, absorbed in deep communion with her deities.

Perhaps she will not notice.

He drew his coin pouch out of his pocket, twisted a corner into a dense knot, and gently pressed the button, hoping the Scorpion craftsperson had oiled the mechanisms. No needle shot out this time, but Yojiro could hear the faint spin of a pulley.

A panel the size of a cartwheel slid open in the wall to Yojiro's right, silent as a breath. He froze.

The shugenja's prayers droned on, undisturbed. Yojiro slipped into the opening moments before it shut, enveloping him in darkness.

He waited for several minutes, pressing his ear against the panel door, listening for any reaction from the shugenja, but he heard nothing. The ashen smell of dust and spider silk tickled his nose. There was no fleck of sunlight in this strange, walled passage, so his eyes could not adjust.

He had not thought to bring his candle and fire striker on the daytime outing, so he cautiously spread his hands out to feel. The passage, about as narrow as the length of his katana, was walled with splintering wood that gouged and pricked at his skin. He stumbled upon a raised plank in front of him, the first step of a steep staircase leading up toward the back of the shrine, behind the relief. Warily, he crawled up the steps, keeping his hands before and above him. The stairs groaned beneath him ever so slightly, like the grim, faint moan of the dying.

A sharp, searing pain raked one of his hands, so he snatched it back. Feeling his flesh in the dark, he perceived that a fine cut had opened across his palm. He traced the pain in a straight line.

Razor thread.

Drawing his wakizashi, he sliced the air in front of him, hearing the *ping* as the wire snapped against his blade. He continued up, his short sword now before him.

Finally, after he had crawled the height of the shrine, his weapon collided into another door. Finding the handle, he cautiously slid it open. Gray streams of light filtered in from a few fist-sized air vents in the far wall, illuminating a small room with a sloped ceiling. He figured he was in a tiny space between the vast relief and the back wall, just behind the eaves of the shrine. A few brass oil lamps dangled, hovering over what appeared to be a red-pine workbench scattered with tools. Yojiro lit one with a nearby steel fire striker. His stomach pitched.

Beneath a scattering of long iron needles, clay pots of oozing black paste, and sets of shackles, the surface of the workbench was spattered with dried blood. Years of stains had pooled into the wood, warping its surface slightly, crusting into a cruel, blackish veneer.

Ignoring his stomach, he studied the instruments without touching them. They looked like tattoo lances, meaning the pots were full of foul-smelling pigments. The chains were on the slimmer side, meant to secure the wrists and ankles of a young person, though not quite small enough for a child.

On the wall above the workbench hung a leather diagram of the human body, front and back, with strange symbols etched all over the skin. They looked just like the marks on Takao's arm, a secret language scrawled in serpentine crescents. Next to the grim drawing hung a scrap of kimono, upon which was embroidered the Scorpion crest.

Obo, what did you discover here?

Yojiro's throat tightened as his heart trembled in his chest. This was the secret that drove Obo to the brink with fear ten years ago. The secret the Scorpion would kill to keep hidden. This was why Obo had begged Motome for help, for protection. This was what Aramoro knew and wouldn't say.

How could the Scorpion hide such depraved rituals? How could Aramoro, Kachiko even, defile the purity of their station with these wicked secrets?

He needed to confront Aramoro and get the answers. Now. Ignoring his writhing stomach, Yojiro ripped the diagram and the silk crest from the wall, rolled them up, and thrust them into his breast pocket. He blew out the lamp and stumbled quietly back down the stairs, white-hot anger beginning to boil in his chest.

He cursed Kachiko for threatening him. He cursed her for condemning his honor. He clenched his fingers so tight it nearly snapped his knuckles.

She will answer for this. So will Aramoro. I will tell Motome. I will tell Toturi. I will tell the emperor that there is rotting flesh in the depths of my clan. I will expose it to be burned with the light of the sun, cleansed from this world.

Yojiro spread his fingers wide to search for a latch to open the panel in the wall. It was tucked into the side. Yojiro pressed it, again using his coin pouch. The panel slid open, blinding him for a moment with the sun. He blinked. The shrine was empty. Even the praying shugenja was gone. But he no longer cared who saw. The truth needed to be revealed.

He strode out into the sunlight, searching for Motome. He rushed around the other shrines, weaving in between priests and worshipping visitors. Several of them gave him flustered glares as he shoved past them to look into a building only to hurry out again, but he ignored it. He needed to tell her. His heart galloped.

She was not in the temple. Frantic, he darted out of the compound's gate into the street. Though several dozen reverent pedestrians bustled in both directions along the road, Motome's tiny figure was not among them.

Maybe she returned to the reformatory.

He scurried down the street in the direction of the Merchant Quarter. Its dark alleys loomed ahead. He plunged into one, only to nearly crash into the front door of a pickle shop. The store's sign clattered as he barely nudged it before halting. A dead end.

Not waiting for his eyes to adjust, he backed up and tried another. He rounded the corner, nearly running now.

Suddenly, he slammed into a hulking figure. He cracked his head against its shoulder and nearly tumbled to the ground. Grunting, he clutched his bruised skull in both hands.

"Please forgive me," he stammered, his cheeks flushed with panicked shame. "I did not see you."

As the stars left his eyes, his shoulders tensed. His hand flashed to his katana. He had crashed into the muscular arm of a man bearing a red silk palanquin on the opposite shoulder. The brute snarled and cursed under his breath.

"What is it?" that cruel, hissing voice called from behind the crimson curtain. It lifted, revealing the ratty face of Ikku.

CHAPTER NINE

"Ah, Magistrate," Ikku chuckled as his servants lowered his palanquin to the ground. He stepped out, whirling his scorpion pipe in eager fingers. "It is pleasant to see you again so soon. You just caught me on my way back from my morning prayer to Daikoku-no-Kami for today's fortune. It seems he feels particularly generous today."

"I do not have time to meddle with you, Ikku," Yojiro grumbled. His hand clenched around the silken ties of his katana hilt.

Ikku's bellowing laugh filled the close confines of the alley, reverberating in the overbearing eaves. "Time can be bought, magistrate. Your choice, as always."

Yojiro's thumb raised his katana a degree, threatening Ikku, but the crime lord merely gestured to his minions. Ikku's six gangsters snatched thick mountain-ash *tetsubō* hidden beneath the palanquin. Swinging the slender clubs bound with iron rings, they moved to encircle Yojiro. The samurai drew his sword fully, hoping his steel would deter them.

"I will cut through each one of you if I have to," he warned, crouching into a striking stance.

"My loyal servants have toppled your kind before, magistrate," the crime lord said indifferently. "Get him."

The gangsters hurled themselves at Yojiro, careful from experience to coordinate their swings in the narrow space. Yojiro ducked under the arm of one to escape the circle, but they all swung around, shifting their formation to catch him in another ring against the opposite alley wall. One criminal swung at Yojiro's side, and as he moved to dodge, a second tough aimed high, ready to strike Yojiro's head as it came within reach. Yojiro dropped beneath the swing and sprang up on its back side, slashing clean through the headhunter's wrists on the way up, but a third brute had already caught Yojiro in the thigh with his tetsubō. Luckily, the end of the club hit the wall, dispersing the force, but Yojiro's knee still buckled in pain, and he fell, that side of his body crumpling into the ground.

Keep moving. You need to clutter their timing!

Continuing the motion from his fall, Yojiro tumbled out from under a hail of blows. The end of the alley loomed dangerously nearer as the gangsters drove him toward the corner. He leaped forward, taking the offensive, slashing in a wide arc to gain ground. One brute lunged, wildly smashing her cudgel down on top of Yojiro's katana, forcing his cut down into the cobblestones. The steel rang against the stone, and the shudder vibrated up his arms into his shoulders.

They are trying to break my sword! I need to end this!

He reclaimed his momentum, slashing down into the gangster's unprotected neck. Slicing through the bone, however, Yojiro's blade stuck. He jumped, wrenching it free with the counterweight of his whole body, but the delay mistimed a necessary dodge as a fifth criminal's club, aimed high, crunched into the side of his head.

He couldn't see. A metallic ringing swirled inside his skull, and he collapsed on the street, his katana slipping from his limp fingers. Time slowed as muffled cries rent the air, preceding the final blows. He could only wait. The street was cold.

No new blows fell. Someone was lifting him, shaking him in the dark.

"Yojiro!"

It was Motome.

"Yojiro! Wake up!" He opened his eyes. He could only see her mouth. "Yojiro, you need to breathe."

She tried to lift him, but he slipped out of her arms, doubling over in the street. As he hunched over on the cobblestones, nausea swept through him, shuddering in his spine and his belly. After a few moments, Yojiro breathlessly nodded his thanks to her, the searing pounding of his lungs still refusing to abate. He eased down, leaning back against the wall, the cool wood steadying his head. Slowly, his breath returned, and it merged into a laugh, relief gradually releasing the rigidity of his body.

"Motome-san," he wheezed, mirth painting his voice. "Thank you."

"Are you OK? Just moments ago, you looked dead."

He tried to nod, but the resounding pain in his head cut him short.

"Give me a few more moments to collect myself," Yojiro replied.

"I'm so sorry I left you. When I finished with the priest, I could not find you, so I thought you had gone to the Temple of Daikoku without me."

Yojiro smiled weakly. "And I thought you had headed back to the reformatory, so we went opposite ways."

As his sight refocused, a body came into view. And another. Motome sat back on her heels, jitte firmly in hand, its forked prong streaked with blood. All around her lay the gangsters, unconscious or dead, some with broken wrists and fingers, a few missing teeth – or, in one case, hands. Ikku, too, lay a little distance off, limp and crumpled in a heap like a cast-off garment.

Motome, still somewhat winded from her own skirmish, laughed, relief relaxing her face from her intensely concentrated battle scowl. "We did not leave an offering at the Temple of Daikoku, Yojiro-sama," she said. "Your bad fortune is still following you."

Yojiro pulled his purse from his kimono and tossed it onto the heap of defeated rogues. "Our offering," he wheezed, "to Daikoku-no-Kami. He can have the whole pile."

Motome smiled and cleaned her jitte on a handkerchief before sliding it back into her obi. "I think he will be pleased. How does your head feel?"

Yojiro caressed the dull lump forming behind his ear. An ache beat deep within it. "Nothing debilitating."

"As long as you can walk." She helped him to his feet. Her warm eyes grew grave, wilting her smile somewhat. "I have bad news, Yojiro-sama."

Her sorrow sharpened his focus. "Oh?"

Then he remembered his own bad news. His wicked discovery in the garret in the Shrine of Onnotangu. His chest clenched.

"Not here," she said, steadying Yojiro's gait with a hand at his elbow. She gestured toward the shadows. "In private."

He nodded. The secret chafed inside his soul. Seething. Rioting. It bound him up, the Scorpion shame tangling around him in thick cords, suffocating him.

I will tell her everything. I will expose the rot. Then I can be free.

They shuffled down the street toward the reformatory, Yojiro leaning on Motome's strength.

"What?"

Yojiro's jaw dropped. He pressed his fingers into his eyes, the answers in his head splitting into a hundred new pieces, renewing the whirl of confusion. He drooped beneath the weight of them, the clashing possibilities taking the floor out from underneath him.

"You were right to be suspicious of him," Motome nearly wailed, her voice weak and bitter with regret. She slumped down upon a zabuton in her office, clutching at the silk cushion with sorrow-clenched hands. "Kitsuki Obo was a child stealer. The priest at the Temple of Amaterasu said as much. Those awful rumors I heard in the North Rim were true. I was such a fool to trust him!"

"Dazzled by hope's bright star," Obo had written about her in his journal. He had deceived her from the first day.

"What did the priest tell you?" Yojiro asked, pacing around the room, the knot on his head throbbing, nearly urging him into a frenzy.

"He remembered the Kitsuki visiting the temple every few months, always on the first day of the month as we suspected, the day of the black moon, just as the sun was setting. He made offerings in the Shrine of Onnotangu, and he would always be accompanied by a teenaged street orphan from the Fishers' Quarter. The priest always knew because they smelled so strongly. The Kitsuki would come with a different youth each time."

Yojiro cringed.

A different youth. Every few months. For ten years.

Gruesome images wavered in his mind. The needles. Shackles. The workbench awash in blood.

He gritted his teeth. "Did the priest know why the Kitsuki brought them there?"

"No," she mumbled, "but he always pointed to the relief while whispering at length. The priest thought maybe he was teaching the orphans the story of the kami, but when none of them ever returned, he simply judged the man to be a poor missionary."

Yojiro recalled the diagram he had taken from the wall in that wretched place. The pattern dictating which serpentine symbols Obo undoubtedly chiseled into the youths' flesh.

Takao... Takao had one branded upon his arm.

Yojiro snatched the pleasure-house ledger from Motome's desk and thumbed through the earlier entries, skimming each name she had marked as those coinciding with the first day of the month. He passed Aoi's name near the front. Several dozen new-moon names into the register, he found it.

"Month of the Tiger, first day. House of Foreign Stories. Takao."

Yojiro nearly dropped the book. The ledger was not a list of Obo's encounters at pleasure houses. This was a coded archive of his rituals. He had recorded the names of his victims.

Both Takao and Aoi had gone through this ritual, tortured at Obo's hand. Yet they called him "sensei." They were his pupils, students who mourned his loss. Takao had even threatened to kill Yojiro for coming too close to their secret. A secret he would kill to protect... Was this ritual their secret? What had Obo done to them?

Yojiro flipped through the names once more. Takao. House of Foreign Stories. Aoi. House of the Morning Star. The geisha-house names varied, barely half a dozen matching Takao's house and many more coming from the House of the Plum Blossom. Perhaps they expressed a code... some encrypted description of the outcomes of the ritual? Aoi had said that there had been other pupils, but that they had abandoned the school after Obo was killed.

"What is it?" Motome asked, interrupting his thoughts. She had already started taking down Obo's slips of paper from the wall, her fingers listless with regret, shoving them into their maple-wood box. "Have you found more damaging evidence against his character?"

Yojiro tried to ignore her as his mind raced through the events, straining to connect them.

A Kitsuki investigator is sent to Ryokō Owari to find shinobi.

He becomes delusional while looking. He recruits one of the Emerald magistrate's yoriki. He lies to her and his superiors, feeding them false information. And yet, he gives Seppun Motome secret clues to his wicked vice, kidnapping youths to torture. However, those tortured become his pupils. He is then murdered… by the Scorpion?

His entire body shuddered in confusion. He feverishly combed through the chaos of clues that lay piled around them, pinned to the walls, tucked into boxes, thrown in baskets.

The pieces will not come together. They simply do not fit.

Yojiro spied the basket of Obo's bloody clothes. The clothes that had been too wide. Taken from someone else. Retailored to fit.

The truth settled down on him, like a frozen mist, chilling his heart.

I need proof.

He snatched the jade dragon ring and stuck it on, then tried it on different fingers in a wild juggle. Inside the rim of the ring, a piece of green-stained wax had refitted it to accommodate a smaller finger. Yojiro discreetly ripped the wax away. The ring now sagged enormously, even around his thumb, an ornament meant for broad, stocky fingers.

Yojiro seized the porcelain urn of Obo's ashes and broke the sticky prayer seal. A dusky scent eased out of the jar. Muttering an apology to the deceased, he snatched up Motome's writing brush and stirred about inside the urn for any bone fragments, careful not to touch the defiling pieces of the dead. A few charred bits rose to the top. Finally, what he was looking for breached the surface of the ash. One finger bone. It was delicate, from a finger even thinner than his own, a finger from a hand too small to wear this ring without the wax.

"Yojiro-sama?" Motome stared up at him, her mouth and cheeks trembling with dread as he fished the bones out with chopsticks and folded them up in a scrap of paper. "What are you doing?"

"I need to speak with Aramoro," Yojiro said, slipping the bones and ring into his pocket and mashing the wax seal shoddily back into place on the urn. "Now."

"What is this about?"

Yojiro merely stared straight into her light eyes. They were wide, warm, but somewhat fearful. "Trust me."

CHAPTER TEN

Aramoro was in the reformatory's gravel courtyard, taking a guarded stroll for air and sunlight, three dōshin escorting him from behind, keeping an obviously intimidated distance from "the Whisper of Steel" and his cruel tongue.

"What have you come to see me about, lapdog?" Aramoro growled, disgust still contorting his wild, unshaven face. "Have you come to beg?"

Yojiro eyed the guards, who might still be in earshot.

"Shall we sit? Perhaps at the edge of that waterfall?" he suggested, pointing to Seno's eavesdropper guard. Aramoro smirked. The water crashed across the stones, frothing in boiling chaos above the principle "Meiyo", muffling their words as they spoke.

"I know that you did not kill Kitsuki Obo," Yojiro said. He drew the finger bones, ring, and green wax from his pocket, showing them to Aramoro in the paper they were wrapped in only for a moment before hiding them again. "This ring is too large for the dead man lying in that urn, yet it is Obo's ring. And the clothes the dead man wore the night you killed him. They had been tailored to fit the man in the urn, altered from the size of a man who would fit this ring."

"Clever observation," Aramoro chuckled. "What does it mean?"

Yojiro drew out his single remaining letter from Obo's desk. "I found this letter from the Kitsuki investigators dated one month ago. They claim not only to have informants in our own spy network, but also to suspect us of using shinobi. They sent Obo to Ryokō Owari twelve years ago expressly with the purpose of finding them. However, in this letter, they warn Obo of a man named Soshi Ezo, a dangerous Scorpion shinobi who was rumored to still be alive after faking his own death ten years ago."

Aramoro's smile grew darker, taunting even. "And did Kitsuki Obo find this Soshi Ezo?"

Yojiro folded his arms, refusing to falter at the trick question. "He did, but not after receiving this letter telling him to find Ezo. He actually found Ezo ten years before the letter. I read an account from his journal that suggests that ten years ago, he discovered a terrible Scorpion secret. Kitsuki Obo found evidence that a group was tattooing their bodies in dark rituals to grant themselves the ability to become one with shadows. This made him delusional, his mind frantic with fear as every shadow appeared to be an enemy. However, his nightmares became reality. He was intercepted and silently replaced soon after by Soshi Ezo. Then Ezo, who adopted Obo's identity, worked to hide what Obo had discovered by lying to the Kitsuki investigators ever since."

"So, you suggest that I killed Soshi Ezo and not a Kitsuki investigator like everyone believes? Why would I do that? He sounds quite useful."

"You would only kill someone like that if ordered to. And that order would only come if he were a danger to our clan – if he threatened us in some way. With his 'kagenari', he must have. This explains why the clan picked you to take care of Ezo. Only the Whisper of Steel could cut down a shadow."

Aramoro rubbed his coarse chin in amusement, his angular teeth flashing in the sun. "Me, take down a shadow master? You flatter me. How do you know Ezo used kagenari?"

"The Kitsuki investigators knew and wrote about it in their letter. Apparently, Ezo was infamous for his skill with it. The investigators called him the most dangerous shinobi our clan has ever produced."

"Still, I don't why you would think such a ... magnificent asset would deserve death."

Yojiro swallowed, the complex strands of the story finally weaving together.

"I met two of Ezo's pupils who knew. They refused to tell me why their master was killed, yet unwittingly revealed the reason to me. The young woman was an exceptional illusionist, trained by Ezo to impersonate others quite well. The other pupil, a young man, I saw was marked with the kagenari shadow brand. From what I discovered about the school and its rituals, however, it seems that both must have been given the shadow brand, but only the young man could wield it."

"Interesting. Go on."

"For the students, neither of these abilities were secrets they felt they needed to protect by killing me. This means that our clan was not threatened by these secret arts. No, what these pupils needed to hide was a secret that endangered them personally."

Aramoro clapped, a raw amusement staining his bedraggled face. "And what was that?"

"Ezo did not fake his death strictly to become Obo. Rather, he faked his death to escape from the Scorpion. To avoid punishment. An execution, even. I think his habit of forcefully branding his students might explain it. After faking his death, he fled here but secretly longed to return to the Scorpion's good graces. I found this in his workshop." Yojiro withdrew the tattered Scorpion crest Ezo had pinned to the wall next to his kagenari diagram. "He came to a Scorpion city, he destroyed a significant menace to the clan, and he purposefully fed false information to more clan enemies, hoping to regain the Scorpion's good graces. He worked tirelessly for ten years at it before revealing himself and his good work to the clan once more. However, since he had been unable to refrain from his original sin of torturing people, you killed him."

"Clever, Yojiro," Aramoro leered, his smile dangerously calm. He dipped his hand into the fountain, tracing circles upon the water's glassy surface. "You almost have it all right."

"What did I get wrong?" Yojiro paused, reviewing his story. Obo's delusions. Ezo's impersonation. Aoi and Takao.

"Now permit me tell you a story, Yojiro," Aramoro said, his eyes dimming as he delved far into his memories, his fingers plunging deeper into the fountain pool. "Decades ago, Soshi Ezo and I trained at the same fighting schools, learning the same techniques and following the same path. We even learned ninjutsu, mastering all the discreet arts. However, we eventually parted ways when he took the oaths to become an actual shinobi, a path I could not follow, as I was a noble's son. 'You are too conspicuous,' they said.

"However, the real reason, Yojiro, was because my family did not want me to give up Bushidō. You see, shinobi become *hinin*, the lowest of castes. Those who deal in filth and excrement. Those who touch the dead and torture the guilty. Those who relinquish their bodies to others' pleasure. I was too important to become a warrior with no honor, no identity, the lowest status in the Celestial Order. My primary duty was to continue being a Bayushi samurai. But Ezo's was not."

"So the clan has been using dishonorable warriors for that long?"

"What clan hasn't, Yojiro?" Aramoro grunted. "Do not judge the vine for adapting to the shape of the tree it grows on. The Scorpion only ever do as they must. We do not cower from our duty."

Yojiro bit his lip. "So Ezo became shinobi, for the clan."

"Yes," Aramoro continued. "Yet somehow, he relished it. He enjoyed the freedom of a life without Bushidō, without the constraints of the Celestial Order, without needing to adhere to tenets like righteousness, sincerity, or honor. Yet, a shinobi still has their own rules. However, as a dishonored man – despite having been given purpose by a Great Clan – Ezo sank deeper into his depravity, beginning to ignore the shinobi code, acting less like a loyal retainer and more like a wild demon.

"And just as you say, about ten years ago, Ezo was discovered experimenting with kagenari, more dishonorable than poison, crossing a new line of corruption. His tests killed many of his fellow students, and the masters of his shinobi school executed him."

"But he faked his death?"

"Yes. His sensei underestimated his abilities, not knowing the extent of his kagenari. He faked his demise and escaped to Ryokō Owari with a few of his followers. Yet, he was not careful. To the Dragon's credit, Obo discovered Ezo mere weeks after his arrival."

"But he became delusional, afraid of the shadows that chased him."

"Wouldn't you? Ezo and his followers immediately removed him as a threat. However, Ezo did not kill Obo to win back his status as you say, to become the servant of a Great Clan again. Instead, he relished his complete autonomy, acting selfishly, whimsically, wildly as rōnin. He killed Obo and stole his identity in order to hide in plain sight. No one was looking for a gold-trade minister, and a Kitsuki investigator would be privy to secret information that could warn Ezo of danger. He thrived in the Fishers' Quarter amid the lower castes, far from eyes trained to detect illusions, a ruler among worms. No one knew of the infiltration until a few months ago, when somehow our spy network caught wind of an acting and infiltration school secretly operating here.

"As our scouts dug deeper, they found rumors of kagenari being used, stories among the peasants about magic brands and those who could step between shadows. That's when our informants discovered that Ezo had established his 'Shadow Den Dōjō', where, as you say, he continued to experiment on his pupils, low- and high-caste alike, most of whom did not survive. We do not know how many he successfully granted his abilities, but we do know of his two youngest, the least discreet. Takao, who was branded with shadow. And Aoi, who somehow did not die during the ritual but whom the shadow brand could not stain.

"You see, Yojiro, his threat to the Scorpion was much more than the dispensing of young people. Ezo actually tampered with the powers of Heaven, degrading the Celestial Order and mocking the Three Oaths by establishing a rogue school – one without clan or purpose save his own. You see, Yojiro. He became ninja."

"Ninja," Yojiro repeated. The word felt bitter on his tongue, having changed so much in the last few days.

Then Seno had truly been onto something. He must have somehow witnessed something that proved Ezo's arrival in his city ten years ago. "Truly capable, though unwise," as Obo had observed in his notes.

"And this threatened our clan's very existence," Aramoro continued, jerking his hand from the water, as if bitten by a serpent. He clenched his fist. "Because of rumors of his success with Takao, several Scorpion shinobi leaders were willing to legitimize Ezo's Shadow Den Dōjō, adding it to their ranks. However, that was before the Dragon Clan got hold of the information. We learned that the Kitsuki had not only heard of Ezo and his execution but also suspected that he had faked his death. This meant Ezo was a liability. If we laid claim to such a character, turning a blind eye to his selfish corruption, our clan would risk being forever disgraced, perhaps even disbanded. And so, I was sent to eliminate him."

Yojiro frowned. "But why did you let yourself get caught? Surely, a more subtle elimination would have avoided political contention while not provoking the Kitsuki investigators."

"I wanted to provoke them!" Aramoro said, grinning. "Ezo and I had a long discussion about this when I spoke with him the day before his death. He did not agree with my decision in the end, and he tried to escape, but his death was swift. The least I could do for an old friend."

His own fight with Takao flashed inside Yojiro's head. He had barely survived, saved instead by luck and Aoi's interference. For Aramoro to have slain a shadow master in a dark street, without sustaining any injury, must have been an amazing feat.

"The involvement of a high-ranking Scorpion in the death of one of their investigators serves two functions," Aramoro continued. "The first is that our clan has sent a warning to the Dragon that not only do we know about their investigators' schemes here in Ryokō Owari but also that we do not allow them to act with impunity. Thanks to Ezo's convenient work over the last decade, we know they have no proof with which to come forward and accuse our clan of dishonorable acts. Threat of a public scandal dares them to reveal what they know, and if they take the bait, it will be the Kitsuki School of Investigation's downfall. Imagine them making the same mistake as that fool Seno! Calling the Storm Tigers ninja? Public disgrace is inevitable."

Yojiro bit his lip. "And what is the second function of your arrest? Is this where I come in? To punish me by forcing me to clean up after your public declaration of war on the Dragon Clan?"

"Ha! A task worthy of Kachiko's vengeance," Aramoro laughed, rubbing his hands together. "But no. Our goals were much less petty than that, Yojiro. I allowed myself to be arrested to send a public declaration to anyone, whether Dragon or Scorpion, that we, as a clan, will never tolerate ninja. We will hunt down and destroy all those who would defile Bushidō. We will punish those who would tamper with the Celestial Order and serve only themselves. And that, Yojiro, includes you."

Yojiro's stomach lurched.

"Me?"

"Yes, Yojiro. Your failure at the tournament of the Emerald Champion was indeed unfortunate, but it also reeks of disobedience. Of selfish independence. Kachiko and several daimyō were worried that your behavior might lead you to betray our clan someday."

"I did not…" His voice crumbled before the memory of his vehement resolve at the Temple of Amaterasu. He had been ready to betray them. To exterminate them. To disband their clan. To be free of them forever. He was thinking as a rōnin, ready to burn down the world, as Denmaru had said. He could no longer call that honor. Only selfishness.

Yojiro sank down into his collar and crossed his arms. His heart, pricked through so many times by his clan in only a few weeks, felt raw. Fatigued. Yet…

This was an exile of redemption. Ezo's life had been a parable Kachiko wanted me to see. Ezo walked the depraved road of the rōnin, a masterless samurai. Adrift on the waves, lacking the surety of a life in service to a Great Clan.

"*Will you do the same, lapdog?*" Aramoro's twisted grin and sneering eyes seemed to say. "*Will you cling to your own whims, your own selfish desires? Will you destroy yourself, and force us to destroy you?*"

Yojiro steeled his face. He would not give Aramoro the satisfaction of seeing him bow.

"The next time I see you, Aramoro," Yojiro simply whispered, "you shall be a free man."

He turned and walked away, beckoning the guards to take Aramoro back to his cell. Motome ran up to him, her warm eyes bright with excitement.

"Did he tell you anything? Did he confess?"

Motome looked different. Smaller. More gray. Somehow, his eyes had changed. His body quaked under the solemnity of the moment. From the depths of his soul, through the muddled mists of confusion and worry, a pillar of clarity emerged.

He was a Scorpion, and without that, Bushidō was hollow.

He pulled his high collar a little higher around his neck, shielding more of his face.

"He did not confess," Yojiro said, heading toward the exit, away from Motome. "Aramoro is innocent. However, I know who killed Obo. Gather your dōshin and meet me at the Fortuitous Wind. Our murderer might still be there."

The lies burned his tongue as they left his mouth. He almost welcomed the sting.

CHAPTER ELEVEN

Back in the Fishers' Quarter, Yojiro followed the gutter up to the Fortuitous Wind. The stench. The smoke. The shadows. None of it bothered him now. His purpose remained fixed. His promise to Toturi seemed small next to the impending disgrace of his entire clan. If the Scorpion could stand against ninja, to right their own wrongs and cleanse their ranks, they must be preserved to serve as Rokugan's underhand.

As Yojiro approached the inn, Denmaru and his squad strode by on their patrol. Yojiro hailed the Thunder Guard captain and humbly bowed to him.

"Captain Denmaru," he began, his words stumbling over his newfound humility. "Forgive my ignorance. You and your soldiers put out that fire in the Licensed Quarter the other night, didn't you?"

"You were looking for any excuse to hate us. Your own clan. Just like that Otomo."

"You were right. I ignored the signs even when they happened right before my face, like with the Storm Tigers. Otomo-sama has been fabricating evidence of ninja for years now, hasn't he?

Thanks to you, he failed last night, didn't he? So, he clumsily tried to implicate me."

"He burned down his own mansion seven years ago to do it, too," Denmaru grunted, folding his arms across his armored chest, the scars on his hands and face stretched tight in his resentment. "He claimed he saw a ninja there on the rooftop. He nearly set the entire Noble Quarter ablaze. So, you see why Hyobu-sama and I stop him when we can."

Otomo must have seen one of Ezo's students. Perhaps the waterfalls were not so foolish.

Yojiro's heart twitched, the weight of his upcoming task pressing down on all his bruises. He bowed and made a final farewell to Denmaru, and he entered the inn.

This time with no dishrag welcome.

Instead, Aoi, impersonating Jin once again, slumped over a straw broom, struggling with shaking hands to clear the last little grains of sand from between the floorboards.

Takao, again disguised as a fisherman, scrubbed the walls with hot water and ash, his brow furrowed in concentration.

Neither spoke to the other. The common room was empty, as if their silence had driven away their business.

"Jin-san, Ebi-san," Yojiro greeted them, wary of the dim corners of the room, his hand hovering ready to draw his weapon if necessary. "Good afternoon."

"What do you want?" Takao hissed, his hand lowering to his side, indicating the location of a hidden dagger.

Aoi grabbed Takao's arm, ignoring the threat. She propped her broom against the wall.

"Good afternoon, magistrate," she said, bowing, attempting her best old servant imitation. "What can this humble servant do for you?"

"Much better, Aoi-san," Yojiro said, sorrow creeping into his heart, threatening to crush his resolve. He clenched his teeth. "Now, if you would be so kind as to reveal yourself."

"If you wish," she said, warily, sharing a skeptical glance with Takao before obliging. Her young face, wet eyes, and long hair appeared. She still wore the old man's clothes, but they fit her young woman's body, their appearance on Jin's frame having been part of the illusion. "What can we do for you, Yojiro-sama?"

Yojiro moved closer to them, lowering his voice to a whisper. "One of you needs to come with me."

"What for?" Takao snarled, ready to break free from Aoi if necessary.

"To be arrested for the murder of Kitsuki Obo, the man who sold street orphans to geisha houses throughout the city. This will keep the secret of Soshi Ezo, the man who branded youths with kagenari magic in his rogue shinobi school."

Takao and Aoi looked at each other, alarm stretched across their faces.

"Why us?" Takao demanded. "Aramoro is the one who killed Ezo-sama. And he got caught. He should take the blame."

"Aramoro-sama needs to go free," Aoi whispered, clutching tighter at Takao's arm, fear at the realization blanking her eyes as she stared into space. "For the clan."

"I can exonerate him," Yojiro explained. "I have enough evidence to use against either of you, but if one of you will confess, it will expedite things. You only have a moment to decide–"

"In here!" Motome shouted in the street. The three Scorpions turned to see the yoriki plunge into the inn with a dozen guards crowding in through the entrance.

Takao snatched Aoi's hand and bolted up the stairs, quick as lightning.

"Stop!" Motome yelled. She and her dōshin barreled past Yojiro in hot pursuit, their feet shaking the entire dilapidated building as they ascended after the young couple. Yojiro walked after them, knowing the two shinobi would use their abilities to escape, so speed was of no consequence. Takao had more than likely melted into shadow already, but Aoi only had one trick.

Motome and her dōshin spread out, pounding on all the doors and rushing into the rooms, the shouts and surprises of the tenants ringing in the air. The sound of crashing upstairs indicated she was tearing furniture away from walls and flinging belongings from closets, thorough in her search for two people who had apparently vanished. With many rooms in the inn, her search would surely last a few more minutes, despite the help of her guards.

Yojiro waited at the bottom stair. An old woman hobbled toward him, her back bent and her head bobbing in fear as she trembled down the steps to avoid the violent noise from above. Despite the posture, Yojiro could see the woman's movements were greatly exaggerated, not a steady, wary descent after decades of frailty. He put his hand on the woman's shoulder.

"You know, Aoi-san, you are a better choice than Takao for many reasons," he whispered into her ear.

"No. We shall not surrender," she said, her incongruous young woman's voice quivering in fear, lending an intense innocence to her wrinkled eyes. Motome's voice shook the ceiling as she ordered her guards to open all the windows and look down into the alleys, to climb onto the roof if necessary. Aoi swallowed. "We can escape."

Takao burst from the darkened crack of a backroom door, having doubled back for Aoi. He lunged at Yojiro, dagger in hand.

"Let her go!" he hissed, striking, but Yojiro had already learned Takao's attack patterns, and found them easier to navigate by the light of day. He dodged and then snatched Takao's arm where the shadow brand was hidden.

"This cannot be found on the body of a prisoner," Yojiro calmly stated, his heart breaking for them as he pleaded with Aoi. "This secret must be kept. Aoi-san, I know that somehow, the shadow brand did not stay on your skin. You healed without gaining its power."

Takao struggled in his grip, trying to shift the blade into the other hand. Yojiro twisted the wrist, and the knife fell to the floor.

"Aoi-san," Yojiro continued, keeping his voice low to avoid Motome's attention. "I know that Ezo still kept you, even when the shadow brand did not stick. He trained you in his impersonation craft instead. He gave you purpose. If you do this, you can keep Ezo's secret safe."

"Don't listen to him, Aoi," Takao interrupted, struggling in Yojiro's grip. "He is manipulating you. The Scorpion Clan murdered Ezo! And now they want to murder us, too!"

However, Aoi's old-woman face dissolved into her own, and her own shoulders hunched over in resignation. She turned to Takao, her dewy eyes wet with real tears. "I am sorry, but Yojiro-sama is right." She frowned, a world-weariness tainting her young face. "And without Ezo-sensei, we have no master. We must return to the Scorpion, rejoin the clan. Or else we have no purpose."

"We have purpose!" Takao insisted, his own hurt twisting his mouth into a bitter scowl. "You and I can carry on Ezo's school."

Aoi shook her head. "Ezo's school is nothing without a clan, Takao. I've long thought this. We must do our duty to the Scorpion. I may be expendable to them, but through this, I find meaning." She turned to Yojiro, putting her hand on his arm. "I will go with you, Yojiro-sama."

"No, Aoi," Takao whispered, wrenching free of Yojiro to grab her shoulders and shake her. "I will not allow you to sacrifice yourself for this."

Aoi smiled at her lover, a last, sweet smile commanding all her lingering courage. "Do you remember our first lesson from Ezo-sensei? About loyalty to him as our master? You and I still live by it. Your anger is an expression of loyalty toward our sensei, honoring his death and seeking revenge against those who wronged him.

"My sacrifice will be my loyalty toward Ezo-sensei's school, to hide you, his greatest success."

Takao's face softened long enough for her tears to fall onto his hands in their final shared moment.

Within seconds, Motome crashed back down the stairs.

"Yojiro-sama, you caught the girl!" she panted, fumbling down the steps with her guards. She gestured for them to bind Aoi. "Where is the boy?"

"He was just a bystander," Yojiro said, twisting his fingers into painful knots in his pockets. Takao had completely vanished. "No need to look for him. We have the person we came for."

"Yojiro," Aoi called to him as they finished binding her arms, an intense hope struggling over the despair choking her voice. "Do you believe in reincarnation?"

Yojiro stared at her, wondering, begging the Heavens for the first time in his life for the celestial wheel she longed for to be real.

"For those who keep the Celestial Order with duty and devotion, another life is promised," he said, his face growing solemn, relaxing into his next words, as though he were about to lie. He was not sure of their veracity. But he would tell her anyway. "If the Heavens care for any of us, you will be reunited in a future life, Aoi-san."

With that, the guards took her away.

"What was that about?" Motome asked as they abandoned the inn. She still had her jitte clenched tightly in her fist, as if afraid of an assault from some unknown source.

Yojiro straightened his collar again on either side of his face, shielding himself from the world of shadows.

"Some lies we just need, Motome-san," he said, turning to look at the gutter. The trickle of brown sewer water glittered as it ran downhill to empty into the Bay of Drowned Honor. He could no longer smell the stench.

EPILOGUE

Yojiro leaned over at his worktable, a slab of cherrywood before him, glowing warm under the undisturbed sun through his open windows. He slid weary fingers over the grain. A dark ripple here. A pale river there. The solitude of his craft calmed him. The strain of his mission to Ryokō Owari still trembled in his tired heart. The betrayal. The tragedy. The darkness. He had traded his own soul for a life. But he had also given up Aoi's life for their clan.

Soshi Aoi had confessed to killing Kitsuki Obo in revenge for his part in her sale to a geisha house as a child, only one victim of many. Her verbal confession was enough to convict her, and she would be executed within the week. Shosuro Takao had disappeared, taking the instruments of the Shadow Den Dōjō's rituals with him, leaving no hints of his next move. Yojiro hoped he would not see the shadow-branded shinobi again, but he was sure that revenge would drive them together again one day. Aramoro was released without penalty for his lack of involvement in the murder, though he stayed on in Ryokō Owari to enjoy the luxuries of the Licensed Quarter as a free man. Kitsuki Obo's ashes and belongings were on their way back to the Dragon Clan, although Yojiro knew the shipping caravan would be attacked by brigands, ensuring that everything, including Obo's ring, clothes, and desk, would be lost. Seppun Motome was praised by no one for her involvement in the case, many of her clues having been largely unneeded in convicting Aoi, and Otomo Seno had no interest in such minor murder cases anyway. Instead, he had written his long letter to the Emerald Champion, reporting on his many exploits in purging his city of ninja, though he was still awaiting a reply.

Yojiro sighed. Motome had written a long parting letter to him, which he still kept in his breast pocket, next to the new ochre silk coin purse she had sent.

"I must admit that my bias against the Scorpion hindered my evaluation of Obo's sinister activities, an advantage he pressed for a decade. While I am still far from trusting the Scorpion in my city, I now know that there is more than Scorpion crime to look out for. I will attempt to work more closely with Captain Denmaru rather than against him, as you advised. In turn, I hope that you can continue to use your influence, and your sense of duty and honor, to move other Scorpion, especially those in the capital, to mete out true justice."

The irony of her words slapped him in the face. He had betrayed her most of all. However, there had been no choice. Their relationship of trust had been sacrificed on the altar of necessity along with Aoi. To loyalty. To the Scorpion.

"*When you visit again, I will fulfill my promise to take you to the Temple of Daikoku,*" she ended, forcing Yojiro to smile in spite of himself. "*Your friend, Motome.*"

Yojiro pressed his sharp wood knife to the pulpy surface of the cherry block before him. A single wood shaving bloomed before his blade like the petal of a new flower.

I should propose some policy changes to Champion Toturi about Ryokō Owari, to do her a favor. Perhaps starting with a promotion.

A heavy rap at the door drew his attention.

"Enter," he called, setting his tool down in deference to his visitor.

The shōji screen slid open to reveal a tall, shadowy figure. Yojiro flinched instinctively, his hand already at his katana. He crouched in a defensive stance and prepared for the worst. However, no shinobi or brigand emerged from the dark. Instead, the open door revealed a grotesque visage of a crimson oni, fully fanged and horned. Its form was dressed in opulent red and black silks, the minute patterns woven into the brocade flickering like a rippling tide of fresh blood in the sun. Through the shining pits where the oni's eyes should be glimmered an unfathomable cunning. The man in the mask was the Scorpion Clan Champion, Bayushi Shoju.

Yojiro bowed low, lower than he ever bowed, as Shoju entered, mild tremors of fear and awe spreading throughout his chest. Though he had met the Clan Champion many times, he had never had a personal audience, let alone a personal visitation.

"Shoju-ue. You bless my workshop with your presence. Please, forgive the disorder."

Shoju waved away the flattery with a black-lacquered fan, uncharmed by the formality. The oni mask completely concealed his facial emotions, exaggerating every slight move of the body into a crucial language, mesmerizing to behold.

"You returned triumphant," Shoju boomed, his deep voice echoing from the depths of his oni mask, likewise devoid of telling tones or strains, his motives and intentions fully veiled. "My brother is free, and our clan is above reproach. Kitsuki Obo's scandalous activities in Ryokō Owari Toshi have swung the pendulum of power back to the Scorpion. The Dragon have been weakened, particularly our enemies among the Kitsuki investigators. You have done well."

"I humbly thank you for your praise, Shoju-ue," Yojiro said, bowing again.

"I was even impressed with your actions during the tournament of the Emerald Champion, Yojiro-san," Shoju continued, taking up one of Yojiro's carving knives from the worktable and deftly spinning it in his fingers. "By giving Toturi that riddled hint, ensuring his win against Aramoro, you proved you could choose our clan interests over even Lady Kachiko."

Yojiro swallowed.

Lord Shoju knows the whole truth… And yet, he is the only Scorpion who sees the tournament in this way. Not as a failure but as a benefit. Why?

"You might have suspected that you were chosen for this mission in Ryokō Owari as some form of test," Shoju continued, absently inspecting Yojiro's wood block. "My wife believes she was testing you, trying your limits of sacrifice… of self-debasement… of pain." He plunged the knife silently into the wood where it stood quivering, a trembling spire in the new slab. "However, I wanted to see your limits, too, Yojiro-san. I wanted to measure your loyalty to the Scorpion, even in the face of our most precious secrets. The dishonorable existence of shinobi proved the perfect trial.

"You are obviously ready for more crucial tasks. More powerful influence. You are ready to take your place at my side and help me save Rokugan."

"My lord," Yojiro stammered. He hoped his faltering sounded like surprise instead of distress. The last fleeting hope of a life like Motome's – simple, honest, honorable – seemed to fade forever with those words. "I thank you."

"We shall speak again," the Scorpion Clan Champion replied.

Shoju departed as suddenly as he had appeared, leaving the doorway dark and empty. Yojiro slid the door shut and wrenched his knife free from his cherry plank. The tip was undamaged, having been slid perfectly into an invisible weak spot in the grain.

Yojiro wiped the sweat from his palms and calmed his breath.

Will working with Shoju mean more autonomy, more choice?

Again, he attempted to carve into his cherry block, this time starting from the hole that Shoju had left. The wood curls came away easily, but all he could manage to do was widen the pit, deepen the hole. He scoffed at himself and threw the tool down.

No, working with Shoju will only mean more sacrifices.

More lies.

He stared at the uncarved wood. He would begin again tomorrow. The surface would wait, a form still full of a thousand possible truths. As a craftsman, he could shape it however he wanted. When the time was right.

ACROSS THE BURNING SANDS

DANIEL LOVAT CLARK

For Mom, who taught me to love horses, birds, the outdoors, and long journeys.

CHAPTER ONE
The Way Station

I rode past two white trees.
It grew so dark I could hardly see.
Tried to go home, but never again.
I'd ridden clean out of the realms of men.

The attackers were poised to kill them all in three ways. The first was the spear and bow, the spilling of blood: the honorable path, in other words. The killers, who wore furs and leathers and stank of animal fat, carried torches, axes, spears, and crude bows. Although Shono and his party were samurai and the brigands were just Tegensai mountain folk come down from the Pillar of the Sky, only a fool would think that death did not rest at the ends of those weapons.

I am no fool. I have seen death come too suddenly, too soon. He remembered another battle, the feel of his sword in his hand as it bit flesh.

The second way was via the animals: horses and camels, but mainly horses. One hundred of the beasts were kept in the paddocks of the way station. If the ambushers could kill or steal those beasts, Shono and his samurai would never reach the next way station alive.

Tegensai have little use for our horses in their mountains, except perhaps to feed them to their dogs and the mountain trolls. But it didn't matter why they might want the mounts – only that Shono's party would die on foot.

The third was water. Always water – on the Sand Road, even there on the knees of the Pillar of the Sky mountains. A heavy stone cistern lay on the rise above the way station. The lid must have weighed as much as thirty warriors, but it could be moved or broken. If the water were poisoned or befouled or spilled into the thirsty dust of the Sand Road, they would sicken and die, humans and horses both.

Shono's life was an inch from ending in three different ways, but what of it? *Does a samurai not live at all times three feet from death?* He walked from the yurt with no sign of fear. *Mitsuko is dead. I was to make her my wife, and instead I made her a corpse. What have I left to lose?*

Shono drove a handful of arrows into the dust at his feet, seeing his mother's grave face as she sent him west. *"To treat with the caliph in al-Zawira."* As if the entire clan couldn't see it for what it was: *sending her broken son away.* He drew, loosed – as calm, as numb, as in the practice yard. His arrow struck true, and a man died. *What of it?*

"Lord Shono!" Three of his retinue, weapons in hand, surrounded him. Yumino was wearing her armor – *Does she sleep in it?* – but the Bokudō brothers were like him, protected only by an Ujik-style *deel* of dyed wool. "Lord Shono," said Yumino again. "We should get you away from here."

"No," he said. His voice, his orders, but Shono watched, heard them happen, as if he were someone else watching another person standing in his skin. He commanded only by force of habit. "Yumino-san, to the cistern. Naosuke-san, Naotaka-san, see to the horses."

"That's right, send the shepherd to tend the horses," quipped Taka.

"Plenty of goats between us and them," added his brother. But they went; of course they did. Only city people would mistake the nomads' free spirit for a lack of discipline. Shono knew better.

So Shono stood alone again, plucking a harvest of death from the sandy soil at his feet and sending it streaking into the chaos and dark. Each shot stung at his wrist where his bracer should have been – he almost felt it. Most of his arrows found their mark, sending Tegensai warriors sprawling. Others vanished into the dark. Shono saw no difference between the two from his place outside his own mind, watching himself at work.

Soon the arrows were spent. *What of it?* He cast his bow aside and drew his sword. Two of the raiders rushed toward him, one armed with a spear, the other with an axe in her hand. Shono flowed like water, the way his instructors had taught him, wondering if he was about to die even as he knocked the spear aside and stepped inside its reach. The thought did not frighten him.

His sword flashed in the flickering light of the torches and the raiders' spreading fire, intercepting the second brigand's arcing axe blow at the wrist. Axe and hand tumbled into the night. Shono never stopped moving, driving his hip into the spear-wielding brigand and sending him stumbling back. The man shouted something in the language of the Tegensai, and Shono's sword finished its long arc, up and around and back across the raider's chest. It wasn't a fatal wound – the layers of leather and fur cut before his skin – but it was enough to cause him to drop his spear and drive both hands to his breast to stop the blood flow. No samurai, this raider – and young, inexperienced. Shono killed him in another heartbeat. Drove his sword into the man's stomach, watched him fall, gasping for breath.

Just like Mitsuko. For a moment it was her gasping at his feet, the wind snatching her last words from him. It was her blood on his sword. Mitsuko, his betrothed, the hope for peace between Unicorn and Lion. *Dead by my hand, killed as much by my mother's choice as my blade.*

Footsteps behind him. He turned, too slow, still seeing Mitsuko – would he see her again, now? Was this it? A Tegensai raider screamed forward, hurling her spear. It was true, the sweet frisson of perfection that he had felt so many times when an arrow left his bow. It would take him in the heart. He was neither surprised nor afraid. *So I end. What of it?*

But then Taka was there, Bokudō Naotaka, the shepherd's son from the north. According to Rokugani custom, he was *jizamurai*, a vassal warrior not truly noble, not truly peasant. But in the free-spirited Unicorn Clan, a man like Taka could rise to a great station based on his deeds and his skill – deeds like saving Shono's life. The spear took Taka, instead, as he hurled Shono to the ground.

"'See to the horses'," Taka groaned. "Shono, you ass. As if we would let you fight alone." Then he lay still.

The Tegensai raider lay dead on the ground, Taka's own spear protruding from her chest like a slender tree. Taka's eyes stared at nothing, his face ashen gray.

Mitsuko dead by my hand. Taka dead by my incompetence.

Shono shook his head, scattering windblown dust from his face. *Suke.* He found the other Bokudō brother at the horse paddock, scimitar flashing as he drove a raider back. *Yumino.* She was atop the cistern, her spear flicking forward and back like a lunging serpent. *The others.* Ide Ryōma – language tutor, advisor, friend – hurled a bucketful of water at a burning yurt.

Iuchi Shoan – who'd saved his life as a child and been his auntie ever since – tended to a wounded warrior in the doorway of the stone block house of the way station. Other samurai and *ashigaru* lay dead or fought the raiders. His party had numbered twenty warriors when they left Khanbulak. How many raiders were there? Fifty? How many of his own were still alive? A dozen?

They're all going to die. They followed me, and I'm going to get them killed.

He spared a moment to shut Taka's eyes, then started moving. There was no thought, no genius moment of strategy, only the knowledge that to do nothing was to watch a dozen more Takas die in front of his eyes. He rushed to the paddock, took another bandit from behind, and vaulted the fence. "Suke-san, open the gate," Shono said, finding Umeboshi and leaping atop the blood bay's back. No saddle, no stirrup; only a fool or the best rider in the world would fight like this from horseback.

Suke opened the gate, and Shono rode out with a shout. He gripped Boshi's flanks with his knees, one hand tangled in the horse's dark mane; it was barely enough to keep him ahorse. Umeboshi was half in a panic, the smell of blood and fire and the stinking Tegensai all in his nostrils, and eager to rush forward. Shono urged him toward the closest knot of raiders, where two of his retinue were pressed back-to-back. He slashed at the closest raider as they thundered past, a weak strike given his lack of footing but enough to disrupt their formation, send them scrambling. His warriors took advantage of the distraction and retreated, regrouping at the way station.

Shono kept riding, scattering Tegensai warriors as he ran, ducking under a hurled spear here, a flickering arrow there. Umeboshi screamed as Shono wrenched him back to the fray time and again. Boshi lashed out with his hooves, shattering bones, screaming and biting. Then one of the Tegensai raiders plunged a spear into Umeboshi's side, and he fell. Shono barely tumbled free in time, failed to keep a hand on his sword.

Not Boshi, too, Shono thought. A ridiculous concern – what did a horse matter compared to the human lives dying around him? *Compared to Mitsuko.*

But the raiders ignored the horse, leapt over him and around him as Boshi struggled to rise again. Two of them: one holding a spear, the other drawing a glimmering long knife. Shinseist prayer beads dangled from the wrist holding the knife. *The Lion reject Shinsei, the Tegensai accept him, and both try to kill me.* Shono reached to his hip and drew his *wakizashi*. He backed away, turning his head and letting his senses drift across the battlefield in the Shinjo fashion, searching for a path to safety. He heard hoofbeats.

"Now you die, *chi-gye*," the spearman growled in broken Rokugani. Then the point of a lance burst from his breast, and he fell as a frothing horse galloped past. The bandit with the knife had enough time to turn before a scimitar flashed in the dark and his head fell from his shoulders. A great black horse reared, bellowing, in front of Shono, its rider booming in the dark.

"Cousin!" Chagatai called. "It seems the Moto come to the aid of the Shinjo once again!"

CHAPTER TWO
The Sand Road

Behold the setting sun; it leaves a trail of gold.
Someday I will follow it as Shinjo did in days of old.
To ride into the Burning Sands where the nights are icy cold,
That is my destiny, for only Ki-Rin could be so bold.

They left the way station the next day, descending from the Pillar of the Sky mountains and riding into the endless sweep of the Plain of Wind and Stone. Red hills lay like a crumpled blanket before them, edging on a rolling expanse of black and yellow earth. Ribbons of sand lay against spurs of rock, and flats of dusty clay were interrupted by ragged scars left by the infrequent rivers of the Burning Sands. A few clumps of blue-green marked where hardy shrubs clung to what life they could eke out of the land. *Beautiful and empty. I could ride into that expanse and be gone forever.*

Chagatai's warriors added to Shono's party made their group almost forty strong, with over a hundred horses. Shono, Chagatai, Yumino, and Ide Ryōma rode apart from the main body, where the thunder of hooves and dust of the trail was less oppressive.

The conversation, however, is stifling.

Moto Chagatai kept up a steady flow of boasts and chatter throughout the morning. He praised Shono's horse – the blue roan Tsubasa that day, while Umeboshi recuperated – and pronounced the virtues of his own, a black stallion named Daichin.

"Your horse is very fine, cousin," said Shono.

Chagatai proclaimed his love of hunting, asking his cousin if he fancied their chances of finding any worthy game on their ride today.

"I have never been so far west," said Shono. "I must bow to your superior expertise in this matter, Chagatai-san."

A mistake. The man will pounce on my weakness.

"So you must, Shono-kun," agreed Chagatai. "It is a wise lord who knows when to accept the wisdom of his betters."

"And a wise officer who can offer his expertise when it is warranted, yet hold his tongue when his silence is preferred," observed Ryōma. The little man's round hat was pulled down against the sun, and his lazy way of slouching atop his horse gave the impression that he was asleep. "We were speaking of hunting. In your opinion, Chagatai-sama, are we likely to find any worthwhile game on our journey today?"

"How can we speak of hunting, with our friends' ashes still warm?" asked Yumino.

"Dead is dead," said Chagatai. "The rites have been said and the Lords of Death appeased, and the ashes ride east with my messengers to be returned to their families. Meanwhile, we who live must ride on."

"And we must eat," said Ryōma.

"Yes," agreed Chagatai. "As for game, we may see a deer or

two when next we find water, but I fear they will have fled the sound of our hooves. I did see two fine birds in your baggage, cousin; perhaps falconry can fetch a hare or two between us."

"Those birds are intended as gifts for the caliph," said Ryōma.

"Some exercise may do them good," Shono allowed. He turned Tsubasa back to the main column.

In so doing, he bought himself a frigid reception from Suke, who found an excuse to ride to the far end of their party. *I earned that.* But if Suke's mood persisted, or spread, it could make his warriors unruly, erode their discipline. *I cannot lead them if they do not trust me. They will not trust me if I do not trust myself.* Watching himself from the outside, he saw what he should do, the overtures he should make, the balance of command and friendship. But it was impossible. There was nothing inside him to make the connection with. *Perhaps I should step aside. Retreat to a monastery; would that make things right?*

He accepted the birds from his groom, Tanaka, and rode back to Chagatai. Suke's mood would have to wait. *As will my own.*

They distributed the hawks and rode out farther from the main column, sending the birds aloft when a rabbit burst from a scrap of scraggly bush. Chagatai's bird made the kill, and he rode off to collect it with a chuckle.

"Shono-sama." *She doesn't even touch the reins.* Yumino nudged her sacred steed over to where Shono sat on Tsubasa. "I worry that Chagatai is trying to get you away from the protection of the column."

"Ah," murmured Ryōma from Shono's other side. "You, too, are wondering at the coincidence that those bandits just happened to attack a way station for the first time in years as the Shinjo heir was passing through."

Chagatai, trying to kill me? The thought neither surprised him

Legend of the Five Rings

nor frightened him. *Would that balance the scales?* "You forget, it was Chagatai who rode to our rescue. Without his intervention, I would be dead. So might we all be."

Yumino grunted and turned away, her horse moving instantly from a standstill to a gallop.

"She thinks that she's failed you as a *yōjimbō,*" Ryōma said. "Take care not to sting her pride any more than is necessary, Shono-sama. The Battle Maidens swear no oaths, waste no words on empty promises. That she has chosen to serve you is a mark of high honor."

"Yumino-san did her duty, and I am still alive," Shono said. "What more could either of us ask for?"

"As you say," said Ryōma in that tone that meant the opposite. He quieted again and appeared to fall asleep in his saddle.

When Chagatai returned, he had a fine dust-brown rabbit hanging from his saddle, and the caliph's bird perched proudly on his gauntlet. "Your hawk is still aloft, Shono-san," he called. "Does the bird refuse your commands?"

"She cannot refuse commands I have not issued," said Shono.

"A curious sentiment – one who never gives an order is never refused. Tell me, is this how you intend to rule, when you become khan?" Chagatai sidled Daichin into step as Shono urged Tsubasa forward. Ryōma and Yumino fell in behind.

"The emperor rules," said Shono. "The khan leads."

"Have you a different opinion, Chagatai-sama?" asked Ryōma. "Your own father is the Moto khan; has he taught you the difference between a ruler and a leader?"

"Let the Ide shave words apart for their meanings," said Chagatai. "We Moto prefer actions to words. My father, Ögodei Khan, rules the western lands well and leads our armies when he must. When I am khan, I will do both with brilliance."

"Khan of the Moto," asked Yumino, "or Khan of Khans? You forget your station, Chagatai-sama."

"*Che*," breathed Chagatai, shaking his head. "And why not? I have the kami's blood in my veins, the same as my cousin here. Where is it written that the Khan of Khans must always be a Shinjo?" He held the rabbit aloft. "I can hunt, I can ride, and no one alive is as deadly on horseback as I; the Unicorn would be lucky to have a khan such as me." He glanced sidelong at Shono. "Especially in a time of war, *ne*?"

A war I gave us, with Mitsuko's blood on my sword.

"You do not choose the khan," growled Yumino.

"Ha! No, I don't. But perhaps someone should. A *quriltai*, as in days of old. Let the Unicorn choose who will lead them."

For a moment, Shono wanted it. *If I step aside, let Chagatai be khan, I could – what? Will it bring her back? Will I forsake my duty?* Bushidō forbade such thinking. He hoped that keen pulse of longing hadn't shown on his face.

"I could kill you where you stand for such disloyalty," hissed Yumino.

"You could try," laughed Chagatai. "But be at ease, Yumino-san. Shono is in no danger from me. That is what you fear, is it not?" Rolling with his horse's gait, Chagatai carefully hooded his hawk, placing her on the horn of his saddle. "You wonder at the bandit attack, at my convenient arrival. Well, it was no accident. I rode west when I received word from my aunt, Moto Rurame Noyan, about a spy captured in Khanbulak." He turned in his saddle and smiled, broad and smug like a hunting cat. "If I ever wish you dead, cousin, I'll do the job myself. I won't be sending brigands to accost you on the road."

"It's likely someone did, though," Ryōma mused. "An enemy without Chagatai-sama's refreshing forthrightness."

Shono raised his hand, and his hawk fell from the sky with

a shriek to perch atop his leather gauntlet. "There is no sport to be had here," he said, "and the column is drawing ahead of us." He put his heels to Tsubasa's flank, and they broke into a gallop.

Two days later, they reached the Hidden Valley, where the Ganzu family made their home. The journey was uneventful, aside from a spirited chase after a wounded antelope that put Chagatai, pink-faced with the thrill of the hunt, in a gregarious mood for more than a day.

Shono spent the journey studying his cousin, his thundering moods. Chagatai was as wild as the desert through which they rode, as sudden as a grasslands storm, a Moto to the bone. Shono tried to imagine him at a formal court occasion, sitting meekly through a tea ceremony or – Fortunes, kami, and Lords of Death forbid – in audience with the emperor himself. *A wild stallion loosed in a porcelain maker's workshop. There would be no survivors.* Chagatai was everything the Empire thought of the Unicorn: wild, free, fierce, quick to laugh, quick – according to himself – to love, terrible to anger, generous, and almost completely lacking in social graces. Yet he was beloved by his fellow Unicorn. When one of the ashigaru started up the traveling song, Chagatai joined in enthusiastically. His verses celebrated the legendary Moto skill in battle while also alluding to their great prowess as lovers. Shono himself couldn't find the music within him. *Perhaps my mother would approve of Chagatai. Didn't she break off her engagement to Ikoma Anakazu, knowing it might mean war with the Lion Clan, out of fear the Unicorn might cease to be ourselves? When we put on the silk robes of court, climb down from our horses, and bow to the other clans, do we abandon what makes us who we are? Would a khan like Chagatai earn us the respect we have been denied?*

He had no answers. He wished to share his thoughts with Ide Ryōma, explain how his murder of his betrothed had tainted him, how stepping aside for Chagatai could make things right. Except if he did that, if he admitted to the weakness of his thoughts, he would lose the respect of Ryōma and everyone who served him. *This is not Bushidō.* Instead, he tried to imagine what the little Ide would say: "*It is also the Unicorn way to adapt, to new environments or to new people. We adapted when we stayed with the Ujik and adopted the Moto into our clan. We must adapt again now that we are returned to Rokugan.*" Chagatai could never change who he was. Shono could never ask him to, no more than put the wild hawk on the wing in a cage. *Something beautiful would be lost forever. Is that the burden of the Khan of Khans, to put themselves in the cage and keep their clan free?* And was his mother's choice sacrificing her own honor to preserve Unicorn freedom, or was it sacrificing the honor of her clan to break herself out of the cage? *Will we ever agree on an answer to that one?*

Shono's musings were brushed aside as the Hidden Valley appeared before him. He'd had no warning as they approached it. In all directions, he'd seen nothing but the desolation of the Burning Sands. The Pillar of the Sky mountains were a gentle bruise in the sky behind them, and the sweep of rock and sand extended like an ocean all around. Then, suddenly, they were atop a rise looking down into a broad river valley, green with water and filled with box-shaped mounds of baked earth. Roadways of weathered wood bridged mound to mound, and people in striped robes with turbans wrapped around their heads made their way throughout what must have been a city, only Shono could see no buildings. One man arrived at a mound like any other, took leave of his companion, and then descended a stair into the earth.

"Welcome to the Hidden Valley," laughed Chagatai. "It makes an impression, does it not?"

"They live beneath the earth," Shono said at length.

"Indeed they do," said Chagatai. "As you might, in this sun-scorched land. And it has the advantage that, as no rooftops or towers rise above the fall of the river valley, the whole village is invisible from more than a dozen yards away."

"Can these people truly be Rokugani?" breathed Yumino in wonder.

"Some in the Imperial Court might say the same of the Ujik," said Ryōma. "But in point of law, no; the Ganzu are Unicorn by our custom, but not of Rokugan. Our holdings beyond the emperor's proclaimed borders are… a special case."

"The emperor cares not whether his subjects live above or below the ground," declared Chagatai, "so long as they pay their taxes."

"And we care not," said Shono, "so long as they have water."

Chagatai's eyes were upon him as they gathered at the head of the switchback trail on the valley slopes that led to a broad paddock at the downstream edge of the village. *Is even this a test? Does Chagatai see some weakness, some failing in how I respond to the Ganzu?* He couldn't fathom the *noyan*'s game. He couldn't fathom his own response to it. So, he ignored it, as best he could.

This eastern bank was given over mainly to the strange sunken city, its narrow courtyards and orchards recessed between raised earthen walls and roads. The western bank was entirely agricultural, with fruit-laden trees in uneven rows and squares of black earth bearing a crop of some sort of grain, its stalks nearly doubled over with the weight of their seed. Seeing so much lush greenery after weeks of some of the least hospitable landscape he'd ever encountered was a surprise that left Shono feeling untethered, adrift in memory as much as place. He did his best to keep it from showing in his face. "They water their fields from the river," he observed.

"Only river worthy of the name for a hundred *li* in any direction," Chagatai said. "Although I confess I've never ridden west of here to see for myself."

"Their city has no walls, no defenses." As their horses filled up the paddock, Shono climbed atop the fence for a better view. "And no horses to speak of. Some camels."

"Their warriors are brave enough, but the Hidden Valley's true defenders are the hundreds of li of desolation all around them. Even their river gives up and runs into dry clay only a little way downstream, in the dry season."

"But the Sand Road leads straight here."

"In times of peace, yes," said Ide Ryōma. "I understand the Ganzu have a few tricks they can employ if they fear an enemy may approach along the Sand Road."

Iuchi Shoan, who stood up in her stirrups and squinted upstream toward the river's source, murmured half to herself, "Some magic, too, I shouldn't wonder." The shugenja had passed most of the ride in silence, and Chagatai laughed aloud.

"She speaks!" he chuckled. "And not just to the spirits!"

Shoan's brow wrinkled, and she turned her attention to the Moto. "Do you always treat your elders so disrespectfully, Chagatai-kun?" she asked. "Perhaps I'd be more willing to speak to you if you had anything of interest to say." She clucked her tongue and steered her horse toward the path down into the valley.

"If I didn't know better," said Chagatai as he followed, "I'd think that Shoan-sama didn't like me."

Shono nudged Tsubasa after Daichin. "Ryōma-san, tell me more of the Ganzu."

"The Ganzu were happy to swear fealty to Shinjo Khulan Khan

in 1010," said Ide Ryōma. "But they were forced to surrender to the caliph in 1072 when he attempted to conquer the Sand Road. The better part of their warriors marched east and joined with the White Horde and the Battle Maidens, who broke the Nehiri advance and reclaimed the lost land in 1074."

"And *only* the lost land," grumbled Chagatai. "The Shinjo khan forbade the sacking of al-Zawira then, and so the Moto stayed their hand. Had I been khan, the caliph would have been cast down and his city made a warning to those who would raise a hand against us." He swung down from Daichin and led the stallion into the paddock.

"And then the Unicorn would trade with whom, precisely?" Ryōma asked, dismounting his shaggy dun, Patience.

"Some new king would rise in the region to trade with, I am certain." Chagatai waved a dismissive hand. "And there's still the Ivory Kingdoms."

"Ryōma-san, you said the Ganzu *marched* to join the White Horde?" said Shono. "On foot?"

"The Ganzu are a hardy people. Some of them survived."

Shono looked at the smiling people around him, bowing to him as they went about their business. *My people, when I am khan.* He saw Chagatai stretch expansively and then swagger toward the center of the village. *Or Chagatai's, if he has his way.* A vision of the Unicorn under Chagatai Khan swam in Shono's mind: war on all fronts, a harvest worthy of the Ujik's Lords of Death. *It would be easier for me to let Chagatai take my place, to shirk my duty. But Bushidō commands otherwise. Duty, loyalty, righteousness – they forbid me to step aside.* But did they also command him to do so? Should there be no consequence for Mitsuko's blood on his hands?

"Come!" said Chagatai. "The Ganzu khan will want to make us welcome. It will be nice to sleep in a proper bed again;

these houses are no yurts, but they're better than the dusty ground!"

They walked on one of the valley's elevated roads, making their way toward the only buildings Shono could see that rose above the flat plain of the general plan. One Shono took for the daimyō's manor, if daimyō was the term to use for the Ganzu leader. The other's dome-shaped roof suggested it was some sort of temple. He stepped back to where Iuchi Shoan walked, threading prayer beads through her fingers. "Auntie," he said, "to which god is that temple dedicated? Surely the Ganzu do not honor the kami?"

Shoan shook her head. "No, Shono-san. They follow a new gaijin tradition. Followers of that faith are called Qamarists, and you will see many of them when we reach al-Zawira; this caliph you ride to treat with calls himself the Protector of the Qamarist Faith."

"Who or what is Qamar? A god?"

"As to that, you will have to ask a Qamarist priest. My knowledge does not extend to the matter."

Chagatai was right: they slept well that night. The next day, they remained in the Hidden Valley as guests of Ganzu Hama, the daimyō, or khan – in the local language, the *khutun*. She received Shono, Yumino, and Ryōma in her garden in the cool morning light shortly after they broke their fast.

The khutun was a small woman, her hair gray and her spotted hand clutched around the head of an ebony cane. She was dwarfed by the heavily laden fruit trees of her garden, hobbling along beneath them as if in some far-off forest and not in a tiny square of earth surrounded on all sides by her palace. But this tiny woman from a tiny family had no fear of treating Shono as if he were an errant grandson. "It has been many years since a member of the Great Khan's family deigned to visit my valley," she said, leaning on her cane.

"My mother sends her respects," Shono said. "I know that she would be very glad to visit your city and see its wonders for herself, if the war and matters of court did not detain her." It was probably even true. He had often heard Altansarnai Khan lament that her duties did not permit her to travel as much as she would like.

"Yes, your war," Hama tsked. "A shame. Though I hear that you have made a name for yourself on the battlefield."

"News travels swiftly," Shono said. "But I fear it is exaggerated. My warriors and I won a battle, nothing more."

"And killed the woman to whom you had been betrothed to do it. Not many would have the stomach for such a thing."

Mitsuko filled his vision, screaming, knocking Taka aside and killing his horse. She came for him, for Shono – their blades clashed. His sword plunged into her stomach.

That was then. Focus on now, you fool.

"The betrothal was broken when Matsu Mitsuko attacked Hisu Mori Toride," said Yumino. "My lord Shono's duty was clear. His course was decided, and his honor demanded he follow it."

Was that for Hama Khutun's benefit, or for mine? And how long had he been silent, lost in his memory, that Yumino had felt compelled to speak for him?

"Honor," observed the khutun. "And was it honor that caused your mother to break her engagement and give the Lion the excuse they needed to attack in the first place?"

Ryōma bowed deeply. "The fault belongs to the Ide. The treaty said 'according to custom', and we understood that to mean according to the custom of Rokugan, where the samurai of the lesser family joins the greater. But the Ikoma insisted after the treaty was signed that it meant *Ikoma* custom, where the bride joins the groom's family. A dreadful oversight on our part."

"Hmph," snorted Hama. "You mean that the Lion believe their daimyō outranks our Khan of Khans."

"My mother would have been forced to abdicate her post," Shono said.

"And all of Rokugan would see that the Unicorn are no better than a vassal family, in the eyes of the Great Clans," said Yumino.

"Instead, all of Rokugan sees that the Shinjo break their word, then task the Ide to take the blame," boomed Chagatai from atop the garden wall. He took a step to a nearby ladder, then slid down it to join them.

Yumino stiffened at Shono's side. Her hand had a stillness to it as if she were very carefully refraining from gripping her sword.

Chagatai may not have sent the Tegensai to kill me, but he has just stabbed me in the heart. Shono's nostrils flared as he took a deep breath, seeking stillness. The sweet summer smell of the garden and the richness of black earth filled him, along with the leathery tang of Chagatai. "What would you have done in my mother's place, cousin?" *What would I have done?* "Bowed your head, let your clan be diminished?"

Chagatai grinned like a wolf. "I would have marched right into my wedding day and come out with Ikoma Anakazu's head for thinking he could cheat the Unicorn."

"So, my cousin objects to the way in which Altansarnai Khan broke the engagement," said Shono. "He finds it insufficiently treacherous and bloody-minded."

"Does not Bushidō command us to commit fully to our course of action?" laughed Chagatai. "There's no sense in betrayal by half measures, not if your honor is already forfeit."

"I shall keep your words in mind, Chagatai-san." *For the day when you betray me.*

The Ganzu daimyō insisted they spend a full two days as her guests. Shono would sooner have ridden on immediately, but their herd – especially Umeboshi – was exhausted. *Every day I am gone is another day for the war to turn against the Unicorn. Another day for friends and family to die,* he thought. And then: *and yet you are half-hoping you never return. Make up your mind, Shono.* Agony to be away from his clan, agony to return to them.

He instructed Tanaka and Suke to see that the horses were well watered and fed and given a chance to recover. Though Suke was still cold, he at least did as he was told.

Shono sat quietly in his place of honor at the khutun's right hand during the dinner on their final night. Chagatai, at the khutun's left, was the center of attention. He told his own version of the battle at the way station, one in which each Unicorn left a dozen dead and dying bandits at their feet. Yumino ground her teeth and glared, even when Chagatai spared a few phrases to describe the terror she inspired in the Tegensai as she danced atop the cistern. She did not relent until Chagatai described Shono's bareback charge as demonstrating "courage worthy of a Moto". *But not of a khan.* Chagatai was walking a careful path, lifting up everyone around him, but himself more than the rest. *Was he tutored in the fine Moto art of boasting, or does it come naturally?*

Ganzu Hama laughed and applauded Chagatai's tales from atop her ebony throne. Each armrest was carved in the shape of a lion-dog resting a paw atop a pomegranate. The wall hangings were a mixture of silk and wool, eastern and western materials combined, and all the furnishings were of excellent quality, but with disparate styles so haphazardly juxtaposed they left Shono unsteady on his feet. The manners of the Ganzu were the same: some of the reserved formality of a Rokugani court along with the easy laughter of the Ujik and some other habits that Shono took to be of western influence. *They are a people of the crossroads. More Unicorn than the Shinjo, in some ways, although they are no horsemen. They explore by letting the world come to them.*

He said as much to the khutun in a quiet moment the next morning. The old woman had accompanied them to the paddock and was leaning on her ebony cane as Shono checked Tsubasa's tack.

"You are perceptive, Shono-san," said Hama. "We have been Unicorn only a short time by the standards of the other families in our clan, I know. And even the Moto are treated as outsiders and newcomers in Rokugan. But it is more than an accident of geography that binds us to the Unicorn Clan. Not every tribe in this region joined with Shinjo Khulan Khan willingly."

"How often do you leave this valley?" Shono asked.

"Rarely. We do not grow enough extra grain to support great herds of horses and camels, especially through the dry season when the river slows to a muddy trickle. But there is no way to cross the Burning Sands, in either direction, without stopping at our holy river. People have been coming to this valley for as long as cities have risen on either end of the Sand Road. And they will continue to do so until those cities fall."

No time soon, I trust. Shono mounted, still considering. Chagatai fell in beside him as they clattered across the bridge to the western bank.

"Surely your duties are discharged now, cousin," Shono said.

"Not at all," said Chagatai. "Your mother charges the White

Horde with the defense of the western border, and the Unicorn claim all the land to the edge of al-Zawira. I will ride with you the whole way, Shono-kun!"

Shono let Yumino's steady glare speak for him.

CHAPTER THREE
The Dead City and the Crooked City

Far-off al-Zawira
Lies now where we once made war.
Nothing of those kings still stood,
Paid in full for Shinjo's blood.

The Burning Sands changed color as they rode, from red, to black and yellow, to a blowing, drifting gold. The final passage was the hardest; were it not for the way stations with their cisterns, half of Shono's horses would have died. After only a few hours of the unfettered sun, Shono adopted the loose head wrapping of the Ganzu and found that it helped. Most of the party soon followed suit. They shared a way station with a Nehiri caravan one evening. Every member of the Rokugani contingent bought a cloth of clean white cotton to wrap around their head. Shono had never loved an article of clothing so much in his life.

A simple pleasure, but even those have escaped me since Mitsuko's death. He clung to it, to any sign that things were returning to normal – that he was returning to normal. *Bushidō insists I maintain face in the presence of tragedy. My duty makes no allowances for grief.*

So, I will feel none. He nearly convinced himself. If nothing else, he was too hot and tired to think about anything else.

Soon enough, they crested their final wave in the sea of dunes and saw the shining ribbon of the King's River wending its way from west to southeast. On the southern bank lay green fields and orchards at least as lush and vibrant as those of the Hidden Valley, all the more inviting for the blistering heat of the day. On the northern bank lay only drifting sand and baked clay, with a few clusters of buildings, most of those ruins.

Where the river crooked from west to south rose a city that sprawled out of sight into the distance, its bright banners and painted domes glimmering in the sun. *It must be twice the size of Khanbulak. It must be larger than Otosan Uchi, the Forbidden City.*

"Al-Zawira," Ryōma pronounced beside him. "Seat of the caliphs for the past six centuries. Our most important partner in trade for the past two."

"What do they all eat?" wondered Chagatai, for once quieted by the spectacle of it.

"The Nehiri have all the land between the King's River and the Queen's River, some hundred li farther south, irrigated and blooming," Ryōma shrugged. "They call this region the Cradle of the World. I call it the World's Garden."

Behind him, Shono heard Shoan gasp. "Auntie?" He turned to see her gesturing to a cluster of ruins on the near bank, her hand clutching a prayer talisman so fiercely he wondered that neither broke.

"I recognize some of those symbols. That's foul sorcery."

"That," said Ryōma, "is the Dead City, and it's where we will be making our camp."

Of course it is. "I trust there is some reasonable explanation for this?" Shono asked as they rode closer.

"This was once part of the Empire of Rempet, dominated by

sorcerer-kings and self-proclaimed children of the sun. When Shinjo was here almost a thousand years ago, she cast down the sorcerer-kings and destroyed their idols. It was thanks to our efforts that the Nehiri were set free from bondage and rose to create their own empire in the World's Garden."

"I suppose the locals avoid the place for fear of some curse or another?" asked Shoan. A massive statue – a radiant sun flanked by spreading wings – loomed above them as they rode, as much a promontory or cliff as a work of art.

"No one will trouble us here," Ryōma agreed. "And it serves as a regular reminder of the might and generosity of the Unicorn to periodically renew our claim."

Within the broken walls, Ryōma took charge, directing servants and samurai to caches of supplies buried under drifting sand. Shono found a broken old statue to stand on, letting his hair blow in the cool breeze off the river while Ryōma worked. He stood and watched the city shimmer in the heat, its colors shining and bright. *I've never seen a city like this before. Hardly anyone in Rokugan has.*

Something about the thought sat ill with him. *In Rokugan, peasants die in the same village they're born in, seldom venturing more than a few dozen li in any direction. Even samurai rarely travel outside their clan's dominion.* Of his party, not even Ryōma had ridden this far west before.

"When was the last Unicorn mission here, Ryōma-san?" asked Shoan as the encampment sprung up around them.

"Two years gone, Shoan-sama," said Ryōma. "With no official Imperial sanction, we dare not maintain a permanent embassy here, but we visit often enough to warrant storing some supplies in the Dead City."

"Who led that delegation?" Shono asked.

"Ide Ashijun, before his ascension to Emerald magistrate. Most of what I know of the situation here comes from his notes."

"And it's safe?" asked Yumino. Her hand hadn't left her sword since they'd passed beneath the crumbling sandstone arch at the city's edge.

"There's nothing here but sand, rock, and a few broken statues," said Ryōma. "Just be sure to check your boots for scorpions in the morning." He climbed up on the broken statue to stand at Shono's side. "My lord, will you ride directly to the caliph?"

"Is that what you recommend, Ryōma-san?"

"Yes, my lord."

"Then we shall do so."

"Ha," boomed Chagatai. "Well, then let's go."

"Not you," said Shono.

"Eh?" The burly Moto halted halfway through his turn toward the horses.

"You are not part of this diplomatic mission, Chagatai-san." *For which we can all be thankful.* "If you will stay, stay, but I charge you to guard the camp."

"Hmm," growled Chagatai. For a moment, Shono thought he would refuse. *Nothing is wrong. He will obey. You will treat with the caliph, and all will be well.* "It will be done," Chagatai said eventually. He stalked away, calling for his lieutenants.

"Ryōma-san, you will accompany me." *So that I don't wind up one foot in the stirrups, but of course we don't mention that. Face. Confidence.*

"Of course." Ryōma bowed.

Shono turned and found Yumino sitting astride her dapple gray, Kiso, with Umeboshi's reins in one hand and Ryōma's shaggy little beast Patience on her other side. *Of course Yumino will not allow herself to be left behind.* "Then let us waste no time, Shono-sama."

"Kiso is high-spirited," Shono observed as he mounted. "Is he the best choice for a city?"

"He will not enjoy it," Yumino admitted. "But as your yōjimbō, I wish to have my best weapons at my disposal in the event of any attack, and Kiso is one of the blessed herd. By any measure, an Utaku steed is a Battle Maiden's best weapon."

"Then we must honor Kiso's sacrifice," said Ryōma as he mounted Patience. "Let us all pray to the ancestors that our mission is successful."

Shono reached for a prayer and found nothing. Instead, he simply led them up the slope and out of the encampment.

"What is our mission, precisely, Ryōma-san?" Yumino asked. "If I do not overstep to ask."

"Our war with the Lion complicates our relationship with Caliph Harun al-Hakim," Ryōma said from somewhere beneath his hat. "Lord Shono's charge is to ensure that the caliph remains our friend and doesn't seek to take advantage of our distraction. The last thing Altansarnai Khan wants is a war on two fronts."

"Is the caliph a man to be cowed by force, or won by flattery?" Yumino wondered.

"An excellent question. And so you see why this is a task only the son of the Khan of Khans could attempt, for he has both arrows in his quiver."

Do I? "It seems to me that my arrows are a breeding pair of Shinjo horses, a fine silk gown, and two trained hunting falcons." He turned in his saddle to see that the gifts were following, Ryōma holding the lead rope. "The caliph is a rich man. Whatever it is he wants, these gifts are surely not it."

"The gifts are necessary, and you're forgetting a hundredweight of tea," said Ryōma. "But you are correct. Our better hope is that the khan sends her son and heir to treat with the caliph. That's a mark of great respect."

"And Shono-sama is a great warrior, as well," Yumino added. "His victory at Hisu Mori Toride secures his reputation."

Mitsuko dying as the wind threw embers into the sky. "You are magnificent in battle, Shono," *she said.*

Shono put his heels to Boshi's flanks and broke into a gallop.

CHAPTER FOUR
The First Audience

An Ide rode to Uchi-san
In the summer when days were long.
He waited for an audience there,
And rode home with snow in his hair.

The bridge into the city was an oddity. Flat-topped barges floated atop the river, lashed together into a single path. Camels laden with goods from desert tribes, Nehiri warriors with their faces hidden beneath black scarves, white-clad pilgrims in billowing robes all walked across the bridge as if it were solid ground. At the fore and aft of each barge was mounted a curving prominence of gilded wood, hung with a lantern, and beneath the deck of the bridge slept or lounged a bargeman with a long pole.

"The Bridge of Boats," Ryōma proclaimed. "It can be dismantled if an invader or flood threatens and is easily reassembled when the danger has passed."

None of their horses passed over the bridge eagerly, but they put up only modest protests. Even Kiso offered only a flick of the ears to show his displeasure.

"I presume our caliph lies within," Shono said, gesturing to the towering white walls perhaps a li away.

"Indeed," said Ryōma. "That's the Round City, the oldest and most prestigious district in all of al-Zawira." He peeked out from beneath his hat and grinned, and Shono was reminded that his language tutor was not much older than him. "Also the roundest."

The city was a confusion of scents, sights, and sounds that exceeded anything in Shono's experience. The spices of cooking food, the smoke of burning incense, and the stink of a great mass of humans and animals all living atop one another was enough to leave him nose-blind. The constant dull roar – of merchants hawking their wares, lovers quarreling in gardens, donkeys braying in the streets, the faithful raising their voices in prayer, musicians playing their beautiful creations, even the sparking cough of fireworks streaking into the sky – overwhelmed his Shinjo-trained sense of hearing as well.

And the people! Black-skinned Bandar and pale-skinned Suhilim and people of every shade in between. Nehiri with their long robes and brightly colored head scarves, Sogdans with the brilliant patterns on their long coats, and other peoples Shono could only gape at, each in clothing and adornment more unusual than the last. One tall, pale man with hair the color of copper had an outlandish ruff of lace around his neck. A woman with skin the color of unfired clay had brilliant jewels embedded in her nose and ears, with a golden chain running between them. A lean man with what looked to be tattooed writing crawling all over his face and naked arms capered and danced, while a small whirlwind with burning eyes of fire spun and pranced alongside him to the music of two pipes in the man's mouth. Al-Zawira made the diversity and splendor – and the squalor – of Khanbulak look like a candle before the sun.

Yumino stared straight ahead as they rode. Ryōma again looked half-asleep in his saddle, but by slight shifts in his shoulders Shono surmised he was studying the crowd as intensely as he was. *It's a sort of freedom. Riding into the endless plain, or vanishing into the mass of humanity. Either way, I could go and never return.* It was a seductive thought. Shono tried not to think it too loudly. *Remember your duty.*

When they approached the walls, guards in steel caps wrapped with black scarves crossed their spears to block their passage through the gates. "Who rides armed to the Round City?" demanded one guard in Nehiri.

Ryōma nudged his horse to the fore. "Shinjo Shono, son of Shinjo Altansarnai of the Unicorn Clan, comes to the Round City to treat with Caliph Harun al-Hakim," he replied in the same language. "We come in peace and bearing gifts."

A woman appeared in the shadows of the gate beneath the mighty walls. "And you are greeted in peace, Shono ibn Altansarnai al-Shinjo." Her voice was thunder and honey, commanding attention like the oncoming storm, yet she herself was nothing more than a shadow, with two eyes glowing like a cat's in the darkness. "Please," she said. "Follow me."

They passed through the gate and rode for several long, echoing seconds beneath the wall. When they emerged into the light, Shono at last had a chance to study her. She was tall – taller than him – a bright slash of color against the black uniforms of the guards. Her robe was saffron-orange with a black fringe, and she wore gold at her ears, throat, and waist. Deep-red garnets sparkled on her bronze fingers, and her eyes were like liquid gold.

"The stables are here," she said, gesturing just beyond a number of tall, muscular servants. "Please, allow them to take your horses."

Shono dismounted and handed Boshi's reins wordlessly to

the closest servant. The others did the same, and then Ryōma coughed and stepped forward. "These two are gifts for the caliph." He managed to combine gesturing to the horses with removing his hat and bowing. "Would it be proper to leave them here, or to bring them directly to his presence?"

"The caliph does not care to have beasts roam freely through his Inner City," the woman purred. "The servants will ensure all your gifts are delivered to their proper destination."

Ryōma bowed. "Thank you, *sayidah*."

"Let us proceed," she murmured, and they followed her deeper into the Round City, where another set of walls rose above them.

The silence as they walked in the woman's shadow grew deeper and more awkward. Ryōma was in agony, eyes wide, hat turning a slow circle in his hands. Yumino seemed unimpressed, the classic cool and collected Utaku as she watched everything with glimmering, dark eyes. Shono sought something to say to break the silence.

Their arrival at the gate beneath the inner walls suggested a topic. He gestured above them. "These walls are impressive."

"They are," the woman agreed. "Built in the second century. There is no other wall to equal it in all the world."

"The Kaiu Wall in Rokugan is taller," said Shono. "And longer, by hundreds of li."

"I am certain the Shinjo prince has seen many large and strong walls in his life." As they proceeded into the shadows beneath the wall again, the woman seemed to vanish in the darkness, only her golden eyes and the flash of her smile visible. "But you misunderstand. The walls are celebrated in the Caliphate for their impressive feat of describing a perfect circle." In the dim light, the garnets on her fingers sparked as she traced a circle with both hands. "Two of your li across, and perfectly round." As they emerged into the light again, Shono saw that she was smiling.

"I will let you decide if this feat is worthy of the celebration it enjoys."

"As you say," Shono said. "You called me a prince. I fear you are mistaken; we reserve such a title for those of Imperial blood. Perhaps your language makes no such distinction?"

"If you are to treat with the caliph as an equal," said their guide, "then a prince you shall be."

Shono glanced over his shoulder, to where Ryōma was doing his best to remain serene. *The caliph raises my status, to raise his own.* Shono thought of Chagatai.

"And what is your role here, my lady?" Shono asked. "Are you a princess?"

The woman laughed, and Shono had a sudden impression of a stalking tiger. "Hardly. I am called Mandana. I serve the caliph as his chief advisor."

"And your family? Your people?"

"I am Mandana bint No One al-Nowhere. Just Mandana."

"To rise to your position is no easy feat for a woman from Nowhere," said Shono. "The caliph must value your advice highly."

"All who hear me speak value my advice," Mandana said, her voice a velvet purr. Shono could well believe it. He half-wondered if there was some sorcery behind her words, to hold his attention so. *The sorcerer-kings are dead and gone. Shinjo-no-Kami killed them.*

"I have heard you called the Tiger Woman," said Ryōma. "Your fame spreads even to Rokugan."

Does it? Shono wondered. *It is the first I have heard of her.*

Mandana smiled, just like a predatory cat, all teeth and no warmth. "I like that. It makes me sound very dangerous. But have no fear, *sadah*. You are safe from me while you are guests of the caliph."

Beyond the wall, the confusion of tightly packed but elegant houses on either side gave way to sprawling palaces and manor houses, gardens alive with calling birds and babbling fountains. The avenue before them ran toward a tremendous building surmounted by a blue dome that sparkled in the sun. Other avenues ran to join it, spokes of a wheel running toward the axle. "The Grand Temple," Mandana said. "Built in the fourth century. It is the largest Qamarist temple anywhere, even larger than those in the City of God."

"Is it where I am to meet the caliph?"

"The caliph has many palaces," Mandana said. "Today he receives you in the Judge's Court. It is on our right, just here," and indeed, they had arrived.

More guards stood at the gates to the palace gardens, and as he entered, Shono felt the difference between his home and this strange place with its round walls. The Shinjo were not great keepers of gardens, preferring to do their contemplation on the open plain or in a wild forest, but the gardens Shono had explored in his youth were all carefully manicured to present an illusion of the natural world. Were it not for the paths and lanterns, one might be forgiven for thinking a Rokugani garden was a natural collection of plants and stone. But no such error was possible for the garden in the Judge's Court. Paths ran in straight lines, intersecting at precise angles, and arranged together in a pattern of perfect symmetry. Flowers and trees grew in ordered ranks, the configurations of their colors and perfume mathematical in their perfection. *What do I have to offer someone from such a different world? What is it he wants?*

Shono paused a moment in the garden. "Do you enjoy gardens, my prince?" asked Mandana.

Memories rose, as clear and fragrant as the flowers around him: Mitsuko, racing through the garden in her uncle's estate. Laughter. The thrill of evading her maids and nurse, together. *We were fourteen?* He put the thought aside. *Nothing is wrong. I will not allow my musings to distract from my duty.*

"Less than I once did," Shono said. "Take me to the caliph, if you please, Mandana-sama." She smiled as he used the Rokugani honorific despite speaking Nehiri, then led him to the doorway. A carpet hung across it in lieu of a door.

"The caliph awaits."

Shono bowed and entered, Ryōma at one side, Yumino scowling at the other. They passed under the arch into a long gallery, light and airy with tall empty windows on two sides.

Mandana stepped forward and announced them, her voice swelling to fill the entire hall. "Presenting His Excellency Shono ibn Altansarnai al-Shinjo, prince of the Unicorn Clan, Noyan of the Blue Horde, and heir apparent to the khan."

Seeing no place to remove his boots, Shono led the others in a steady walk down the length of the gallery. Their feet clopped on a mosaic floor of red and white stone. Courtiers, guards, and hangers-on from a dozen nations watched with naked interest as Shono's party crossed the room. *Come gawk at the barbarian. Within Rokugan or without, it seems everyone finds us a spectacle wherever we go.*

The caliph sat at the far end of the gallery atop a small mound of striped cushions. He was a stout man, his hair and beard more gray shot through with black than the other way around. Shono placed his age at nearly sixty and his height at just less than his own. His skin was perhaps a shade darker than Shono's, with a warmer golden tone. Aside from the jewels sparkling at his fingers and throat and the size and magnificence of his turban, Shono might have overlooked him as just another courtier in this far-off land.

Behind him was a collection of people, mostly quite young, mostly quite beautiful. They had skin as fair as porcelain or as deep as Hama Khutun's ebony throne or anywhere in between.

They wore Nehiri-style caftans and robes, for the most part, their hair hidden under scarves or turbans or other headdresses. Shono resisted the urge to run a hand through his own loose-flowing hair. *Perhaps I should have made an effort to dress as a local.* He couldn't tell if the caliph's attendants were ornaments or advisors, or perhaps both.

The one closest to him wore a fawn-colored robe, her head wrapped in a scarf of deep burgundy. Her robe was cinched with a belt of gold medallions, and more medallions lay hanging from her throat and resting on her deep-brown forehead. Her eyes shone darkly in the shafts of light streaking in from the windows. Her lips were turned down in an expression of distaste, smoothed into bland serenity as Shono approached.

"That is Saadiyah bint Abdul Rahim al-Mozedu," murmured Mandana at Shono's side, matching him stride for stride. *Saadiyah, daughter of Abdul Rahim, of Mozedu*, Shono translated. "Watch out for her, *sayid*. You have no friends in this court save perhaps for me, and she is the cleverest of the caliph's little birds and has no reason to love the Unicorn."

If Mandana is my closest friend in this court, I may as well throw myself to the wolves. Shono bowed before the caliph as Mandana climbed the dais to stand one step below the most powerful man in the west.

"You stand before Harun ibn Mahmour ibn Ja'far al-Hakim, Caliph, Defender of the Faith, Sultan of al-Zawira, Beloved by God, and Supreme Leader of the Qamari Peoples," she said, her voice ringing throughout the audience hall.

Shono straightened, and his eyes fell on Saadiyah and her penetrating, considering gaze from beneath her burgundy head covering. Unbidden, Mitsuko leapt to his mind. *Our first meeting, that look of dubious contempt. To think that we would go from that, to love, to war.* "Great sultan," Shono began.

"Caliph," murmured Ryōma.

"Great caliph," Shono amended. *Put Mitsuko from your mind. A samurai does his duty; he does not moon about after lost love.* "I bring gifts from my mother, the champion of the Unicorn Clan, daimyō of the Shinjo, and Khan of Khans." Servants stepped forward, and he found his tongue, speaking with more confidence than he felt. "We offer two trained hawks, for I understand falconry is a sport beloved by both our peoples. I had the training of one of these birds myself; my mother trained the other. Let the speed and keen vision of a hawk on the wing represent always your great wisdom and mercy."

A low murmur spread through the assembly. *But is it approval, or dismay?* He carried on as a servant presented the next gift. "We offer a gown of the finest silk, woven and sewn by artisans of the Crane Clan, the finest in the Emerald Empire. We hope that this priceless treasure may find favor with all your court." The gown had been made to order according to the specifications of some Ide expert or other, possibly Ryōma. Its sky-blue silk was embroidered with gold thread and studded with pearls. It even seemed that it might fit the caliph's stout frame adequately well.

With a thump, two servants placed a chest between them at the caliph's feet. Shono bowed as the servants opened the chest for all to see. "And finally, a hundredweight of the finest tea in the Emerald Empire. Let it be a warm reminder of the riches that both our peoples gain when we trade freely along the bountiful Sand Road."

The servants closed the chest again, and it, along with all the other gifts, vanished into the crowd. The caliph frowned down the length of his hawklike nose at Shono and stroked his beard.

Mandana broke the silence with a soft purr. "Prince Shono is forgetting the most priceless of his gifts, a fine breeding pair of Shinjo horses. I had the pleasure of seeing them stabled in the Middle City."

"Curious," said Saadiyah. Her voice had none of Mandana's power, but it rang clear and steady like a bell. "Has Prince Shono perhaps forgotten that it was our horses in the Cradle of the World that enriched their bloodline and made them what they are today? Does he imagine that our herds are in need of improvement?"

"Now, sister, mind your words," said Mandana with another smile. "You speak of 'our horses' as if you or any Bandar were there all those centuries ago."

"Naturally not, my lady," said Shono. He cast about for some perfect words to say. "Our horses are as much a symbol of Unicorn esteem as a treasure in their own right. I would not presume to advise your own horse breeders of their business, but in any case, adding our horses to your herds remains a symbol of friendship between our two peoples."

The caliph spoke at last. "You speak of two peoples," he said in a wheezy voice. "Which two? Shinjo and Nehiri? Rokugani and Qamarist? I think perhaps the situation is more complex than that."

"I'm certain I do not know what you mean," said Shono, truthfully.

"Perhaps not," said Harun. "Perhaps we shall discuss it in more detail at a later date. But you must be tired and hungry from the road." He clapped his hands, and Mandana, Saadiyah, and all the rest of his attendants bowed as he rose. "Let us retire to the Dancer's Palace for dinner and amusements."

The entire court assembled, swiftly and according to some protocol Shono could not ascertain, into a procession. First came a small, perfumed man with a great parasol, which he carried above the caliph's head. Next went the caliph, flanked by two guards in coats of gold brocade. Shono found himself walking between Saadiyah and Mandana, a startling and unsettling pair of escorts to be sure. Saadiyah made no effort to hide her appraisal as she studied him or to hide her dismay at what she saw. Mandana, on the other hand, could barely be bothered to spare him a glance. Yumino and Ryōma were both gone, lost in the parade. "Is it normal for the caliph to shift to a new palace for a meal?" he asked.

"As I said, the caliph has many palaces," murmured Mandana. "And as a great lover of palaces, he uses each according to its particular strengths."

"Be glad that our procession today takes us through the Silver Garden," said Saadiyah. "You have no such wonders in your kingdom, I believe."

Fortunes bless and preserve me, she is worse than a Crane. She might as well call me "barbarian" while she's at it.

Shono glanced about as the procession snaked through a round gate and stepped down into a grotto hidden from the avenue outside by an intricately carved screen. The garden within was a lush profusion of green plants and murmuring fountains, and the whistles and trills of unfamiliar birds perfumed the air as surely as the colorful flowers blooming everywhere Shono looked. "It is a fine enough garden, I allow, but–"

"Just wait," Mandana smiled.

"Have no fear, foreigner," said Saadiyah. "The Silver Garden has yet to display its principal treasure."

Ah, there it is. "Foreigner."

A few paces later, the procession passed through an arch of blooming trees and came into a large central court, as perfectly square, Shono assumed, as the Round City was perfectly circular. In the center rose a tremendous tree that glimmered in the evening light. Every leaf, every bough, shone with reflected sun and lantern light, glimmering at turns silver and gold as Shono's perspective shifted. Perched on the tree everywhere he looked were birds of gold, with feathers of precious stones, each bobbing and singing and trilling in a complex symphony. The limbs of the tree rustled as if stirred by a breeze, though the air was still, and water trickled along its roots, giving only a hint as to the intricate mechanism that allowed the whole to function.

"The great tree of the Silver Garden is made from over a ton of precious metals," Saadiyah proclaimed proudly, her gaze fixed firmly on the improbable tree. "The finest philosophers and engineers from throughout the Qamarist world worked together on its design."

"It isn't sorcery, then?" asked Shono.

"Not at all," Saadiyah said. "The ingenuity of humankind alone is responsible for this wonder. The engine is powered by the flow of water."

Both women seemed to be awaiting some sort of response from him. Shono wondered what he should feel: awestruck wonder, as Saadiyah seemed to expect? Or amusement, as Mandana fairly radiated? He felt neither. *"Your tree is very nice, but I am numb inside because I slew my betrothed in battle"* is not something a samurai should say. "It is magnificent," he said at length.

Soon they were all arranged again in the Dancer's Palace, where long tables formed three sides of a square, and all the diners sat on the outside edge. Shono was directed to a seat between Saadiyah and Mandana again. The other guests each sat cross-legged on a cushion, but Shono set his cushion aside and sat in the Rokugani fashion. Yumino, who had been seated at the utter edge of the horseshoe to his right, did the same, but Ryōma, only a few seats past the caliph to his left, sat on the cushion as if he'd done so all his life.

Once everyone was seated, the caliph clapped his hands again, and silence fell. "We welcome our guests from across the Burning

Sands, may God the Comforter shelter them," he called. "And we offer these tokens of our esteem."

A flood of servants emerged, each bearing a gift. The first approached Shono and bowed low, presenting a jeweled scabbard with a gold-chased hilt emerging from it. Shono glanced at Ryōma, who nodded slightly. *This isn't Rokugan. Refusal is neither expected nor required.*

"I thank you, great caliph," Shono said, taking the sword and drawing it. The steel seemed to flicker in the fading light of the day, ripples of dark and light flowing down the blade. *Blood would scarcely show against that pattern.* Its balance in his hand was perfect. *This sword has never killed anyone I loved. It's more than I can say for my own blade.* "It is exquisite," he remembered to say after a time.

"The secret of watered steel is known only to Qamari smiths," proclaimed the caliph. "There is no other steel like it in all the world for strength and flexibility."

There followed gift after gift. A tunic so dense with gold brocade it stood on its own atop the cushion. A magical amulet, proof against any poison, from Mandana. A saddle of exotic wood, leather, and ivory. Gold medallions for his belt. A dagger whose hilt was carved jade. Yumino and Ryōma were not forgotten, either; a silver tea set and cups in gaijin style for Ryōma, gold and jewels for Yumino. With each gift, Shono fumbled for his courtesies while the caliph boasted of its extravagance.

At last, only one gift remained: a tiny, intricate bird fashioned from white gold. Purple amethysts served for its eyes, and delicate ivory feathers adorned its ruff. A golden key protruded from its side. "You are meant to turn the key," suggested Saadiyah, as if guiding a child. Shono swallowed his annoyance and did so. The bird turned its head, fluttered its wings, and sang a liquid flow of soaring beauty.

"It is beautiful," admitted Shono. "And cleverly made. This is akin to the birds in your Silver Garden?"

"The caliph's Silver Garden," Saadiyah said. "But yes."

For some reason, Shono thought of his exchange of gifts with Mitsuko, when their betrothal was formalized. He had given her the very finest horse in his stable. She had given him a copy of Akodo's *Leadership* that had been in her family more than six hundred years. *I sent it back to her mother. I wonder if it arrived before or after I sent her Mitsuko's corpse?*

"You do not care for it?" Saadiyah asked. "Perhaps it is too delicate for your nomadic ways?" Shono glanced at her, startled from his memories.

What must my face have looked like? "I admire this gift intensely," he said. "Forgive my rudeness. My journey has been long."

"In that case—" Mandana smirked "—I apologize for what you are about to endure."

"For shame, Mandana," chided Saadiyah. "To speak so ill of the caliph's entertainments."

"Does not the Prophet command honesty?" asked Mandana with perfect innocence.

"What great trial must I now brave?" Shono asked, setting the jeweled bird aside. One of the servants whisked it away, as they had all the previous gifts.

"Dinner," said Saadiyah.

Dinner proceeded through over a dozen courses, and each course was accompanied by its own folly or performance. First, a man emerged with a strange instrument, like a *biwa*, and sat and warbled at the assembly. Then came another man, naked from the waist up, who flourished a variety of swords, then swallowed each sword to its hilt. Two women were next, who gyrated their bare stomachs as they danced. Meanwhile, Shono was served a plate of olives, then a round of bread and a dish of aromatic bean spread, then a delicate flaky grain steamed with pine nuts, then goat stewed with spices and vegetables from the breadth of the Cradle of the World, and on and on. With every course, servants walked among the diners, pouring a fruity purple wine from silver jars.

The caliph set the pace, eating and drinking more than anyone else at the table. Shono found that he had no appetite, and he forced himself to eat a few bites of each new dish for the sake of politeness. *A year ago, I would have enjoyed this feast.* He left his wine untouched, to keep his head as clear as he could manage, and saw that Saadiyah had turned her cup upside down, to prevent the servants from pouring into it. Mandana, Shono noticed, had neither plate nor cup before her and was offered nothing by the servants.

"You are abstaining from the wine?" Shono asked.

"The Prophet warns against the vice of alcohol," Saadiyah said.

"And you, Mandana-sama?" Shono winced as he realized he had just spoken in Rokugani. He made to try again in Nehiri, but Mandana answered as if she had not noticed the gaffe.

"I will eat later. I am here simply to advise the caliph, not to partake of his amusements."

"I see." Shono glanced across the room and past where a dozen beautiful young people were dancing in a most acrobatic fashion. Yumino had her untouched cup of wine to one side, but Ryōma sipped happily as the woman seated next to him laughed at something he had just said. No one else was abstaining from the vice of drink. "It seems your people do not think much of the Prophet's warning, in general."

"The court takes its cues from the caliph," said Saadiyah. "Some previous caliphs have gone so far as to ban wine entirely within the lands where they held sway. Others maintained that the grape is

God's creation, and therefore there can be no sin in its enjoyment."

"Harun al-Hakim is from the latter school of thought," said Mandana. "Such liberality makes him popular among the noble classes, and particularly among the vintners."

"A toast!" bellowed the caliph, lifting his great silver cup high. "Shinjo! Raise your cup, to the friendship between the Qamari Empire and the Unicorn Clan!"

"To our lasting friendship," Shono said, with less power and conviction than he had intended. He set the broad silver cup down again as the caliph drank.

When he had swallowed his wine, Harun wiped his beard and mustache with the back of his hand, then turned to study Shono again. "Tell me, Shinjo," he said. "You are your mother's heir, are you not?"

"I am," Shono said.

"Yet you are her youngest son, I am told." *Told by whom? What spies do you have in Unicorn lands?* The caliph gestured with one fat hand, the gems sparkling. "You have an older brother. Is he addled in his wits? Deficient in his manhood? Why are you the heir, and not he?"

Because my brother is too much like you, and would enjoy this feast with its dancing and wine more than I. Shono took a breath. "My brother, Yasamura, has no desire to be the khan, nor do his skills and temperament lend him easily to that role. My mother chose me, instead."

"But he was firstborn," said Saadiyah. "Chosen by God to be her heir. Who are you, and who is your mother, to set aside the will of God?"

"The kami in their wisdom gave my mother three children," Shono snapped. "She chose the best from among them as her heir." Heat rose in his cheeks, and Shono took a breath. *Calm. This woman is trying to provoke you.*

The caliph grunted and took another swig of his wine. *It could be worse, old man. It could be Chagatai sitting here.*

As he studied the crowd, Shono murmured to Mandana, "The caliph keeps referring to the Qamari. I thought the people of al-Zawira were Nehiri."

It was Saadiyah who answered. "They are, in the main," she said. "But I, as you can see, am not. Nehiri, Suhili, Sogdan, Bandar – these are matters of parentage and geography. But all who follow the teachings of the Prophet are Qamari, and Caliph Harun al-Hakim claims dominion over all Qamarists, as the Prophet's rightful heir."

"I see." *The dome of the temple, rising above the gardens of the Hidden Valley.* "And if some Qamarists owe their fealty to some other empire?"

Saadiyah smiled, elaborately innocent. "Then some might say they are either traitors or infidels."

Oh no.

CHAPTER FIVE
The Second Audience

The white pine forest of Hisu Mori glistens in the snow.
To that place of perfect stillness still my spirit longs to go.
I'll bring my beloved thither and uncover her eyes to show
Her the heart that beats within me, and my love she soon
  will know.

After dinner, they were escorted to a palace set aside for their use: the Prince's Palace, according to their guide. Their baggage was already in the residence when they arrived, and a small army of servants attempted to help Shono undress before he chased them from the room. *It took me two years to get comfortable with Tanaka. I don't even know these strangers' names.*

With Yumino standing guard in the hallway outside, Shono was alone for the first time in longer than he could remember. He massaged his aching feet, unclasped his belt, and crossed to the window, where a carved screen blocked a clear view from the outside but did little to keep out the gentle night breeze or the moonlight. He sat and breathed in the perfume of the garden outside. *The Nehiri love their gardens nearly as much as the Rokugani, strange as those gardens are.*

He sat and stared at nothing and felt tears well in his eyes. *Every wonder I see I want to share with her. And every time I think of her, delight turns to ash in my mouth.* Was this the first time he had truly been alone with his grief since Mitsuko's death? There was no privacy on the road, and he had spent barely a full day in his mother's camp upon his "victorious" return from the battlefield before being dispatched on this new mission.

"I know her loss must grieve you," she had said, her voice low and gentle. The woman who was both the champion of the Unicorn and his own mother. Seldom had the difference between the two felt so stark.

"Grieve you." As if Altansarnai Khan could possibly understand. *Grief is for the loss of a loved one. I defeated an enemy in battle, Mother, just as a noyan should, as a samurai should. She may not even be dead.* Mitsuko had been breathing, barely, when he walked away, after all. He had abandoned her to die alone. *Perhaps some brave peasant came to her side and nursed her back to life. Perhaps she yet lives, cloistered at a monastery, just waiting for the war to be over so she can be united with me once more.* He let the fantasy grow, nurtured it, until the sound of footsteps in the hall outside shattered him back to reality.

Shono wiped at his eyes. He stood, wrapping his robe around himself in something resembling decent order. When he turned to the doorway, he found Ide Ryōma kneeling, awaiting his acknowledgment as though he were about to pounce.

"Ryōma-san," said Shono. "Can it wait until morning?"

"Respectfully, my lord Shono, no." Shono gestured, and Ryōma rose, stalking into the room and speaking in a low growl. "We must discuss your frankly dismal performance today and ensure that tomorrow goes more smoothly."

"I am certain I don't know what you mean, Ryōma-san," grated Shono.

"Do you think the caliph didn't notice you failing to drink his toast?" Ryōma slumped to sit atop a cushion, propped up against the wall. His eyes were cast down, his body slouched, just as falsely asleep as he ever was in the saddle. "Did you think that perhaps he was delighted with your obvious boredom with his amusements? Do you think your missteps of the language project Unicorn strength? Kami keep us, Shono-sama; your mother gave you this task because you needed time to grieve, but that doesn't mean it's not important!" Ryōma pursed his lips, as if misliking the taste of his own words. *Well, finally someone says it. She sent her broken son away.*

"None of that matters," Shono said.

"Does it not?" Ryōma leaned back, blowing out his lips like an annoyed horse. "His first gift to you was a sword, Shono-sama."

"Should I have refused it?"

Ryōma groaned, sweeping his hat from his head and rubbing at the baldness so revealed. "I do not know. Perhaps it is not your lack of focus that is the problem. Perhaps Altansarnai Khan has given us an impossible task." *When she meant to give me something so easy I couldn't fail.*

"You are my advisor and tutor in these matters, Ryōma-sensei." Shono turned his face to the garden once more. "What do you advise?"

"There will be another audience tomorrow. You must refer to Harun only as the caliph, or the Master of the West. Make no mention of the Qamari Empire or the Qamarists as a people."

"The Ganzu," Shono said.

"Not only them," Ryōma growled. "There's a Qamarist temple outside Khanbulak, did you know? By now, how many of the Ujik follow the creed of the Prophet?"

"I don't know. How many?" *And how many Ide, for that matter?*

"If even one *ordu* is Qamari, the caliph could use them as an excuse for war."

"So, what are we to do? Cast down the Qamarist temples, forbid any creed but the Tao of Shinsei? This is not the Unicorn way. Even Moto Chagatai more devoutly favors the Lords of Death than Shintao."

"It is not the Unicorn way," Ryōma agreed. "And in any case, forbidding the Qamarist faith would only hand the caliph all the excuse he craves for a war."

"Then what? A show of strength? Remind him that war with the Unicorn would cost him more than he could hope to gain?"

"Perhaps so. I find myself wishing we had brought Moto Chagatai, after all."

He thinks Chagatai is a better warrior than me. "To what end? Chagatai speaks not a word of Nehiri. It took me a month to practice it to your satisfaction, and that after years of study as a child."

"Chagatai can't help but project the threat of violence with every movement he makes. No words would be required." *While I project what, the hollow shell of a man grieving the death of his beloved? Does the fact that I slew her, one of the finest warriors of the Lion Clan, in single combat enter into the matter at all?*

"I think you will find, Ryōma-san, that I can be very violent as well, when need be." Shono found that he had stepped forward, dropped his hand to where his sword would be had he not cast his belt aside.

Ryōma raised his hands, open palms toward Shono. *What am I doing, threatening a pacifist?* "Forgive me, my lord. It is late, and we are both exhausted. Think on what we have discussed. I will apply myself to find some peaceful solution, something other than ceding control of the Sand Road to the caliph." He tugged his hat back into place and lifted himself to his feet, bowed low, and left Shono to his grief.

• • •

Shono slept, but not well, and was the last to join the others for breakfast the next morning. The servants, a woman his mother's age with her face hidden behind a red veil and two men with identical perfumed beards, had offered up a meal of olives, figs, and dates, as well as coffee served from Ryōma's new samovar, which the little Ide drank with obvious relish.

"We must keep the Sand Road open," he said, "if only because coffee does not grow in the east."

"I prefer tea," said Yumino, wrinkling her nose over her cup.

"So, our gifts were not laced with poison or anything so crude?" Shono asked as he sat.

"No," said Ryōma. "I inspected them all thoroughly. I have, ah, sent that magic amulet on to Iuchi Shoan."

"Wise," Yumino grunted. "I do not trust that Mandana. I think she is a sorcerer."

"Our Iuchi shugenja have learned much from the sorcerers of the west," Ryōma pointed out.

"I do not think Shoan would trust her, either," Yumino said, placing her silver cup on the table.

"I think that Saadiyah is worse," said Shono, as he accepted a cup of coffee from one of the bearded servants. The jeweled bird stared at him from where it perched on the table before him. *Should we be speaking so frankly? Is it possible one of these servants speaks Rokugani?*

"She insults you and our entire clan," agreed Yumino. "If she wore a sword at her hip, I would have challenged her to a duel by now."

"Dueling–" began Ryōma.

"Is forbidden only between Unicorn, and only to the death," said Yumino. "Shinjo-no-Kami was the essence of compassion, but she was also a warrior. She understood the demands of honor."

"Speak plainly, please, Yumino-san. Do you have reservations about my honor?" Shono took a fig and nibbled, just as if he didn't fear the Utaku's answer.

"I swore no vow to serve you, my lord," she said. "Battle Maidens never do. We live our honor with actions, not words. That I choose to be at your side says everything I need to say about your honor."

"But..." said Ryōma. He popped an olive in his mouth with an impish smile.

"But I see that you are... unbalanced," she said with a cool glare at Ryōma. "You need not be. Shinjo-ue is the one who broke the engagement, not you. Mitsuko is the one who attacked Unicorn lands. You did only as Bushidō required and behaved as well as could be expected. Your loyalty to your clan and your family is proven. You gave Matsu Mitsuko an honorable battle and an honorable death."

"An honorable death is still a death," said Shono. "And a poor betrothal present."

Yumino nodded. "As you say, my lord." She set down her cup and stood. "I will check on our horses while you dress, Shono-sama, if you can spare me."

"What I can't spare is the horses. By all means, ensure they are being well treated." He chewed thoughtfully for a moment after she left. *If only things were so simple.* He envied Yumino her easy confidence, her belief that honor alone was sufficient. *I think the past few weeks have proven that it is not.*

After breakfast, he dressed under the fussing attentions of three servants – *but not the same three as served breakfast; no, we wouldn't want you to learn their names or get comfortable* – and Ide Ryōma. He wore as many of the gifts the caliph had bestowed upon him as he could manage, beginning with the brocade coat, then the new medallions on his belt, and his new sword. "It's not rude to go armed in the caliph's presence?"

"He made no attempt to disarm us yesterday," said Ryōma. "Even Yumino. In any case, he can hardly object to your carrying the sword he gave you." Ryōma himself bore no weapons, not even the wakizashi to which his status as a samurai entitled him. Most Ide subscribed to some version of a pacifistic philosophy, but Ryōma was one of the few who would not even wear a sword, let alone draw it.

So Shono wore the sword, and the rest of his finery, and the three of them proceeded to the caliph's pleasure gardens.

Saadiyah called them "the Gardens of Earthly Paradise" when she met them at the gate. "There is no danger within; your bodyguard can wait here."

Is it stronger to insist she come, or to show that I have no need of her protection? "Yumino-san," he said in Rokugani. "Avail yourself of what pleasures these gardens have to offer. I will call if you are required." She bowed and stepped to the side. Ryōma scurried away to consult with a cluster of courtiers in bright colors, leaving Shono at the mercy of the caliph's advisor.

"Is Sheikha Mandana not joining us today?" Shono asked.

"She will do as she pleases, that one," scoffed Saadiyah. "Come. Let us walk a little in the caliph's garden." She turned and led Shono down a path laid with intricate mosaic patterns, surrounded on all sides by flowering trees a little higher than Shono was tall.

"The caliph seems to have a garden and a palace for every day of the week," Shono observed.

"More than that," laughed Saadiyah. "And more still beyond the city walls." She flicked her fingers dismissively. "Have you no gardens to equal this one in your homeland, Shinjo?"

And so the insults begin. "There is a great variety of beautiful gardens throughout Rokugan," he said carefully. *Shall I boast of our great beauty, far in excess of the caliph's? Or display humility?* He had no easy answer. He settled for honesty. "I suspect which gardens are the most beautiful is a matter of personal choice. The Crane, for example, arrange their gardens just so to achieve perfect balance and harmony. We Shinjo prefer gardens that have a touch of wildness to them, with flowers and trees to remind us of the extent of our journeys. I have heard that the gardens of the Scorpion are dark places, full of secret turnings and hidden grottoes."

"Is there no mathematical principle that guides the arrangement? No symmetry?" For perhaps the first time, Shono could believe he heard some honest curiosity and interest in Saadiyah's voice.

I must be imagining things. "If you are asking whether the gardens of my homeland resemble the gardens of the caliph, they have little in common."

"And which do you prefer?"

Sensing a trap, Shono tried for honesty once more. "In truth, I prefer the open plain to any garden I have ever visited in my life."

"Why, Shinjo, I believe that is the first sensible thing you have said."

"My lady?"

"You prefer the work of God's hand over the efforts of mere mortals. I can scarcely find fault with your opinion." She came to a halt beneath a tall statue of white marble, a djinni contemplating a crow perched on its hand. "Do you know what this statue represents?"

"I recognize the djinni. It resembles illustrations from some of the scrolls my father showed me when I was a boy."

"This is called *The Djinn Hear the Prophet's Word.* The prohibition against speaking the Nameless Prophet's name, to shield him from Name Magic, has often been interpreted to extend to his likeness in works of art. So, the crow represents his teachings in many such works."

"The djinn follow the Prophet's Word?" Shono tried to imagine elemental kami who would celebrate the wisdom of Shinsei, a shugenja who would preach to a kami rather than pray to them. He had no success. *Djinn are not just kami by another name. They are something else entirely.*

"Some do. Others reject it, just as with humankind. I show it to you because this statue, this event, the rise of the Prophet's Word – they all came about after the Unicorn Clan toppled the empire of Old Rempet from its position on the Throne of the World."

"That was hundreds of years ago."

"It was indeed," Saadiyah agreed. "But the actions of your ancestors are still keenly felt in the Cradle of the World today. Some still cry out for vengeance, even though the sorcerer-kings were cruel tyrants who enslaved human beings and djinn alike. Others look to the caliph, and they wonder: if the Unicorn toppled one ruler, might they end the reign of another?"

"It's not our way to interfere in the affairs of gaijin kingdoms," Shono said. "My ancestors destroyed Rempet because it stole Shinjo-no-Kami from us. Your caliph need fear no such vengeance unless he commits some similar crime." He let his fingers brush the hilt of his sword, to let the implication linger.

"What crime did Caliph Ali al-Walid commit, that Shinjo Khulan Khan felt compelled to conquer all his lands east of the King's River?"

He was weak when Khulan Khan was strong. "I do not see your people clamoring to dwell on the east bank," Shono said instead. "The people east of the river are not Nehiri. They are Unicorn, and have been for generations."

"But they are also Qamarists," said Saadiyah. She shook her head and raised a finger to forestall his objection. "But all that is beside the point. The history between east and west has been one of mutual neglect punctuated by occasional conquest and war. Is it any wonder the caliph is wary of you, of your intentions?"

"It seems, sayidah, that I should be having this conversation with the caliph."

Saadiyah turned and resumed walking down the garden path. More statues of beasts and djinn arose on either side. A horrible one-eyed giant here, an *ifrit* there, a monstrosity part-eagle, part-lion, with the face of a human being on the right. "It's best for everyone if conversations with the caliph, may God preserve him, are all worked out beforehand," she said. "You and I can speak more frankly than you and him, without the chance of a diplomatic incident."

"You want to control what the caliph hears and says?" Shono wondered. "Is he your puppet, then?"

Saadiyah laughed, suddenly, a quick sharp bark with little mirth. "He's wild, a force of nature. He can no more be controlled than the storms on the Sea of Jewels. Only pray to God for good weather."

"I wonder which you fear more: the Unicorn, or your own caliph."

"Wonder no more," she said. They had passed beneath a trellis crawling with a flowering vine, and at the end of the long walkway sat Caliph Harun al-Hakim beneath a pavilion of shimmering silk. "It is the caliph, long may he live, whom I fear – whom all Qamarists fear. Who else threatens more ruination than our own ruler? The worst you can do, Shinjo, is storm our city and put us to the sword."

If I didn't know better, I'd think she wanted war between our people. "What is it you wanted from this conversation, my lady?" *Perhaps I don't know better; perhaps war is her aim.*

"I wished to learn the measure of the man who would treat with my caliph," she said. "Is he kind? Cruel? Foolish? Wise? Weak? Strong?"

"And have you reached a conclusion?"

"Foolish. Exactly as I would expect from a barbarian prince."

"If you are so concerned about the militant and warlike Shinjo armies, my lady, you might gentle your tone and choose your words with more care," Shono growled. *A shameful lapse of face,* he chided himself. *Perhaps Yumino had the right idea, and I should challenge her to a duel here and now.*

"Foolish, and easily riled," Saadiyah amended. She turned to look directly at him, arms serenely at her side. "You are wearing the sword the caliph gave you. If you must, draw it and cut me down, and then we will all understand exactly what sort of man you are."

She's right. I'm letting my pride and my grief interfere with my duty. He took a breath, then bowed deeply. "Forgive me, Saadiyah-san. Such an outburst is unbecoming. It is as you said: here we can speak frankly. It was wrong of me to take offense."

Saadiyah blinked. "What is it you want from this conversation, Shinjo?"

"I wish to do my duty. To ensure peace between my people and the caliph."

"Simply done. Cede all claim to the rulership of the people of the Sand Road and let the caliph, God shower blessings upon him, administer trade along its route. You will have peace forevermore."

"You have taken the measure of me, Saadiyah-san," Shono said. "But I have had little opportunity to study the caliph."

Saadiyah cocked her head, reminding Shono of nothing

so much as a curious bird – of the jeweled bird perched on his breakfast table. "Is there anything you could learn about the caliph, God protect him, that would induce you to accept such terms?"

"If you believe I would never accept the terms, why offer them?"

"Why indeed," she said, and turned away. With a gesture, she indicated the caliph beneath his pavilion. Harun lifted a golden chalice of wine and laughed at something Shono could not see. "By all means, my prince. Take the measure of the man, but he will not receive you today. The caliph wishes to rest after the exertions of yesterday, and his magnificence is taking his pleasure in these gardens. Should a similar urge take you, servants will prepare a place for you to watch the amusements."

"The fact that the servants have not already done so suggests you know what my response will be. Tell me, my lady. What do you think of your lord?"

"The great and merciful caliph is beloved by God and all his subjects," said Saadiyah without even a trace of hesitation. "His generosity and kindness is matched only by his temperance and diligence."

Shono watched as the caliph spilled wine down his front, spreading a dark purple bruise across the yellow and red stripes of his caftan. Harun glanced down at the stain and laughed again, leaning back on his mountain of cushions. "And his wisdom?"

"Is matched only by his patience and firm sense of justice."

"I believe I understand you, my lady." *In meaning if not at all in character.* He bowed and turned to go.

"Prince Shono," she said. He paused. "If it came to war... would you win?"

While fighting the Lion at the same time? Not likely. "My people celebrate the five winds," he said. "North, south, east, and west, and the central wind that blows above them all." He turned to face her and found her head cocked in the same curious-bird pose she had adopted earlier. "We divide our forces into five armies – five hordes – both to celebrate the five winds and, as Shinjo did long ago, during our travels." *And never mind that the Green Horde never returned, or that the Purple Horde stands disbanded except in times of great extremity.*

"It hardly matters how many armies you divide your forces into–"

"In all our previous wars with the Caliphate," Shono said, "no more than two hordes have ever been required." With that, he bowed, and took his leave. Saadiyah watched him go, lips pursed and head cocked to one side.

It did not take Shono long to explore the entirety of the caliph's garden. A large pool dominated its center, where the caliph's pavilion overlooked a fountain and a small space for dancers and singers to perform. Smaller pavilions ran off to the side, where various courtiers and functionaries sat on their own, observing the amusements or doing their best to be observed. The caliph was accompanied by several of the same gaggle of young, beautiful attendants from the earlier audience at the Judge's Court, but no one seemed to be troubling him with affairs of state. His chief occupations were drinking wine, eating delicacies offered to him by silent servants, and laughing or cheering at the performances. *How can a man behave like this and be counted a great ruler? How can his followers witness this behavior and simply accept it?* Shono took a breath. His anger was not with the caliph. He turned away.

Shono found Ryōma sitting under one of the pavilions to the side with three Nehirim arrayed around a game board of polished mahogany. The little Ide stood as Shono approached.

"Shono-sama," he said, bowing. "May I please introduce Captain Izad of the caliph's guard." The woman across the board from him stood and saluted stiffly. She was solidly built and wore a brocade coat in black and gold that had a stiffness that suggested armored scales were sewn into it. "And Sheikh Rashid ibn Ahmed, a Qamarist priest." The man to Ryōma's left stood and offered his hand. Shono shook it. *Ah, is that where we get the custom from?* Rashid wore a long white caftan and a neatly trimmed beard.

"A pleasure to meet you, Prince Shono," he said.

"And last, Father Nestor, of the Nasrenes." The man to Ryōma's right stood and shook Shono's hand as well. He was broad in belly and shoulder, with a long bushy beard streaked with gray and an impish twinkle in his eye.

"Don't worry about me," boomed Nestor. "I'm no one important, but the game needs four players, you see."

"I'm not familiar with the Nasrenes," Shono said.

"One of several religious minorities to be found in al-Zawira," said Ryōma. "I believe it's a tradition that has its roots even farther west."

"Don't get either of these priests started," said Captain Izad. "Given half a chance, they will talk your ear off about God, or philosophy, or anything else that catches their fancy."

"Guilty!" boomed Nestor.

"We do enjoy our theological debates," Rashid admitted with a smile.

"I would not distract you from your game, Sheikh Rashid, Father Nestor, captain." Shono bowed. "But perhaps I can join you for one of your discussions of God later." *Perhaps a priest can explain more of the caliph's role in this mixed-up society than I have learned so far.*

"I would welcome that, my prince," said Rashid. "Look for my temple on the western edge of the Market of Books."

Shono thanked him and took his leave. *I will gain nothing more here,* he decided. *Perhaps Mandana has more cryptic wisdom to share.*

CHAPTER SIX
Gods and Wine

Utaku Chiseko,
Who rode with Shinjo long ago,
Told her men they must not drink.
They swore their vows with a wink.

As he left the garden, Shono found Yumino falling into step behind him. She asked no questions and offered no commentary, simply following as he walked the streets of the Inner City. Without a guide to lead them, Shono found the streets simple enough to navigate in their mathematical regularity, but devoid of any strong indication of where to go. Aside from the towering dome of the Grand Temple, each palace in Round City looked much like the last in its uniqueness. For a moment, Shono feared he would lose his way entirely and be unable to locate the Prince's Palace, but turning a corner, he found himself before the whimsical silver tree and regained his bearings.

In the end, he had to ask one of the black-clad guards for directions to Mandana's quarters, which proved to be in a tower built into the wall itself. The guard who directed them made a ward against evil and hurried away once he learned where they were trying to go.

"Stay away from that one, sayid," he said. "Even djinn fear to cross her."

Shono translated for Yumino's benefit as they approached the tower. "You see, Yumino-san. Someone shares your opinion of Mandana-sama."

"No," she corrected him. "That man fears her. I merely mistrust her. There is a difference, my lord."

Shono thought about that one as they walked through the empty plaza leading up to the wall. *Is that the way of things? I mistrust the caliph, but I do not fear him. Perhaps I should. He could have me killed on a whim.*

Something dragged Shono out of his reverie as he stood before the narrow door to Mandana's tower. The bricks that rose above him were the color of the desert sand, and the silence that hung over the area was as oppressive as the blazing sun high ahead. Shono looked up, and up and up to the top of the tower, where a vulture fluttered its wings and peered down at him.

"My lord?" Yumino asked.

"Do you smell something?" Shono murmured. She shook her head no. He shrugged and knocked on the door. The lengthening silence swallowed up the sound of his knuckles rapping on the sun-warped wood. Shono shifted his weight, casting his senses around the tower, the wall, the plaza surrounding them. He turned away, peering into the shadows cast by the closest palaces, set a bowshot away from the walls. *Something is wrong. It's as if I'm being watched, but no one is there.*

At length, the door opened. Nothing and no one greeted them save the smell.

The smell. *Fortunes, kami, and Lords of Death, the smell.* Shono reeled as the smell slowly unfolded around him. A stink like a charnel house, like old meat left too long in the sun, like rot and corruption, like an infected wound. Yumino wrinkled her nose and dropped a hand to the hilt of her sword.

"My lord?" she murmured.

"I think we'd best see what's inside, don't you?" He stepped through the door.

Within was a broad, undecorated chamber. A large table stood in the center of the room, its surface scarred and splintered and stained a dark, disturbing red. Chains, some ending in hooks, hung from the ceiling of the room. A smaller table stood close at hand, covered with shining metal implements of pain and butchery. A hole, like a well shaft, sat a little off-center in the lowest part of the flagstone floor, obscured by a rusting iron grate.

How many people have died here? How much did they suffer before the end came? The smell was worse here, coming and going in waves, tendrils of stench wrapping around him.

"Who opened the door?" Yumino murmured.

"I did!" boomed a voice, and suddenly a man stood between them. He was tall – head and shoulders taller than Shono – with skin the color of polished lapis lazuli. His bare feet were planted on the stone of the tower floor, and his arms crossed across his bare chest. He wore a Nehiri-style turban, baggy pants, and golden chains around each wrist.

Yumino's hand was on her sword and she had fallen to a fighting stance by the time Shono stopped her with an upraised hand. "I am Shinjo Shono, guest of the caliph," he said, gagging from the stench. "I seek Sheikha Mandana."

"I know who you are, Prince Shono," said the man. *The djinni,* Shono decided. *No human could have surprised me so utterly, could have just appeared in front of me like that.* "You may call me

Ma'aruf." He gestured to the stair against the wall. "My mistress is in her chambers, upstairs. I am commanded to escort you thither."

Shono noted the chains at Ma'aruf's wrists. *Commanded? Mistress?* He thought of the statue, the bird perched upon the djinni's hand. "Does not the Prophet forbid slavery, of both humankind and djinn?"

Something sparkled in the djinni's eyes. *Red eyes, like chips of garnet.* "So I have heard, sayid. This way, please."

They climbed quickly upward and through a door set in the ceiling, leaving the djinni behind.

"So," came Mandana's voice of honeyed stone. "You have seen the final fate of those who would defy the caliph and earn my wrath. Are you very shocked? Are you displeased?" Shono did his best to control his gorge. There was no thought left for the dispassionate face of Bushidō; he would consider it a triumph not to vomit all over the stone mosaic floor in this new, much more attractive apartment. "I see that you are. Tell me, my prince. What punishment do you Unicorn have for traitors and thieves?"

A dressing screen, carved with fanciful birds and roaring cats of every description, stood against one wall. Mandana emerged from behind it, wearing a long, loose robe, her bountiful hair piled up atop her head. She tied it in place as he stared, dumbfounded. "Has the cat eaten your tongue?" she asked with a musical laugh. "Ma'aruf, I commanded they be unharmed." The djinni appeared among them and bowed his head.

"Thieves are… branded or exiled," Yumino gasped out from Shono's side. *Mandana is speaking Rokugani,* Shono realized with a start. "It's forbidden to shed Unicorn blood, so traitors are wrapped in a carpet and trampled to death by horses."

"I doubt very much that the traitors care whether they suffer your fate or mine, in the end." Mandana crossed to a table near the wall and poured a red liquor from a crystal decanter. "May I interest you in some wine? I find a glass does a tolerable job of clearing the smell from my nose."

Shono took a ragged breath, looking behind him. A door had fallen shut across the staircase, blocking out the worst of the smell. Already he could breathe again. "Your offer is too kind," he managed. "We cannot accept; we come unannounced and uninvited."

"But not unwelcome," Mandana purred, swallowing a mouthful from her porcelain cup. "You have found me just finishing my bath, but if you will both wait a moment, I can dress properly to receive you." She gestured to a Nehiri-style table and cushions, then vanished behind the dressing screen again. "Ma'aruf, offer them any food or drink within this tower, and tend to them as a servant would."

"As you wish," the djinni said.

"We should leave," whispered Yumino.

"Mandana-sama asked us to wait," chided Shono with more bravery than he felt. *In her own strange way, Mandana has been more honest with me than anyone else in this city. Surely murdering me and my yōjimbō in her apartments is not in her interests.*

They sat, Rokugani style, and looked around the room as Ma'aruf folded his arms, nodded his head, and vanished in an eyeblink. There were exotic carvings in wood and stone adorning the walls, golden lamps burning with smokeless flame, and shelves upon shelves of books and scrolls from every corner of the world. The windows were tall and narrow, as befit a fortification, but the light they admitted reached every corner of the room and made it feel larger than it truly was.

Ma'aruf returned, again simply appearing in the middle of the room, now holding a tray with a Rokugani tea service upon it. Wordlessly, he set cups and poured tea – no proper tea ceremony, but tea, nonetheless.

"Quite the comfortable lair for a wicked sorceress, no?" Mandana asked as she emerged from behind her dressing screen once more. She wore a gown of golden silk, with elaborate gold jewelry adorning her otherwise bare, muscular arms. "That is what you believe, is it not?" She sat herself on a cushion between them, smiling her predator's smile. There was no teacup for her.

"It is a … surprising contrast from the room below," Shono said after a time.

"How diplomatic, my prince. Yes, anything would be, I suppose. But that is where the drain is located, and executions can involve quite a bit of blood." She gestured at a door in the wall. "I usually come and go from the wall-walk, as do my guests. A more … picturesque route."

"You are the caliph's executioner, then?" asked Yumino. A good samurai, she did not allow the frown in her voice to touch her face.

"Sometimes. The difference between me and some dullard with an ax is that before a traitor dies, I can learn something worthwhile." She splayed her fingers out on the surface of the table, and for a moment, Shono had the image of a tiger's claws, idly scratching deep grooves in the wood. "Is that why I have been graced with your presence? Have you come to learn?"

"Always, Mandana-sama," Shono choked out. "Saadiyah has shown me that when negotiating, it is best to know not only the issue to be discussed, but also the people with whom one sits and speaks."

"So, you come to me to learn more of the caliph? Or of lovely Saadiyah?" Her smile had all the amusement of a cat contemplating a bird.

"I come to learn more of you," Shono said. "Are you not the caliph's most trusted advisor?"

Mandana's laugh was like a waterfall, thundering and beautiful. "So, you saw beneath her veil and found the contempt Saadiyah has for our dear caliph, did you?" She waved a hand to dismiss any protestations Shono might muster and fixed him with a golden stare. "Saadiyah has her reasons to hate me, and Harun al-Hakim. Yet she is clever and clear-sighted, and the caliph values her advice despite it all. You see, the caliph is a man who knows the value of his tools and has the wisdom to deploy them to their best effect. You see a man who is indolent and oblivious, but in fact, he is an able administrator with the good sense to delegate his day-to-day responsibilities."

The cup of tea sat in front of Shono. The djinni stood behind. *People. Tools. All the same to her, to the caliph she serves.* "Are you one of the caliph's tools?" Shono asked. *Is a samurai a tool? Bushidō gives us all roles to play. Mitsuko was a good samurai, a tool disposed of by her lord. But we Unicorn are not so callous with our people. We wouldn't even treat a horse so callously.*

Mandana's smile didn't waver, but her eyes snapped to him. "The caliph has been good to me. He finds me useful, as I find him."

A strange sort of honesty and honor. Shono held her gaze. *Useful.* "And Ma'aruf. Do you find him useful?"

"Prince Shono, are you objecting to my treatment of my servant?" She snapped her fingers. "Djinni, tell him. Do I mistreat you?"

"No, mistress."

"I merely wonder if you might put golden chains around my wrists, or the wrists of my people, should I misstep," said Shono.

Mandana smirked.

"What will Harun ask of me, Mandana-sama? What is the price

of continued peace between the Caliphate and the Unicorn?"

"You must return the lands and peoples conquered by Shinjo Khulan Khan. You must give us the Sand Road."

"The lands and peoples of the Sand Road never belonged to the Caliphate."

"They are Qamarists. That makes them part of the Caliphate."

"Some of them are, and some of them are not. None wish to be fitted for chains."

Mandana spread her fingers before her, as if to ward off Shono's displeasure. "Ma'aruf is not my slave, sayid. He is paying off his debt to me, nothing more. Ask any priest: slavery is forbidden by the Nameless Prophet." She stood and gestured to the door behind them. "Perhaps you would prefer to take the upper exit, along the wall?"

After leaving, they walked along the top of the wall to the closest gate, finding a stair down to the street level there. The guards at the gate made no move to stop them, so Shono and Yumino proceeded to the Middle City and soon found themselves in the midst of a crowded market, where awnings of colored cloth held back the blazing sun, and stacks upon stacks of books and scrolls threatened to spill out into the street at every turn. "The Market of Books," Shono said.

"Look, my lord," said Yumino, plucking a codex with a faded blue cover from the nearest pile. A single Rokugani character, meaning either "love" or the name "Ai," adorned the cover. "A pillow book, and so far from Otosan Uchi?"

The bookseller leaned over the wall of books that separated him from the street and began haranguing Yumino in rapid-fire Nehiri. She replaced the volume, bowed, and backed away.

"Come," Shono said. "I wish to find Sheikh Rashid's temple. It is not far from here."

The temple overlooked the Market of Books just as Rashid had promised. It was only slightly larger than the homes and shops that crowded the streets nearby. Its principal distinguishing feature was a tall spire with a balcony, where several crows lurked, doing their best to stay out of the hot sun. The temple sat at a corner, with doors on both facing streets, and Shono found himself chased away by a fearsome older woman who gasped and veiled her face with her head wrapping when he entered. "What are you doing?" she shrieked. "This entrance is for the women; go around, go around!" Shono apologized and bowed his way out while Yumino stared with a hand on her sword, unsure how to respond. Shono went to the other door, where he was met by a laughing man of perhaps forty years, with a neatly trimmed dark beard on a Nehiri face that seemed well made for laughter and smiles both – Rashid ibn Ahmed.

"Prince Shono," he said. "So good to see you again. Come in, come in. The women's side of the temple is set aside for their privacy; they do not welcome intruders."

"Are you a priest only for the men, then?" Shono asked as he removed his boots in the entryway and followed Rashid through a wide room covered with intricately patterned rugs.

Rashid gestured to the long wall to his right, which Shono saw was more of a screen, its carvings and designs blocking casual vision but not sound. "A prayer leader on either side can preach to the faithful on both sides of the screen. The Word of the Prophet is intended for men and women alike – for all people – both human and djinn."

"You preach to djinn?" Shono thought of Ma'aruf standing in the temple. It seemed impossible.

"I would, if any came when I sang the call to prayer. They are children of God, just as we are, although their role is somewhat different in our world."

As Rashid led him into the garden behind the temple, Shono was silent, thinking back to what Iuchi Shoan and his father, Iuchi Daiyu, had taught him of the history of their *meishōdō* magic. It was learned during the fall of Rempet, he recalled, a century or more before the birth of the Qamari Prophet. He wondered if any Iuchi shugenja had ever read the Word of the Prophet, to see what role the djinn played in the Qamarist idea of the world. *Perhaps I should invite Rashid to return to Rokugan with me; our shugenja could learn much from him.*

Rashid led him to a small game table in the corner of the garden, where a blooming tree warded off the worst of the burning sun. Father Nestor in his dark robe already sat at the table, smoking from a silver pipe. "Rashid," said the big man. "And Prince Shono! What an unexpected delight."

Shono bowed. "You are too kind."

Rashid spread out his cream-colored caftan and sat on a cushion. "Now, Prince Shono, I do not think you came to me to speak of djinn, nor to play *shatranj*. Ask your questions."

"I seek to understand the way of your people," Shono said. "To understand the thinking of your caliph and find a path to peace between the Unicorn Clan and the Nehiri."

"There is your first problem," said Nestor. "I am Nehiri, but you need fear nothing from my quarter. There will be peace between you and me, between all children of God."

"God, the Bringer of Peace, desires peace on earth between all humankind," said Rashid.

"I fear I do not understand you," Shono said. "Do you each speak of different gods? In Rokugan, we find it helpful to give the Fortunes names, so that we can tell one from the other."

Rashid smiled and shook his head. "The sorcerers of Rempet used the True Names of humans and djinn alike to command them. To speak a god's name is to invoke them, just as the sorcerers of long ago." He gestured heavenward. "So, we will swear by the light of Lord Sun, or beg for the grace of Lady Moon. Yet also we acknowledge that these old deities are but facets of the same God."

"So you have but one god, with many names. It seems quite a chore for a single god to manage the affairs of Heaven."

"Nothing is beyond the power of God the Almighty," said Nestor. "And so you see, there is some question whether we Nasrenes and the Qamarists worship the same God, by different names, or if only one of us worships the true God and the other a false idol."

"By extension, the same debate applies to your religion as well, Prince Shono," said Rashid. "The Word of the Prophet is for all humankind. Including you Rokugani."

Shono bowed slightly, doing his best not to smile. "We have no need for the Word of the Prophet in Rokugan – we have our own. Thanks to Shinsei's wisdom, there is no debate as to which god is true and which is false. Our priests commune with the kami and the ancestors regularly."

"Your religion seems a very practical one," said Rashid, laughing. "No wonder you believe so easily."

"My belief is not required," Shono said. "That the kami Shinjo founded my clan and led us on our great journey across the Burning Sands is a matter of historical record. That her divine blood runs in my veins, as my ancestor, is likewise not a matter of faith but of fact. The prayers of the shugenja to the kami are answered directly, and none can doubt their efficacy after seeing the miracles they work. We in Rokugan have daily, irrefutable proof of the role of the kami and the Fortunes in the Celestial Order. Even the power of the Ujik Lords of Death is not in dispute."

"Are you a scholar of your Celestial Order, Prince Shono?" Rashid asked, setting aside his own pipe.

"I have read the Tao of Shinsei," Shono said. *Most of it, anyway.* "But I would not call myself a scholar, no."

"I suspect that if you spoke to a scholar of your own religion, you would find that there is considerably more debate and disagreement as to the nature of your Celestial Order than you suppose."

"Perhaps so," Shono allowed. "But we were speaking of your own – ah – faith."

"Quite," said Rashid. "I understand you treat with the caliph. Understand that the caliphs are the inheritors of the authority of the Nameless Prophet. The Prophet was the commander of great armies, the supreme master of a nascent empire that brought peace and order to the Cradle of the World, where only chaos had reigned before."

"Thanks to that kami Shinjo of whom you are so proud," Nestor interjected. "It was she, and the al-Qamari, who cast down Old Rempet."

"You'll just confuse the boy," Rashid sighed. "The al-Qamari were a secret order opposed to the Sun Kings. They called themselves the Children of the Moon, and they held their meetings and did their acts of rebellion at night, far from the sight of Lord Sun. When the Prophet brought his teachings to the Cradle of the World some two centuries later, his followers took up the name of the al-Qamari to rally around."

"And that is why you call yourselves Qamarists?" Shono asked.

"Yes," allowed Rashid. "And why sometimes you see the silver disc of the moon used as a symbol for our people."

"But not just the Nehiri people. We have Qamarists who owe their fealty to Shinjo Altansarnai Khan, my mother, but most of our people follow the Tao of Shinsei. I must assume that some do both."

"And that is what must be complicating your relationship with the caliph, eh?" Nestor chuckled.

"It isn't a matter for laughter, Father," said Rashid.

"It is when I have no part in it for good or ill. You see," he turned back to Shono, "the Prophet never established a formal priesthood to interpret his Word. It's up to each of his followers to do that for themselves. This man," he slapped Rashid on the shoulder, "that you call 'priest', would better be called 'teacher'. And yet the great and powerful after the Prophet's death – or disappearance; that's a matter of some debate as well – decided to promote one of their own to take the Prophet's place as the speaker of the Word and the Protector of the Faith."

Rashid sighed. "Almost as soon as he was appointed, the first caliph faced resistance and controversy. The first great schism of the Qamarist faith was between those who rejected the office of the caliph and those who obeyed. Since that time, the caliph has enjoyed more ceremonial and theoretical power than true dominance over the Qamari world."

"And this caliph is the worst of the lot," Nestor said.

"Father!" protested Rashid.

"I'm no Qamarist; I can say it without committing blasphemy," Nestor said, chuckling again. "And you agree with me, or you'd cast me out of your garden directly." He turned to Shono and leaned forward, slapping the table with his palm. "Listen. Harun al-Hakim is a wicked man. He never met a vice he did not enjoy, nor a sin he would not happily commit to gain more wealth and power for himself. And his followers know it. He must resort to hostage taking, blackmail, and the threat of his armies to keep the emirs and sultans of the Cradle of the World and the Sea of Jewels under his thumb." *With the way he drinks and the pleasures he insists on sharing with his allies, I can well believe it.* "The Prophet forbade sorcery, yet the caliph always keeps a sorcerer close at hand. Why, except that she offers him power?" *Mandana.*

"The Prophet forbade the enslavement of djinn," said Rashid. "To read such a law as a ban on sorcery is not a settled thing."

Nestor held up a hand. "I am certain our guest cares little for the nuance of our theological debates. You cannot deny that the caliph's reign has met with less than universal acclaim from the priests throughout the Cradle of the World."

Rashid sighed. "I cannot. Nor do all his emirs and sultans follow his lead with perfect loyalty."

"If the caliph were to achieve some great triumph," Shono conjectured, "such as extending his rule to include Qamarists in foreign lands, might that secure the loyalty of many of those priests and emirs?"

"It might," said Rashid.

"And if the caliph were to suffer some great defeat, such as losing a war with a foreign power, might he contrariwise suffer a general revolt against his tyranny?"

"Hah," laughed Nestor. "The caliph keeps the children of half his emirs hostage in the Round City. Freeing even one of his caged birds could be enough to throw the caliph into a war against his own people."

"Recall, Father Nestor, that even if you proclaim a different faith, you must still bow to the law of the Sultan of al-Zawira." Rashid sighed and stood. "It would pain me to see you dragged to the caliph's dungeons."

Or to Mandana's tender mercies. Shono stood as well, sensing their audience was at an end. "I thank you, Rashid-sensei," he said.

"Sensei?" asked Rashid.

"Ah, it means 'teacher'," Shono answered.

Nestor barked a laugh. "Hah! What did I tell you?"

"I hope I have given you the guidance you need to find a path to peace, Prince Shono."

"So hope we all," said Shono. He bowed to Nestor as well. "And my thanks to you, too, Nestor-sensei."

As Shono stepped into the street again, soon followed by Yumino through the other door, he saw Rashid appear on the balcony atop the tower overhead. In a high, clear voice, Rashid began to sing, a warbling call that seemed to dance above the rooftops. "God is great!" he sang. "There is no god but God, and we know Him through His Prophet!"

"The call to prayer," said Saadiyah from behind him. Shono turned and bowed. *Am I truly so distracted, to let a courtier sneak up on a Shinjo-trained scout?* "How did you find Sheikh Rashid?"

"He is a wise and amiable man," Shono said. "I was unaware you were familiar with Sheikh Rashid."

"No? There are few teachers in the city who can match his insight into the Word. I favor his temple for prayer and scholarship whenever I can."

"I would not keep you from your prayers," Shono said, bowing.

"Thank you. I hope that your visit was fruitful." Saadiyah bowed her head and walked through the women's door into the temple. The black-clad guard who was her shadow stopped outside the door and assumed the intimidating blankness of guards everywhere.

"You do not pray?" Shono asked the man. He received only an annoyed glare in return.

Shono let his feet lead him as he left the temple. Yumino walked silently two steps behind him, and he thought, and watched, and listened. *By the laws of the Caliphate, it seems the Ganzu belong to them as much as they are Unicorn.* He could see a path forward, redrawing the border at the Hidden Valley, still controlling most of the trade. An adjustment to the tariffs in both directions; details for Ryōma to consider. It would be a stiff loss for the Unicorn, a loss of face for Shono, and a great victory for Harun al-Hakim. But it would prevent a war. *Mitsuko, screaming, sword drawn.*

A small intake of breath from Yumino snapped Shono's attention back to the present. Chagatai swaggered down the street toward them, gazing around himself in frank amazement. *What is he doing here?*

"Cousin," said Shono, falling into step at Chagatai's side. "I had not looked to find you in al-Zawira."

"No?" asked Chagatai. "I would not come all this way and then not see its splendors for myself, cousin."

"I had not looked to find you in al-Zawira, because I instructed you to guard our camp."

"And guard it I shall," said Chagatai with an easy wave of his hand. "I have a dozen Moto warriors at my command, Shono-san. They are each capable of standing guard for a few hours while the rest of us take our leisure in the city."

"And if misadventure should befall them in the city?"

"Then they are hardly worthy of the claim of being a Moto warrior, are they?" He reached out one hand and clapped Shono on the shoulder, a blow that might have felled a lesser man or a small horse. "Come, cousin. Let us find what passes for a sake house and get drunk."

The idea of doing as Chagatai was doing, and taking leave of his responsibilities for a few hours, was suddenly very attractive indeed. Shono would rather climb on a horse and ride into the sun and never return, but since that didn't seem to be an option... "Yes," Shono said. "Let us."

•••

Finding a sake house was harder than Shono thought it would be, and he found himself remembering Saadiyah's words that the Prophet warned against the excesses of wine. At length, they settled for buying a few bottles of deep burgundy wine from foreigners in tunics the same color with gold patterns dyed into the hem and sleeves. The strangers spoke no Nehiri that Shono could identify, nor any Rokugani, but they understood the word "wine" well enough, and so they made a merry company, walking the streets of al-Zawira with jugs of wine in hand.

"To foreigners," Chagatai cried, lifting the clay jug in his hand and throwing back a long mouthful of wine. "May they always flout the Prophet's laws to our benefit!" Shono followed suit; he found the taste almost repulsively sweet, but after a few swallows it produced a most agreeable warm feeling in his belly.

"Yumino-san, do not wrinkle your nose at us. Drink!" Chagatai waved his jug in her direction. She took it and sniffed suspiciously, then tried a tentative sip. Chagatai guffawed and drank directly from the bottle, apparently content with this victory.

"How do you find the city, cousin?" asked Shono after another swallow. "You speak no Nehiri, I think? How do you navigate?"

Chagatai shrugged. "The people are friendly enough, and all half-terrified of the fearsome Unicorn who have twice brought their city to its knees. As for the language, I find that pointing and waving a fistful of coins works as well here as it does in Khanbulak. Half of being welcome anywhere is believing that you should be."

"And the other half is coin?"

"It helps!" Chagatai lifted his bottle. "To money, which flows along the Sand Road and makes our clan the equal of those others with more history and connections to their name."

"A samurai should not concern themselves with such mercantile matters," Yumino reminded him.

"No? The Ide certainly do, and we should thank them for it. Only the truly rich can afford to ignore matters of money and trade." He paused in his swagger, pursing his lips at the sight around them. From the trading house where they had purchased the wine, the three samurai had wandered toward the river and now stood in a district of tall warehouses with vaulted roofs, workshops for the construction and maintenance of riverboats, and long, low tea shops and cafés with dying trees in their courtyards. The buildings all had a slightly shabby air, crumbling here and there with weathered and warped doors and shutters, where there were any.

The people lining the street were even more ramshackle. Some had the broad shoulders of laborers, but most were scraps of flesh hanging from bones, with the enormous bellies of starvation. Some had mangled or missing limbs, but others showed no sign of what, if any, misfortune had cast them into their current extremity.

"As you say," said Shono. *Tools with no use. Discarded.*

"Have these people no ordu to care for them?" Chagatai wondered. "Where are their families? What is wrong with this city?"

"There are beggars in Unicorn lands, too, cousin."

"Not so many, not even in Khanbulak. And not so… desperate." Chagatai grunted and turned his back, leading them away from the river and toward a more prosperous prospect. "If money truly didn't matter, I'd say let the caliph have the Sand Road, let him trade with the Ivory Kingdoms and cut us out. But while our war with the Lion remains unresolved, we cannot afford to give up any of our wealth, power, or influence at court. I'd not see my clan sitting with a big belly on a beggar's blanket."

"So, you admit that steel alone is not enough to win a war," Shono mused. "Cousin, you surprise me. The Moto have a reputation for a more simplistic view of conflict."

"Well, I blame your bloody ancestor saddling us with Khanbulak," Chagatai groused. "We've grown civilized these past generations. Clearly, we'd like that feeling to go away as soon as possible."

Shono laughed, and they drank again.

"You are in a better humor than has been your habit these past few weeks," Chagatai observed. "Are the caliph's amusements delightful, then?"

"The caliph's amusements are tedious," Shono admitted. *But I do feel almost… well.* He paused a moment to study the spires of a nearby temple. "But I am a Shinjo. My chief delight in this city has been meeting its people and learning their strange customs and beliefs."

"Some stranger than others," Yumino muttered.

"*Eh?*" asked Chagatai.

"Yumino-san is still unsettled by our meeting with the caliph's pet sorcerer," Shono said.

"Tall woman, glare like an eagle, moves like a hunting cat?" Chagatai asked. "I saw her. 'Strange' is the word."

"Careful, cousin, you sound almost as if you admire her."

"That woman is not one to admire," Yumino said. "She has no honor, and only false courtesy."

"One sip and our little Battle Maiden is as chatty as a fat old veteran," chuckled Chagatai. Yumino flushed and looked down at her wine. "Enough of the caliph and his pet sorcerer. Let us drink to absent friends." He poured a mouthful of wine to the dusty street. Each of them raised their drink.

The faces of the fallen swam in Shono's vision: those who had ridden with him in battle and those who had fought against him. *Mitsuko. Taka.* "To absent friends," he said, and drank.

"Tell me true, Shono," said Chagatai. "Is this what you want from your life? Is this what you see in your future as khan, traveling to the court of those who hate you to make compromise after compromise? To watch your clan being worn away like a riverbank – a treaty here, a scrap of paper there?"

"Leave it be, Chagatai-san," groaned Shono. "What will be will be, and I will do my best."

"Just as your mother does," said Chagatai. "She signed her treaty, agreed to her marriage, watched as the Lion gobbled up the best the Unicorn had to offer, stripped our clan of its dignity... and then she said 'no', and she took up her sword, and stood up for her people!"

"She broke her word," growled Shono. "She dragged her honor – our honor – behind her horse. For her people? Or because she wasn't willing to sacrifice her own happiness for the good of the clan?" *Five winds, how long have I been swallowing that anger?* He staggered, suddenly exhausted. It felt like a dam had burst, like a torrent had flowed out of him and left him empty. He tried to fill the emptiness with another swallow of wine.

"Is that what you think you did?" Chagatai asked.

"What?"

"When you rode to Hisu Mori Toride. Did Altansarnai Khan order you to lead the battle against your betrothed?"

"No," Shono said. "She would have spared me. But the Lion tasked Mitsuko with that first attack for a reason. They wanted me to back down, to look weak. What choice did I have?"

"You could have stayed behind to garrison the castle. You could have led a counterattack elsewhere into Lion lands. You could have reinforced any of the other villages along the border. Instead, you and your pride rode straight into a battle that any Unicorn commander could have handily won." Chagatai leveled a finger at Shono, a lance at his heart. "You made that choice, Shono-san. And it destroyed you."

"Do you think me so weak?" hissed Shono.

"I think you have thought of nothing since I joined your party except riding west and never returning."

Have I been so transparent? "I have done my duty. I will do my duty. I will serve my clan, always. My mother taught me that... by word if not by deed. The clan comes first."

"She is the Khan of Khans!" roared Chagatai. "She *is* the clan!"

"Khans come and go!" shouted Shono. "Someone else could do the job if she stepped aside." *Did she refuse the marriage because she thought I was not up to the challenge? Fortunes, is that why I'm so upset, because I feel like my mother told me I'm not good enough?*

"I'm glad to hear you say it, cousin!" cheered Chagatai, veering so quickly from rage to delight that Shono felt unhorsed. "Very well, I accept!"

"Forgive me, I lost track," said Yumino, pink-faced. "Did Chagatai-san commit treason again?"

"Unclear," Shono admitted. "Best to blame it on the wine and indulge his childish fancies."

"I know I retain my youthful beauty, Shono-kun," Chagatai said, smoothing out his mustache with one finger, "but I believe I have a few years on you." He hauled Shono away from the wall he leaned upon and draped one arm over Shono's shoulders. "But cousin! I am pleased to see you fighting back. You are in good humor. Is it a woman?"

Shono shook his head, fighting back laughter. *If it's a woman, it's in quite the opposite way you mean, cousin.*

"A man, then? It's not me, is it?" He slapped Shono on the back. "Alas, my heart is not free at the moment, Shono-kun; ask again when our mission is concluded."

"I'll be sure to keep it in mind," Shono drawled.

It was only later, staggering back to the Round City as the sun pinked the eastern sky, that he found cause to wonder: how had Chagatai been so familiar with the caliph's desires and the state of their negotiations?

CHAPTER SEVEN
The Lion and the Unicorn

A Lion met a Unicorn,
Underneath the forest's horns.
The Lion spoke uncivil words.
We answered him with sharpened swords!

By the time he reached the gate of the Inner City, Shono was at least partially sober, although the lack of sleep gave everything a glass-edged tint, as if his world might shatter if he moved too swiftly or spoke too loudly. He therefore at first dismissed the sight of Saadiyah atop the wall above the gate.

Upon emerging in the Inner City, however, Shono turned and saw her still silhouetted there against the light of the eastern sky. She was shrouded, as ever, beneath a long gown of light-brown cotton, but by now Shono had the sense of her stance, her walk, her scent. Not knowing why, he climbed the stair to stand beside her. Yumino remained at the foot of the stair.

"Prince Shono," Saadiyah said as he approached. "You are early emerged from your lodgings." She glanced at his coat, his disordered appearance. "Or perhaps late returned from a night of celebration."

"I have been exploring your city," Shono said. "Mostly, I will admit, a wine shop, at the suggestion of my cousin Chagatai-san." He turned his face to the wind, let it blow through his hair. For a moment it felt like the freedom of the Golden Plains. But just a moment.

"Chagatai-san. This must be Moto Chagatai, the famed warrior?"

"Famed mostly by himself," Shono said. "I have never met a more proud or boastful man." *Except perhaps your caliph.*

"There is much more to see in al-Zawira than wine shops," Saadiyah chided. "Just think! The Court of Wisdom lies within sight of these walls, and instead you chose wine." She nodded in the direction of a sprawling palace, at least the size of any of those in the Inner City, with elegant curving domes and columned courtyards, that stood perhaps two li to the south. "The finest scholars in the Caliphate are gathered there to share their knowledge. Did you know, at the command of Caliph Abbas al-Mansour, the scholars of the Court of Wisdom marched into the desert with their tools." Here she held up an intricate instrument of bronze.

"A strange sort of... compass," Shono guessed.

"A type of astrolabe," she corrected. "Though I am not surprised a barbarian such as yourself is unfamiliar with it. Using this, we can measure the height of the stars above the horizon. The scholars of the court carried these, and other tools, and they went out into the desert where it is flat for many mīl around. They took a sighting of the North Star, and then they marched perfectly north in a straight line, taking careful measurements all the while. When the North Star had risen precisely one degree in the sky, they marked their progress, then returned to the beginning and did the same to the south. When the North Star had sunk precisely one degree, they again marked their progress. Do you know what they found, *sayid*?"

"I do not," Shono said. "I suppose they discovered some relation between the height of the star and their distance traveled, but I cannot guess what it was."

"Of course you cannot. In both directions, a journey of fifty-six and two-thirds mīl was enough to move one degree beneath the star. From this, the scholars calculated the size of the entire world: twenty and a half thousand mīl around." Saadiyah sighed and gazed again at the Court of Wisdom. "To know the size of the entire world, merely from observations here in its cradle. That is the wisdom of the court. I would give much to visit."

"But as you yourself say, it is near at hand. Are you truly forbidden to pass through its gates?"

"Its gates are no barrier to me," Saadiyah allowed. "Yet forbidden from making the journey I am, all the same." She puffed her cheeks and blew out her lips, like a horse whickering its disapproval.

"It seems odd to me that the caliph would trust your counsel, yet not trust you with freedom of the city."

"It is not for the likes of you or me to question the decisions of the caliph," Saadiyah said.

Shono took a breath and cast his senses wide. *There.* Two guards, on the wall with them in the shadow of the gate to the left and the tower to the right. *She daren't speak ill of the caliph in their hearing, I suppose.* "I believe I understand you, my lady." He paused a moment, considering. "I don't believe you've told me anything of your father, Abdul Rahim, or of the Mozedu."

"Mozedu is a city," she said, slipping her astrolabe into a bag and the bag over her shoulder. "It lies across the Sea of Jewels, not far from Lake Bandu-Xosa, and is one of the richest trading ports in all the Caliphate, save only perhaps al-Zawira itself, or Ninua on the Conqueror's Sea." She closed her eyes and leaned against the parapet. Her face... softened. "I can still remember the smell of the sea, the sparkling light of the water in the morning. I remember the hills overlooking the city, where we grow olives and oranges."

"And your father?"

"My father is the emir of Mozedu. He is respected among the Bandar, both the highland tribes and the merchant princes of the coast."

"Little wonder, then, that the caliph is so protective of you. Surely if he allowed any harm to befall you, he would make a powerful enemy."

Saadiyah favored him with a sharp look. "As you say, my prince. I must take my leave and see what duties the caliph has for me today." She bowed and made her way down the stairs. Shono remained a while longer, thinking, before he and Yumino returned to the Prince's Palace.

When they arrived, they found Ryōma sitting at breakfast, already dressed in the Nehiri fashion.

"You have become Nehiri, Ryōma-san," Yumino said. Indeed, Shono had scarce recognized him. *Even his smell has changed.* "Perhaps we should all adopt the local style of dress? It seems to be the equal of our own for modesty and comfort."

"You should bathe and perhaps sleep an hour, if you can manage it," Ryōma said. "You look as if you have drunk some poor wine seller out of their stock."

"With Chagatai-san's help, we just might have," admitted Shono. He staggered toward his room to follow Ryōma's advice but was pulled up short by the Ide calling his name.

"Shono-sama. What was Chagatai-san doing in the city?"

Ryōma had set down his coffee and now slouched, perfectly still in that apparent slumber that meant he was thinking very hard.

"You find that suspicious as well?" Shono asked. "Good. That suggests I'm not being paranoid."

Shono retreated to his room and collapsed, clothed, on his bed. After far too little time, he was awoken to bathe and dress. His dressing-room servants, a trio of women who compensated for his nudity with their own head-to-toe modesty, fussed at him while he considered, and as a token of peace, he ultimately elected to follow Ryōma's lead and dress as much in the Nehiri fashion as he could manage, in a sky-blue caftan embroidered with crawling vines, with a head scarf of white cotton. Only his Ujik-style belt, from which hung his two swords, remained to mark him as a Unicorn. *And my face.*

By the time he was dressed, Saadiyah was seated in the dining room, laughing at some joke of Ryōma's. "You look every inch the prince today," she said, smiling at his costume. "I am commanded to escort you to the Court of Beasts, where his magnificence hopes you will enjoy a bit of sport."

"By all means, Saadiyah-san, lead on."

She bowed precisely and led them through the door. Once her back was turned, Shono filched a handful of olives and figs from the table and, on a sudden impulse, plucked the jeweled bird from its place. He tucked the bird into his caftan and followed, eating what he feared might be his only meal for the day.

The Court of Beasts was past the Silver Garden and near the great wall on the other edge of the Inner City. It had its own tall walls, carved and painted with animals of every description, some of which Shono dismissed as chimerical fancies. The gate through which Saadiyah led him had a rearing horse standing to one side, a snarling lion at the other, and an eagle with wings spread above.

Who is the eagle? Shono wondered. *Does the caliph set himself in that role? A vulture would be more apt, if he hopes to pick over our corpses after the Lion have finished with us.*

Within the walls, the Court of Beasts proved to be a modest collection of buildings arrayed around a large oval area. The trees and flowering plants that Shono had come to expect from Nehiri gardens still served as natural barriers and markers of paths, but all led to the center, where a number of broad pavilions offered shade for the crowd of courtiers, soldiers, and ministers gathered to watch the spectacle in the oval.

As they approached the center, they passed a large bronze cage on their right, which contained a stunted tree and a colorful chorus of dispirited birds. The building to their left proved to contain its own cages, each displaying a different exotic animal.

"The caliph enjoys putting beautiful creatures in cages, it seems," Shono murmured.

"The caliph takes great delight in displaying exotic animals from the far corners of the world."

I'd rather our hawks had flown away in the Burning Sands than languish in a cage like this. Shono took a breath and stilled his face. They were approaching the edge of the oval, and he could see the caliph sitting atop an enormous cushion and laughing at some folly in the ring.

Shono smelled blood, and his fingers twitched toward the hilt of his sword. *No. If the caliph wants you dead, he'll do it quietly, in secret. Like bandits on the road.* Servants swarmed in the oval as Shono and Saadiyah came to rest against the rail. The servants carried baskets of sand, rakes, and other tools of gardeners, which they used to clean away pools of blood. A cart vanished through a gate to the left, with the corpse of a bull sprawled atop it. Shono wondered what had become of the victor of the last contest.

The caliph was only a few strides to his right, and he gestured

Shono closer. "Welcome, Shinjo," he said in his wheezing voice. "I understand that you Unicorns are great lovers of beasts, and so I thought to delight you with some of my treasures."

"You are too kind, my lord." Shono's stomach twisted. *People and beasts alike are things to him. I will like what is to come even less than singers and dancing girls.*

"I have a particular treasure that I think you will find especially pleasing," Harun said. He raised one hand, and his rings glinted in the light. "Do you know what it is? I was very lucky to add it to my menagerie, you know; I was half-convinced they were mythical."

"I couldn't guess, my lord."

"It is a unicorn!" chuckled the caliph. "Here she comes now."

The gate at the far side of the great oval swung open, and a creature trotted through as servants and grooms scattered from its path. It was, arguably, a unicorn, with a single horn rising from above its nose and four feet stamping on the sandy ground. But it was as unlike the unicorn of Shono's clan crest as seemed possible, as unlike the stories as he could imagine. It was gray, its skin warty and tough-looking, with three toes on each foot, and it was practically hairless, with no flowing mane or indeed any grace or beauty to its appearance whatsoever.

"You see?" bellowed the caliph, as much for the crowd to hear as for Shono. "Fat, stupid, and ugly. The perfect unicorn in all respects." Shono heard Yumino, ten paces away, stiffen, felt her hand fall to her sword.

Yet it moves swiftly enough, seems strong and proud. And as for stupid, that I think remains to be seen. "My lord is mistaken," Shono said instead. "The true unicorn was a spirit of light, of fire and water, and the savior of my clan on our journey. This is an animal, although an uncommon strange one, I admit."

"Stories have a way of changing in the centuries since they were first told," the caliph said. "Who knows what the Shinjo of ages past thought when they first encountered this majestic beast?" He chuckled again, then raised another hand. "But I did not bring it here merely so we could see it trot in a circle. My prince, I give you... 'The Lion and the Unicorn!' We have prepared this spectacle just for you."

Muscular servants stepped forward, grabbing hold of chains laid in the sand of the oval. They pulled, straining and grunting, and hidden doors opened in the ground, one in each of the four directions. From each came a roar or a scream, and from each leaped a tawny-furred lion. They were thin, rangy beasts, half-starved and hungry for blood. The message could not be less subtle: the caliph was well aware of the Unicorn war with the Lion, and what was more, he intended to profit from it. *Well, now we know who was behind the spy Chagatai's aunt uncovered in Khanbulak.*

The crowd roared with the lions as the unicorn stamped and galloped in its circle. The lions stalked, screaming to one another as they took the measure of their prey. *Three lionesses, one male. How appropriate.*

"Thirty dinar on the male to make the kill!" roared the caliph, his high, wheezy voice strengthened by his bloodlust.

"I will take your bet, my lord," said Shono. "I will bet thirty horses against your thirty dinar that the unicorn is the victor."

"Hah!" bellowed the caliph. "You are walking home, then, Shinjo."

"Do you have thirty horses?" asked Saadiyah. Her arms were crossed across her body, and she alternated between looking at the ground and peering at the animals in the arena.

"Not in al-Zawira," Shono admitted. "I suppose I'd better not lose."

With another roar, the first of the lionesses struck. She leapt upon the unicorn's back, her claws scrabbling for purchase on the beast's rough skin. The unicorn bellowed and spun itself around, but the lion clung to it tenaciously.

"First blood to the lion!" shouted someone to Shono's left. *Yes, it had been.* He remembered Yumino arriving to breathlessly report the death of the Battle Maidens' commander at Hisu Mori Toride, Utaku Hisako. *Slain in a duel by Matsu Mitsuko. My betrothed. Herself cut down in battle by my hand.*

Another lioness leapt for the unicorn, but the horned beast thrashed its head into her path, and the lion fell with a yowl. Blood streaked the unicorn's horn and pooled around the fallen lioness. As she struggled to stand, the unicorn trampled her into the sand until she lay still. *That beast must weigh two tons,* Shono marveled.

The crowd howled, some in dismay, others in excitement. The male lion, with a booming roar, finally hurled itself into the fray. It grabbed hold of the unicorn's face and shoulder with each mighty paw and bit into the beast's neck. The unicorn bleated in a high-pitched wail, then surged forward, carrying two lions as if they were dolls. It slammed itself and the male lion into the sturdy rail so hard the wood splintered, then galloped away before veering back and charging again. The lion clung, biting harder, perhaps knowing that its only hope of survival lay in stopping the unicorn's rampage, until the third time the creature slammed it into the rail. There was a terrible crack, and both railing and lion fell to the sandy earth as the unicorn staggered away. Blood ran from its neck, and its sides heaved with the force of its ragged breathing. But it still stood. The lioness on its back kicked ineffectually with her hind legs, growling in frustration.

The third lioness stalked away, looking for her opportunity, but the unicorn chased after her. The lion yowled in fear and leapt up toward the railing, where several of the caliph's guards, including Captain Izad, rushed to shove the beast back into the ring. The unicorn lowered its head, charged, and slammed its horn into the lion's flank, then flung it to the side, and the dying creature hurtled into the crowd of onlookers, after all.

"Perhaps you should increase your bet," Saadiyah suggested as the crowd fled the dying lion, and cursing soldiers ran forward to finish it with their spears.

Shono shook his head. "It's a test of endurance now," he said. "The unicorn is losing blood, and all the lioness on its back need do is stay there until it dies."

"Then is all lost?"

"The poor creature is half-starved. She may have no strength left, either."

The crowd seemed to have lost its taste for the amusement as the unicorn shuffled around the arena, its tail spinning, its sides heaving as it grumbled for breath. The lion on its back occasionally cried out, sometimes gnawed at the beast's spine, leaving no appreciable mark on its tough skin. Long minutes passed as the caliph grew increasingly agitated. Mandana, at the caliph's side, stared fixedly at the pair of animals until Saadiyah pulled her attention away with a murmured comment, perhaps about preparing the next spectacle.

By the time the lion fell, gasping, from the unicorn's back, Shono half-expected the unicorn to promptly fall to its knees and expire. Instead, the creature found a new surge of energy, which it used to gore, kick, and trample the exhausted lion into a bloody mass.

The caliph shot to his feet and stalked away, most of his courtiers scurrying after.

"Put that monster out of its misery," snarled Mandana, then followed.

Shono forced himself to watch as Captain Izad summoned a dozen archers and they loosed shaft after shaft into the unicorn until it fell to its knees and lay still. The soldiers approached with spears, and one of them nearly died when the unicorn gave one last charge, but finally they knocked it to its side and stabbed it in its soft underbelly.

"What a beast," said Captain Izad. She turned to Shono and pressed a purse into his hands. "I believe the caliph owes you these thirty dinars, Prince Shono."

Shono juggled the heavy purse in his hands, then tossed it back. "Please ensure all these animals receive funerary rites appropriate to warriors of their courage. Whatever you do for your army's horses will be fine."

Izad nodded, and Shono turned away to find Ryōma, Yumino, and Saadiyah waiting for him, the only other people left in the Court of Beasts.

"Saadiyah-san," said Shono. "You may tell Caliph Harun that I enjoyed the entertainment very much. Tell him I suggest that we arrange for a hunt the next time he wishes to visit Unicorn lands, that he might see how we sport with such noble beasts."

Ryōma interjected. "Perhaps we might arrange for the caliph to visit the Hidden Valley, to see one of the splendors of the Burning Sands for himself. The Unicorn welcome visitors to our lands outside of Rokugan proper."

"As you say," said Shono.

"I will tell him, my prince," Saadiyah said.

"I am no prince," Shono said. "I am Shinjo Shono, heir to Shinjo Altansarnai, of the Unicorn Clan. I am a samurai of the Emerald Empire, the Noyan of the Blue Horde, and the future champion of the Unicorn and daimyō of the Shinjo." He let himself smile, then, and felt it a feral thing. *Perhaps that "unicorn" was a better symbol of my clan than I first believed.* "And you, Saadiyah-san, may call me Shono-san."

"I will tell him, Shono-san," Saadiyah said, and bowed. Then she was gone, and Shono was alone with his yōjimbō and his advisor.

"What now?" Yumino asked.

"Ryōma-san, that message felt fairly direct; do you agree?"

"Yes, Shono-sama. It was a calculated insult and a threat. I am no longer hopeful that we can resolve this matter through negotiation, even if we were willing to surrender the Ganzu."

"Don't look so discouraged, Ryōma-san. It's not your fault that the caliph is a wicked man who never wanted peace."

"Che," Ryōma growled. "Every time the Shinjo draw their swords, it is because the Ide have failed."

"And what of the Moto?" asked Yumino.

"I refuse to take responsibility for the Moto," Ryōma said.

Shono surprised himself by laughing. There was a fire inside him, a warm and comfortable anger that could substitute very well for happiness. "Nor should you, Ryōma-san. I think it is time for you to ride to the camp and share what has transpired here with Shoan-sama and the others. A messenger must be dispatched to Khanbulak."

"It will be done," Ryōma said with a bow.

"Now, Yumino-san, let us find some place comfortable to wait for the caliph's next move."

"Why not leave now?" Yumino asked. "If the caliph has no desire for peace, shouldn't we leave before he takes our heads?"

"The caliph is not the only person in this city with whom we can negotiate."

CHAPTER EIGHT
The Silver Garden

Like the hawk who takes to the wing
To see the world spread around her, I sing
Of hidden glens and ancient trees and waterfalls.
The world is large, but we humans are small.

Shono led Yumino back to the Silver Garden to await whatever would come next, while Ryōma went about his mission and the sun climbed down from its zenith toward the horizon.

"Not the Prince's Palace?" Yumino asked.

"I prefer to be outdoors," Shono said. "I cannot currently gallop across the Golden Plains, so this will have to do."

She nodded and occupied herself with a careful survey of every entrance and exit the garden had to offer. Shono stood beneath the silver tree and studied the branches and the bejeweled birds. Their songs were not very similar to those of any birds he well knew, but allowing for artistic interpretation, they sounded very like birds, and the craftsmanship was exquisite. He thought of the little mechanical songbird Saadiyah had given him.

Saadiyah. The caged bird. He thought of Father Nestor's description of the caliph's plight. *The caliph seeks war to prove his strength to his recalcitrant subjects, and he seeks to conquer the Ganzu to prove his virtue to the prayerful. But he can do neither if his power is threatened from within the Caliphate by even one rebel emir.* He reached inside his caftan and touched the jeweled bird where it nestled against his heart.

But then he heard footsteps in the garden as the sun set, and he turned to find Chagatai stepping from between the trees, Yumino at his heels.

"Cousin," said Shono. "Did Ryōma's message already make the camp?"

"No," said Chagatai. "I have been in the city for some hours. What message did Ryōma carry?"

What business could he have had in the city? "A warning, for my mother. I now believe that the caliph was behind the attempt on my life outside Khanbulak. He has always sought war with the Unicorn, from before I arrived in al-Zawira."

"Not so, cousin," said Chagatai. "I have just come from a most illuminating conversation with the caliph and his pet sorceress." Shono's eyes narrowed. "He offers me peace and friendship for the Unicorn for all time, as well as a ton and a half of gold and other rewards."

"Chagatai–" Yumino growled, her hand drifting to her sword, but Shono silenced her with an upraised hand.

"This is a matter between me and my cousin, Yumino-san. Stay your hand." She nodded and stepped to the side, where she could put herself between them at a moment's notice. "And what is his price?" Shono asked, at length. He felt his fingers itch, willed his hand to stay away from the hilt of his sword.

"I believe you know it. He demands the fealty of the Ganzu and sovereignty over the Hidden Valley. He wants a new treaty that grants him rights of direct trade with the Ivory Kingdoms, rather than being forced to go through us and grant us tariffs."

"Is that all?"

"No," said Chagatai. "He also offers to make me Khan of Khans."

"Che," growled Shono. "You did always say you would kill me yourself if you wanted me dead. So, is that it, then? Have you come to kill me, or to hear my counteroffer?"

"That is what you Shinjo do, is it not? Bargain and cajole, make deals, and then break them?"

I am not my mother. The warm fire of anger in his belly kindled to a roaring furnace. He felt himself harden, like steel. "My counteroffer," he said. He looked up, to where the great silver tree spread its boughs over his head. *A ton and a half of gold. The caliph's limitless gold, against what?* His fingers brushed the hilt of his sword. *Against my steel.* "My offer is this, Chagatai-san: I offer you nothing. You are a samurai of the Unicorn Clan or you are not. I am the heir to the Unicorn. You will be the Moto khan when your father steps aside, and I will not suffer a khan whose loyalty can be *bought*. Raise your sword against me, and I will cut you down. Call your quriltai, and I will defeat you before them. Otherwise, fall in line and remember your honor."

Chagatai stalked forward, reminding Shono of nothing so much as the lions in the oval arena. *But I am a Unicorn.* "That, Shono-sama," Chagatai said, grabbing Shono's hand with his own, "was the correct answer. Perhaps you have the makings of a khan, after all."

Shono took his hand from his sword. The fire in his belly flickered, grumbled. *I'm almost disappointed. Honored ancestors, give me an enemy to fight in open battle.*

"Listen closely, cousin," Chagatai continued. "The caliph didn't send me here to kill you; he has his own killers. I came to warn you. Even now, they surround us."

Shono glanced to Yumino, who stood with sword in hand and poised to kill Chagatai with a single stroke.

"I hear nothing," Shono said. He closed his eyes. The gurgle of water, the trilling of the birds, Yumino's tense breath, Chagatai's heart pounding with excitement. Footsteps on the street outside the garden. "A dozen soldiers, armed and armored. We are surrounded."

As he spoke, the caliph's black-clad guards came rushing into the garden, scimitars and spears in hand. Captain Izad stood in their midst, her face stone. "Prince Shono," she called. "I am commanded to bring you into custody on the charges of treason and wicked sorcery."

"Your charges are nonsense, captain," said Shono. "I am not the caliph's subject and therefore cannot commit treason against him. And as for sorcery, you'll pardon me if I laugh."

"Nevertheless."

"I take it I am wanted dead or alive?"

"Alive is my preference," said Izad. "But the caliph will be satisfied with your head." She nodded, and her soldiers advanced, spears and scimitars at the ready.

They had been speaking Nehiri, but soldiers with weapons raised was a statement clear enough for both Chagatai and Yumino. "'Make me Khan of Khans,'" Chagatai grumbled as he drew his sword. "This caliph has no honor at all." Yumino glanced at his sword, at Shono's face, and shifted her attention to the soldiers surrounding them.

"If Lord Shono does not make it through this battle, Chagatai-sama, you die, too," she promised.

"There's only a dozen of them," Chagatai scoffed. "If the caliph had known I would be here, he would have sent three times as many."

Taka dying at the way station. "Shono, you ass."

Shono drew his sword, the watered steel rippling like shadow in the gleaming silver light of the tree. *I want to live.* "Less talking," he said. "More killing. Come, you dogs!" he cried. "See how the samurai of Rokugan fight! When you get to whatever hell awaits you, tell them the Unicorn Clan has returned to these lands!"

"Tell them the Lords of Death have come!" bellowed Chagatai.

The soldiers bellowed their own war cry and rushed forward, lunging with their spears or raising their scimitars.

Yumino was the first to strike, silently raising her katana high, then bringing it down and through her opponent's skull in a fatal blow. She danced away, circling her next foe as he roared and rushed forward. Chagatai, too, rushed the oncoming killers, slamming his shoulder into the first of them and sending him sprawling. The Moto's scimitar swung in a deadly arc, and one of the soldiers lost both his hands in a single stroke.

For his part, Shono flowed like water and stepped around the jab of an assassin's spear. With his empty hand he gripped the spear shaft, and with his sword he lopped his assailant's head from his shoulders. The watered-steel blade parted cloth, flesh, bone as if they were paper. Then Shono was air, leaping back as two more of the killers pounced, leaving them to crash into one another in the space he had just vacated. He touched the fire in his belly and raised his sword once more, cutting through both attackers with two quick strokes. As he kicked the bodies away, he heard Chagatai curse.

"Shono-san, remember when I said the caliph should have sent three times as many warriors?" Chagatai pointed to where another group of soldiers approached, stringing bows. "Killing the caliph's entire army will take all night!" Chagatai complained as he beat back another foe, only to find himself confronted by Captain Izad. The stocky Moto snarled and lashed out, but the Nehiri captain caught his scimitar on her shield, and only

Chagatai's surprising quickness saved him from the whistling arc of her cudgel.

"No need to kill them," Shono called. "Only to escape." He lifted the spear he had taken from his earlier opponent and hurled it into Captain Izad's shoulder, driving her to her knees. "Captain, please tell the caliph that we decline his hospitality."

He ducked under another attacker's slash, scraped his sword along the woman's shield, then jumped back as Yumino's blade burst from the guard's throat. Chagatai reached his side a moment later, bleeding from a wound on his arm. The three of them ducked around the silver tree, putting it between them and the archers.

"Right," Shono said. "Yumino, it's time you went and fetched your strongest weapon. We'll all need horses to get out of here alive. Chagatai, get to the Dead City; keep everyone there safe. The caliph will be trying to kill us all at once, I think."

"And you, Shono-sama?" Yumino asked.

"I have an important new alliance to make," he said. He pulled the jeweled bird from his caftan and tossed it to Yumino.

She tucked it into her kimono without a word, her mouth a tight line. *She wants to argue, but battlefield discipline is the only thing the Battle Maidens value more than their sacred steeds.* "Hai," she said. "Kiso and I will find you when I have the horses." She ran from the garden so fast she may as well have already been on horseback.

"Good hunting, cousin," said Chagatai. They clasped hands once more, then Chagatai rushed forward, cutting down the closest guard with a whoop. "Ha ha! Chase me, you gaijin dogs, or are you afraid?" He ducked behind a tree as an arrow hissed past where he had been standing, still booming challenges and increasingly crude insults in Rokugani.

Then Shono was alone, save for the oncoming guards and a

wounded Captain Izad. He let them corner him against the garden's wall, then climbed up and over it as nimble as a mountain goat. *Follow if you can.* Dropping to the avenue on the far side, he jogged into the shadows of the next garden in line.

The streets were deserted in the silver darkness of the full moon. Shono made his way toward the Court of Beasts. *I should have bothered to discover where she makes her lodging. Perhaps I can catch her scent where I last saw her, follow her that way.* He saw no servants, no passersby he could interrogate. Except – there. Someone stood in the darkness before him, a deep blue fading into the shadows.

No heartbeat. No scent. "Ma'aruf," Shono hissed.

"God's blessings upon you, Prince Shono," Ma'aruf said, striding forward. "I am commanded to deliver you to my mistress."

"I would rather not kill you, djinni."

Ma'aruf laughed. "I feel the same way, my friend." He vanished and appeared again behind Shono. Shono raised his sword – *too slow* – and Ma'aruf's arm came down like a falling mountain on his head.

CHAPTER NINE
The Night of Ghuls

Around me spreads a golden sea.
A more bountiful land I'll never see.
As far as I ride and wherever I roam,
The Golden Plains are always my home.

Shono awoke to the smell: the rotten, choking smell, as if a *nerge* hunt had finished directly atop an open mass grave. When he managed to peel his eyes open, he was unsurprised to find himself lying flat on his back on the table in the center of Mandana's chamber of blood. He tested his wrists, his ankles, and found them all bound tightly. *But I am not dead yet, so she must want something from me.*

He turned his head and found Ma'aruf standing as still as a statue in the gloom, garnet eyes glittering. In an instant, Ma'aruf was at his side, dabbing carefully at a cut on Shono's arm. *When did I get that? During the battle? Or after?*

"Fetch your mistress," Shono said on his second try, his throat broken and torn like the Burning Sands themselves. "Let's get this over with."

"No need to fetch me." Her voice filled the room. It came from nowhere, from everywhere, from the shadows. Shono had the briefest impression of something huge, awful, a demon from his nightmares, but then Mandana herself stepped into his vision, smirking. "Welcome to my home, my prince."

"Spare me your courtesies, sorceress. They ring hollow while I am tied to your butcher's block." *What are you doing, you fool? If you are going to survive this, keep a gentler tongue in your head.* Shono struggled to rein in his anger, but it was running wild, an unbroken stallion. *Have a care it doesn't buck you off.*

"Courtesy," Mandana said in Rokugani. "That is one of the tenets of your Bushidō, is it not?"

"It is," Shono said. "And as it happens, attacking guests and locking them in charnel houses is a grave lapse of honor."

"I have never found a code of honor or justice that was not broken more often than it was followed," Mandana mused. She crossed to the table at the edge of the room and examined each of the sinister instruments there in turn, then paused to consult a thick book bound in pale leather. "Even your own mother dishonored herself, did she not?"

This is how it will be, even if I survive the night. Everywhere I go, my honor is sullied by what my mother did. "She made her choice," Shono said. *Yet not all join Mandana in condemning my mother's decision.* "Had she made a different one, you would find fault with that, I am certain, saying that she dishonors herself and my clan by allowing herself to be reduced to a mere daimyō's wife." He turned his head away, and his gaze fell upon Ma'aruf again. "We Unicorn value freedom as much as honor."

"Freedom? That is not Bushidō," Mandana said. "Or have I been misinformed?"

"A samurai lives for others. Protects others. Shows compassion to others. We find that compassion in celebrating our freedom."

"Fascinating. It really is as unworkable and nonsensical a creed as the Word of the Prophet, open to whatever interpretations and justifications the mortal mind can devise." She crossed to the table and leaned over him, grinning down into his face. Her hair fell loose, brushing against his cheek, and the smell of wet blood came with her. Shono surged against his bonds, lunging forward to kick her, bite her, anything, but only elicited a dry chuckle. "The things people do, the lies they tell themselves, all to hide the truth that they cannot face: power over others is everything."

"Power over self is paramount," Shono snarled. *Shinsei said that. I think.*

"Oh, poor deluded prince. If you had any power over yourself, you would stop me from doing this." With casual, effortless suddenness, Mandana reached out with two talon-like fingers and plucked Shono's left eye from its socket. His vision forked, swam, turned in on itself, and then exploded in red-hot pain and blood. He heard screaming and realized in some detached, still-reasoning part of himself that it was his own. When his vision cleared, it was blurred and strange, false feeling as though he were still drunk. But he saw clearly enough to watch Mandana pop his eye into her mouth like an olive, chewing and swallowing with evident relish. He felt himself fall down into the table, into his own head, his vision narrowing as if peering through a long tunnel, his hearing awash with his own heartbeat. *Don't black out. She's distracted. Do something.*

"Why?" he croaked.

"When we negotiate with your mother, sell you back to her, you'll be my creature. I will see through your eyes – eye, I suppose. Your mind, your soul, will belong to me. This is just the first step."

"I'll die, first."

"Only if I permit it. And I do not permit it." She returned to her book, studying its pages. "That is all for today, I think. If we press the issue too quickly, you might get your wish, and we can't have that." She moved away, on his blind side. *I have a blind side.* Footsteps on the stairs, the creak of the door. Her voice filled the room, salt and furnace thunder. "Ma'aruf. Make our guest... comfortable." He heard her smirk, and then the door closed again.

Ma'aruf appeared at his side. "My mistress calls you our guest, sayid. But if you were truly our guest, and so due proper hospitality, you would have called God's blessing upon this house."

"Ma'aruf." Shono felt his mouth moving, felt words spilling out, but he was standing outside again, watching it happen. "Ma'aruf, why do you serve such a monster? Surely she does not deserve the loyalty you show her. Help me."

"It is not a matter of loyalty." The djinni shook his head. "Ifrits such as I are bound body and soul by our word and bargains. I must obey the particulars of my mistress's commands. I cannot simply set you free. But... she has named you as her guest." He leaned forward, his garnet eyes glimmering. "Perhaps she was speaking poetically. For if you were truly our guest, and protected by guest right, you would have called God's blessing upon this house."

His vision swimming, Shono slumped against the table. "I see," he said. *How might Rashid put it?* "May God, the Bringer of Peace, bless this house."

"Another of the names of God might have been better chosen, but I thank you all the same, sayid." Ma'aruf bowed and began working at the ropes that bound Shono's wrists with fingers as powerful and unyielding as stone. "These ropes are clearly too tight. You must be uncomfortable."

"Thank you," Shono gasped. He turned his head to watch Ma'aruf work, and his head exploded in fresh pain. *She ate my eye.*

"Would our guest like any refreshment? Perhaps a beverage or delicacy that would be difficult or impossible to acquire here in the city?" Shono gaped at the djinni, who sighed theatrically. "The Prophet commands us to offer our guest the finest refreshments that are within our power, and my powers are prodigious."

"*Airag*," Shono said. *He is… helping me.* "Fermented mare's milk. Only brewed in Ujik and Unicorn lands. If you please."

"An excellent choice, sayid. Why, I believe it will take me the better part of an hour to locate such a drink and return."

"Why are you doing this?" Shono flexed the fingers on his left hand, felt blood returning to them. *He was right; I am much more comfortable with the ropes loosened.*

"It is an uncommon prince who takes notice of a lowly servant." With that, the djinni crossed his arms, nodded his head, and vanished.

One hour. I wonder if he meant a Rokugani hour, or a Nehiri hour? It didn't matter. Shono twisted, grunted, felt his skin chafing and tearing beneath the ropes, strained his whole body. He tried to cast out his senses in the Shinjo way, to locate Mandana in the tower above him, but the pain of his eye and his wrists kept snapping him back to himself. It was impossible to concentrate. *It doesn't matter. Either she discovers me while I work to escape, or she doesn't.*

He freed one hand, then the other, then sat up on his third try to pick at the ropes binding his feet. Minutes passed, his blood pounding in his ears. Finally, the ropes came away, and he staggered to his feet, leaning on the table as a wave of dizziness attacked him. *The whole world looks wrong. I can't tell how far away anything is.*

He stumbled across the room, avoiding the iron-gated well in the center, and braced himself against Mandana's table. An oil lamp, vials and flasks of oil and who knows what else. The insidious book. Implements of torture, gleaming in the lamplight. Shono watched from outside his body as he grabbed hold of these last and hurled them to the floor with a strangled cry. *She ate my eye.*

Gasping, he crawled down the table to the end. His belt with its gold medallions rested there, swords still attached. He grabbed hold of his sword's hilt. He would draw the watered-steel blade, climb the stairs, and kill Mandana. *Don't be a fool. You couldn't kill a half-drowned rabbit right now. You need to escape, find Saadiyah, and complete your mission.*

"Shono!"

"My lord!"

That was easier than I thought it would be. Yumino stood in the doorway, sword in hand and Saadiyah behind her. The samurai stalked into the room like a hunting cat, but Saadiyah simply rushed to his side.

"Your face," she said.

"I will live."

"Not if it gets infected. Hold still, Shinjo, you're not going anywhere like that." One delicate hand splayed open against his chest, holding him in place while the other stroked his face. "Tell your bodyguard to stay alert, please; I will need a few moments."

"I might as well remind her to breathe." Even so, he translated Saadiyah's request.

"Hai."

"You two don't share a language," Shono said while the gaijin selected a bottle from Mandana's array. "How did you find each other?"

"She showed off the jeweled bird I gave you until someone pointed her at me. Then she said 'Shono' enough times that I got the general idea. It was no great leap to suppose that you'd gotten yourself into some trouble. This will hurt."

"Everything hurts," Shono said, but when she twisted his head back and poured a stinging, ice-cold pool of fire into his missing eye, it was all he could do not to scream. By the time he could breathe again, she was pressing folded cotton against his face and wrapping a length of cloth around it. "My lady," he gasped, "I had planned to rescue you from the caliph's captivity, but I see that I got it the wrong way around."

"It's only to be expected from a barbarian."

"Still, I think it best if we flee the city together."

"Yes, let's."

"Shono-sama," Yumino hissed.

Mandana stood in the doorway, blocking their exit to the street beyond. "Somehow you have disposed of my djinni and called your allies to you. I congratulate you, Prince Shono. Few manage even this much of a fruitless and doomed escape." Her voice thrummed through the air like the promise of gathering thunder. With each word she seemed to swell with power.

"Kill her," Shono said in Rokugani, and Yumino leapt forward with a soundless scream. Her sword glimmered in the lamplight but cut only shadow and smoke. Mandana had vanished. "To the horses," he said, but the door slammed shut.

"You fools have no idea of the extent of my powers." Mandana's voice prowled in the shadows, stalking on tiger's feet. Shono shifted, his sword in his hand, straining to find her.

"You do not frighten me, sorceress," said Saadiyah. She busied herself at Mandana's tool bench, her back to the room and showing no care.

"Do you think your precious learning and your benevolent god will protect you from me?" Mandana chuckled. "Will you conjure him down from Heaven like the sorcerers of old?"

"To conjure by the name of God is akin to Name Magic, which is forbidden," Saadiyah said with infinite patience, as if returning to an old argument. "God the Most Bountiful has already supplied his children with everything they need. There is no need to resort to sorcery."

"And what tool has your god provided you with against me?" growled Mandana.

"Bandages, a jar of lamp oil, and an open flame," Saadiyah said. "Shinjo, where?"

"There!" He heard, felt, Mandana gathering herself to pounce, and he pointed. Saadiyah spun and hurled a bottle, its mouth stuffed with burning cotton. It struck the stone floor of the chamber and spread a lake of dancing flame, which revealed Mandana, staggering and shrieking.

Yumino stepped forward and cut, sending black blood streaking against the far wall. Mandana howled and faded into the smoke, until only the howl remained.

"Is she dead?" Yumino asked.

"Doubtful," Shono said. He crossed to the door and hauled it open. "But I'll not stay to find out."

"What is that noise?" asked Saadiyah.

Shono paused, focusing his senses. Mandana's final howl wasn't lingering – it was being answered. From down below. *Down the well.* Ten thousand screams, from ten thousand ruined throats, and drawing closer. "We should leave."

Saadiyah nodded, scooped up Mandana's pale book, and followed the samurai out the door.

Outside, Kiso and Umeboshi were waiting, restless but loyal.

Yumino vaulted easily into her saddle, then kept a vigilant eye out as Shono clambered atop his own horse.

"What now?" Yumino asked. Shono made to answer, then saw that she was looking at Saadiyah.

And now those two are best friends. Of course they are. Shono offered a hand and pulled Saadiyah up behind him. "We must leave the city at once, my lady," he said. "Any suggestions?"

"Rashid's temple," Saadiyah called, pointing, and they were off, every hoofbeat a knife of fire through Shono's head.

The gate dividing the Inner City from the Middle City stood open, to Shono's surprise – until he saw the corpses of the guards still lying across the paving stones. "Your handiwork?" he asked Yumino.

"Saadiyah is the one who convinced them to open the gate," she said. "I like her. You chose well."

Chose what? But then they were at Rashid's temple, and Saadiyah slid off Boshi's back and raced to the doorway.

"Sheikh Rashid," she called softly.

The priest emerged and stared. After a moment, he sighed. "Saadiyah, horses were not part of the plan."

"I know," Saadiyah apologized. "You'll have to bring them around to meet us. Everyone will be looking for the three of us; no one will think to stop you with our horses."

"Or we leave the beasts here."

"Not an option," said Shono, with a glance at Yumino. *But why can't they simply come with us? What is this plan?*

"We'll need them when we reach the other side," Saadiyah said. "This is nearly two weeks early; the boat isn't ready."

"May God the Shepherd look over us," Rashid sighed. "Yes, of course."

Shono relayed the important points in Rokugani as he and

Yumino dismounted. Shono reached for the bow that Yumino had thoughtfully placed in its case on his saddle, but a throb of pain surged from his missing eye. He cringed, lifted the weapon and the quiver, and handed both to Yumino. She took them with a wordless nod.

Rashid took both horses by the reins and vanished down the street. Saadiyah led them into the temple. *Through the men's entrance. I suppose to hell with propriety tonight.*

Perhaps sensing his surprise, Saadiyah called over her shoulder. "God will forgive us, I hope, for using his temple so callously. But if nothing else, we will need Rashid's lamp to go any farther." She plucked a small bronze and glass oil lantern from a low table, where Rashid had left it alongside an opened book, then led them into the garden – the same garden where Shono, Rashid, and Nestor had passed that agreeable hour in conversation. She led them to the shatranj board and gestured to it. Yumino stepped forward, grabbed hold, and shoved the thing aside, revealing a narrow passage and a crude wooden ladder.

Shono stared with his one remaining eye. "Did you know about this?" he asked in Rokugani.

"No," said Yumino. She brushed off her hands and began climbing down the ladder.

"She speaks not a word of Rokugani; how is it that she is better at giving you orders than I am?"

Saadiyah climbed down next, holding the lamp. Shono stopped on the second step down, grabbed hold of the game board, and found that it was cunningly arranged on tracks. He was able to close the entrance up behind them quite easily.

"How long have you been planning this escape?" he wondered aloud.

"Four years," said Saadiyah. "When I turned sixteen, I vowed to escape and free my father to act against the caliph's tyranny, or to die in the attempt and free my father to act against the caliph's tyranny."

"A decision worthy of a samurai," Shono said as they crept down the narrow, cramped tunnel. "Where does this tunnel emerge?"

"If the calculations I performed this morning on the wall are correct, in a temple outside the Pilgrim's Court."

An astrolabe can be used to measure distances. "I see," said Shono. "How often are you wrong?"

"I thought you were an idiot barbarian when we first met," she said. "So, never."

It took nearly a quarter of an hour to reach the end of the tunnel. When they did, Saadiyah pointed to the digging axe leaning against the tunnel wall, then at the ceiling. Yumino understood instantly and swiftly cut through the last few finger widths of sandy earth, finding a smooth, straight-edged stone beyond. Yumino kept digging and cutting, and the entire square flooring tile was soon revealed.

"Ah," sighed Saadiyah. "Another ladder or short stair here would have been a clever idea."

"We'll make do," Shono said, stepping forward and making a stirrup of his hands. Yumino stepped up, braced herself against the stone, and pushed. With a terrible scrape, the stone came free, and she hauled herself up into the space above. "You next, my lady," Shono said, and Saadiyah stepped into his hands as well. Shono lifted, Yumino pulled from above, and Saadiyah was soon through the hole, too. Shono's own jump nearly made him black out again, the throbbing in his eye socket was so bad, but between them, the women managed to drag him up to lie, gasping, on the intricately beautiful floor of the temple.

"Now we see if Rashid has made it," Saadiyah whispered. She

pointed to the empty hole, and Yumino wordlessly replaced the tile, then brushed away the dirt and grime that marked where they had come through. Saadiyah paced to the doorway, where a sliver of silver moonlight spilled across the floor. "He's not here," she whispered.

The three of them emerged from the temple to find the city streets utterly deserted. "Something is wrong," Saadiyah said. "The Pilgrim's Court should have some visitors, even at this time of night."

A sickly howl echoed across the rooftops. *Just like the voices from Mandana's well.* "Demons walk the streets tonight," Shono said. "We should be glad innocent people have enough sense to shut their doors."

He'd spoken in Nehiri, but Yumino at least understood his tone and his expression. "We must find Kiso," she said. "And the priest."

"Give me a moment," Shono said in Rokugani. The square in which they stood was a large one, flagged in white stone that shone in the moonlight, surrounded by temples and other buildings whose purpose might be visible by daylight but were a mystery now. One such building had a low, flat roof and a stunted cedar tree giving it some shade. Shono jogged to it, handed his swords to Yumino for safekeeping, and began to climb. Every movement sent his vision swimming and his entire body throbbing with pain, but eventually he gained the roof.

Once there, he cast his senses wide, as his sensei had taught him. There were a handful of schools in Rokugan that taught perception and the art of seeing truly. The Kitsuki method was justly famous – the Hiruma scouts had no equal in the Shadowlands – but Shono still believed that the Shinjo school exceeded them all. *Time to prove it, Shono. How hard can finding two terrified horses be in this city?* He closed his eyes – his eye – and listened, hearing the hissing, screeching, howling progress of the monsters, feeling the sound warp and echo as it passed through the city. And then – there! A scream, and a muffled curse – Rashid was not equal to the challenge of two spirited Unicorn steeds, it seemed.

"This way," Shono called. Yumino tossed up his swords, and Shono snatched them from the air at a run.

With Yumino racing along the street below, Shono leapt from building to building, until he slid down an arched dome and landed on a roof overlooking a place where two streets met. Rashid was still struggling with both horses' reins, and the hissing howl was closer than ever.

"Rashid-sensei!" Shono shouted. "Let them go and run for your life!"

Rashid looked up to where Shono stood. For a moment nothing moved, then a piece of shadow dropped from a rooftop across the way and loped toward Rashid. The priest dropped the reins, and Kiso and Umeboshi both bolted down the street toward Yumino. Shono drew his sword, the watered-steel blade cutting through the moonlight, and leapt from the rooftop with a shout. He hit the ground running and managed to get to Rashid just as the thing grabbed him and drove him to the cobble-stones.

The thing had the shape of a man, with ragged black clothing and a scrap of cloth wrapped around its face. In bad light, when it wasn't moving, it might have looked like just another masked killer, right down to the sword at its belt. But its eyes glimmered gold in the moonlight, and its filthy nails were as long and sharp as claws, the skin of its hands a putrid off-white. Shono cut it across the chest and sent it sprawling. The blow would have killed a human being, but the thing stood up and *hissed*, scrabbling for its own sword. Shono swung again, cutting through its neck and sending its head bouncing across the cobbles and into the dark. The body fell like a marionette with its strings cut. Three more of the things dropped down from rooftops, eyes shining in the moonlight.

"Sensei, can you stand?" Shono asked.

Yumino arrived astride Kiso, Shono's bow in her hands. She loosed an arrow, and another, while Shono helped Rashid to his feet. The priest was clutching a wound on his arm where the monster's teeth or talons had found their mark. "A *ghul*," he gasped. "Evil sorcery. A demon bound in the corpse of a human."

"How do I kill it?"

"Remove the head, pierce the heart, or burn it with cleansing flame," Shono translated for Yumino while he helped Rashid onto Kiso's back.

She slipped the bow back into its case. "I'm not the archer you are, Shono-sama. I'll focus on cutting their heads off." She drew her sword, wheeled Kiso as if by a thought, and cut down the first ghul that leapt for her.

"Better to run than to fight, Yumino-san," Shono said. "Make for the river. The Bridge of Boats."

"Hai," she said, and she galloped away.

Shono whistled and found Umeboshi trotting toward him, Saadiyah already in the saddle with her skirts bunched up around her legs. "You ride, Saadiyah-san?"

"My father taught me to sail and my mother taught me to ride, but I haven't done either in years." She awkwardly pulled herself back to perch on the rear horn of his tall Shinjo-style saddle, and Shono mounted gingerly.

"Some skills, once learned, are never lost. Let's hope riding is one of them."

He turned Umeboshi in a tight circle, then kicked his heels

into the horse's flank. "Ya!" The three of them surged forward, following in Yumino, Kiso, and Rashid's wake.

Hooves clattering on cobbled streets, they dashed through the night-clad city. Houses and shops, temples and manors streaked past, their shutters closed and lights doused. It seemed a different city from the one Shono had ridden through only a few days before, as empty as a graveyard. *And as full of death.*

They twice more met with ghuls as they rode. A group of three stood hissing and sniffing where two streets met, and Shono and Yumino rode them down without a pause, swords flickering in the moonlight. Boshi shied away from the monsters, but Kiso rode on unperturbed.

The next group of ghuls leapt rooftop to rooftop, their hissing giving way to the howling of desert jackals. Some of them had weapons in their twisted dead hands, and one or two even loosed arrows in the riders' direction.

"Shono-sama!" Yumino called, racing ahead of him. "The demons are keeping pace!"

It was so. Fast and agile as they clearly were, the monsters would never be able to catch a Unicorn on horseback … unless that Unicorn was burdened with an extra rider. Slowed by the weight of Rashid and Saadiyah, their horses were not pulling away from the hunting ghuls. *Had I two eyes, I might use my bow, pierce their hearts as we ride. But at my best, I might have scored one hit in five when aiming for the heart, and I am not at my best.*

"Ride on," he called forward. "Once we rejoin the others, perhaps Iuchi Shoan will have a solution for our problem." They rode on. Blood pounded in Shono's ears with the hoofbeats pounding on the street. He felt fresh blood on his cheek and realized his eye socket was bleeding again. Shono stood in his stirrups, urging Umeboshi on with each heartbeat, with each sway of his saddle. Saadiyah clung to him, rocking back and forth and silent with her own thoughts, her own fears. *A samurai does not feel fear, no more than he does grief.*

After an eternity, the Bridge of Boats came into view. But no sooner did they approach than Yumino reined Kiso into a tight, clattering circle. "My lord!" she called. "Look."

The crews of the barges that made up the bridge were scurrying back and forth across their decks, pulling ropes and untying each barge from its neighbors. Already the bridge was beginning to pull apart. Saadiyah leaned to see past his back and gasped. "We are too late," she said.

Shono did not pause but spurred Umeboshi on to still-greater exertion. "Shinjo!" Saadiyah called. "You must be either mad or the finest horseman alive to attempt this!"

"I am a Unicorn," Shono breathed, and then they were clattering across the deck of the first boat.

The second boat was a few feet off true, but there was still no water visible between the two boats' hulls, so Boshi took the gap at a brisk trot. Hoofbeats behind announced that Yumino was following, and an arrow striking the deck ahead announced that their pursuers had switched their tactics.

Good. At least they won't be rash enough to follow us. With a wordless shout, Shono urged his horse on to the third boat, then across a widening gap to the fourth. The fifth and sixth had become fouled together, and Umeboshi crossed them at a canter as an arrow shattered the lantern hanging at a barge's stern and spread flame across the deck. Umeboshi shied, but Shono kept his seat and Saadiyah clung even tighter.

The seventh boat was already pulling free with enough water between it and the previous barge that Shono could have lain down in the gap. Umeboshi took the leap as Saadiyah screamed on his back, and for a moment they flew. *Every hope we have for success comes down to whether my horse is strong and fast enough.* Then they landed on the other side and kept on, crossing the eighth and ninth.

Saadiyah's scream of fear became a whoop of delight, then a cry of alarm as an arrow embedded itself in the wood of Shono's saddle. "That was lucky," Shono called, as more fire spread ahead of them.

"Will your horse ride into fire?"

"He will if I tell him to," Shono said, and dug his heels in.

They jumped to the tenth boat, clear over the pool of flame, and the arrows were now falling behind them. They ran across the tenth to the eleventh boat, jumped to the twelfth, and then splashed into the water only a few paces from the shore and hauled out of the river.

"We made it!" exulted Saadiyah. "We're alive!"

Kiso climbed the bank just downriver, Yumino still sitting tall in her saddle. Rashid was slumped over the back of the horse, his white robes stained red where an arrow had pierced his shoulder.

"Rashid!" Saadiyah cried. She slipped off Umeboshi and rushed to the priest's side.

Shono turned and studied the far shore. The river was now a confusion of boats, several on fire, with no evidence there had ever been a bridge. Dark figures, hunched and loping like animals, ran back and forth on the far bank, but none seemed willing to brave the river. "They don't like water?" Shono wondered.

"Thank the kami for small favors," Yumino muttered. "We're out of bowshot, too."

Shono turned his attention to their charges. "Rashid?" he asked.

"He'll live, I think," said Saadiyah. "If we can get him down off this horse and give him some medical attention."

"We can't stop here," Yumino said. "The Dead City is only minutes away."

"Do what you can for him, Saadiyah-san. Then get back on the horse."

"I'm not a physician," Saadiyah complained, but she tore a strip of cloth from her underskirt and fashioned a bandage from it, wrapping it tightly around Rashid's wound with Yumino's assistance.

"Che," Yumino muttered. "We'll need to purify ourselves after this."

But then it was done, and Shono hauled Saadiyah up onto his horse and they rode for the Dead City.

"We're riding *to* the Dead City?" Saadiyah shouted as they approached. "That place is cursed, they say! We should be riding in the opposite direction!"

"That's where my people are," Shono called back. "I'm surprised to find you superstitious, my lady."

"We have been pursued most of the night by monsters out of a children's story. Some small amount of superstition is not just rational, but wise."

"No time for wisdom now," Shono called. He drew his sword. "The ghuls are here, too."

The sounds of battle greeted them as they approached the Dead City, and ghuls swarmed at the edges of the encampment. Hissing and howling as they hurled themselves at the Unicorn, they were naked or draped in rags and burial shrouds, their flesh pale and bloated where it wasn't bruised or green. Their mouths were ragged wet holes, marked by the occasional shine of white teeth and the writhing of long, wormlike tongues. Their eyes were pale in the moonlight, shimmering like an animal's at the edge of the firelight.

The remaining Unicorn were hard-pressed. Most were on foot, and a trail of corpses showed where they had fought a retreat through the crumbling city gates to their current position at the summit of the winged sun statue carved into the rocky outcropping overlooking their camp. A ragged band of surviving ashigaru, led by Bokudō Naosuke, held the line against an endless tide of ghuls, while behind them Ide Ryōma handed arrows to a pair of Moto archers and Iuchi Shoan tended to a wounded Moto Chagatai. The horses and camels in the paddock at the edge of the ruined city, although in a panic of screaming and braying at the smell of the ghuls, at least were unharmed.

"What now?" Yumino asked. Her eyes flicked from the melee, to the paddock, to Shono, and back again. *As my yōjimbō, she feels obligated to grab the horses and run. As a Battle Maiden, she cannot abandon our companions to their fate. I am not the only one who can feel torn in two.*

Shono drew his sword. "Saadiyah, Rashid. Dismount, please." The anger was back, a warm fire in the pit of his belly. *These are my people Mandana is killing.*

Saadiyah slipped off Boshi, then helped Rashid down from Kiso. "What are you going to do, Shinjo?"

"My auntie there is a sorcerer." Shono indicated Shoan with a nod of his head. "I'll tell her what Rashid told me about these beasts, and we'll see if she can find a solution. If not, we cut our way to the horses, and everyone who can mount rides east as fast as they can, and everyone who can't dies."

"Take this," Saadiyah said. She pressed the sinister volume from Mandana's lair into his hands. "It might help. May God the Defender of Justice protect you."

"And you," Shono said, then turned Boshi in a tight circle. "We get this book to Shoan," he said in Rokugani. Yumino nodded. "Ya!"

They rode forward, trampling over or threading between the first few ghuls as it suited them. As they reached the denser pack of ghuls climbing up toward the Unicorn on the winged sun, they swung their swords, cutting heads and limbs as they pressed forward. The shock of each impact of his sword made Shono's missing eye throb with delirious pain, but he pressed on. The horses, too, did their part, lashing out with hooves and on occasion teeth, cracking bones and tearing putrid flesh with each blow.

Suddenly, Chagatai loomed before them, roaring his battle cry and sending ghuls sprawling with a sweep of his scimitar. "Cousin!" he cried. "Come, join us! Let us all greet the Lords of Death together!"

"Not today," Shono said, galloping through the gap Chagatai had made him. He held aloft the book. "Unicorn samurai!" he called. "Iuchi Shoan is the key to our salvation. Each moment we buy her is a chance that we all might live. For Shinjo and the emperor!"

"For Shinjo and the emperor! For the Lords of Death!" came the call from a dozen Unicorn throats, and Shono was vaulting from Boshi's back, racing to Shoan's side.

"So!" boomed a voice. "I have found the Iuchi sorcerer at last."

"No," Shono breathed. He placed the book in Shoan's outstretched hands and spun around.

Ma'aruf stood ten strides away, within the circle of Unicorn warriors even now fighting against the ghuls. "Your airag awaits you in my mistress's tower," he said. "Now stand aside, that I may kill the sorcerer."

"Never."

"So be it." Ma'aruf folded his arms, nodded his head, and vanished. But Shono was already moving, his watered-steel scimitar glimmering in a flat arc, and when the ifrit appeared behind him, the blade sparked and slid along the stonelike skin of his chest. Shono raised his sword for another strike, and Ma'aruf slapped him with the back of his azure hand. Shono went sprawling while Ma'aruf ran a finger over the chip the sword had cut from his chest. "I don't believe a mortal swordsman has ever cut me before," the djinni said.

Shono pulled himself to his feet, gritting his teeth against the pain of his head and eye and the fresh agony of what must be a broken rib. "Fortune favors the mortal man," he said, and he leapt forward, pure fire, unleashing all his anger and hurling it along the edge of his sword. Ma'aruf lifted one arm to block his blow, as if dismissing a child wielding a willow switch, but the sword sparked again and flaked another chip of the djinni's strange body away.

"Enough of this!" Ma'aruf boomed. "I am commanded to kill the Iuchi sorcerer and any who would stand in my way. I would not harm you, Prince Shono, but you leave me little choice!" He shifted, his bare feet scraping across the stone as he struck: low, low, high.

Earth. Shono read the djinni's style as he danced, like air, away from each strike. *And why not? He has the fortitude of iron and the strength of a mountain.* He blocked one of the djinni's strikes and staggered back, ears ringing and arm aching. *Perhaps literally.*

Shono spared a glance at Shoan. She was hunched over the book with Ryōma, gesturing over a diagram in rust-red ink. *No help there.*

Shono flowed like water, moving with the djinni's next strike and slashing at his legs. *If I can break his stance, I have a chance.* But his sword merely screeched and sparked and left another tiny chip in the djinni's flesh. *Or stone. His stance is so solid he may as well be part of the rock below.* Then Shono blinked. *I have only ever seen his feet planted firmly on stone. He didn't even walk up the stairs with us.*

Then Ma'aruf's fist slammed into his shoulder and sent Shono crashing to his knees. The scimitar skittered away, fallen from numb, nerveless fingers.

"My apologies, sayid," Ma'aruf said, lifting his fist again.

"Spare me," Shono said, and he lashed out with his leg. He surged to his feet, one foot positioned behind Ma'aruf's knee, hip slamming into the djinni, sending Ma'aruf off-balance. The djinni staggered, one foot lifting from the rocky ground, and Shono flowed, water, behind him, blending *ki*, wrapping his arms around the ifrit's chest and *lifting*.

"What!" Ma'aruf bellowed. "Impossible! My strength is of the very earth. You cannot hope to best me in a wrestling match!"

"I believe I just did, sayid," Shono gasped. He held Ma'aruf a finger's breadth above the ground, the djinni kicking and flailing with only ordinary human strength. *And he isn't so heavy as he looks, once you get him off the ground. But I can't do this forever, and if I let even one foot touch the ground he could kill me with a single blow.* "Tell me, my friend. What, precisely, were Mandana's orders to you?"

"'Find and kill every Iuchi sorcerer in the Cradle of the World and the Burning Sands,' she said. 'Let nothing delay you. Kill anyone who would stand in your way.' I have found one, and so I must kill her."

"Shoan-sama!" Shono called.

"Nearly ready, Shono-san," she snapped. "This is slightly more difficult than it looks."

"I'm sorry, Auntie." Shono twisted and hurled Ma'aruf to the ground, as far from Shoan as he could manage. "Iuchi Shoan, I cast you out from the Unicorn Clan. You are *rōnin* from this day forth, and no longer may you bear the name Iuchi."

"What?" she gasped. "My lord Shono, please, what–"

"I'm sorry, Auntie," he said again. "Finish your spell or we all die." He turned to Ma'aruf. "Did you catch that, or should I repeat myself in Nehiri?"

"I understood well enough," Ma'aruf said. "Well played, my prince. Mandana will be extremely vexed when I return to her."

"You have the entire Burning Sands to search for any other Iuchi sorcerers that may be lurking there. It seems to me that you should be very, very thorough and take your time before you go anywhere near your mistress again."

Ma'aruf smiled. He folded his arms, bowed his head, and vanished. Shono groaned, found his scimitar, and limped to Shoan's side.

"Auntie," he said.

"I have its name, Shono," Shoan said in a hoarse croak. She looked up from where the book was opened on her knees. Shono's eyes slid away from the crinkled pages, the rust-colored ink, the crawling writing and unsettling illustrations.

"Whose name, Auntie?"

"The demon that binds these ghuls." She stared up at him. Her eyes were red with tears and exhaustion. She trembled. *She's afraid.*

He thought of his father. *"Meishōdō is Name Magic. To know a thing's name is to know its nature, and that knowledge means you can control it."* Daiyu fondled the charm at his throat. *"If you're willing to pay the price."*

"Do it," Shono said.

Shoan nodded and struggled to rise. *She's my mother's age. She looks twenty years older. What troubles her more, me making her rōnin, or that book?* She placed a hand on Ryōma's shoulder and stepped forward. She raised her hands above her head, holding a small piece of rock the same color as the walls below. *A piece of the city itself.* Then she began to sing.

It sounded like the call to prayer, Shono decided, but mournful and foreboding rather than celebratory and humble. But it wavered high above them all, and the ghuls paused as if to listen. When she finished, Shoan cried out in Nehiri, blended with some other language Shono didn't know. "Ho! Go forth! *Tawil at-Umr! Talmat, talmat!* I release you from this binding, *Qlifot!*"

A great wind tore through the Dead City. The ghuls raised a chorus of hisses, howls, yips, and roars as sand surged in a swirling torrent. When the wind faded, the ghuls were gone; the camp, such as it was, lay in ruins; and a cloud of black and red dust danced and twisted in the sky, leaping over the river and settling over al-Zawira.

"No," choked Shoan.

"Good work, sorcerer!" bellowed Chagatai. "You have just saved all our lives."

"But at what cost?" Shono asked.

Shoan pointed a trembling hand at the city, then busied herself with tucking her hair, disordered by the great wind, back behind her ears. A wide white streak ran from her temple to the tips of her previously jet-black locks. *And yet, I do not think that is the price of which she despairs.*

"What happened?" Shono asked again.

"Those creatures, they were all the same demon," Shoan managed after a few deep breaths. "It was bound into service against its will. I set it free." She nodded toward the city. "And now it is taking its vengeance. I fear the city may not survive."

"Let us hope the monster confines its vengeance to Mandana alone," Shono said. "For now, we live, and Mandana and Harun will be in no immediate position to pursue us." He turned to Ryōma. "It's time to snatch a stalemate from the jaws of this defeat."

As the sun came up, Shoan saw to Rashid's wounds – using traditional medicine, ignoring the water talisman of healing at her belt. *Was that her choice, or out of respect for Rashid's Qamarist aversion to sorcery?*

Shono outlined the plan he had half formed when he went looking for Saadiyah. Ryōma listened, nodding, and soon took up the thread, outstripping Shono's explanation. "A pledge of warriors and matériel, mutual defense," he said, clapping his hands and warming to his subject. "Let the deal stand public, and then let the caliph respond. If we give him a chance to back down, then throw in, oh, a three percent reduction in tariffs and a ceremonial pilgrimage from some Ganzu; he'll be able to save face, and we can prevent any further escalation of the conflict."

Saadiyah snorted. "I wouldn't mind a little escalation, if it ended with his indolent rump off the throne and Mandana's head on a pike."

"What if we want him gone?" Shono asked. "Or what if he refuses?"

"Then it's war, but with the caliph fighting on two fronts while we do the same, it's one that we might actually win," Ryōma shrugged.

Saadiyah took a deep breath and released it, smoothing her now-bloodstained robes. "Let us hope it does not come to that. The Prophet commands peace and brotherhood among all humankind."

Shono fought back a smile. *So, she wars between her desires and the Prophet's Word just as I do with the demands of Bushidō. We are more alike than she thinks.*

Ryōma stood and led them to where Shoan was attending to Rashid in the shadow of one of their few remaining tents. "Shoan-sama," he said. "Sheikh Rashid." He spoke first in Rokugani, then quickly repeated himself in Nehiri. "Between the two of you, we must find a marriage ceremony that will satisfy all parties."

"A what?" Shono asked, following after.

"Of course," Saadiyah said. "That is the traditional way of sealing an alliance in my culture; is it the same in yours?"

"Quite the same nearly everywhere the Unicorn have traveled," Ryōma assured her. He produced paper and a writing kit from somewhere about his person. "Let us discuss the precise terms of the marriage contract – and the alliance. My lord Shono is quite wealthy, of course, and more than willing to pay a generous bride price."

"I won't be a junior wife," Saadiyah said. "I'm his primary wife; I want that down in ink."

"I … have no other wives," Shono said, in a daze.

"That makes it easier," Saadiyah nodded. "I have no other wives, either, at the moment."

Ryōma shoved his hat back and glanced up at Shono's face. "We could have a period of courtship, of course, Shono-sama. Or we could make some other match; perhaps Chagatai, or your sister or brother, or does Lady Saadiyah have any siblings?"

"Two older brothers," Saadiyah said, "but–"

Shono cut her off. "No," he said. "I am not my mother. We will not be spending months on delicate negotiations of this and that point, only to break our word in the end." He turned to where Yumino stood nearby, staring out at the city. "Yumino-san, what is it that you said? Utaku swore no vows, she simply lived her honor?"

"Hai," Yumino said. "Words can get in the way. They can be twisted, interpreted. Actions are where your honor lies."

"I like her," said Saadiyah when Ryōma had finished translating. "So, Shinjo. What is it to be?"

Words were required, sadly, and they spent hours on the terms of the alliance and the contract. It was largely as Ryōma had first proposed, although Saadiyah proved to be a shrewd negotiator in her own right – she would not relent on shipping rights until Shono pointed out that the Unicorn did not control any ports, nor any coastal territory at all. In the end, she insisted on adding them anyway. "Because who knows what might happen in the future?"

The practical upside was that al-Zawira would remain the hub of trade with the east, but Mozedu's merchants would be able to travel as far as Khanbulak. There were details regarding soldiers and matériel to be rendered as aid in the event of war against the Caliphate, and different details against other enemies – including the Lion. *Really a ceremonial contribution for this current war, but that's all we need.*

"Very well," said Ryōma at last. He offered Shono his seal.

Shono took it, feeling its weight in his hand. *If I do this, I've turned my back on Mitsuko entirely.*

"Show some courage, Shinjo," Saadiyah said, perhaps misreading his hesitation. "We could both have it much worse."

Shono thought of Mitsuko. *I could have had it much better, too.* He took a breath and stamped his seal on the paper. "As you say, Saadiyah-san."

"And what now?" Shono asked as he brushed Umeboshi's mane out. Ryōma slouched nearby, letting Patience nose at his sleeves for a treat. *The horses will recover from the terror of last night faster than we will.* "After… the ceremony. Do I ride west, to meet with her father? Or east, to introduce her to my mother?"

"That will be up to you, my lord," said Ryōma. "And I am at your disposal. Chagatai can carry word of what transpired here back to Rokugan as easily as either of us can. And while your mother would sorely desire you to return to the fight against the Lion–"

"Would she, I wonder?" Shono rested a hand against Umeboshi's neck, feeling the quiet warmth and solidity of the horse. *Would that I could be so calm.*

"...but if you feel that your attentions are required here, to maintain tranquility, she cannot have any objection." Ryōma bowed to him, shoving Patience away with one hand. "I am happy to draft a letter to both sets of parents, whichever course of action you choose."

"To maintain tranquility." *I could stay in the west for years. Forever, even; securing the alliance with al-Mozedu is as great a benefit as most khans' sons bring their clan. Let Chagatai rule the Unicorn. Don't I deserve to rest?*

He thought of his brother, his sisters. *And how would they fare, in a Rokugan with a Moto Great Khan? Would I never see them again? No. I cannot leave the Unicorn to Chagatai's mercy. He may be a great warrior, but a khan needs to be more than that. We need a khan who knows when to make war and when to make peace – and how to do both.*

He thought of his mother's decision, the choice to plunge them into this war, the one that he had so resented. *An impossible choice. Just as Hama Khutun said, just as Chagatai said.* He whistled Tsubasa out of the herd and brushed him as well.

But at length, it was time. The Unicorn survivors, all twenty of them, gathered outside the Dead City under an ancient olive tree, looking down upon the river. Shoan and Tanaka came to find Shono, to purify him and dress him in his finest clothes.

"This will be the last service I do for you, Shono," Shoan said.

Shono nodded, swallowing the lump in his throat. He wanted to speak to make it right, to restore her to the Unicorn Clan. *But I cannot. What a samurai does, he does with his whole heart. I could not simply pretend to cast her out, not if I expected a djinni like Ma'aruf to accept it as done. And once done, I cannot simply undo it, not without dishonoring both Shoan and myself.* "Auntie," he said.

She brushed his comment aside. "You don't call me that anymore, Shono-sama." She took a deep breath and sighed. "Not the wedding you hoped for, I know. A gaijin bride, and a rōnin priest."

"It doesn't matter," Shono said. "I am ready.

ABOUT THE AUTHORS

KATRINA OSTRANDER has served as editor for media tie-in novellas spanning multiple genres including cyberpunk, fantasy, Lovecraftian horror, and science fiction. As the Creative Director of Story and Setting for Fantasy Flight Games, she oversees the internal and licensed development of proprietary IPs, including *Arkham Horror* and *Legend of the Five Rings*. She has also written for or developed over a dozen roleplaying game products, including adventures, supplements, and core rulebooks.

katrinaostrander.com
twitter.com/lindevi

ROBERT DENTON III lives in the New River Valley of Virginia with his wife and three spoiled cats. He's written extensively for the *Legend of the Five Rings* setting, including dozens of short stories, contributions to the fourth and fifth editions of the *Legend of the Five Rings Roleplaying Game*, and his first novella, *The Sword and the Spirits*. As an author of tabletop roleplaying games, his works include *Tiny Taverns: A Slice-Of-Life Fantasy Roleplaying Game* and the underwater fantasy setting *Destiny of Tides*.

twitter.com/ohnospooky

MARI MURDOCK is a freelance writer living in Utah. She has been writing for the tabletop gaming industry since 2013 with writing credits from companies such as Alderac Entertainment Group, Green Ronin Publishing, Gallant Knight Games, and Fantasy Flight Games, where she is best known for her work on *Legend of the Five Rings*. Though she has written many different genres, she loves projects that let her take inspiration from her Japanese roots. When not writing or gaming, Mari is most likely doodling monsters, cooking Asian fusion, or reading pulp fiction. She currently lives in Salt Lake City with her husband.

marimurdock.com
twitter.com/murdock_mari

DANIEL LOVAT CLARK is an author and game designer in the Twin Cities, Minnesota. He lives with a daughter, a dog, two cats, and a wife who may technically qualify as a third cat. Dan has a degree from the Barrett Honors College at Arizona State University, and learned most of what he actually knows working at Fantasy Flight Games in Roseville, Minnesota.

danlovatclark.com
twitter.com/danlovatclark

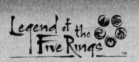

Volume 2
coming soon

THE GREAT CLANS OF ROKUGAN
THE COLLECTED NOVELLAS VOLUME 2

Collects these heroic adventures,
including a new novella of the Lion Clan:

Deathseeker by Robert Denton III
The Eternal Knot by Marie Brennan
Trail of Shadows by D G Laderoute

ARKHAM HORROR™

Riveting pulp adventure as unknowable horrors threaten to tear our reality apart.

A bold thief unleashes an ancient monster, a mad Surrealist tears open the boundaries between worlds, horror movies capture crawling dread, dark incantations which fracture reality... explore the uncanny realms of Arkham, and beyond.

DESCENT
LEGENDS OF THE DARK™

Epic fantasy of heroes and monsters in the perilous realms of Terrinoth.

A reluctant trio are forced to investigate a mysterious city, but in doing so find themselves fighting a demonic atrocity, and a holy warrior is the only hope of salvation from a brutal demonic invasion...

A trio of legendary figures reunite to solve a mystery but instead uncover treachery and dark sorcery.

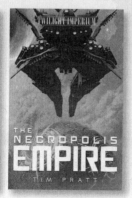

WORLD EXPANDING FICTION
Do you have them all?

ARKHAM HORROR

- ☐ *Wrath of N'kai* by Josh Reynolds
- ☐ *The Last Ritual* by S A Sidor
- ☐ *Mask of Silver* by Rosemary Jones
- ☐ *Litany of Dreams* by Ari Marmell
- ☐ *The Devourer Below* ed Charlotte Llewelyn-Wells
- ☐ *Dark Origins, The Collected Novellas Vol 1*
- ☐ *Cult of the Spider Queen* by S A Sidor *(coming soon)*

DESCENT

- ☐ *The Doom of Fallowhearth* by Robbie MacNiven
- ☐ *The Shield of Daqan* by David Guymer
- ☐ *The Gates of Thelgrim* by Robbie MacNiven
- ☐ *Zachareth* by Robbie MacNiven *(coming soon)*

KEYFORGE

- ☐ *Tales from the Crucible* ed Charlotte Llewelyn-Wells
- ☐ *The Qubit Zirconium* by M Darusha Wehm

LEGEND OF THE FIVE RINGS

- ☐ *Curse of Honor* by David Annandale
- ☐ *Poison River* by Josh Reynolds
- ☐ *The Night Parade of 100 Demons*
   by Marie Brennan
- ☐ *Death's Kiss* by Josh Reynolds
- ☑ *The Great Clans of Rokugan, The Collected Novellas Vol 1*
- ☐ *To Chart the Clouds* by Evan Dicken
   (coming soon)

PANDEMIC

- ☐ *Patient Zero* by Amanda Bridgeman

TWILIGHT IMPERIUM

- ☐ *The Fractured Void* by Tim Pratt
- ☐ *The Necropolis Empire* by Tim Pratt

ZOMBICIDE

- ☐ *Last Resort* by Josh Reynolds
- ☐ *Planet Havoc* by Tim Waggoner *(coming soon)*